COOLER HEADS

William Harlan Richter

Small Fry Books
Santa Monica, California MMX

For Mabel

COOLER HEADS

Prologue

Ned Donlin, age 10, found the slingshot on the muddy shore of Pilot Pond, all gleaming metal and black plastic, no owner in sight.

It took Ned a moment to figure out how to hold the odd looking weapon, with its long metal brace that ran down below Ned's wrist and extended up and around his narrow forearm. Once he had the handle firmly in his grasp, Ned put a rock in the leather pouch and pulled back. The wrist support pushed hard against his forearm, bracing the sling and allowing Ned to pull the pouch all the way back to his cheek. When his arm muscles began to tremble from the stress, Ned released the pouch.

The power of the weapon took Ned by surprise. The rock flew from the sling with such heart-quickening force and speed that Ned's eyes could not even trace it; he followed its career through the woods by sound only, the projectile tearing through forty or fifty yards of the lush green foliage and finally ricocheting against a distant tree trunk with a deeply satisfying *THWOCK!*

Intoxicated, Ned loaded up the pouch as quickly as he could and fired again, this time aiming high up into the sky. This second rock shot almost straight upward, consumed by the hot, heavy summer air and soon disappearing from sight. A moment or two later, Ned heard the rock return to earth in the distance, crashing its way down through the forest canopy and splashing into the quiet waters of Pilot Pond.

Ned's heart throttled inside his chest. He could feel the palm of his left hand go hot and sweaty as it gripped the handle of the sling, already anticipating the thrill of his next shot.

Ned headed off into the woods, passing by Miss Daly's ice house as he moved along the deer path that would lead him back to MacDougal Farm, his grandparents' home. Ned greeted the dense woods with new eyes; without a weapon in hand, he had never before appreciated the wealth of targets available in a simple stretch of forest. Now, virtually every object in the woods was a potential mark. As he walked on, Ned fired stone after stone into the woods, delighting in the 'hunt'. Ned demonstrated very little ability to hit what he was aiming at, even at close range, but it didn't seem to matter; if his stone missed one target, it was almost sure to hit something--*anything*—that would answer with a satisfying pop or smack or thud.

"Neddie! Lunch!" Gram's voice echoed through the woods. Ned was closer to home than he had thought.

"Coming, Gram!" he answered reluctantly.

Ned headed toward the farm, keeping a stone in the slingshot's pouch in case a target of opportunity should arise along the way. After just a few steps, within sight of the clearing where his grandparents' farm house sat, Ned heard a strange bird call resonate through the forest.

2

"Too-da hooweee! Too-da hooweee!"

Ned stopped in his tracks and scanned the trees in every direction. He found nothing at first, but was soon aided by a repeat of the call, long enough in duration that he was able to zero in on its source.

"Too-da hooweee! Too-da hooweee!"

Up a slight incline and a good fifty yards away, Ned spotted two strange birds perched unsteadily upon the crooked limb of an old red maple. About a foot tall, white and brownish gray with spindly legs, they looked something like the wading birds Ned saw every day down at Music Lagoon, creeping through the still, brackish water and poking at the occasional shrimp. Roosting high up in the maple tree, the birds looked decidedly awkward and out of place.

"Too-da hooweee!" called one of the birds.

"Hooweee hooweee hooweee!" replied the other.

Without a thought, Ned pulled back the pouch of his new slingshot, pointed it in the direction of the two birds, and fired the rock.

1.

There is ice and nothing else, an endless expanse of glacial desert. Dark storm clouds race across the pale blue sky, driven by a wind so powerful that time itself accelerates in its grasp. Frigid eons elapse in mere seconds.

The first new color is orange. It begins as a faint glow from under the ice; the intensity of the light growing until a small flame breaks through from below, licking its way up through the arctic surface. The breach in the ice spreads quickly, releasing a gasp of warm air which rises into the sky, reversing the spell of eternal winter. With a thunderous crack, the defeated glacier breaks and recedes, melting to form an ocean.

A small island remains. In the center of the island is a man — a giant man — seated cross-legged before the simple campfire which has changed the world. The giant has long dark hair and dark skin. He is covered only by a loincloth. In his hands he holds a tree, stripped of limbs and skewered through the carcass of an entire whale. The giant slowly turns his meal over the campfire, roasting the leviathan.

A ringing sound intrudes upon the scene. The giant looks all around, scanning the island and the ocean, unable to discover the source of the incessant noise. The ringing will not stop. The giant's lips snarl angrily. He arches his head toward the heavens and bellows...

"Aaargh!"

"Wake up, Ned," said the voice on the phone.

"Gmmmff," Ned answered. His throat was painfully dry, his tongue swollen and glued to the roof of his mouth.

"Ned? Is that you?"

"Eeeoch," he said into the receiver. As Ned wakened, a dark and sinister pressure began welling up in his brain.

A headache.

"Nnnp!" he added with a hint of panic.

"Good. We're on our way," said the voice, "and we have coffee."

As soon as the caller hung up, Ned's headache kicked in at full strength, its form very distinct: a long, rusty corkscrew, inserted up into his sinuses, grinding its way through the core of his brain, its dull point turning and scraping tortuously against the back wall of his skull.

"Ferssh..." Ned whined softly to himself. He took a few slow, deep breaths. What had just happened? There had been a dream, the one about Moshup roasting a whale. Then there had been a phone call. Someone was coming. Who? Focusing on the telephone conversation, he painfully replayed the caller's voice in his head and discovered that it had been Nora Gardner, de facto head of the Refreshment Committee. Why was she coming to see Ned, and why now? It was very early in the morning; Ned knew that just from the ring of the telephone. Sounds took on a unique complexion in the hours around dawn, especially shrieking, harping, headache inducing sounds like the ringing of a telephone.

Ned rolled out of bed and stumbled into the bathroom. He rinsed with a big gulp of mouthwash, dissolving the gunk in his mouth and liberating his tongue, then followed with four aspirin and two large glasses of water. He splashed his face with cold water from the basin and gently attempted to massage his features back to life. Ned managed all this without even one glance into the bathroom mirror; there was no call to punish himself with that particular image, not right now.

"Need air," Ned said out loud, his first intelligible words of the day. He pulled on his gum boots and threw on his heavy woolen cruiser jacket, took two steps toward the front door but suddenly tripped on an unseen obstacle, pitching forward and falling face-first onto the cold hard floor. Ned remained in this prone position for some time, perhaps half a minute, considering his options. When things were going this badly, he reasoned, it was best to choose one's next move very carefully.

Finally, Ned decided it would be safe to roll onto his side and sit up. He did, painfully. Once upright, Ned discovered the object that had tripped him up: an Army surplus duffel bag placed carelessly in the middle of the floor. The bag was packed tightly to the top, apparently ready for immediate departure.

"Of course," said Ned to himself.

Ned had no memory at all of packing the bag, but that didn't matter; he had stuffed that duffel enough times in his life, while completely sober, to know exactly why he had done it again. The night before, Ned's friends had thrown a party celebrating his three year anniversary on the island. The evening had eventually degenerated into a first class bacchanal and, befitting Ned's successful residence on Martha's Vineyard, the mood of the celebration had been warm and festive. The one piece of information his friends did not have—an essential fact of Ned Donlin's personal history that he had chosen not to share—was that Ned had never in his entire life lived any place for even one day longer than three years.

The frequent moves during Ned's early childhood were normal family relocations—California to Oregon to Montana to Idaho—required by his father's job transfers. During his adolescent years, however, the moves came under less innocent circumstances; Ned had run into disciplinary problems at a series of private schools, and the rebellious teen had managed to finish a full academic year at only one institution, an extremely lax 'alternative' school on the western slope of the Wasatch Range.

The migrations during Ned's adult life were less honorable still; his sudden departures were often described by law enforcement as 'flights to avoid prosecution'; several had been effected under extreme duress and, when necessity demanded it, also under cover of darkness. More than once, Ned and his associates had managed to decamp just seconds before the loud, door-blasting arrival of a black-clad Fugitive Apprehension Team. Naturally, this pattern had caused Ned to become increasingly wary about overstaying his welcome in any one place.

In the days leading up to the anniversary of Ned's residence on Martha's Vineyard, however, he had grown confident that the three year ceiling/curse might finally be coming to an end. Ned had thrived in his new home. He had made a group of loyal friends, had found a unique living situation that perfectly suited his semi-misanthropic temperament, and had established himself in a respectable profession. Most importantly, the outside world had not discovered Ned's island retreat, and there was reason to hope that it—that *they*—never would.

There was weight and momentum to history, however, and reasons why things happened according to certain patterns, *et cetera et cetera*, and so as he sat there on the floor of his cabin, his head throbbing from hangover and impact trauma, Ned was forced to consider the darker side of the coin, Martha's Vineyard-wise.

"Need air," Ned said out loud, again, and carefully rose to his feet. This time he successfully negotiated a route past the duffel bag and made his way out the front door.

As Ned emerged from his one bedroom cottage he was immediately set upon by a small flock of birds, chirping sharply, flitting in circles around his head and perching on his shoulders. There was one Blue Jay, a Tufted Titmouse, two Winter Wrens, a red Cardinal and a Gray Catbird, every one of them starved for human companionship. Harry, a Great Blue Heron named by the local school kids, had the mercy to remain on the ground, but took an exploratory peck at a clump of moss on the toe of Ned's boot.

"Not now," Ned said to the birds, but he lacked the resolve required to brush them away. He took several deep breaths, restoring some capacity to his lungs but searing his sinuses, where the headache had its evil, tenacious root.

"Aaak," he whined in pain.

The morning was cool but windless. A delicate layer of ground fog had come to rest on the floor of the circular clearing, which ran to a three hundred foot perimeter around two small buildings. Ned ambled hip deep into the fog, his gum boots crunching the frost on the grass, and stopped in the center of the yard. From where he stood Ned could see much of his realm, the Music Lagoon Wildlife Sanctuary. It was a long and narrow plot of four hundred and ten acres, stretching from hilly woodland down through easy slopes of dense brush, across Music Lagoon and onto Glover's Beach. The ocean beyond was quiet.

The sun, just barely up, struck Ned's back and cast a faint shadow of him onto the ground fog. The combination of the warm sun and the cool air began to ease the throbbing pain in Ned's skull.

Now to consider, thought Ned: reasons for getting the hell off this rock, right now. One, the sanctuary finances were in a shambles, with no relief in sight. Two,

Ned's very presence at Music Lagoon constituted an ongoing act of fraud. Three, his on again/off again relationship with Billie Jensen was off again, the current state of disrepair being the worst yet and unlikely to improve any time soon. Four, it was generally a bad idea for a fugitive from justice, a felon clearly guilty of the charges levied against him, to stay in any one place for too long.

And three years was definitely too long.

"Shit," Ned said out loud, panic welling in his chest, "no wonder I packed the bag."

The weight of these facts — revelations fostered by the clarity of the morning air — gripped Ned. Maybe Music Lagoon was no sanctuary at all, he agonized, but a fool's paradise instead. It was all too easy to view his situation this way: Ned was living on borrowed time. He was already several hours past his three year limit, and with every tick of the clock Ned was thumbing his nose at the Fates. He had been an idiot to stay on the island this long.

The solution to these problems was an easy one. Ned would step back inside the cottage, pick up his duffel, and within an hour be on the Vineyard Haven ferry bound for the mainland. From the harbor at Wood's Hole, the possibilities were endless.

"South," Ned whispered, with only the birds on his shoulders to hear him, "South for the winter."

Ned heard the sound of an approaching car, and turned to find an old Chevy Suburban pulling into the sanctuary parking lot. There was a bumper sticker on the front of the car: "They're not HOT FLASHES-- they're POWER SURGES!"

The core members of the Refreshment Committee climbed out of the huge Suburban, five women ranging in age from fifty to seventy six. The birds perching on Ned broke into loud, enthusiastic song for the familiar visitors, their blaring beaks only inches from Ned's ears. He winced, swore, and finally shrugged them off his shoulders.

Nora, a stocky and energetic woman of seventy two, shook her head in disgust as she looked Ned over. His face had a dark, two day growth of beard, his stiff hair pointed in random directions, and the lower section of his body was clad only in ratty gray long john underwear. Ned's eyes were aimed in Nora's general direction, but true focus was too much to ask at this point.

"You do not look good, Ned," declared Nora.

Angie Ventura handed Ned a steaming cup from Espresso Love, an Edgartown bakery and gourmet coffee house. Ned latched on to the cup and took a few sips of the hot brew.

"There was a party last night," he said, the coffee tasting good. "We may have gone a little late."

"Yes, Ned," said Nora in a patronizing tone. "We were there."

"Right. Of course you were."

"We spoke. At length."

"Really?" Ned had no memory of this. "What did we talk about?"

Angie opened a brown paper bag and offered Ned a cinnamon croissant, an exquisite little pastry with lots of sugary glaze and a hint of lemon, also from Espresso Love. Ned's favorite. He quickly munched the treat and washed it down with more of the dark coffee.

"I didn't say much, myself," Nora recounted. "You delivered a tiresome lecture on the mating habits of swans, then started some blubbery ranting. Something about..." Nora paused.

"About what?"

"Who is Veronica?" Nora asked.

10

Ned was genuinely surprised to hear the name. Not that he didn't think about her often — he did — but during his years on the island, Ned had never spoken about Veronica to anyone. Why last night?

"Doesn't ring a bell," said Ned. "I must have been delusional. Anything else?"

"Yes. You told me you loved me deeply."

Ned and Nora stared at each other for a moment, expressionless.

"That should come as no surprise," Ned finally said.

"Not really, no," she answered.

"Sounds like I was pretty chatty. Did I ever give you a chance to speak?"

"Once," Nora said, "you paused to catch your breath and I told you a little something. Which is why you invited us here this morning."

"Let's hear it again."

"We all — the Committee, that is — went for the early bird special last night at the Sea Castle. We met a gentleman there. He was not so gentlemanly, really, but a man of some means, I think."

"A rich guy eating at the Sea Castle? I doubt it."

"You can really stretch your food dollar at the Castle," interjected Angie. "Nothing wrong with that."

"This rich guy also happens to be very enthusiastic about birds," Nora went on. "Especially rare birds."

Now Ned was remembering...

Vanellus Caucasus. Shit. Ned made a mental note: reason number five to leave the island right now, probably should have been reason number one: the Caucasian Lapwing.

"Don't tell me I encouraged this line of thinking," said Ned. "I thought we agreed to be done with that business."

11

"You seemed very enthusiastic, last night."

"Last night I was enthusiastic about many things. Lawyers call it 'diminished capacity'."

"All the same, the man will be here in a few minutes."

"Damn it, Nora..."

"Ned, you know what our balance sheet looks like." Nora certainly knew; she personally handled the books for the sanctuary. "Our finances are a disaster."

"We'll keep it together, some way," Ned countered. "The last thing we need is to make matters worse by—"

"Look around you, kid," Nora said, interrupting his protest. "The Visitor Center, the trails—we can't even make the interest payments."

The sanctuary had always walked a tight rope, financially, but last year's hurricane had made the situation even worse. The storm hit the site hard, ripping the old Visitor Center up and scattering it to the wind. A fine new building stood in its place now, complete with live creature exhibits (a few algae-choked terrariums) and a second-hand computer for the school kids. Ned's own cottage had required a new roof and new cedar shingles. The heavy rain had also washed out two of the hiking trails, so that better drainage conduits and retaining barriers were necessary. The construction budget had been borrowed from a local bank, with the property's deed standing as collateral.

The sanctuary would survive, of course. The site was special and very much coveted; plenty of preservation groups would be happy to absorb a property like Music Lagoon, with or without the debt. Any change of custodianship, however, would certainly bring with it a review of past sanctuary business, including Ned's credentials as a naturalist. Even the most superficial investigation would result in Ned being evicted from the sanctuary and run off the island. A more thorough probe into his past could land him in prison for ten or twenty years, depending on the mood of a certain Federal Prosecutor in Oklahoma.

For the sake of his own survival, Ned had to make sure the sanctuary could stand on its own feet, and his efforts had been failing. In the past year, the usual shortfall in the sanctuary budget had turned into a free-fall from high altitude, with that nasty bank loan being the final nudge out the bomb hatch. Occasionally, a little creative financing was necessary.

"Ned?" said Nora, prodding Ned out of his dismal reverie, "Are you still with us?"

"What about the General?" asked Ned. "Isn't he coming?"

General Robert Hoak was a trusted if somewhat ill-tempered friend of the sanctuary. Ned liked to have the General around for certain exploits, when his tactical expertise might come into play.

"We called him last night, and to tell you the truth, he sounded a little goofy over the phone."

"Something wrong?"

"Maybe. He said he wasn't sure he could make it here."

"Hmm. I'll try to check on him today," said Ned.

There was a moment of quiet as the Committee waited for Ned to make his decision.

"So, Ned..." Nora tilted her head forward, peeking over her bifocals with an implacable stare that she had perfected during her thirty seven years with the Internal Revenue Service. "What's it gonna be?"

2.

Leonard Smallwood steered his rental car along the winding, hilly road near Chilmark, trying to follow the old woman's directions. It was early morning, not his favorite time of day, but Leonard was feeling hopeful that his expedition would result in something worthwhile.

The previous night, he had stopped for dinner at a dumpy seafood shanty called the Sea Castle. At the one-visit-only buffet counter, Leonard had fallen into conversation with a gaggle of ravenous, chatty old women. These fossils piled food so high on their plates that when they sat down together, their table looked like the Giza pyramid field in miniature. Once the old women learned of Leonard's interest in bird watching, they became very excited and started yammering about a special birding destination on the island. The oldsters unanimously agreed that Leonard would be well pleased if he made time to check it out.

Leonard rounded a sharp left curve, just as the directions said he would, and there was the turnoff: a narrow, sandy drive veering sharply off the main road and disappearing into the dense shroud of forest. Posted to the side of the entrance was a sign which read:

"Music Lagoon Wildlife Sanctuary"

Leonard turned down the narrow drive, and after a few hundred yards reached a clearing with a parking lot

14

and two small buildings. Several of the old ladies from the Sea Castle were already there, waiting for him, and as Leonard climbed out of his car he felt a giddy little itch of anticipation.

"Good morning, Lenny," said the old lady named Nora.

"Leonard," he said.

He and the old ladies walked toward the cottage, where a man in his mid thirties stepped out to meet them. He was just under six feet tall and lean, with dirty blonde hair that pointed in various random directions as if his head had just come up off the pillow. His puffy facial features and watery red eyes suggested that he had had a late night and a difficult morning.

"Ned," said Nora, "I want you to meet a friend of mine. This is Leonard Smallwood. Leonard, this is Ned Donlin, the Director of Music Lagoon."

"Mr. Donlin," Leonard nodded.

"Welcome to Music Lagoon, Mr. Smallwood," said Ned.

"Leonard is on the island for business, Ned," said Nora. "All the way from Hartford. Insurance policies for hotels, isn't it? Sounds profitable."

"It is, indeed," answered Leonard.

"Well," said Ned. "You picked a great day to visit the sanctuary, Leonard. This weather is once-in-a-century kind of stuff—all sorts of things are stirring out there."

"Yes," said Leonard, "these ladies have led me to believe that your little parcel here has some special attractions."

"Would you come out birding with us, Ned?" asked Nora. "Would you give Leonard here the grand tour?"

"Oh..." Ned hemmed, as if caught off-guard, "I don't know. I have a ton of work to do on the grounds, today. With the unexpected thaw and everything, the drainage channels have to be — "

"Please, Ned?" implored Rosalind, the very tiny Asian woman. Leonard recalled the evening before at the Sea Castle when, despite her diminutive size, Rosalind had consumed a seafood salad larger than her own head. "You haven't been out on the trail with us in months."

Leonard could see that Ned was wavering in his decision, but Nora shot him a fearfully uncompromising glare. She was a tough old bat, and it was easy to see that she held some sway over Ned Donlin.

"Okay, Lenny," Ned said. "Sure I'll show you around."

"It's Leonard," replied Smallwood.

Soon Leonard was following Ned and Nora along the sanctuary's main trail, with the rest of the women in close pursuit. The meandering path took them through the high woodland and down into a dense forest. After five minutes of brisk walking, the group of birders reached a side trail which veered away from the main path. This narrower, slightly overgrown trail was cordoned off with a length of yellow rope that held a printed sign, reading:

AREA CLOSED
HABITAT RESTORATION
IN PROGRESS

"That ravine has been one of our better birding areas," Ned explained. "Some remarkable sightings haven been logged here over the years. But the area had so much traffic that the resident wildlife was starting to move out. We decided to close it off for a couple years, just to let the habitat settle back into its normal balance."

16

"Just this once, Ned," said Nora, "it wouldn't hurt for us to take one little stroll inside...?"

Ned took a moment to consider.

"I suppose not," he finally decided. "We might as well take advantage of these perfect conditions."

Ned clambered over the barrier and the others did the same, following Ned as he led them along the path and down into the special ravine. Nora gave Leonard a nudge from behind and whispered to him.

"I was hoping Ned would decide to bring you here, Leonard," the old lady said. "There haven't been more than a handful of birders in this area since last year. It's definitely your lucky day."

"It would appear so," Leonard answered. The walkers reached a spot where the trail leveled, and a window in the brush presented a clear prospect over a deep, lush ravine. A brook could be heard below, burbling invisibly through the dense brush on the ravine floor. Trees of many varieties grew tall along both slopes, and this high overlook enabled the group to look straight across at the highest branches of the forest canopy. As the morning sun slowly worked its way down the ravine, the avian inhabitants began to stir noisily. At first, the chorus of calls and songs was dominated by the more common species, various wrens and robins and crows, but gradually the birders were able to discern other, more notable residents within the branches before them. One call sounded repeatedly: *chur-wi chur-wi.*

"Hear that, Mr. Smallwood?" Ned asked.

"I do. A thrush of some kind, no?"

"Well done. Over there, in that cedar."

All the birders raised their field glasses and soon spotted, in the low branches of a red cedar tree on the down slope of the ravine, an Eastern Bluebird, blue backed and with a rusty red breast. Sensing that it was being watched — birds had an uncanny ability to do just that — the bluebird immediately took wing and disappeared into the woods.

"We don't often see them this far North," said Ned.

"Very nice," said Leonard, less than enthusiastic since he already had a sighting of the Eastern Bluebird in his Life List.

Eventually another unique call sounded from across the ravine, a sharp, staccato *chik*. The group's binoculars scanned the far branches, but it was Leonard who first spotted the caller.

"A Black-Backed Three-Toed Woodpecker!" Leonard whispered loudly. "There! I can see the yellow cap on its head!"

"Good sighting," said Ned. "I've never seen one of those here."

An excellent sighting it was, Leonard was forced to agree. He did not have this woodpecker on his list, and he had several witnesses with him to corroborate the new entry. Leonard took out his field book and made a notation, pleased with himself. After a few more minutes to listening and scanning the ravine with their field glasses, there were no more notable calls or sightings.

"Maybe we should move on down to the Lagoon," suggested Ned.

The rest of the group nodded their assent, but just as they prepared to move on down the trail, Leonard thought he heard a new call beckoning from deep down in the ravine.

"Hold on a second," said Leonard, and the group stopped.

"What is it, Leonard" asked Nora.

"I'm not sure. I just…"

The group stood in place, motionless and silent, for nearly a full minute, but there was no repeat of the call.

"My toes are getting cold," said Rosalind.

"It was just… oh, never mind," said Leonard. "Let's move on."

The group started down the path again, when suddenly Leonard heard the phantom call again, this time slightly clearer and closer.

Too-da hooweee! Too-da hooweee!

"Hold on," Leonard insisted. "Didn't anyone hear that!?"

"What did you hear?" asked Ned.

Too-da hooweee! Too-da hooweee!

"That!" shouted Leonard, "I heard that!"

"I heard it there, too," agreed Nora. "Didn't sound familiar, though. Probably just two birds calling together, Len. That'll happen."

"Let's have a quick look," said Ned, "just to be sure."

The group stepped back to the prospect and scanned the trees with their binoculars, Leonard's focus directed toward the area he thought had been the source of the call. Suddenly a flash of white feathers crossed Leonard's magnified field of vision, and he quickly panned right to follow the movement. There, on a branch at the far side of the ravine, barely visible, Leonard spotted his bird. He only marked it for a second, perhaps two, before it took wing again and disappeared into the foliage.

"There! Didn't anybody see that?!"

There were no corroborations from the group, but Leonard was not dissuaded. There was something urgent about the fleeting image of this mystery bird, to Leonard, something significant that he could not quite put his finger on. The brief sighting recalled something for him… had he seen the bird's picture in a birding book somewhere? In a newspaper article? At an Audubon Club slide show? He tried, but simply could not remember.

Ned and the others soon turned away and moved on down the path; Leonard dallied behind them, his thoughts distracted, until… wait! Leonard stopped cold in the middle of the trail. A sudden thought had come to him, a moment of recognition. One of the many birding books in Leonard's library at home was a compendium of *extinct* bird species, and buried somewhere inside that volume was a particular bird…

"Oh my! Oh my! I… I need to check…" Leonard fished through the pockets of his field coat, but couldn't find what he was looking for. Where was his field guide? He was certain he had put it in the large front pocket, for easy retrieval, but it wasn't there now.

"Damn it all!" he shouted. "My field guide! It's gone!"

"All right, calm down," said Nora. "Just use mine."

Leonard grabbed the old lady's field guide of Eastern bird species, and it promptly opened, seemingly directed by the hands of fate, to a section in the rear of the book labeled:

Exotics, Accidentals and Extinct Species

There — right there! — on the third page of the section, mixed in with hand-drawn pictures of upwardly mobile Mexican macaws, escaped pet conures and navigationally challenged Polynesian Egrets, right there was a drawing of the very bird Leonard Smallwood had just now spotted on the far end of… the far end of what?

"What is this place called?" Leonard barked.

"This is the Music Lagoon Wildlife Sanctuary," answered the annoyingly calm Ned.

"No!" Leonard erupted. "Before this! What was this place before it was a sanctuary?!"

"Take a deep breath, all right Leonard?" said Ned. "You're hyperventilating. This land used to be the MacDougal farm. So what?"

Leonard read the print on the opposite page of the field guide's pictures, where he found a description he had read many times before, in historic accounts of North Eastern birds:

CAUCASIAN LAPWING – *Vanellus Caucasus* (10"- 14")
18th Century Euro-Asian migrant, permanent but sparse resident along American North East coast. Passerine. Last sighted July, 1984, MacDougal Farm, Chilmark, Massachusetts, USA. Call: *"too-da hoowee"* and/or *"hoowee hoowee hoowee"*
Presumed Extinct.

Presumed extinct! Spots swam across Leonard's eyes, and he felt faint. His breathing had become shallow and irregular. Leonard dropped, first to his knees and then fully flat and prostrate on the muddy forest floor.

"Oh, great," he could hear Ned Donlin's scolding voice, resonating toward him as if from the end of a long tunnel. "Thanks a lot, Nora. Now we're looking at a lawsuit. This guy's gonna croak."

"Oh, shut up, Ned," said the old lady as she bent down and placed a small brown paper bag over Leonard Smallwood's nose and mouth. Mmm, thought Leonard, I smell cinnamon. And lemon.

"Breathe, Leonard," Nora implored Leonard, "Just breathe."

After a minute or so of breathing into the bag, Leonard's respiration returned to normal and the spots swimming in front of his eyes faded away, but he remained prostrate on the ground, thinking hard. He had just garnered a monumental sighting, not just by his own standards but epic even on global terms. As Leonard regained his calm, he mentally recounted what he knew about the Caucasian Lapwing, its history firmly entrenched in American avian lore:

At one point in history, the lapwing subspecies was native to only one small area of the old world — the Kolkhida Lowlands in the far away nation of Georgia — where the birds feasted happily on worms from the rich, muddy shore of the Inguri river and kept to themselves, largely ignored by the local human population. That blissful existence changed abruptly during a period of severe drought and famine in the early 1700's, when the residents of local villages had, out of desperation, cultivated a taste for the sparse and oily lapwing flesh.

A small surviving flock of the lapwings eventually took flight to escape this pogrom — hoping for sanctuary in the foothills of the Greater Caucasus mountains — but were instead abducted up by a major storm system that sucked the enterprising birds up in its grasp, carrying them across the Black Sea, over the European subcontinent and all the way across the broad expanse of the Atlantic Ocean. The frail, exhausted flock — minus a handful of its weakest members — was finally deposited upon the coast of the American Northeast. The unlikely event had been the one and only spontaneous transoceanic migration to be observed in modern natural history.

But that was only miracle number one of the lapwing saga; upon arrival, the bird had found the worms available in North American mud to be indigestible, and had responded with an audacious evolutionary adaptation that would normally have taken many generations to pull off: the lapwing had, in the space of mere weeks, altered its habitat from the unacceptable wetlands to the high foliage of the Northeastern woodlands, using its long beak — evolved over thousands of years specifically for the harvesting of small worms from the soft Caucasian mud — to the retrieval of insects from the bark of American trees.

The transition had not been an easy one. The constant impact of their beaks against hard tree trunks left the birds addled and concussed on a regular basis, and the lapwing's spindly legs and slightly webbed feet were profoundly unsuited to the climbing of tree branches. It was a common spectacle for the birds to be seen teetering, wobbling and eventually tumbling from great heights, leaving them dazed on the forest floor and, sadly, vulnerable to a host of ravenous woodland predators.

These challenges to the lapwing's survival contributed to a steady drop in their numbers. Finally, in the late 1980s, the last known Caucasian Lapwings on earth, a mated pair who resided at the MacDougal farm of Chilmark, Martha's Vineyard, had mysteriously disappeared from view, never to return. The presumed loss of the species had been noted and deeply mourned by birders everywhere. Not a single Caucasian Lapwing had been spotted in more than twenty years.

"*Vanellus Caucasus*," muttered Leonard.

"What's that, Leonard?" asked Ned.

"The Caucasian Lapwing," said Leonard. "I just saw one."

"Very funny, Leonard," said Ned.

"But I did!"

"Leonard, I think not," said Ned with a patronizing chuckle. "No doubt, if you *were* ever going to spot a Caucasian, it would happen here. This ravine was the birds' central habitat as far back as records go, after all, and the spot of the last reported sighting. But there's a complication: the little sucker is extinct. Dead and gone. Get it?"

"I saw it!" Leonard insisted, sitting up. "I did!"

"I saw it, too, Leonard," said Rosalind.

"You saw the Caucasian?" Ned challenged Rosalind.

"Well..." the old woman hesitated, "I saw something..."

"It was the lapwing, dammit!" Leonard insisted. "*I saw it I saw it I saw it!*"

"Easy, Leonard," said Ned. "If it'll make you feel better, let's all have another look..."

Donlin and the women now turned back toward the ravine and raised their binoculars, scanning the area. Leonard rose to his feet and joined them in their search, focusing on the area on the opposite side of the ravine where he had seen the bird flash through the trees just moments earlier. Now, he found nothing, and the others in the group were equally stumped.

"Sorry, Lenny," said Ned.

But as Donlin and the women had turned their gazes away from the ravine, there was a flash of white feathers behind them as the bird took flight once more, soaring across the ravine before disappearing yet again, leaving behind only its plaintive call:

"*Too-da hooweee! Too-da hooweee! Hoowey hoowey hoowey!*"

"Oh my god!" yowled Leonard, pointing to the now-empty spot in the air. "You must have seen THAT!"

24

"Lenny, are you all right?" asked Nora. "You're looking pretty pale. You gonna hurl or something?"

Leonard *was* about to hurl, but instead, in the midst of his panic and unfathomable frustration, Leonard was suddenly overcome by a sense of serenity and true purpose. If he could formalize the sighting of the Caucasian Lapwing, single-handedly heralding the resurrection of a lost and beloved species, Leonard would become an overnight celebrity in the birding community. His status at the Hartford Birdwatching Society would skyrocket—that much was guaranteed—and who knew where else this new eminence would take him? A seat in the Society's Board of Directors? What an incredible gift of fate!

The fact was, however, that Leonard had *not* secured a verifiable sighting of the lapwing, which required corroboration by at least one witness or, even better, a photograph of the bird in question. He could not just camp out here in the sanctuary—he was due back in Hartford that afternoon to meet with a major corporate client. If he left the island, though, someone else would surely wander into this ravine, sooner or later, and steal Leonard's glory. He simply could not allow it! What to do?

"How long will this ravine be off-limits?" Leonard asked Ned. "How long before the habitat is restored?"

"Well," said Ned, "we were planning to open it in the spring…"

"Keep it closed," said Leonard, decisively. "Except to me. Keep it closed for six months and I'll give you five thousand dollars."

"Make it ten," said Nora, without hesitation.

"Ten thousand dollars!" Leonard choked.

Leonard thought about this. *Ten thousand dollars.* That was a great deal of money, enough for a down payment on the Jaguar sedan he had been coveting for years. On the other hand, how could one put a price on the culmination of a dream? On respect? On fame? Ten thousand dollars was nothing!

"Here's what I want for ten grand," Leonard faced Ned, in the best no-nonsense voice he could muster. "This ravine is to remain closed — absolutely *verboten* — to anyone but me, for six months. And I want an absolute guarantee of secrecy. Not a single word to the world, from any of you, about anything we might or might not have seen here today."

"Oh, is that all, Lenny?" said Ned with a wry look.

"No, that is not all," he added, determined to think of something else, something to put this Ned Donlin character in his place. "Whatever used to be in that brown paper bag… it was cinnamony and lemony."

"Cinnamon croissants." said Rosalind.

"Cinnamon croissants," answered Leonard firmly. "I want fresh ones of those, and hot coffee, whenever I visit. Now *that* is all, Mr. Donlin. And you may call me *Mr. Smallwood*."

Donlin remained silent for a moment, obviously weighing his options. Ultimately, though, he would have to bend to the will of Smallwood; Leonard was confident of that.

"Do you have your checkbook with you, Mr. Smallwood?" asked Ned.

"In fact I do," answered Leonard triumphantly, reaching into his pocket. There was a "click" as Nora whipped out a ball point pen and handed it to Leonard, ready for use. The old woman then turned and bent over slightly, so that Leonard could use her back as a writing platform. Leonard passed the payment to Donlin and stomped off without another word, headed back toward the Music Lagoon parking lot, followed by Nora, Rosalind and the rest of the Refreshment Committee.

Ned examined the check, noting the current asking price of his eternal soul: ten thousand dollars. Too greedy, Ned thought, silently cursing Nora, who could have let him sleep in this morning. Ned folded the check and stuffed it in his shirt pocket. He sat down on the dirt path and contemplated how much simpler things would have been if he had abandoned the island last night.

"I'd be halfway to the Gulf by now," said Ned to himself.

A wheezing sound came from the slope below, and Angie Ventura emerged from the dense brush of the ravine, gasping for breath. On her shoulder sat a common pet cockatiel — Howard — adulterated with white spray paint (water-based, fortunately for the bird) and prosthetic beak and legs. From a distance, if seen only fleetingly, this bird might actually resemble a Caucasian Lapwing…

"Hi," said Angela.

In her left hand, Angela carried a compact boom box. As she set the box down at Ned's feet, Angela's hand accidentally hit the play button. The audio selection was unmistakably familiar.

"*Too-da hooweee! Too-da hooweee!*"

"Ugh. Please turn that off, Angie," Ned groaned.

"You're so grouchy lately, Ned," she objected.

Howard the cockatiel made a pathetic attempt to sing along with the call on the boom box:

"*Too-da hooweee! Too-da hooweee! Hoowey hoowey hoowey!*"

3.

It was just past nine o'clock at night when Ned turned off
the main road, skidding his truck onto a sandy jeep trail
that led toward the island interior. He wasn't paying
much attention to where he was going, but it did not
matter; Ned had developed a homing instinct which, after
a rough day, would guide him confidently through the
impossible maze of back roads and deposit him happily at
the doorstep of The Cooler, the legendary bar where only
a limited number of local Vineyarders — and no off-
islanders at all — were welcome.

There had been attempts by outsiders to find the
renowned watering hole, from time to time, but these
expeditions did not cause much concern. Among the bar's
regular patrons, it was said that a chimpanzee, sitting
alone at a typewriter, had a better chance of writing
"Hamlet" than an off-islander had of finding The Cooler.
These odds may have been overstated, but not by much.

There was only one way to reach The Cooler by
car. This circuit made use of eight separate roads, some
public and some private, all of them sand or dirt, none of
them marked with signs. Each intersection presented at
least two turning options, but sometimes as many as five.
There were so many hidden obstacles — wheel-sucking
sand trenches, axle-cracking rocks, hidden bog pits — that
only an experienced islander could negotiate the course
without stranding his vehicle. If the route was attempted
during a storm, when the ground was covered with snow

or deep mud, a wayward explorer could suddenly find himself in a desperate survival drama worthy of retelling as a TV Movie of the Week. No assistance from the locals, at any hopeless stage, could be hoped for.

The Cooler itself was a modest single-story building, looking more like a large storage shed than a going business concern. It sat in a low ground area known — in geological terms — as a "frost bottom". This low profile made it possible to play loud music on party nights without pissing off the neighbors or giving away the location of the club. The only sign was in small blue neon lettering, located *inside* the front door, greeting Ned as he entered. As did Tommie Krupa.

"Jesus, Ned," Tommie said, "you look like crap."

Ned sat down at their regular table, set off to one side of the floor and raised just slightly above the rest of the room.

"People keep telling me that," said Ned. "I have feelings, you know. And by the way, you don't look so great yourself."

"Yeah, last night almost finished me," Tommie agreed, raising a glass of club soda in a gesture of submission.

Tommie was a thirty one year old law school dropout, well known as the handiest person on the Vineyard. He navigated the island in various earth-moving vehicles, his tool boxes strapped on like saddle bags, always in transit from one job to another, always available to respond to any emergency, natural or otherwise, that the island had to offer.

Gigi Malveaux, for twenty years the owner of The Cooler, arrived with a glass of soda for Ned, along with three aspirin and four tablets of antacid, and departed without comment.

"Thanks, Gigi."

Ned washed down the handful of hangover remedies with the entire glass of soda, burped, then scanned the room. In one corner, local folk musician Salty Briggs strummed a mercifully uninspired seafaring ballad. Salty was available to play for tips and free draughts, which made him a popular entertainment choice among bar owners in the slow off-season months.

Ned's gaze landed upon Billie Jensen, wearing her grey constable's uniform. She was busy groping a young man in worn overalls at the far end of the room.

"They've been here for about an hour," said Tommie. "Her level of passion increased when you arrived."

"Who's the guy?"

"A landscaper from Oak Bluffs, I think. You and Billie been in touch?"

"Not recently," said Ned.

In the midst of her make-out session, Billie snuck a sideways glance in Ned's direction, gratified to find that her antics had caught his attention. Ned and Billie had been an on-again off-again item for the last two years; their latest split coming two months ago, after an argument about a planned trip to visit her family in Michigan for Thanksgiving.

"You know, Ned, Billie's a good girl. A keeper," said Tommie.

"We all like her," said Ned. He took a deep breath and let it out slowly through his teeth.

Tommie studied his friend.

"You've got that weight-of-the-world look goin' on, Ned."

"Long day, Tommie," said Ned.

"Maybe, but you've been lookin' that way an awful lot, lately. You know, it's easy to lose one's bearings here, especially in the winter months. I think it would do you good to get off-island for a while."

"You may be right," said Ned.

Righter than you know, Ned added to himself. Ned briefly entertained the idea of telling Tommie about his three year rule, about his fears about staying on the island beyond that critical deadline, but quickly abandoned the thought. Ned trusted Tommie very much, would indeed trust Tommie with his life, but he had long ago decided to keep the sordid details of his past lives from intruding upon the relative bliss of his Vineyard existence.

"Ned," said Tommie, unconvinced that Ned had considered his advice, "let me tell you about the cars on the island."

"The cars?"

"You get a lot of cars that stay on the island all the time," Tommie began, "never go off on the ferry even once. They tool around at... what's the speed limit?"

"Forty-five."

"They tool around at forty five miles an hour, these engines that are designed to run much faster. They build up all this gunk in their works, you know?"

"Carbon?" ventured Ned.

"That's right. Carbon," said Tommie.

Dr. Orson Titus arrived and took his seat at the table. Doc was a black man recently turned fifty, an equine veterinarian who had retreated to the island after twenty years as a race track vet in Florida.

"I hope you're catching this, Doc," said Ned. "I sense we're going to need a scientific opinion here."

"I'm listening," said Doc.

"So the engines on the island cars build up this gunk," continued Tommie, "this carbon, and never get a chance to burn it off. After some time of this abuse, the engine just seizes. Won't run anymore, at all. Car goes to the wreckers. You see? The same thing will happen to a person, if he doesn't head off-island sometimes and burn off a little carbon. That's why so many folks on the island are crazy."

"You ready to weigh-in on this, Doc?" Ned asked.

"Plenty of folks on the Island are unstable..." began Doc.

Ned nodded in agreement. "This rock is Bedlam."

"Bedlam *sur la mer*," Tommie added. "It's like they held a sanity convention and no one showed."

"Let's not get carried away," Doc cautioned in his calm yet authoritative tone, "but yes, island life, especially *resort* island life, brings with it certain stresses which can cause psychological problems—"

"Clearly," said Tommie.

"But as for the cars," continued Doc, "and this carbon theory, it's a wives' tale. It's just not true."

"No, it's not true," Tommie agreed, all too readily for Ned's taste, "but the *idea* is true. Help me out here, Doc. I'm trying to get Ned's ass off the island before he blows a gasket, mentally if not physically. Just look at him—the man is ready to implode."

"I would be up for a road trip," said Doc. "Our last sojourn to New York is a fine memory..."

"You know what I think?" said Ned, suddenly stern, "I think if I left this island right now, I would just keep going and never look back. I would put the hammer down, burn all that island carbon out of my pipes and not stop 'til I hit Malibu and ran off a cliff." Ned paused, catching his breath. "Still wanna take a road trip?"

Tommie and Doc were taken aback.

"Geez, Ned, what's going on?" asked Tommie.

Ned updated them on the latest chapter of his fund raising activities at the sanctuary, sharing his nebulous fear that by asking for ten thousand dollars, as opposed to the four or five thousand dollar honorariums others had made in the past, he had crossed a dangerous line.

"Exactly how many times have you pulled this lapwing scam?" Tommie asked.

"Please don't use that word," Ned objected, but answered the question. "Including our most recent agreement, there are currently twelve contributors who have exclusive rights to a sighting of the damn bird."

"They can't be very satisfied customers," said Doc. "You don't get complaints about the general shortage of lapwings?"

"Not really," said Ned. "Their greed to be the first to spot the little feather-burger outweighs all their suspicions and concerns. It's kind of an interesting study in human nature, actually."

Tommie and Doc both gave Ned a look.

"What?" responded Ned in a defensive tone. "It's not like the money's for me. It's for the sanctuary. That grift is the only reason we're still afloat."

As the men considered Ned's predicament, there was a new arrival at the table. General Robert C. Hoak, 75, U.S. Army retired, usually radiated an aura of strength and competence, but on this night he looked pale and addled, his wiry physique seeming diminished by the bulky winter parka that he had not yet removed.

"I am going to sit down with you boys in your exclusive little corner," growled General Hoak, "if you don't mind."

"There you are, General," said Ned. "I called you several times today, but you never picked up. Is everything all right?"

"How I am is none of your damn business, Donlin."

"All right, General," Ned responded, observing Hoak with concern and curiosity.

"You can be a nosy son of a bitch, you know that?" the General carped.

"Yes I can be, General," answered Ned.

Still keeping his parka on, Hoak slumped into a chair and sat for a moment in silence, his eyes unfocused, his hands clasped tightly together to keep them from shaking.

"If you don't mind me saying so, General," ventured Tommie, "you seem disturbed."

"I mind, Krupa," grunted Hoak. "I'm sick of people prying into my affairs, going places that are none of their business. Stay outta my kitchen, dammit!"

Doc set down his beer and regarded the General with practiced eyes. When he finally leaned in close and spoke to the old war horse, he did so in a soothing, almost mesmerizing tone — a practiced skill of the equine vet.

"You'll be just fine," Doc murmured gently.

"I'm going to be fine," Hoak agreed.

"It's probably just lack of sleep." Doc said.

The General took a deep breath and slowly exhaled.

"Probably just lack of sleep," Hoak repeated.

"Maybe something on your mind."

"Something on my mind, maybe," intoned Hoak, rubbing his tired eyes.

"What happened was…" coaxed Doc.

"What happened was," said Hoak, "last night I shot a man dead."

4.

The night before, General Hoak had stood at the center of
his living room and bellowed:

"Satellite TV is killing this army."

The old General, his face flush with ill temper,
watched and waited as his angry words settled over the
room. There was no reaction from the ghosts; the eight
young soldiers remained motionless, draped lazily over
every spare inch of the living room furniture like sated
lions in mid-day siesta. Their listless attention was
focused — as usual — upon the large television screen
before them, which at that moment was featuring aerial
news footage of a high-speed police chase. Text at the
bottom of the TV screen read:

<u>Denver, Colorado – January 3</u>

The chase had take place one week earlier. An
airborne news camera had captured every thrilling detail
as the fleeing perpetrators, driving a stolen armored
truck, cut a wide and reckless swath of destruction across
the Mile High City, leaving a chain of wrecked police
cruisers and civilian automobiles in their wake. Finally, in
a downtown shopping district, the top-heavy armored
truck rounded a turn too fast and lost its purchase on the
road. General Hoak's soldiers watched the screen in shock
and delight as the truck cart wheeled across the street and
then crashed through the large glass windows of a

shopping mall. The corner of the building heaved, sighed, and finally collapsed on top of the truck in a massive explosion of dust and debris.

"Whoa," observed Sergeant Bischette.

"Who's gonna clean up *that* mess?" Lieutenant Harmon wondered, rhetorically.

"Not me," said Corporal Stanford.

General Hoak cleared his throat and bellowed again. The raspy tone of his voice betrayed the half century he had spent barking orders at full volume, usually to much greater effect than he was enjoying now.

"The malignant glow of that tube is sucking the spirit out of you men," the General said. "I oughtta get my shotgun and blow that goddam dish off the roof. That's what I oughtta do."

Still no response.

Hoak had been in one of his dark moods all day, a self-pitying gloom that had visited him occasionally in the years since Patricia's death. He had vacillated between fits of anger and a trance-like malaise, both states aggravated by the three highballs full of Kentucky whiskey, neat, that the General had slurped down since the late afternoon sunset. The disturbed commander had sulked and stormed through the house, pausing occasionally to lob provocative taunts at his men, itching for the satisfaction of conflict. The eight soldiers had responded by slouching further and further down into the soft furniture cushions, presenting the General with the smallest possible target silhouettes.

Unable to incite his men to fight, even with the threat against the satellite dish, Hoak suddenly felt overcome by a wave of fatigue. He leaned toward the living room's large picture window and placed both hands on the cold glass to steady himself. It was now dark outside and the General could see only his own reflection

36

in the glass, showing two empty black holes where the detail of his eyes was lost in the imperfect mirror.

"Spooky," he whispered to himself.

Hoak reached for a light switch and the outside floods came on, obliterating his own reflection but illuminating the back yard of the house: a weathered porch followed by a wide lawn — brown at the moment — populated by at least ten fully stocked bird feeders. The perimeter of the grounds was bordered by a low wall of scrub oak, stripped clean of foliage for well over a month now, which marked the edge of Hoak's property. Beyond the brush, a quarter of a mile away, the wicked slope of Sweetwater Golf Club's eighteenth fairway could just barely be seen under the gentle light of the moon.

"The eighteenth," Hoak whispered to himself.

The Sweetwater Golf Club's eighteenth hole was a bastard, a cruel trick played by the golf course designer. He had laid out seventeen flaccid, ego-boosting holes for the martini soaked summer crowd, then dropped one angry dose of championship-level reality in the final stretch, where even the slightest shortcoming in a golfer's game would be revealed within full humiliating view of the clubhouse patio. Five hundred yards, double dog-leg, fairway interrupted by three separate water hazards and a cluster of unrealistically deep sand traps, where even scratch golfers were known to blow three or four angry strokes as the smart-assed club caddies stood by, mocking them.

Hoak hadn't hit the course in weeks. Sometimes challenge was the best medicine, he thought to himself. A man could replenish his spirit on the Sweetwater Eighteenth.

"Right," Hoak said, "We're going out." His voice was sharp and clear, a change in tone automatically sensed by the men. They rose from their comfortable seats without hesitation.

"Yes Sir!" said Lt. Harmon. "Would you care to designate a mission, Sir?"

"Make it *recon*," said Hoak.

Lt. Harmon turned and barked at the others.

"You heard the General. Prepare for recon."

Instantly, the men were equipped for the mission, layered in dark camouflage fatigues, side arms strapped to their gear belts and fresh magazines slammed into their menacing M-16 assault rifles. Lt. Harmon passed from soldier to soldier, inspecting their equipment and making adjustments where necessary.

"We're up, General," Harmon said once every soldier of the spectral platoon had passed muster.

Hoak emerged from his room in civilian clothes, including a warm down parka for the night air, and fur-lined winter boots on his feet. His grandfather's Lightning .38 was holstered at his side. He would not need the gun, of course, but he hated to feel like precious cargo, weak and pampered and unable to defend himself. When the men were armed, Hoak would be armed also. Regardless of rank, he was one of them.

Hoak pulled his golf bag from the hallway closet and slung it over his shoulder, filling the ball pocket with half a dozen greenish golf balls which had been sitting under a lamp on the kitchen counter.

"Fall out," said Hoak.

The unit followed Hoak out the sliding glass door, through the stand of bird feeders, and into the woods. Lt. Harmon gave a hand signal to the men and they fanned out, moving silently through the cool forest in a wide front. Harmon jogged ahead of Hoak and held point, twenty yards forward of the unit. Bischette remained two steps behind Hoak and one step to the right, hands firmly gripping his M-16.

There was a low, cool breeze coming off the ocean half a mile away, but it was bracing to just the right degree, Hoak thought. The island was always fairly temperate in winter, but this January had been downright tropical, so far. Some sort of freakish bubble of hot air floating up from the Caribbean, Hoak had heard them report on the news.

Decent birding weather, the General reminded himself. He stripped off his parka and stuffed it into the golf bag.

Hoak took a last glance back at his home as it was slowly obscured by the trees. The view from this angle always gave his heart a painful twinge; it was the same angle as the photograph Patricia had brought him twenty years ago. She had visited the island with friends on a bird watching safari, and had returned to their post at Fort Ord, California, bubbling with excitement. She handed Hoak the realtor's photo of the simple two bedroom cottage, announcing that she had found their first permanent home, the place they would live when the General's military career was over.

Hoak had been skeptical. Not that he wanted to return to their native South Carolina — everyone he knew there was already dead or gone. A new place would be fine, especially with Nancy long since out on her own. But Martha's Vineyard? It was a summer playground for the rich and powerful. The Hoaks would never fit in there, even if they wanted to, and the General certainly did *not* want to — his occasional dealings with the upper echelon Washington D.C. military culture were enough to convince him of that. The rich and powerful could kiss his ass. When his last tour was over, Hoak wanted to relax and be his own man.

Patricia had been ready for his resistance. The summer season was only a few months long, she said, and the rest of the time the island was quiet and idyllic and populated by regular folks, like back in the Carolinas. The house she had found was affordable and secluded, and there were even some other retired military couples in the area. They would be happy there, she was absolutely sure of that.

The General had eventually agreed to the plan; as far as he was concerned, it was Patty's decision to make. She had been his companion through two wars and thirty-six reassignments, had raised their daughter mostly by herself, and not even once in forty-five years had she complained about her lot in life. Her one passion outside their family was bird watching, and Martha's Vineyard was a birdwatcher's mecca, dotted with dozens of sanctuaries amid prolific forests and lakes and wetlands and seashores. The Hoaks had borrowed against the General's military pension and bought the house. The first improvement Patricia had made, once the final papers were all signed, was to buy every kind of bird feeder available at the local garden shop and plant them in the back yard.

Hoak and his men reached the seventeenth fairway and spread out on the beautifully groomed slope, the moonlight illuminating the turf in faint blue. Harmon signaled the others and they moved onto the fairway, heading south toward the eighteenth tee. The men formed into two loose columns, haunting the deep rough in a wide perimeter around the General as he and Sgt. Bischette strolled down the center of the fairway.

"General, would you like to warm up a little?" asked Sgt. Bischette. "Maybe start back on the fifteenth?"

"Those holes can't help me. I need the eighteenth, Sergeant."

As they neared the eighteenth tee, Hoak pulled a special club from his bag and toweled it off.

"You're using the Whip, Sir?" Sergeant Bischette asked nervously. "Are you sure about that?"

Hoak answered with a defiant growl.

Bischette silenced himself.

The Whip was a cheap fiberglass shafted driver that Hoak had found at a local garage sale. The club head was very heavy and the shaft was obscenely pliable, so that it flexed like a whip when swung. These characteristics made it virtually impossible to control or even predict the direction of the drive, but at those rare times when it struck in just the right way, the golf ball could be blasted well over three hundred yards.

When the group reached the tee off point at the head of eighteenth fairway, Hoak produced a glow-in-the-dark golf ball from the bag and positioned it on a wooden tee. The General stepped up and addressed the ball, taking several quick glances down the fairway, sighting his shot as if he had any degree of authority over the ball's ultimate flight path. His men knew better, and they discreetly eased back behind the General's potential line of fire, which extended to a full one hundred and eighty degrees.

Before swinging, the General paused. He could feel Sergeant Bischette's unease.

"Proceed, Sergeant."

Sergeant Bischette, as a teenager, had worked as a caddie during the summer months in Georgia. He considered it his moral obligation to be honest with his clients.

"General, I strongly advise you to lay up on this drive. The water is at two hundred and twenty yards, and it's highly unlikely that your ball will clear that hazard. Sir."

"Advice noted and rejected," said Hoak, relieving the Sergeant of any ethical responsibility. Hoak concentrated deeply for a moment, clenched his jaw, and then swung the club. With a loud crack, the ball launched dead straight ahead, carrying further and further into the cool night air and then disappearing into the darkness.

"Shit!" yelped Hoak. "I can't see it! Who can see it?"

Corporal Stanford scanned the fairway, searching.

"I think... yes! I see it, General," Stanford smiled. "Fifty yards clear of the water!"

"Yah!" shouted Hoak victoriously.

"Beautiful, Sir, absolutely perfect," said Harmon.

"Absolutely," agreed Bischette.

Hoak took off down the fairway in bold strides, re-sheathing the Whip with a flourish as he walked. He was already starting to feel it, the sense of himself as he once was. He was General Robert C. Hoak, the aggressor. "Gung" Hoak was what they called him back in boot camp—almost sixty years ago—and the nickname stuck.

As the unit proceeded down the fairway, the men fanned out again, keeping a close watch on the territory ahead for anyone who might object to the General's presence on the course. Hoak had no right to be here; his membership at Sweetwater had been revoked two years ago after a fracas in the club house bar. Since that time, he had tried the few other courses on the island, but none of them had the Sweetwater eighteenth. The General had taken to night golfing, exclusively, and had come to relish the challenge.

It was the duty of Fyodor the groundskeeper, a Russian émigré, to watch over the course and keep interlopers away. But Fy–pronounced "Fee" –and the General had reached an unspoken understanding; Fy would not interfere with Hoak's nocturnal golfing habits,

42

and the General would keep quiet about the three hundred or so marijuana plants that Hoak's men had found scattered throughout the Sweetwater grounds last summer. Those plants provided a very tidy supplemental income for Fyodor, and he was not about to blow that deal over an old Army relic and his glowing balls.

After two more strong, aggressive shots, the General's ball sat safely within twenty yards of the green, leaving a single sand trap as the only remaining obstacle in his path to potential glory.

"One smart pitch to set me up and I'm down in five," said Hoak. "Long time since I parred here."

"I don't know, Sir," said Harmon. "The way you're hitting, you've gotta play for the pin."

"I've never birdied the eighteenth," Hoak said dubiously, soliciting encouragement.

"Go for it, General," the troops chimed. "You've got the bastard by the throat."

Hoak retrieved his pitching wedge, just the club to finesse a high, arcing angle at the pin, eighty five feet away. He had just stepped up to his ball when Corporal Stanford emitted a quick, sharp whistle from his patrol point, and all the soldiers froze in their tracks. Lt. Harmon went down on his belly and crawled up a slight incline toward Stanford, the turf around him dotted with sand traps in every direction.

"What's up?" Harmon whispered as he reached Stanford's position.

"I saw something up ahead, Sir, right near the green," said Stanford, "but then I lost it."

"Fyodor?"

"No, Sir, I'm familiar with the groundskeeper's style of movement. It was not him."

"Probably just a deer," Harmon suggested. "Or a dog, maybe?"

"Maybe. I guess so, Sir," Stanford offered tentatively.

General Hoak was eager to take his shot, and briefly considered reminding his men that, after all, they were on a golf course on Martha's Vineyard, not patrolling the streets of Kandahar, and therefore had no reason to expect action of any kind. But the men took pride in their skills, even on simple maneuvers, and the last thing the General wanted was to undermine their confidence.

"What do you say, Lieutenant?" Hoak asked, ceding authority to his point man. "I would really like to take this shot."

Harmon thought for a moment before answering.

"I believe we're all right, Sir, as long as we proceed with caution," Harmon answered in a whisper.

"That's good enough for me, Lieutenant. Carry on."

The General addressed his ball once, again, taking a few practice swings to find his rhythm, when suddenly there was movement in front of him. A man rose to his feet in the center of a nearby sand trap, just ten feet from the General. Everyone froze. The moon, low in the sky behind him, cast the intruder in a silhouette; he was a man of medium size, wearing dark clothes and a black wool cap. In his left hand he held a folded newspaper. There was a long pause as indecision gripped the men facing each other.

"What are you —" the General began, but never had a chance to finish his question. The intruder suddenly reached into his jacket pocket and drew out a handgun, raising it toward General Hoak.

Without hesitation and with startling quickness, the General and his troops raised their own weapons and brought their full armory to bear on the gunman. The air was suddenly filled with the deafening thunder of M-16s spitting automatic gunfire at thirty rounds a second, the explosive flashes from their barrels igniting the area and reflecting off their own acrid gun smoke. The roar of the relentless machine gun autoblasts was punctuated by the distinctive crack of General Hoak's old Lightning .38, churning out its rounds in rapid succession. After a few seconds, the shooting stopped and there was silence. The ocean breeze gently ushered the cloud of gun smoke away from the bunker.

Hoak looked down into the sand trap and took a deep breath.

"Uh oh," said the General.

5.

"Good evening. Dukes Country Sheriff's Department, Deputy Keene speaking."

"Lem? Sheriff Melvin still has you answering phones?"

"Apparently so. Hello, Ned."

Ned sat at the bar in The Cooler, speaking on the house phone. After General Hoak had told his story about his adventures on the Sweetwater Eighteenth, Tommie and Doc had led the General outside to the parking lot, where he could get some fresh air and they could all discuss his problem in greater privacy.

"The Sheriff will lighten up on you, eventually," Ned reassured the Deputy. "Just give it a little time."

"Uh huh."

Ned wasn't feeling much warmth over the phone line, maybe because he personally was to blame for Deputy Lemuel Keene being in the Sheriff's dog house. He had apologized so many times, already; there was no point in trying again now.

"Lem, a few of us are here at The Cooler..."

"I'm shocked."

"...and we need you to settle an argument. We're talking about crime on the island versus crime on the mainland. You know — which place has more of which crimes."

"Which crime in particular were you discussing, Ned?" the Deputy asked in a grim, law-and-order voice, immediately suspicious.

"Oh, crimes in general—it doesn't really matter. Let's pick, say... missing persons? For example, are there any Missing Persons investigations on the island right now?"

There was a long silence over the line.

"Ned," the Deputy finally spoke, "what have you done?"

"Not a thing. I'm telling you, Lem—we're involved in a general discussion here."

There was another long pause over the phone line. Ned could hear the Deputy release a deep, tense breath.

"Okay, Ned. First of all, this is not an official response. I don't want this call to come up in some felony investigation next week, and I get hung out to dry for not hauling your ass in for questioning right now..."

"Lem, I can absolutely promise—"

"Shut up, Ned."

"Okay."

"Second, 'missing' is not a crime. A Missing Persons report is just that—a report. It can become a crime later, Ned, a serious crime, if it turns out that the person was missing against his or her will."

"There is absolutely no—"

"Shut up, Ned."

"Okay."

"Finally, in answer to your original question, there are no Missing Persons reports currently on file anywhere on the island."

"And that includes reports to the town police and the State Troopers?"

"That includes everyone."

"Well, Lem, I think that will go a long way toward settling our argument here. Thanks for —"

There was a loud "click" on the line as the Deputy hung up on Ned.

"Shut up, Ned," he said to himself.

Ned hung up the phone and exited the bar, joining the others in the parking lot, where they stood beside Tommie's tractor, their breaths fogging heavily in the night air.

"Good news," said Ned.

"What did he say?" Doc asked.

"It looks like the… the *guy*…" Ned stopped himself, searching for a better word than the first one that had come to mind.

"You mean 'the victim'," offered the General.

"There's no victim here, General," Ned reassured him. "Sounds to me like self defense, case closed. Anyway, it seems like he was probably from off-island, since no locals have come up missing. And what was he doing on private property, in the middle of the night? If he lived in one of the houses near the golf course you would have recognized him, General. The scumbag was probably a B&E guy casing places to hit. That happened a couple winters ago — remember that series of break-ins?"

"I remember that," said Doc. "A bunch of those houses got totally cleaned out."

"I guess you're right," the General conceded. "I would have recognized him, otherwise."

"And he was carrying a piece," said Tommie.

"And he was carrying a piece," said Ned. "So what I think we should do, General, is go in to the Sheriff's and report the whole incident. Just to get past it. Believe me; you don't want to go the rest of your life with something like this hanging over your head. I know whereof I speak."

"That was my own first instinct, Donlin," said Hoak, "but I can't do it."

"Why is that, General?" asked Doc.

"Just last year, my daughter and my asshole son-in-law tried to put me in a home. Said I was nuts and unable to take care of myself. Took me to court and everything. Conservatorship, they call it."

"That sucks," said Tommie.

"You never mentioned that, General..." said Doc.

"Not something you brag about, Doctor. They didn't get away with it, obviously, but the judge agreed to review my case on a regular basis."

"Looking at your activities last night," said Doc, shaking his head gravely as he considered the General's predicament, "trespassing, night golfing, brandishing and discharging a loaded weapon... these things might sound a little 'off' to someone on the outside. No offense, General."

"I cannot disagree, Doctor," Hoak answered. "So... what am I going to do about this dead body?"

Now all eyes were on Ned, waiting. He slumped against the hood of an old Chevy Impala and sighed.

Again it starts, Ned thought to himself.

It was this damn island. For a quiet little place where nothing ever happened, lots of things kept happening, and sooner or later the worst things seemed to land into the congenial laps of Ned and his friends at The Cooler.

"Okay," said Ned, resigned. "What to do with the dead body..."

"I suggest immediate burial," offered Tommie. "It's my opinion that most problems in life can be solved by covering them with six to ten feet of good soil."

"Except for toxic waste," offered Doc.

"Right, Doc, except for toxic waste," Tommie said agreeably. "As it happens, I've been helping the Sweetwater groundskeepers put in their new drainage system. There's a back hoe already on the course. The eleventh fairway."

"The body is already buried, in a way," said Hoak, "but only a few inches deep. Just off the golf course."

"Oops," said Doc, "We'd better get there before the raccoons find him, or his parts will be all over place."

← ← ←

The four men — Ned, Doc, Tommie and Hoak — split up and re-assembled at the General's house, shovels in hand, where they began their march across the General's back yard, through the deep stand of brush, and onto the grounds of Sweetwater Country Club.

"I don't see why we have to use shovels," Tommie said to the group. "I told you I've been working on the drainage system here. The back hoe is sittin' over on the eleventh fairway. I can have it over here in five minutes."

"Gee, Tommie, that might be a little conspicuous, a loud diesel grinding away at midnight," said Ned.

"Also," said Doc, "while the heavy steel claw is good for moving big chunks of earth, I wouldn't want to go probing around for a corpse with it. Might get messy."

General Hoak groaned in agreement. He was not looking in top form, exactly, but his spirits seemed to have perked up once the group had formulated a plan for keeping him out of trouble, though that plan consisted only, so far, of a second burial, this time deeper and further away from the fairway.

The General and the men finally arrived at a mulchy patch of forest floor just thirty feet or so from the edge of the eighteenth fairway. There in the ground was a shallow hole, dug no deeper than nine or ten inches. The soil and leaves that had once covered the hole had been swept aside, and the hole was empty.

"Oh God," rasped General Hoak. "The raccoons have got him already."

"You sure this is the spot, General?" asked Ned.

"Without a doubt," said Hoak.

Doc bent over the hole with his flashlight and examined the bottom of the grave. He found leaves darkened by a gooey substance.

"Blood and lots of it," said Doc. "Most of it has dried. This is definitely the spot."

Tommie swept his flashlight over the hole, and spread his search to the area around it.

"How about that," he said in wonderment.

"What is it?" Ned asked.

"These sweeping motions where the covering earth is spread out? Those were obviously made by the body — the guy — himself. And over here, see the footprints walking off? Just one set," Tommie said as he looked up at the general. "Looks like your target walked away under his own power."

"But there was blood everywhere!" Hoak said in astonishment.

"General," said Tommie, "looks like you shot yourself a *bona fide* tough guy. He's long gone by now."

"Good God, I buried the poor bastard alive!"

The group silently pondered this macabre development.

"So let's see where this leaves us," reflected Ned. "I guess you're off the hook for murder, General. That's good news, right there."

"Unless he's just wandering around on his last legs, so to speak," said Doc. "A head wound gushing that much blood is trouble, no matter how you look at it. He could just be stumbling around, ready to keel over for good."

"But look at the tracks," said Ned. "More or less straight toward the main road. He was together enough to know where he was going."

"Look here—I think he left something behind," said Doc as he bent over and swept aside some of the loose earth. When he straightened up he was holding a folded section of newspaper.

"It's the New York Times. Opened to the crossword puzzle."

"Biding his time while he was casing the houses," offered Tommie.

"Well, we know he was—is—a smart guy," commented Doc. "This is the Saturday puzzle, the toughest day, and he answered single every space... *in green ink.*"

Ned made a strange sort of involuntary choking sound. Doc shined his flashlight Ned's face—he had suddenly gone pale.

"You all right, Ned?" the doctor asked.

"What color ink did you say, Doc?" Ned managed to ask, weakly.

"It's green, Ned."

"Doc," Ned followed up in an increasingly strange tone of voice, "are the answers right?"

"Huh?" Doc wasn't getting him.

"The answers to the crossword. Are they the correct answers?"

The group regarded Ned quizzically.

"Well, let's see," said Doc, re-examining the puzzle, *"One, Down: the clue is 'Rascal'. Five letters.* Let's see..."

"Could be 'SCAMP'," offered Tommie.

"And what he's got here is… hmm… 'KITTY'. Can't see that, really. Let's try another. *Fifty-two, Across: Blanch. Six letters*. Kinda like what's happening to Ned's face right now. I'll guess 'WHITEN'. Jump in any time, General."

"Uh… how about 'BLEACH'?" Hoak ventured.

"Good. Let's see… our anonymous friend entered 'STELLA'. That's not going to work."

Doc scanned the remainder of the puzzle, surprised and even somewhat impressed by what he found.

"Damn," said Doc, "this guy is wrong about everything. Every square filled in, all the answers fit together, but not one of them is right. Curious."

"I'm not feeling so good," mumbled Ned, clearing his throat of nothing in particular. "Must be all the blood, or something. I think we're done here, huh General? At least for now?"

"I suppose so," replied Hoak.

"All right, then. I'll see you guys later," said Ned.

Ned wandered off in the general direction of the General's house, his course through the woods a bit meandering as he navigated his way absentmindedly and without the aid of his flashlight. His friends looked at each other and shared a shrug, then followed Ned, at a distance, into the darkness.

6.

Veronica returned to the Makoniky Country Inn just before noon, where Clive the Day Manager, a slight and pallid young Englishman, eagerly awaited her return. Clive watched, riveted, as Veronica ambled across the lobby, long and lean in her faded jeans and cowboy boots, striding the bare floor with a loping Western elegance that was unconsciously erotic in every nuance. American girls! Wonderful, thought Clive. Incredibly wonderful.

And here was the part Clive liked best: Veronica's head was tilted slightly forward, so that the bangs of her raven black hair swayed rhythmically as she moved, hiding and then revealing her eyes, back and forth, hiding and revealing. As she made her way toward Clive's desk, her bangs swung aside once more to reveal that her eyes were now focused on Clive, watching him as he watched her.

The Englishman gave a tiny, involuntary whimper.

"Any messages, Clive?"

"No — sorry, Ms. Lodge," said the Day Manager, struggling to disguise his breathlessness. "But your *friends* have returned."

"Well. That's something," she said.

Before she could turn away, he handed her a piece of note paper with a name and phone number scrawled upon it.

"This is a local doctor, a good one," Clive said in a confidential whisper, though they were alone in the room.

"He occasionally even makes house calls. I offered his name to your friends, but they declined."

"All right, Clive," said Veronica, puzzled. "Thank you."

Past the first flight of stairs, out of Clive's line of vision, Veronica retrieved the Beretta automatic from the holster in the small of her back, carefully attaching the silencer that she always kept in a special pocket sewn to her jacket's lining. Out of habit, Veronica ejected the gun's magazine and confirmed the full load of nine millimeter cartridges. There was a satisfying snap as she slid the magazine back into place. The cold metal felt good in her hands, and her body reacted instinctively to its oily, acrid scent; Veronica's pulse quickened ever so slightly, and she could feel a gentle surge of adrenaline run through her veins.

This was a welcome change from the uneventful day she had endured, so far. Restless that morning, Veronica had left the isolated inn to find breakfast and explore the nearby hamlets, Vineyard Haven and Oak Bluffs. The tour had not taken very long, as the towns offered little to distract her. The few people visible in the streets and shops seemed emotionally cocooned; civilized and occasionally courteous, but closed down. *"Closed for the season. Thanks for a great summer! See you next spring!"* So read the signs in the windows of half the shops in town, but Veronica figured the locals should have the same message pinned to their chests.

Jee-hova, she had thought to herself as she strolled the nearly desolate sidewalks of Main Street and Circuit Avenue, *how does anyone make it through the winter here?*

The only hint of drama came during a walk on the gray, storm-tossed beach in Vineyard Haven. There, Veronica came upon a pitiful deer carcass, washed up on the beach, its tiny two-point antler rack tangled with seaweed. Veronica looked across the quiet ocean and saw the mainland in the distance... how many miles? Ten? Veronica guessed that the deer had drowned attempting to escape the island, and she could relate. She planned to be doing the same, soon, hopefully with better results.

Gun in hand, Veronica finished her climb up the stairs and arrived at the door to her suite. In one swift motion, she unlocked the door, kicked it wide open, stepped through the entry and began shooting. *Phhhtt! Phhhtt! Phhhtt! Phhhtt! Phhhtt!* The silenced shots dug into mattresses, drilled holes in the wall plaster, exploded feather pillows and destroyed one lamp as the two male occupants in the room dove for cover, the rounds whispering past their heads. *Phhhtt! Phhhtt! Phhhtt! Phhhtt! Phhhtt!*

An audible *click* signaled an empty chamber in Veronica's gun.

There, thought Veronica, *that felt better already*. Of course, she had missed her kills intentionally, determined only to throw a serious scare into the brothers, and the effect had been achieved. She could smell naked fear in the air, mixed with gun smoke, and Veronica was reminded how well those two aromas complemented each other.

The two men were hidden from sight.

"No more shooting, Ron," one voice pleaded from behind one of the beds. "You have to be nice to me. I got buried alive!"

"Yeah," agreed a second man's voice from behind the armoire, "Don't shoot us."

Veronica slid a fresh magazine into her smoking weapon... *snap*.

"Oh, no," moaned the first voice.

Locked and loaded again, Veronica took a moment to survey the room. Aside from the destruction she herself had just caused, there were other relevant details to the scene. Bloody hotel towels were scattered all over the room. A bag of newly purchased first-aid products was spread out on the coffee table: antiseptics, analgesics, gauze and bandages.

"Come out, come out, wherever you are," ordered Veronica.

"No!"

"Idiots. You're still alive, right? Have you ever known me to miss something I was trying to hit?"

After a moment of consideration, the Friendship brothers, Ricky and Bobby, emerged timorously from their cover positions. The first thing Veronica noticed was the gash in Ricky's forehead, a bloody crease glaring and obscene, with a butterfly bandage incompetently applied to the wound. The action of diving behind the bed had caused the gash to re-open, a gooey stream of blood now seeping out from under the bandage and down the side of Ricky's face. Veronica also noticed, with interest, the men's' attire: both wore dark suits with white dress shirts and ties. Ricky's clothes were beyond filthy, from ground-in dirt as well as blood.

"Hi, Ron," said the bloody Ricky, the older and heavier of the two men, nudging his brother Bobby with an elbow.

"Yeah," Bobby added. "Hi Ron."

"Thirty-six hours you've been gone," Veronica said, forcing calm. "After I told you to stay here in the room—I could not have been clearer on that point—the two of you take off without a word and disappear for a day and a half."

"We'd been four days in this goddam room!" said Ricky. "The TV sucks here, and I ran through all my crosswords. It was too much, Ron."

That much Veronica did know. With their limited attention spans, she should not have expected that the Friendship brothers could stay put. She should have chained them to the radiator.

"Sit down. I want to hear it all," she said. "Right now."

"Ron, you always say we should use more initiative—"

"Are you fucking kidding me?" Veronica growled, "Why in God's name would I say that? I have *nightmares* about you using more initiative."

"But our idea… it's pretty good," Ricky sat on the edge of the bed, genuine excitement in his voice. "You maybe would have been happy with it. Under different circumstances."

"Goddam it, Ricky…" said Veronica, ready to lose all patience.

"Okay, okay, it's coming. We were stuck here, so bored that we started reading these old tourist magazines they got, and they're all about this island. Did you know, the President comes here and stuff? People invite him to use their big houses in Summer time, but maybe even for Thanksgiving or Christmas or whatever."

"So…"

"So there's a Goodwill store in town, and we pick up these suits, probably from dead old people or something. I don't know if you noticed, but there are lots of old people here…"

"You bought the suits using what cash? Don't say you cut it from the Denver take, 'cause we talked about how those bills might be traceable. Please don't say you did that."

The brothers were silent. Veronica bowed her head and sighed.

"Go on."

"So we put on these suits and some dark flier-boy shades and everything, and we drive around and pick nice, big houses and go up and knock on the door. Lots of times, no one's even home — we own those places, outright. Nobody even has alarms, around here. But if someone does answer the door, we put on a good show. We say *'Good day, Ma'am or Sir, whichever, we're from the United States Secret Service —"*

"Oh, no..." Veronica groaned.

"We say to them *'Someone really important — somebody huge! — is coming to stay nearby. We can't say who it is, but we need to do a security check of the residentials in the surrounding area. Would you mind if we came into your house and had a look around?'* And Ronnie, they get these big fuckin' smiles on their faces and the doors swing open like you wouldn't believe, like they just had won the fuckin' lottery or something."

"You didn't take them right then..."

"Of course not, who do you think we are?"

Veronica gave him a look.

"Well, we pocketed some small stuff, but mostly we just cased the places, you know, to come back later for the score. It was going beauty. We got a list as long as your arm, maybe just two nights or three nights work if we hustle hard. And the loot in these houses, Ronnie, these are prime goods. Just say the word and we're ready to go."

"You don't think this was a little high profile — the U.S. Secret Service? You guys spreading around hints that the most powerful man in the world was soon to arrive next door?"

"We told them all it was a big secret," Bobby contributed proudly. "See, that works because of the *Secret* Service part, and that it was a question of American security for them to keep quiet."

"Right," said Veronica, "In that case, they'll definitely keep quiet, like people always do."

"We were very firm," said Ricky.

Veronica glared at him. "Now let's talk about the blood." She motioned to the scattered heaps of soiled, bloody towels and bandages all over the room.

"Yeah, the blood. What happened was, we went to case these big honkin' houses on a golf course," Ricky explained. "I went around back, on the golf course side, and there was someone there on the grass. I remember seein' a gun and a flash and that's all. Bullet musta bounced off my head. I woke up in dirt, Ron!" Ricky rocked his head in remembered distress, his voice cracking and the promise of tears soon to follow. "In dirt! You can't know. You just can't."

"I was goin' through the woods all last night lookin' for him," said Bobby. "Finally found him stumblin' around near the main road this morning. What a fuckin' mess his head is! Have you seen it, Ronnie? Have a closer look."

"I can see fine from here," she said.

Veronica reflected in silence for a long moment.

"We have a job here…" she finally said, calmly.

"What job? Where's this big client you been talkin' about?" protested Ricky.

"We have a job here," Veronica continued, ignoring Ricky's interruption, "and we knew there might be some down time before the job went off, some quiet time, which is not a bad thing considering the fallout from Denver. I don't know yet what the job is, or was, but you may have screwed it."

"Four goddam days and no job!" Bobby protested. "It's not happening, Ron, you gotta see that."

"How did we get here, Ricky?" asked Veronica, her voice laced with a sarcastic hiss.

"Huh?"

"How did we get here? How did we get two thousand miles from Denver to this island? By Greyhound bus or grimy cargo train or some shitheap station wagon that you hotwired?"

"No," Ricky answered quietly, conceding the point. "We came in a jet, Ron. A private jet."

"Yeah," Bobby remembered wistfully, "that was nice."

"Our client's jet. A jet that was waiting when we needed it, where we needed it, just the way it was promised. Just the way this *job* was promised."

The Friendship brothers had no response.

"I don't know," Veronica shook her head despairingly, "I just don't know. Here we are on this tiny island to do a job, needing to lay low, and you boys are out there making a splash. The job may be screwed. And if it is, you better start looking for a shitheap to jack, Ricky, because if this job is screwed, we are not flying out of here in a private jet."

"You're a strong persuader, Ron," said Ricky, hanging his head in shame.

"I'm glad you see my point. And actually, you can forget anything about jacking a car. Because if you boys leave this room again, I will hunt you down and kill you both and after your next island burial, Ricky, you will not be walking away. I promise you that."

"We understand, Ron," said Ricky, giving his brother a nudge.

"We understand, Veronica," chimed Bobby.

"Good," she said. Veronica opened the door and left without another word, being sure to attach the 'Do Not Disturb' sign to the door handle.

The brothers sat in silence for a moment before either of them spoke.

"Screw her," said Ricky.

"Damn straight," agreed Bobby. "She can't tell us what to do. She's not our boss."

"Actually, she is," said Ricky. "But screw her anyway."

"Yeah," said Bobby, "screw her anyway."

7.

Veronica pulled her rental Jeep out of the Makoniky Inn parking lot — with an aggressive spin of knobby tires on dirt — and pointed it toward Edgartown, hoping the long drive across the island would burn off some of the irritation still lingering after her encounter with the Friendship brothers. Though her anger at the Friendships was justified, she could also relate to their impatience. Veronica herself was frustrated that their job had not yet begun. It had been two full days since the client had contacted her with so much as a status update — an unprofessional lapse. As for the brothers, the reckless Secret Service scam was just the latest offence in a series of that reached back many years. Veronica had tolerated these transgressions, over time, because the Friendships' criminal skill sets were useful and because she hated working with new people. Lately, however, she had begun to feel that the brothers caused more aggravation than they were worth. The time was approaching when Veronica would have to make a decision about their future.

Veronica passed a speed trap — a state trooper's cruiser backed into the woods along the road, poorly concealed by the scant winter foliage. She checked her speed, acceptable at forty-seven miles per hour but not suspiciously conscientious. Veronica had noticed that this island was crawling with cops; each town had its own force, plus a full Sheriff's Department and a local

contingent of State Troopers. It was a typical conundrum
for a resort community — too many cops in the off-season,
not nearly enough when the tourist onslaught began.

Halfway along the ten mile drive, a vehicle
appeared in Veronica's rear view mirror, two hundred
yards back, and hovered at that distance. It was not the
speed trap cop, but a civilian pickup truck. She marked
the position of the truck as several miles passed,
maintaining a consistent and unthreatening distance
behind her Jeep. Veronica was always on the alert for
threats from law enforcement or her competition, but had
no reason to believe that she had been made by anyone on
the island. There was a chance the Friendships and their
antics had somehow poisoned the well, but her
intuition — a reliable tool for Veronica — was not yet
sensing trouble.

Veronica sped up a few miles per hour. The
pickup stayed with her for a distance, then turned off onto
a dirt side-road and disappeared. She finished the drive to
Edgartown without further incident, parked on Main
Street and got out of the car, opened her cell phone and
strolled casually down toward the empty sidewalk as she
dialed.

"Speck residence," a small boy answered, over the
phone.

"Hello," said Veronica. "Is Mr. Speck at home?"

"May I ask who's calling?"

"No."

"Okay. In school they said we shouldn't give
information to strangers on the telephone, but you sound
nice."

"Thank you," Veronica said. Here's a kid with
flawed instincts, she thought. The world will eat him
alive.

"You're welcome," answered the kid. "Poppa is off-island."

Off-island. It was one of the first things Veronica had noticed about Martha's Vineyard; any person, place or thing, animal, vegetable or mineral, was first and foremost described as being one of two things, *on-island* or *off-island*. The distinction was critical to the local residents, apparently, having broad significance beyond merely describing physical location.

"Poppa is off-island, huh? Any idea when he'll be back?"

"No, ma'am. No one ever tells me anything," the boy said.

"What's your name?"

"Ripley"

"I'll tell you something, Ripley" said Veronica.

"Really?"

"Yeah. Your father is starting to piss me off." There was gleeful giggling over the line.

"See?" the boy said, "I knew you were nice."

After hanging up her cell phone—with no satisfaction for her effort—Veronica continued down Main Street, looking for an open bar. She had developed a hankering for alcohol; either tequila or scotch would do. She checked the time on her wristwatch, not for permission to drink but as a gauge of her state of mind. *Urge to drink at twelve forty two*, she noted to herself. Past noon, anyway. Anxiety level: four, on a scale of one to ten. She could live with that.

Veronica spotted a bar across the street and headed that way. As she abruptly changed direction, she caught a flash of movement out of the corner of her eye, a human figure quickly stepping out of her line of vision. Veronica did not turn to look more closely—she did not have to. She knew immediately that she was being followed.

Shit, thought Veronica. She knew this would turn out to be the driver of that pick-up truck that had been behind her on the way into town. But who could it be? There were several possibilities, but only a few were remotely likely. She held her course as she crossed the street, but passed the bar without going in. Keeping her stride relaxed, Veronica made her way down Main Street toward the harbor. Casually checking her surroundings the way a tourist might, she scanned the area for an opportunity.

Half a block before the harbor, a small wooden walkway veered away from the Main Street sidewalk toward a cluster of shops set back from the street. Veronica turned down the walkway, passing by several shops before she ducked quickly into the recessed doorway of a darkened boutique. There was one of those signs behind the door's window, crudely printed in faded black marker: *"Thanks for the great season! See you again in April!"*

In this recess Veronica waited silently, moving only to slip her gun out of its snug harbor at the small of her back. Soon she heard footsteps on the boardwalk, very close now. A man. In work boots, Veronica guessed. There was a pause in the steps, for just a moment, but then the man continued on at a cautious pace. Veronica was familiar with the tentative rhythm of her pursuer's footfall; it was the unmistakable sound of a man ignoring his better judgment, driven forward by an irresistible impulse. It was the egregious male flaw, typical and unfailing, upon which Veronica had capitalized so profitably across the years.

"Bread and butter," she whispered quietly to herself.

As the man passed by, Veronica stepped silently out of the shadowy doorway and pressed the muzzle of her automatic against the back of his skull. The man stopped cold and raised his hands, just high enough to demonstrate complete submission.

"Go ahead, Ronnie," said Ned Donlin. "Take me out. Best thing for everyone."

8.

"Are you sure, Ned?" asked Tommie Krupa. "Looks to me like his wood pile is half full already."

"More," Ned insisted.

Tommie was standing beside a five-ton truck, its bed loaded high with firewood logs that were cut to short lengths but still unsplit. He had already dumped a full cord of wood and was unsure about the wisdom of unloading more.

"It's not like this stuff will climb back on the truck by itself," added Tommie. "If it's more than Doc wants, you and him will have to work it out between you."

"More," repeated Ned.

Tommie shrugged and hit the hydraulic lever at the back of the truck. With a groan, the truck bed tilted back, sliding another cord of wood onto the driveway with a loud rumble.

"When," said Ned.

Tommie returned the truck bed to its level position, stopping the flow of logs. Without another word, Ned applied himself to the pile of wood, standing the logs on end and attacking them with a seven pound splitting mawl. He grunted loudly each time as he heaved the mawl up into a high arc, and then let the tool's head weight take over, carrying it's momentum down and through the logs. The wood sounded a deeply satisfying *crack!* as it split, sending the divided sections flying in every direction.

Tommie climbed up onto the truck bed and made himself a comfortable recliner among the remaining logs, lighting a Tiparillo as he observed Ned's furious chopping.

"You just lemme know when you're ready to talk," said Tommie.

Ned did not respond, other than his usual grunt when he again swung the mawl into its arc, splitting the next victim. *Crack!*

Ned, Tommie and the logs occupied the driveway of the Titus house, a large, green-shingled Victorian in the Ocean Park section of Oak Bluffs. Doc Titus and his wife Florence had been hard at work restoring the place since they moved to the island ten years earlier. It was now nearly perfect, a showcase of pristine Cape architecture equal to anything of its kind. Ten years of dedicated work by the Tituses, however, was now blighted by the unsightly mountain of logs that had been so rudely dumped onto their driveway.

Doc emerged from the house, escorting an eight year old girl, Darcy, and her pet, a ferret named Sid. Doc had specialized as an equine vet when he was practicing, and was now supposedly retired, but a sizeable traffic of walk-in patients ended up in his office anyway, pets of every domestic category plus a steady stream of wounded birds from the wild, courtesy of Ned Donlin.

Doc took great pride in his ability to mend the delicate broken bones of the wild birds. This duty, combined with the work on his Oak Bluffs home, had done much to restore the healing spirit that Doc Titus had lost during his tenure as a racetrack vet in Florida, a seventeen year period of virtual indentured servitude in the 1970s and 80s, when he had been forced to practice a form of medicine resembling nothing so much as battlefield triage.

"Sid will eat anything he can get into," Doc was telling little Darcy as they walked together down the front steps of his house, "so it's up to you to make sure he only gets the things I wrote on the list."

"Okay, Doc," agreed Darcy, consoling Sid the dyspeptic ferret with a delicate stroking of his silky neck fur.

"And you have the stomach medicine. Be sure to mix it in every time you —" Doc stopped short as he suddenly caught sight of the massive pile of wood in his driveway.

"Hey hey hey," he protested to Ned and Tommie, "You said *some* wood, guys. *Some* wood I could use, but this is *much* wood, Tommie, *too much* wood. There's got to be two cords here. What am I going to do with all this?"

"Don't look at me," said Tommie from his firewood throne, "I wash my hands of it. This is Ned's doing."

Doc sighed and turned back to the little girl.

"Head on home, Darcy, and give me a call if there are any more problems," said Doc.

"Thank you, Doc," Darcy said. As she passed the firewood truck, she waved at Tommie Krupa.

"Hi, Tractor Tommie," said Darcy.

"Hi, honey," Tommie replied shyly.

"Tractor Tommie?" Doc asked, as Darcy wandered off down the street.

"They had me over for 'Career Day' at the grammar school," Tommie shrugged.

"Really? Under what category?"

"*All of the above*," answered Tommie, puffing proudly on his Tiparillo. "Confirming that I am multitudes. It's the handyman's prerogative, Doc — just sort of floating around, a free agent, doing this and doing that but without specific commitments or labels, having made no irreversible decisions about who I am or my place in the world."

"And thus, blissfully avoiding any sense of your own mortality?"

"Exactly."

"Interesting, Tommie. Thanks for sharing your doomed strategy for happiness."

"Any time, Doc," said Tommie.

Doc turned back to Ned, refocusing on the unsightly problem at hand.

"Now," said Doc to Ned, "what is *your* dysfunction?"

Ned continued chopping without even looking up.

"He ain't talkin'," said Tommie, "but he obviously has some anger to work through."

"It's not anger," Ned blurted angrily as he continued to split the logs. Crack!

"Then what are we talking about, Ned?" asked Doc.

"Lust," answered Ned, without elaboration. Crack!

"Excellent. Lust and related topics I could talk about all day," Tommie said.

"So... you've got some extra lust that you would rather not have?" Doc asked Ned. "And your solution is to deposit upon my previously undefiled driveway a great amount of wood for which I currently have no need, so that you can chop away and exercise — ex_or_cise — the demon lust from your loins?"

"Ooo, Doc, don't stop," said Tommie.

"And there is some anger included," conceded Ned, straightening himself up as he ceased splitting wood for the moment, catching his breath. "Even some fear, maybe."

"Tell us," said Doc.

And so he did.

The night before last, standing with Doc, Tommie and General Hoak over the empty grave in the woods of Sweetwater Country Club, Ned's heart had skipped several beats when Tommie discovered the crossword puzzle near the grave site; the puzzle had been fully completed, in green ink, with no mistakes crossed out yet not a single answer correct.

Ricky Friendship, Ned had realized immediately, *without a doubt*.

Ned tried desperately to reach any other conclusion, but he could not. A crossword with all incorrect answers, but completed in full with no gaps? A unique, antisocial sort of intelligence was required to achieve that feat, and Ricky had been bestowed with just that characteristic—in spades. As for the green ink, Ricky refused to use any other color pen, saying he liked how the green reminded him of money.

So Ricky Friendship was on the island, and where there was a Ricky Friendship, there must also be a Bobby Friendship, for only death—or possibly the penal system—would ever separate the two. Ned also knew, too well, that the Friendship brothers were professional lackeys. Talented in some areas, it was true, but not very successful as self-motivators. Alone, they had neither the will nor the imagination to steer themselves this far away from their home turf, not even if they were desperately on the lam.

Ned had realized, with absolute certainty, that Veronica Lodge was on his island, and he was stunned by that unacceptable development. It was a revelation that he was not nearly ready to share with his friends, and so Ned had hurried off alone, without proper explanation, leaving them behind at the open grave.

The next morning, after a sleepless night, Ned had begun calling the few open hotels and inns on the island, starting with the most remote. The search had not taken very long; the handful of inns still open on the island had few guests, especially in the middle of the week, so the party Ned was looking for would be more than noticeable. By his third call, Ned found himself on the phone with Clive, the Day Manager at the Makoniky Country Inn.

"Good morning, Ned."

"Yep. Listen, Clive, I'm wondering who you've got in the way of guests."

"Now? Uh… well, let me think…"

Ned noticed a strange tone in Clive's voice.

"I'm looking for a woman…" Ned continued.

"Aren't we all? *Heh heh…*" Clive chuckled nervously.

"A particular woman, Clive."

"There's no one of that description here," Clive blurted nonsensically, with the selfish and defensive tone of a child who had discovered a trove of hidden candy and didn't want to share it with his playmates. It was a common reaction to Veronica Lodge; Ned had experienced it himself, and immediately recognized the symptoms in Clive.

"So she's there. Veronica Lodge."

"Yes," Clive acknowledged with a cranky reluctance, imagining his secret candy cache spilling out onto a crowded schoolyard.

"What about friends?" asked Ned, cutting Clive off.

"In a separate room. Two of them."

"Either of them bleeding?"

"Now that you mention it," said Clive, surprised, "bleeding profusely."

Ned had immediately jumped in his truck and driven to the Makoniky Country Inn, parking discreetly in the woods across from the inn to begin an impromptu stake-out. He was sickened to find himself there, hiding alone in his truck, fingers white-knuckled as they gripped the steering wheel. He had the racing heartbeat of a scared rabbit, and the first sight of Veronica, as she left the Makoniky later that morning, did not improve his condition. Her walk, her body, the way her black bangs swayed back and forth as she moved… *ouch*. Ned had suddenly felt like a pathetic schoolboy, an undersized and acne-plagued social pariah, spying on the head cheerleader from behind the bleachers of a high school football field. Pitiful.

Ned had followed her. A face-to-face confrontation seemed inevitable, but he was determined to first find out what he could about her presence on the island. It had to be a job—Veronica was not the vacationing type—but what could possibly bring her here, to Martha's Vineyard, in winter? And what were the Friendships doing on the eighteenth fairway of Sweetwater in the middle of the night? Breaking and entering? No. The notorious and celebrated Veronica Lodge did not travel two thousand miles to jack plasma TVs out of empty summer homes.

Ned followed Veronica as she turned her Jeep onto the road to Edgartown, but after less than two miles her driving pattern had become noticeably cautious—she had obviously picked up the tail. Stealth had never been Ned's strong suit. He was forced to turn off the main road and let her go. He finally caught up with her again in Edgartown, first spotting the rental Jeep and then her, as she stood alone on Main Street, making a call on her cell phone. When she hung up the phone and moved on, Ned followed her on foot, with predictable and familiar results. In less than a minute, he had the cold muzzle of

Veronica's Beretta asserting itself against the base of his skull.

Ned's one satisfaction came when he turned to face her and found genuine surprise in her eyes when she first saw his face. That was a first. Veronica took pride in expecting the unexpected. She even caught her breath, audibly and somewhat dramatically, but that effect was just flattering enough to Ned to make him suspicious.

Probably faked, he thought. Veronica was an excellent performer under pressure.

"Ned?" she whispered in wide-eyed astonishment. The wide eyes faked, *definitely*.

"Yeah, but... you're not here for me, are you?"

"Well, no, sweetheart," she said with a leer, "but I guess I got lucky."

The reunion had not gone well for Ned. His very first move was to offer Veronica quite a lot—namely, the world—to leave the island immediately and never come back.

"Really, Ned?" said Veronica. "The entire world?"

"Yes. You get the world, I'll settle for just Martha's Vineyard. Hold on... throw in all of Cape Cod and the islands, to be on the safe side, and while you're at it, Bolivia."

"Bolivia?"

"In case things here fall apart, which they just might. I'll need a place to start over."

"I've been there, Ned, and trust me—things have changed since the Butch and Sundance days. You and Bolivia are not a match. Let's see... I know! Take Eritrea. I can't go back there, anyway."

"Eritrea?"

"East coast of Africa. Oil reserves, political chaos, tons of potential. Look it up."

"Oil, huh? Anything else to recommend it?"

"Their struggle against Ebola and famine are slowly making headway. Plus the weather is nice. As I remember, you like a dry heat."

"It's a desert? Fine, I accept. So we have a deal?"

"No. Sorry. Can't leave the island just yet," she said, adding with a naughty smile, "Which is good. We have catching-up to do."

Tommie Krupa felt obligated to interrupt the story, at this point.

"Wait wait wait, now," Tommie said, sounding annoyed. "Hold on just a second…"

"What, Tommie?" Ned asked. By this point in his retelling, Ned had taken a break from splitting logs, and was sitting on his stack of freshly split firewood, streaks of dried sweat marking his face, sipping a beer in the afternoon air. A full cord of unchopped logs still waited, a few feet away, to be serviced.

"I just want to be clear on a few things," said Tommie, "to confirm that you are as screwed-up as I believe you to be."

"Go on."

"You were with this Lodge woman two years?" asked Tommie.

"Almost three," replied Ned.

"By the way," Doc interjected, "I know the name Veronica Lodge from somewhere. Is she famous?"

"Not in veterinary circles, no," said Ned. "You might know the name from a comic book, which is where she got it. She needed an alias in a hurry-up kind of way, and she picked the name from a comic in a dentist's waiting room."

"And her real name?" Doc asked.

"She's from a well-to-do family in Phoenix," said Ned. "They're cactus farmers. Aloe Vera barons, actually. Not to be secretive, but Veronica swore me never to —"

"Not important anyway," Tommie cut him off. "So with this woman you experienced many adventures about which you will not be specific…"

"Not at this time."

"…and you shared almost three years of outlaw sex. Now you see this woman again, by surprise, and you're feeling the urges of this kind again. A rekindling, as it were?"

"Yes," answered Ned.

"Get it?" Tommie grinned, "Re-*kindling*? You're sitting on a stack of wood."

"So you have some regrets about that period in your life," Doc took up the inquisition of Ned, "and you don't want to repeat previous mistakes. So you're going to split firewood, here in my driveway, until you are anesthetized by exhaustion, so that you won't have to stand up, like a man, and face these issues from your past?"

In answer, Ned finished off his beer and turned to face the wood pile again, grimly. He set a log up on its end then heaved high his splitting mawl, bringing it down with a sharp report — *crack!* — just as a Jeep pulled up and parked in front of Doc's house. Veronica Lodge and the Friendship brothers stepped out of the Jeep.

"Well, how about this? Small island you got here, Nedly," said Veronica.

9.

Tommie and Doc fixed their eyes on Veronica as she stepped out of the jeep and headed their way, looking her hell's-vixen best in black tights and a warm shearling jacket.

"Oh, boy," said Tommie, a little too loudly, as he ogled an eyeful.

"Amen," agreed Doc.

"Hi, Ned," the Friendship brothers chimed together as they approached the woodpile. Ricky had what looked like a full roll of gauze wrapped around his head, stained in front with a great deal of blood.

"Boys," nodded Ned with resignation in his voice. "To be honest, Ricky, you've looked better."

"Tell me about it," said Ricky.

"We're looking for a Dr. Titus," said Veronica, "A friend gave us his name."

"I'm Doc Titus," Doc stepped forward and smiled brightly, making no disguise of his enchantment with Veronica. Ned groaned aloud at the sight of it, hating to see Veronica's charms infecting his support structure like this.

"My associate here is in need of a little medical attention," Veronica said to Doc.

"Well, I'm actually retired…" Doc said.

"*Please*, Obee-Wan?" said Veronica with a playful smile. "You're our only hope."

"Oh, brother," moaned Ned.

"Okay," said Doc immediately. "Come on inside."

Ned rolled his eyes as Doc led the Friendships into the big house.

Veronica remained out front, with Ned and Tommie.

"Hi," she said, greeting Tommie girlishly. "I'm Veronica."

"Hi. I'm Tommie," grinning like a fool. "I'm a very good friend of Ned's."

"I'm very pleased to meet you. Uh, Tommie… do you suppose I could have a moment alone with Mr. Donlin here?"

"Not a problem," said Tommie, a little disappointed but happy enough to grant Veronica any wish. As Tommie headed for the house, he stopped beside Ned and whispered in his ear.

"Life is short, Ned. Don't be an idiot."

"Thanks for the support, Tom," he said as Tommie disappeared into the Titus house, leaving Ned and Veronica alone together.

"Hi again, sweetheart," said Veronica.

Ned sighed, set down his beer and gripped the splitting mawl with both hands, feeling its weight and destructive capability. An evil thought crossed his mind, where it was intercepted by Veronica.

"You'd never get away with it," she said. "Too many witnesses."

Ned realized she was right, and redirected his evil intent at the as-yet-unsplit cord of wood still stacked before him.

Crack!

In Doc's office, Ricky Friendship took a seat on Doc's big oak writing desk, which Doc always kept cleared and ready for use as an exam table.

"Let's have a look, Mr...."

"Smith," answered Ricky.

As Doc tended to Ricky, Bobby Friendship poked curiously around the study, appraising keepsakes on the shelves and studying Doc's credentials on the walls. Tommie entered and sat down in Doc's rocker, keeping a suspicious eye on both Friendships.

"Okay, Mr. Smith, let's have a look-see," said Doc, unconsciously slipping into his bedside voice as he unwrapped the gauze around Ricky's head, revealing...

"Yikes," Doc exclaimed, "*yech.*"

The gash in Ricky's forehead was badly infected and bloated with puss.

"Holy shit," said Tommie, "that cut's got more colors than a baboon's ass."

"Who did the work on this?" asked Doc, appalled.

"That's me," acknowledged Bobby, testily. "I ain't no doctor. That's why we're here, get it?"

"We've got some cleaning to do, for starters," said Doc. Ricky snarled in pain as Doc injected a local anesthetic into his forehead, and then began working through the infection, clearing a path to the original wound.

"Ahhh! Take it easy, man."

Doc worked at Ricky's skin until only the original gash remained, freshly scrubbed pink now, with just a hint of skull beneath.

"Hmm," said Doc, "what did you say happened?"

"I hit my head," answered Ricky, "I walked into a ceiling beam. It's these old houses around here—all the ceilings are so low. Who were they made for, anyway? Circus midgets?"

"Hit a low beam, huh?" said Doc, noting a dent in the skull where a bullet had deflected. "What caliber?"

"Weren't no pea shooter, I'll tell you that," offered Bobby.

"Shut up, Bob," said Ricky.

"Right," said Doc, and turned to Tommie, "maybe a forty-five, huh?"

"A Colt, just maybe," nodded Tommie. "Full circle on that adventure, eh Doc?"

"What are you talking about?" Ricky asked suspiciously.

"Don't worry about it," said Doc. "We're gonna disinfect this and sew it up. Then you're off the slab."

"Hey, Doc?" Bobby Friendship was taking a close look at Doc's framed medical school diplomas. "How come all your stuff has pictures of horses on 'em?"

"What?" shouted Ricky, alarmed. "You're a goddam vet?!"

"Listen to me, you little pissant," Doc said calmly as he prepared the suture needle and thread, "I am a fully trained physician, better than you deserve, in fact. Regardless of my chosen specialty, I am more than capable of treating your problem with the appropriate level of humanity. If you have any doubts about that, I encourage you to seek help elsewhere."

"Yeah, well, okay. Go ahead," said Ricky, his concerns eased by Doc's professionalism. "No offense, Doctor."

"That's all right," said Doc, addressing the wound again with needle in hand. "Now, this shouldn't hurt. If you feel more than a little sting, stomp your foot twice."

Meanwhile, back out in front of Doc's house, Ned took a break from splitting wood. He sipped his beer again and faced Veronica.

"I may have been a bit antagonistic, before," said Ned. "I mean in Edgartown. Sorry about that."

"It's good to see you, Ned, after all this time."

81

"It's good to see you too, Ron, and I do mean that. Surprisingly. But—"

"But you'd like me to leave as soon as possible."

"It's just that I've put together something resembling a life here, and I'm protective of it."

"I understand, Ned," she replied. "I do. I always figured you for a settlin' down kind of guy."

"Really?"

"I'd like to hear about it—the birds and the turtles and so forth, I mean. Maybe some time later on."

"You know about the sanctuary?"

"I've heard a little. You've got nothing to worry about. Sooner or later, my job here will happen—"

"Stop, please," objected Ned, "I don't want to know anything about it."

"I'll do the job," she continued, "and then I'll be gone."

Ned didn't respond.

"That's what you want, right?" said Veronica.

"That's what I want," said Ned, feeling relatively sure of himself.

Doc and the others emerged from the house. Ricky had a new bandage on his forehead, which was much less swollen now. After a brief argument over who would ride shotgun, the Friendships climbed into the Jeep.

"Ned," Doc said, "Nora called. She says to 'check the Board', whatever that means. Said it was urgent."

"Okay, thanks," said Ned, understanding the message but wondering what could be so important, and guessing it was probably not anything good.

"Sounds like you're getting a call on the Bat Phone, Ned," Veronica teased. "We better get out of your way."

Ned, Tommie and Doc all watched Veronica as she headed for the Jeep. She was just about to climb into the driver's seat when she paused and spun around to look at Ned, her straight black bangs swinging gently aside to reveal her eyes.

Damn it, thought Ned.

"Later, Nedly," she said with a smile, and then to Doc and Tommie, "See you fellas."

Veronica climbed behind the wheel of the Jeep and drove off.

"Wow, Ned," said Tommie.

"Yep," said Ned.

"Ned," said Doc, "this thing about 'checking the Board'…"

"Yeah?"

"Nora actually sounded quite urgent. Panicked, maybe."

"Huh," said Ned. "Okay if I use your laptop?"

Doc agreed, and the three men hustled into Doc's office, where the laptop was already running. With Doc and Tommie looking over Ned's shoulder, he opened the internet browser and went straight to the Audubon Society's own web site, where Ned clicked on the link marked "Rare Bird Alerts" — the section of the site known to Ned as "The Board" — and navigated to the section of the list that covered the American North East coast. In autumn and spring, the peak birding seasons, The Board would be crowded with postings, but at that point there were only a handful of sightings recorded.

"What's Nora's fuss about?" asked Doc, as Ned scrolled through the few recent postings.

"No clue," said Ned. "I don't see anything that would — "

Ned stopped speaking as the answer to Doc's question now appeared on the screen in front of him. The most recent posting on the board was dated and timed for that day, January 7, at one twenty-three PM, just hours earlier. The posting gave Ned a shock larger, even, than seeing Veronica Lodge after all these years. Ned's throat constricted until he could barely breathe, and his heart thrummed at a hummingbird's pace.

"Holy shit," said Ned, out loud.

The posting read:

Vanellus Caucasus?

Martha's Vineyard, Massachusetts
January 12
Uncorroborated
Unconfirmed
See attached file:

"Vanellus Caucasus?" Tommie said, butchering the pronunciation. "But isn't that the—"

"Yes, it is," answered Ned. His fingers trembled as he clicked the cursor twice on the attached file. In a flash, Ned and his friends were staring at a photograph: an out-of-focus, amateurish image, obviously taken with a long telephoto lens and no stabilizing tripod, of a single bird. For all the technical shortcomings of the photo, for all of Ned's own conflicting thoughts (hope and/or dread) about the bulletin's authenticity or lack thereof, it was immediately clear to Ned that he and his friends were, at that moment, staring at the image of one adult female, thought-to-be-long-extinct Caucasian Lapwing.

"Uh oh," said Ned.

"Someone thinks they saw the supposedly extinct Caucasian," asked Doc.

"Yeah," answered Ned.

"Here on the island," said Doc, considering the ramifications.

"Yeah."

"Who else is gonna read this notice?" asked Tommie.

"Every birdwatcher in the civilized world," Ned answered with confidence.

"And what are they doing to do once they read it?" Tommie seemed to sense the answer to this question, all on his own, but he had noticed that Ned was starting to look shell-shocked; he wanted to keep Ned's brain working.

But it was Doc who answered the question.

"They're going to come here," said Doc. "In droves."

"Including your 'special' contributors?" Tommie asked Ned.

"Especially them," said Ned, almost choking on the words. "All of them."

10.

Arnie Speck scurried from window to window, parting the blinds just enough to scan the perimeter of his property. He could barely see from the sting in his eyes; it was goddam January and here he was with rivers of sweat running off his head. As if the shakes and cramps and diarrhea weren't enough. Speck went to the bathroom and pulled out a beach towel, lamely wrapping it around his head like a turban to protect his eyes from the salty deluge.

Where the hell was Fyodor, anyway?

Speck returned to the window to check the north lawn. It looked clear, but wait — over there behind the Webster cottage — there was one in a heavy blue parka, mostly hidden but poking his head out every few minutes to scope Arnie's house. That made three of them in all — three that Speck knew about, anyway. They had hounded him relentlessly on the mainland, in New York and Miami and Atlanta, in airports and in hotels and in the streets. Arnie had deluded himself into thinking that a return to the Vineyard would somehow bring him relief.

He had been wrong.

Now the phone rang, and Arnie scurried to pick it up.

"Dude!" said Fyodor, on the other end of the line, "you are back?"

"Fyodor, goddamit!" Arnie shouted desperately into the phone. "Where are you?"

"Dude, I go by house and see the narcs, they are everywhere. In street, in yard, hiding behind trees —"

"They aren't narcs, you idiot! They're process servers! It's only about subpoenas. Get your Bolshevik ass over here now!"

Arnie slammed down the phone. He had met the Russian two years ago while playing a round of golf at Sweetwater. Back then, the intense pain from Speck's herniated disk had made his life an absolute misery, contorting him into a hunched, pathetic old man who could barely climb out of his golf cart, much less make a decent swing. His doctors kept insisting that surgery was the only solution, but Arnie was terrified of going under the knife. He would never let those hacks cut into him, ever. Arnie figured he would just continue numbing the pain chemically, but after years of constant drug use his prescription meds were about as effective as children's chewable vitamins.

Fyodor, the Sweetwater groundskeeper and sympathetic local dope connection, had slipped Arnie a special pain-killing opiate with a Russian brand name that Arnie had never heard of. The drug, which Arnie inhaled through a nebulizer, was an instant success. After two quick hits, Arnie had straightened out his back for the first time in weeks, suddenly feeling large and in charge as the dope surged through his system. Arnie had golfed one of the best rounds of his life that afternoon — a 74! — hitting off Fy's inhaler every thirty minutes or so to keep his engine primed. Thus began the dynamic state of narcosis that had dominated Arnie Speck's life for the last two years, a delicate chemical balance that had been challenged, recently, by the added stress of Arnie's personal financial crisis.

When he had full access to his brilliant new medication, Arnold Speck convincingly presented himself to the world as a self-possessed and aggressively resourceful businessman, straight and tall and fit. He had felt no back pain at all in almost two years. For some months now, in fact, he had noticed a comprehensive numbness in his entire nervous system. Life was beautiful again, Arnie figured, and it would remain that way as long as he didn't venture from the island — from Fyodor, really — for too long. The few times that Arnie had been careless enough to let his inhaler supply run low, he had quickly devolved into the wretched and desperate junkie that was on display right now.

Arnie felt a sudden balloon of pressure somewhere in his gut and made a dash for the bathroom.

Which way will it come? he wondered, guessing at the last second and sliding across the tile on his knees until he slammed against the toilet and thrust his head inside the bowl. Right answer. A viscous stream blasted up through his throat and into the toilet. He was just finishing off with a convulsive round of dry heaves when he heard a voice behind him.

"Poppa? Is that you in the potty?"

Speck moaned and slumped down on the floor, leaning limply against the toilet bowl as his son stepped into the bathroom doorway.

"Poppa?"

The first sight of his son Ripley, especially after a few days' absence, was always a shock. The nine-year-old was round and soft and warm and vulnerable. Could this really be my spawn, Speck often asked, but it was a rhetorical question only. Arnie knew exactly how he had ended up with a kid like this.

As a young and very successful entrepreneur, a man of working class roots, Arnie had insisted on marrying "above" himself, to a Beacon Hill debutante with an established family name. Their engagement guaranteed full coverage in every society column in the Northeast, and that had been important to Arnie, at the time. He had especially looked forward to melding his confident and aggressive "street" genes with Caroline's refined Boston Brahmin blood line, producing a brood of genetically superior hybrids, innately powerful yet socially adept, who would rule the Speck empire with brilliant success for countless generations.

Things had not turned out as planned, however; the sole and sad result of the Speck's coupling stood before Arnie now, weak of body and cursed with the survival instincts of a lap dog.

Ripley giggled at the sight of his father.

"Poppa, you have a towel on your head! Like a genie!"

"Leave me alone," groaned Arnie. "Go find Anastasia and do your math or something."

"Anastasia has been gone since July, silly Poppa. It's Isabella now."

"Whatever."

Arnie's wife, Caroline, was currently on a spending spree in Milan, leaving her progeny in the care of his latest nanny.

"May I read you my school paper?" Ripley asked, excited.

"No. Go away."

"It's called 'The Devil's Bridge'."

Arnie groaned, trying to raise himself off the floor in order to get away from the hectoring whelp, but Arnie's legs refused to work.

"Trapped," he said out loud.

"*The Devil's Bridge*", Ripley began reading, oblivious to his father's agony. "*A long long time ago, before the pilgrims came to America, the peaceful Wampanoag people lived happy lives on the island of Nope.*" Ripley paused and looked up at Arnie. "*Nope* was what Martha's Vineyard was called back then, Poppa."

How could Arnie ever hand over his hard fought fortune to this babbling simpleton? True, his "empire" was now in the red to the tune of two hundred and seventy three million dollars, and still plummeting, but this was nothing more than a temporary setback. In the usual Speck fashion, he would rise from the ashes and restore his estate to its former greatness. But why bother? So Ripley could inherit the riches, only to be preyed upon by hucksters and parasites and squander it all? More than once, Arnie had daydreamed of trading Ripley in to an orphanage and bringing home in his place a lean, street-seasoned urchin who Arnie could mold in his own powerful image.

It could happen.

"*The Wampanoag people shared the island with giants,*" Ripley continued with his narrative. "*One was an evil spirit named Cheepii Unck.*"

"Cheepii Unck?" Arnie interjected. "I thought the Vineyard giant was named Moshup." Arnie was not entirely ignorant of the native folklore — he had included some well-chosen details, for effect, in the brochure for his latest housing development, his sure-to-be crowning achievement, "Noman's Dunes".

"No, Papa. Moshup was the nice giant who ate whales on a stick, like a corndog," said Ripley. "Cheepii Unck was the mean giant."

"Silly me," said Arnie.

"*One day,*" Ripley continued reading, "*some of the people on the island got an idea. 'We should have a bridge to the mainland,' they said. 'Then we could trade things with the mainland people, and they could come visit us whenever they wanted. We would all be rich and even happier than now. We should definitely build a bridge.'*"

"A bridge?" Arnie muttered.

A bridge between the Vineyard and the mainland! What was it, three or four miles across the water? Was it even possible? Arnie's mind, even in the midst of its spiraling delirium, was suddenly swimming with the potentialities. A bridge! If anyone could pull it off, it would be him. He would call it the 'Speck Span'. He would charge toll and build parking lots and be richer than God.

"But half of the Wampanoag said 'No!'" Ripley continued, *"'We should definitely not build a bridge. We are so happy now and we should not be greedy. The people on the mainland are savages and if there is a bridge they will be here all the time, and the island will be crowded and they will teach our kids bad things. We should definitely NOT build a bridge.'"*

Of course, thought Arnie, *that sounds familiar*. For years he had been battling the local planning commission over projects he had proposed for his island property — parking lots, mini-malls, entertainment complexes, even a few tastefully disguised fast food franchises. The paranoid, xenophobic socialists on the planning commission had fought Arnie at every turn and, at least so far, had won.

"Well? Go on!" said Arnie impatiently. "What happened?"

"Half the people wanted the bridge and half the people did not. They could not all reach a decision, and so they stopped fighting for awhile and went to bed. But the people who wanted the bridge had a tricky idea. They went to Cheepii Unck, the evil giant, and made a deal with him to build the bridge anyway, without all the island people deciding together."

"Good thinking," said Arnie. "Bring in mercenaries."

"They told Cheepii Unck that if he would spend one whole night building a bridge for them, they would give him enough tobacco to fill his pipe that he really loved to smoke."

"Wow," said Arnie, "labor for drugs. These people were vastly ahead of their time." Arnie Speck was actually starting to choke up a little, swept up in an unexpected feeling of camaraderie with the pre-Columbian natives.

"*The other people,*" continued Ripley, "*the ones who were against the bridge, woke up and heard the bad giant at work, but there was nothing they could do. Cheepii Unck was too strong to fight against. 'How will we stop this?' they asked each other. But no one could think of a way to stop Cheepii Unck, so he kept on working. He carried huge rocks into the Sound and threw them into the water to form the bridge.*"

"Wait just a second," said Arnie. "There actually was a bridge? They won?"

"Poppa!" Ripley said, exasperated. "You have to wait for me to finish!"

"Then go on, dammit."

"*Late in the night,*" Ripley went on, "*when Cheepii Unck had already put down a bunch of big rocks, an old lady squaw, who was against the bridge, got an idea. She lit a torch and waved it in front of the face of her big rooster. The rooster woke up and saw the light and thought the sun was coming up.*"

"Oh no…" gasped Arnie.

"*The rooster crowed and crowed and crowed! When Cheepii Unck heard the rooster crowing, he thought it was morning already.*"

"That's monkey-wrenching!" objected Arnie. "Eco-terrorism!"

"*Cheepii Unck had only made a deal to work one night on the bridge, so he stopped working and took all the tobacco the people had and went off to smoke by himself. The bridge was never finished. Today, those big rocks are still spread out under the water in Vineyard Sound. Many ships have crashed and wrecked on the line of rocks that everyone calls* The Devil's Bridge. *The End.*"

Ripley looked up with a proud smile. Arnie was looking worse than ever, completely exhausted and dispirited by the tragic story.

"Urg…" groaned Arnie.

"Are you feeling all right, Poppa?"

"No, I'm not, Rodney."

"*Ripley*, Poppa" the boy giggled.

"Ripley. *The Ripster*. Just tell me one thing, kid. Which way would you vote — bridge or no bridge?"

Ripley burst into breathless laughter, so amused was he by the obviousness of the answer.

"No bridge! Of course, Poppa!" he shrieked.

Arnie felt the abdominal balloon again and twisted himself up until his head was deep into the ceramic bowl. He retched and retched, the bile hurling out of his mouth until his guts were spewed empty. Arnie slumped back against the bathroom wall and stared weakly at his boy.

Tomorrow we'll go to the orphanage, Arnie thought to himself.

"Do Poppa a favor, kid — go get me a big glass of soda water with lots of ice. I think…"

"I'm gonna call 9-1-1," Ripley interjected. "I think you're dying, Poppa."

"You sure as goddam hell are NOT going to call 9-1-1! Go right now and get me — "

But before Arnie could finish his tirade, he was interrupted by the sound of the door bell.

"Thank God!!" Arnie shouted groggily. "Go let Fyodor in!"

"But…"

"Right now!"

Ripley hustled off to answer the door, and Arnie struggled to his feet, stumbling out of the bathroom as best he could. He had finally reached the main hallway, at long last, when footsteps approached him.

"Thank God you're here, Fyodor," said Arnie, trying to focus his bleary eyes. "Give it to me now."

Arnie reached out and groped for the anticipated nebulizer, but instead felt an envelope slide into his hand.

"Arnold Speck?" asked an unfamiliar voice.

"Huh?" Arnie said, confused.

"You've been served."

The stunned Arnie finally focused on the man before him. It was not Fy the Sweetwater groundskeeper at all, but the process server in the blue parka who had been skulking behind the Webster cottage.

"You son of a bitch!" Arnie roared. He lurched toward the process server, who turned on his boot heels and hurriedly retraced his steps down the hallway. Arnie staggered after him in a futile gesture of pursuit. The server raced out the front door, bulling past Fyodor, who was just that moment arriving himself.

"God dammit!" Arnie bellowed, then turned immediately to Fyodor. "Gimme now!"

Arnie rifled desperately through Fy's pockets, finally finding a nebulizer. He stuffed the vent in his mouth and squeezed, deeply inhaling several hissing blasts of the misted narcotic.

With surprising quickness, the drug began having its effect. In just moments, color returned to Arnie's face and the gushes of sweat were stemmed. Arnie's gasping eased into a calm, normal breath, and he curled out of his body's knotted clench, straightening up into a tall, even distinguished looking man of fifty two. It even seemed as if the natural brown pigment of his hair made a comeback, fighting the wave of grey into retreat. The figure now standing in the foyer, almost regal in aspect, was unrecognizable as the suffering, twisted figure that just moments before had appeared on the edge of death.

"Cool," said Ripley, standing awestruck before his father. "That's much better, Poppa."

Arnie stepped to the doorway. His eyes were focusing well now, and he could see across the street, where the process server stood with three or four of his colleagues, grinning from ear to ear, regaling them with the saga of his heroic incursion into the Speck house.

"Every dog has his day," Speck muttered mostly to himself. In his voice, there was no hint of malice or anger. Arnie was too big for that.

11.

Veronica Lodge parked several blocks from Arnie Speck's Edgartown mansion and walked the remainder of the way, as per Speck's instructions. Obviously, he didn't want anyone to make the association between Veronica and himself, but it was a pointless ruse, in her eyes. The town was so quiet now, the local residents so starved for sensory input, that the movements of a stranger would be closely monitored regardless of where she parked or what path she took.

In fact, Veronica could feel eyes following her as he made her way along South Water Street, but they were not the eyes of neighbors; as she approached Speck's oceanfront mansion, Veronica spotted several odd characters posted outside at various spots outside the house, some inside their vehicles and some out on foot, lurking suspiciously. She felt a tinge of alarm, for just an instant, before realizing that these were definitely not stake-out cops. No, the disparate range of their ages and body types alone disqualified them from being The Law. Bottom feeders of one variety or another, Veronica concluded — reporters, maybe process servers. Neither was any threat to her, but just to be sure she pulled a baseball cap out of her bag and put it on, pulling its bill down low over her eyes and putting on a pair of dark sunglasses before she approached the house and rang the bell.

A boy greeted her at the door, a rotund little fellow of boundless good will, instantly identifiable as the kid she had spoken with on the phone.

"I'm gonna get 'A' on this", said Ripley immediately, beaming as he held out his hand-printed essay for Veronica to see. "Would you like me to read it to you?"

"You're Ripley, right?"

"Yes. And that was you on the phone," he giggled, then whispered "the one who was p'd off at Poppa."

"Correct. Ripley, I'd definitely like to hear your paper, some time, but right now I need to see your father."

"Okay. Poppa's feeling much better now. Do you know what we're going to do next week? Me and Poppa are going to an orphanage to visit the unfortunate boys. Poppa even told me to pack a suitcase with clothes, so we could share them with those in need."

"Hmm."

"C'mon," said the boy, taking Veronica by the hand and leading her into the house. "I know Poppa will be happy to see you."

And he was. Arnie Speck was not blind. As Ripley led Veronica into his study, Arnie faced her in person for the first time and understood—intellectually, at least—that she was a rare object of desire. The drug in his nebulizer had obliterated all of Arnie's natural animal impulses, freeing his mind and body for absolute obeisance to the narcotic, but as Veronica sat down before him and leaned back in the softest leather chair, irreverently perching her boot heels on the antique Edwardian tea table, Arnie wondered what it would be like to be with her. He felt a vestigial twinge of desire, frightening him for an instant, but it passed.

"Go play, Ripley," said Arnie.

"Okay, Poppa," said Ripley, waving goodbye to Veronica as he trotted blissfully out of the room.

"Where are we, Arnie?" she asked Speck once the boy was out of sight.

"The mark is en route to the island," Speck said.

"So we're on."

"We are on," said Speck, handing her a large, manila envelope. "Everything you need is in here: a description of what I want and who has it, plus cash to cover your expenses so far."

"Plus the advance, right?" Veronica asked as she opened the envelope and examined its contents.

"It's all there."

Veronica pocketed a thick wad of hundred dollar bills and scanned the rest of the provided materials.

"Environmental Impact Report?" she read out loud, then made a sort of snorting sound to convey her absolute boredom. "*Yawn.* If this is background material, you can keep it…"

"It is not," said Arnie with a hint of impatience at Veronica's dismissive attitude. "In the mark's possession, you will find a genuine Environmental Impact Report, nearly identical to this one. You are to swap this copy with the original. That is the job."

"Fine, then. What sort of security can I expect to be up against? You've never said who the mark is."

"It's all in the package there, as I said, but I think the best course is for you to approach the situation without preconceptions. You will certainly need all your skills. There will be challenges."

"Always. But I'm asking, what kind of challenges?"

"Challenges commensurate with your fee for the job," he replied.

That's a lot of challenges, thought Veronica. The rest of the packet included a series of aerial photos, blueprints, topographical maps, and other printed information.

Veronica noticed one photo in particular, depicting a large country estate of some kind, an architecturally impressive cluster of least eight sizeable buildings surrounded by lush and beautifully landscaped grounds.

"Can I get you a drink?" Arnie asked.

"Beer," she said.

"So tell me," Speck asked as he poured her beer into a frosted pilsner glass, "how did you get away?"

"From Denver? You flew us out. I guess I never had a chance to thank you for that."

"No, I mean from under the collapsed department store," he said, placing her glass of beer onto a coaster on the tea table.

Veronica had never shared with Speck the details of her work in Denver, but the TV clips of the armored car heist were very dramatic, playing the local news in every part of the country for two or three days running.

"I shouldn't admit this," she said, "but it was dumb luck."

"Never apologize for your luck," said Speck. "Everyone has it, of one variety or another, and I don't hire people with the bad kind."

"The armored truck had a very strong superstructure, as you can imagine. It held up fine when the roof came down. We only had a few bumps and bruises."

"And then?"

Yes, the 'and then' had been the tricky part, Veronica remembered well, since the legion of cops who had been chasing them had immediately surrounded the remnants of the collapsed store.

"More luck. The truck landed on its side, right over the stairwell to the basement. We just opened the side doors and dropped down. The stairs led to the service passages of the mall next door. We just strolled up the ramp and away, deposit bags hung over our shoulders. No one gave us a second look."

"It was a good television moment," Arnie sneered appreciatively, "when the police hauled away the last of the debris, only to find the armored truck empty. Priceless."

"Not for the bank, it wasn't," Veronica smiled.

Arnie sat across from her with a glass of ice water, a smug look of confidence and contentment on his face, but... something about Speck was bothering Veronica. Outwardly, he appeared strong and composed and relatively normal, but somewhere behind his watery eyes lurked the barest hint of... something a little "off".

"What about the Friendships?" asked Speck.

"What about them?" Veronica asked casually, wondering if Speck had somehow heard about the brothers' reckless Secret Service con.

"This job will require good sense and some delicacy. Are you confident that they will rise to the occasion? If not, there are some other options. I know of at least one person on the island who could be persuaded to—"

"The Friendships will be fine. I handle all my own staffing," she said with finality.

"As you wish," said Arnie.

Veronica's confidence in the Friendship brothers, of course, was less than she was willing to reveal, at that point. Once she left Speck's house, Veronica got on her cell phone and dialed the brothers' room at the Makoniky Inn. No answer. She tried their cell phone next, and no answer still. Veronica began to seethe. On the off chance that the Friendships had made contact with Ned, she called information and was connected to the number for the Music Lagoon Wildlife Sanctuary. Busy. Very busy, as it turned out. Veronica reached the operator again and claimed an emergency, asking if she could try breaking through the line. The operator checked and came back a few seconds later, saying it would be impossible to break through.

"Why?" asked Veronica, annoyed. "This is seriously life and death."

"Join the club," said the operator, bored. "There are five other parties trying to break through that busy line, as we speak."

Weird, thought Veronica.

"All with emergencies?" she asked the operator.

"Life and death," replied the operator before she hung up.

←   ←   ←

News of the lapwing posting had, as Ned predicted, spread quickly. The first of many urgent calls to the sanctuary came from Dr. and Mrs. Devin Hedge of Hartford, Connecticut, who had made "donations" to the sanctuary in excess of eight thousand dollars. The previous September, the couple had somehow been convinced that they had spotted the Caucasian Lapwing at the sanctuary, but in half a dozen return trips to Music Lagoon, they had failed to discover further proof of the bird's resurrection. These repeated failures had done nothing to diminish their hunger for the honor of the first official lapwing sighting. They were both on the line when Ned picked up the phone.

"What's this about someone spotting a lapwing?" Dr. Hedge started in immediately.

"Well—" Ned tried to answer but was cut off again.

"Oh God, Devin, he's not answering us," Mrs. Devin shrieked. "That's OUR lapwing, isn't it?"

"Folks," Ned said calmly, "there's no reason to panic."

Unless you're me, Ned thought to himself. The sanctuary had only one phone line — they had never needed more — and several very annoyed-sounding operators had tried to break through the busy line, all morning, with supposed emergency calls. Ned had rebuffed all these efforts, all too aware that the calls would mostly be from the sanctuary's collection of "special" contributors, all panicked.

Just like the Hedges.

"We'll panic if we damn well want to," wailed Mrs. Hedge.

"Folks, as you probably saw, the posting of the lapwing photo was anonymous. Meaning no one actually claimed the lapwing sighting on the board, so... the field is still wide open. If in fact there is a lapwing on the island, it will still be possible for you to claim the official first sighting."

"We understand that," said the doctor, "but... why do you think no one claimed the sighting, when they had the photo and everything?"

"Because it's a hoax of some kind," Ned said confidently. "A practical joke. That is the only conceivable reason for someone NOT to put their name on a posting like that. Am I right?"

And Ned knew it was true; there was no good reason why someone would not attach their name to a sighting like this, if it were legitimate. A true — and photographed — sighting of a Caucasian Lapwing, the first in more than twenty years, would be like a Powerball jackpot of the bird watching world. It was, very simply, too big a prize not to claim.

"Dr. and Mrs. Hedge," continued Ned, "You are speaking right now, if I may say humbly, to the world's foremost expert on the Caucasian Lapwing," *which might actually be true*, Ned thought with a certain sense of horror. "Music Lagoon is the ancestral home of the Caucasian Lapwing. When the lapwing disappeared more than twenty years ago, it had last been seen here. If and when it returns, it's reasonable to predict that it will return to this place and, in fact, to the very special plot of land that is our closed habitat; the plot to which the two of you hold exclusive privileges."

"Excellent!" suggested Mrs. Hedge. "We'll be out there tomorrow."

"No no no," pleaded Ned, "you don't want to waste your time visiting now. We'd love to hang you — pardon me, *have* you — of course, but you know how things are in January, birding-wise. There's just not that much to see right now, especially with the noise of all the added air traffic —"

"The what? Did you say air traffic?" asked the doctor.

Ned silently cursed himself.

"Oh, Devin!" the shriek again. "Of course! The posting! Birders will be coming in from everywhere!"

True enough, thought Ned.

In the mere five hours since the lapwing photo had appeared on the Internet bulletin board, private planes and charters had already hit the island like a swarm of black flies. Bookings at the island's inns and hotels were piling up like in record numbers for this time of year. Some places that had already been closed for the season were opening their doors, just to cash in on the occasion. Birders were fanatics — often extremely wealthy fanatics — and few had dared dream of ever seeing the legendary Caucasian, whether they were the first to register the sighting or not. There was little they would not do for the thrill of such an historic encounter, and they were coming to the island now, in force, like sharks to chum.

"That's it!" yelped Mrs. Hedge. "We're on our way over, and that's all there is to it!"

"You're damn right about that, dear," chimed Dr. Hedge. "Donlin, we'll see you tonight."

"But—"

And the Hedges were off the phone, already busy packing their optically perfect field binoculars and hand-tailored safari suits.

"Shit," said Ned as he slammed down his phone.

As soon as he had hung up, the phone immediately rang again. Ned sighed, took a leisurely sip of coffee and then, when he could no longer stand the shrill ringing, finally picked up the phone to field the next desperate call.

"Music Lagoon," said Ned into the phone.

"They're *all* coming?" asked Doc.

"It's a nightmare," said Ned. "I tried to talk them all out of it, but they wouldn't hear it. They will descend upon Music Lagoon in force, and it's only a matter of time before they run into each other at the sanctuary and figure out that they've been, uh…

"That they've been conned?" Tommie offered.

"*Mislead*," said Ned, shooting Tommie an irritated. "They're the victims of a minor misunderstanding."

It was ten at night, and the group was all gathered at The Cooler with drinks in front of them: Ned, Tommie, Doc, Nora, Angela and others of the Refreshment Committee. They had started to trickle in after dark, and by the worried, exhausted looks on their faces they would. Gigi Malveaux, The Cooler's taciturn proprietress, had already extended Happy Hour prices a couple hours past the usual cut-off, as a sign of support in their hour of need.

"We booked them each into separate inns around the island," said Nora. "At least they won't be meeting up over their continental breakfast buffets."

"You might want to help them with dinner reservations, then," suggested Doc, "maybe stagger seating times to avoid overlap. You don't want these people passing their Grey Poupon jars from table to table."

"You've got a point, Doc," said Nora. "There are only what? Two, three good restaurants still open? Left to their own devices, they would bump into each other for sure."

"I'll start calling tomorrow morning," Angela volunteered.

"But there's something I don't get," said Tommie, "This lapwing sighting could be seen as good news, right?"

"How do you figure that, Thomas?" Nora asked.

"Well, Ned's... *fund raising project* is all about who's gonna be first to see this bird, right? So someone has done that, am I right? And they've got pictures. The bird exists... presto! This other still-unknown party takes credit for finding the bird, beating your contributors to the sighting through no fault of your own. It's all over and you're off the hook."

"The sighting is unattributed, Tommie," said Ned, glumly.

"What do you mean?"

"It means that whoever took that photograph is not claiming the sighting for his or her self," said Doc. "The game is still wide open."

"We're being visited, all at once, by all the special patrons of Music Lagoon," said Ned, "who believe that their large contributions to our sanctuary have bought them dibs to claim the first sighting for themselves. If these people meet, and start comparing notes on their dealings with us at Music Lagoon, the shit will really hit the fan."

"Okay, then I really don't get it," Tommie said. "Who would do this? If spotting this rooster is such a big goddam prize, who would go huntin' it down AND put the photo on the public bulletin board but then NOT say it was them who found it?"

"That," said Ned, "is an excellent question."

"Or, rather," suggested Nora, "the question may not even be 'who?' would do it, but 'why?' That's what I'm wondering."

"To understand the action," said Doc, in his most scholarly tone, "look at the reaction. In this case, the reaction is hundreds —"

"Thousands," Angie corrected him.

"Possibly thousands, yes," agreed Doc. "The result of the 'sighting' is thousands of birders, from all over the world, descending upon the island."

"The island hoteliers," suggested Tommie. "Looking to boost business in the dead season? Restaurant owners?"

"Maybe…" said Ned.

"Or," suggested Doc, "they're getting thousands, but it wasn't necessarily thousands that they were after. Maybe it was just one person they wanted to bring to the island."

The group considered this possibility for a moment.

"I don't know about that one, Tommie," said Nora. "Who could be important enough for someone to go to such trouble?"

12.

The voice came over the intercom, strangely disembodied in the emptiness of the jet's central cabin.

"Mr. Vice President? Mr. Vice President?"

Roger J. Paulson, a handsome if somewhat noncommittal looking man of forty-seven, stirred in his large flight chair. His suit pants and dress shirt were hopelessly wrinkled, his tie loosened and askew. The area around him was littered with countless files and reports and coded bulletins.

"Huh? What?" he replied.

"Sorry to wake you, Sir," the clipped, military voice came again over the intercom, "but we're on final approach to the island."

"Oh, good," Paulson said groggily. "What time is it?"

"One twenty two, local. That's AM, Sir."

God, thought Paulson, these trans-polar hops are brutal. What time had it been when they left Laos? It had been damn hot, he remembered that, and blindingly bright. Paulson rubbed his eyes, running through the mental wake-up list he always composed in his mind before sleeping.

Item Number One: *Vanellus Caucasus*.

"Are you using your headlights?" he said loudly into the room, never sure where the intercom mike was located.

"Sir?" Again the disembodied voice in clipped military staccato.

"On approach. Will you be using the plane's headlights?"

"Um… we usually do, Sir," answered the voice with a puzzled tone, "Unless that's a problem…"

"No — use them, by all means. On hi-beam. If any birds, any birds at all, fly into our path, give them right of way."

There was a long pause before the answer came. "Yes, Sir."

"Fine," said Roger Paulson. "Over and out."

Damn right, Roger thought to himself. This whole Caucasian Lapwing thing, it was probably a mistake or a hoax or something. But what if it was true? What if the bird had miraculously returned? It would be a sad ending to the resurrection of the species if the new flock got sucked into the screaming turbofans of Air Force Two. Not to mention, that would mean one less significant entry into the Paulson Codex.

The telephone across the aisle rang, next to the seat where his secretary should be. Paulson glanced around the cabin in vain, hoping against hope that some member of his staff — a butler, a translator, a nurse, even Major Foxbrite — would appear and spare him the indignity of answering the phone himself.

There was no one, of course. Probably the bug, still, thought Paulson. His staff had picked up a little microbial souvenir during their stopover in Laos, a flu bug that had wreaked havoc in both his personal staff and his Secret Service detail. Paulson was surprised anyone was left to fly the plane.

"Hello," Paulson answered the phone in a lame, unconvincing attempt to disguise his voice.

"Oh, hello Sir," said the voice on the line, the smoky Louisiana accent of Special Agent in Charge Rhonda Hipps. "No one there to answer for you, Sir?"

"Nope," said Paulson, reassuming his own identity.

"Any idea where they might be, Sir?"

"Probably in back, throwing up. That seems to be the routine, lately."

"Sorry about that, Sir," said Agent Hipps. "We're doing our best to get the team back to full strength."

Thank goodness for Agent Hipps, thought Paulson. She was always a firm hand.

"Where are you, Hipps?" asked Paulson.

"Down here on the island already, Sir," she answered. "Security will be in place soon. We'll be ready for you, Sir."

"That's fine."

Providing his security would not be much of a challenge for Agent Hipps, not tonight. The Vice President's destination now appeared outside Paulson's window: a small, dark land mass, set against a sea shimmering under the nearly full moon. This was the serene and sparsely populated island of Martha's Vineyard. Now, in mid-Winter, the place would be deader than campaign finance reform.

"And how is the Tarpaulin Center?" he asked. "It's supposed to be wonderful."

"It's nice, Sir," answered Hipps. "It's really very lovely. Quiet, lots of room to roam. Beautiful facilities. I don't know about the birds, yet, but it seems perfect."

"It sounds perfect," said the Vice President. "It sounds like just what I need. What we *all* need. Thank you, Angel Hipps,"

"Sir?"

"*Agent. Agent* Hipps is what I meant. Thank you."

← ← ←

Special Agent in Charge Rhonda Hipps put down the phone and turned to face her detail, those who could still stand, anyway: a bleary-eyed, ashen-faced skeleton crew of ten, plus four dogs, and many cases of sophisticated security equipment scattered all over the refined central lobby of the Tarpaulin Center. The crew did not look well, thought Hipps. There had been group vomiting — projectile — on the transport flight over the North Pole. Some sort of Laotian stomach bug, it seemed. Hipps was sympathetic, but would not tolerate any sort of letdown in their efficiency. The Vice President's decision to come to the island had been made on impulse, at the very last minute, so the lead detail had only been given a few hours to begin their work. The team would have to step up their pace to have the site secure for Paulson's arrival.

"All right, we have an ETA for Sparrow Hawk of twenty-five minutes. Let's finish our scan of the main building, first, then we'll scrape together a team to cover the perimeter."

"Screw Veronica," said Bobby. "She was wrong, and we were right."

"Hm hmm," replied Ricky. He was sitting on a tree stump, a penlight clenched between his teeth, trying to concentrate on his crossword puzzle. His brother Bobby stood nearby, surrounded by fourteen large duffel bags packed full and extra goods stacked up all around, including three projection TVs, a dozen VCRs, several French food processors, and a gallery's worth of watercolor paintings, all subtly rendered island landscapes commissioned and designed to compliment a variety of summer-shaded pastel upholstery.

"Five days here, and she's delivered nothing," said Bobby, "and look at all we got. On our own!"

"Yep," agreed Ricky absentmindedly.

"You're not even listening to me," Bobby pouted.

Ricky sighed as he folded the crossword and stuffed it in his pocket. He rose and joined Bobby amid the heap of loot. Both brothers were wearing their second-hand dress suits, in case of unexpected resistance, but the Secret Service ruse had not once been necessary.

"I'm with you," Ricky said.

"I was saying 'Screw Veronica'," said Bobby. "She was wrong, and you were right."

The brothers had parked deep in the anonymous woods, away from the road, to sift through the goods they had acquired in a strong evening's work. In the course of five hours, they had revisited every unoccupied home they had scouted two nights before—the easy marks. All the goods had been waiting for them, laid out like an appliance smorgasbord "just begging to be lifted", as Ricky observed. Three or four alarm systems had stood in their way, but none had presented a meaningful challenge to the highly experienced Friendship brothers.

"We keep goin' like this," said Ricky, "and we're gonna have to steal an even bigger truck."

"How are we gonna find a fence on this little island, Rick? You know someone?"

"No, idiot, I don't know a fence on Madonna's Vineyard, or whatever this fuckin' place is called. We'll have to fence once we get off this damn rock."

"Off the island? But then we have to take that boat across the water. They'll be lookin' out for us, Ricky, for us and the truck and—"

"Shut up. I know the problems. I got it figured out."

"Really?"

"They got fishermen here, right? We find one of them fishing boats, with all the room in the belly for fish, and we jack it. Stuff all this into the belly and ride it to the other side of the water. We can sell the stuff *and* the boat."

"All the stuff will stink then, Rick," worried Bobby. "It'll stink like fish. No one will want it."

"But check it out…" Ricky reassured him, grabbing a cloth bag from the back of the truck. "When I went to get the truck, I stopped at the store and stole these…"

From the bag Ricky pulled out a handful of car deodorizers, the kind that hang from the rear view mirror. They were purple and in the shape of Martha's Vineyard.

"These," said Ricky, "we hang up in the belly of the boat. I got two hundred. They smell like some kinda flower. We'll get even more cash for the stuff, it'll smell so good."

For a moment Bobby was speechless, rendered mute by the wisdom and foresight of his elder sibling.

"You're my brother…" were the only words he could manage to speak once he had regained his composure.

Bobby reached out and gave Ricky a hug, but in the midst of the embrace he saw something in the distance, over his brother's shoulder.

"Look over there, Ricky," he said. "There's lights that wasn't there before."

With their eyes adjusted to the dark now, the brothers could see just past the woods, where a vast, groomed field of grass lay basking in the moonlight. On the far side of the field, a good quarter of a mile away, they could make out the silhouettes of several large buildings, at least eight of them, with lights now burning in more than a hundred windows.

"Good God damn," said Ricky with a whistle. "Where did that place come from? It's huge, like a compound or a fort or somethin'."

"It's beautiful," agreed Bobby. "All lit up like a Christmas tree."

"We gotta at least scout it out," insisted Ricky.

"Okay," said Bobby, straightening his tie.

The brothers stepped away from their pile of stolen goods and marched through the woods, emerging onto the open field beyond. They crossed the field and within a few minutes were standing at the entrance to the compound's largest building. They primped their suits one last time and then Ricky rang the door bell. They heard steps inside the building, growing louder as they approached, and then the big door swing open revealing a statuesque African America woman—six-foot-three, strong and shapely, in a well-tailored suit.

Agent Rhonda Hipps took a moment to size-up the unexpected visitors; the two men had dark hair and pale skin, with wiry physiques standing less than five foot eight. They wore cheap black suits and dull paisley ties. They were not well shaven. One of them had a large bandage on his forehead, with a shocking seam of stitches peeking out from beneath it.

"Whoa," said the smaller one, involuntarily, confronted by the imposing stature of Agent Rhonda Hipps.

"Good evening, Ma'am," said the one with the bandage on his forehead. "Sorry to disturb you at this late hour."

"No problem," said Agent Hipps. "I was up. What can I do for you?"

"Well Ma'am, I'm Agent Magnum and this here is Agent Callahan. We're with the United States Secret Service. A person of the U.S. Government, whose identity

I can't say, will be visiting soon at the home of one of your neighbors. It's part of our job to do security checks at the homes in the area. Would you object to us having a look around?"

Hipps looked at the two strangers for a long moment, her face betraying nothing.

"Of course," she finally answered, "come right on in."

"Terrific," said Bobby Friendship, as he and his brother stepped into the impressive main lobby of the Tarpaulin Center. "Thanks very much for your cooperation."

13.

Ned rose at about four thirty in the morning, frustrated after just three restless hours of attempted sleep. He had been pestered by dreams, again, featuring a cast of characters that included Veronica Lodge, Billie Jensen, various Wampanoag deities, Nora and the Refreshment Committee, Doc and Tommie, plus several species of avian fauna both real and imaginary.

Ned rubbed his eyes awake, and took a moment to catalog his personal anxiety inventory: first there was Veronica, the siren, a vestige of an exciting but destructive lifestyle Ned had left far behind him, or so he thought. Was it possible for Veronica to carry out her nefarious business, here on the island, without somehow dragging Ned into the middle of it? He was skeptical. Second, was Billie Jensen really shacked up with the landscaper from Oak Bluffs? Ned's unsolicited opinion was that Billie should be with him or remain celibate forever. Third, there were the twelve special sanctuary contributors. The lapwing "sighting" had brought every last one to the island, panicked and greedy and clamoring for Ned's personal attention. If these people ever had the chance to compare notes on their dealings with Ned and the Sanctuary, Ned's life on the island would be torn asunder.

All these were all secondary distractions, however, compared to the one thing that had haunted Ned for twenty years: the bird. *Vanellus Caucasus*. Since the appearance of the lapwing's photograph on the Rare Bird Alert site, Ned had been so distracted with the related complications that he hadn't taken the time to stop and consider, clearly and honestly, the question that mattered most to him:

Could it be true? Had the Caucasian Lapwing actually returned from the abyss of total extinction?

Ned had told everyone—and he was mostly convinced—that the photograph was a prank of some kind or a ruse to further some as yet undiscovered scheme. The bird had certainly not been sighted, because the bird was extinct. Gone. Forever. Which was a mighty long time. The truth, however, was that Ned desperately wanted the sighting to be real. The photograph of the lapwing—and the upheaval that it had brought—could potentially ruin everything Ned had built for himself on the island, and yet... Ned would gladly sacrifice it all if it meant discovering, after so many years of unrealistic hope, that the lapwing had truly returned.

Without rising from his bed, Ned reached to his side table for the color printout of the internet photograph. He squinted, trying to force focus onto the hazy image. He could not. Maybe the bird had moved at the instant the shot had been taken, or maybe the photo was just an imperfect job of fakery. For the first time, though, Ned noticed something else: much of the foliage around the bird, the branches and leaves, was in focus. Ned moved to his desk, set the photo down flat, and brought out a large magnifying glass, last year's birthday gift from Mrs. Calcavechia's third grade class.

Ned turned his desk lamp on the image, and examined the photograph under the glass. The first thing he noticed was the light—it *felt* like dusk. The bird preferred sheltered locations, such as the Music Lagoon ravine. Of course, there were a number of such places on the island, angled in a direction that would receive direct light from a setting sun in January. Ned quickly catalogued, in his mind, the locations he knew that fit this description.

Ned turned his attention to the foliage visible in the photograph. Most of the branches were clear of any leaves, consistent with the season. But to one side, and in the background, there was some scant foliage remaining. Certain tree and plant species held out longer against the cold, naturally, changing colors and shedding at slightly different rates; this was especially true on the island of Martha's Vineyard, which occupied a spot in the ocean where two divergent tides met, each influencing weather conditions differently, resulting in subtly variant conditions of moisture, temperature and wind force from one area of the island to another.

In the photograph, Ned could make out some remaining leaves of cedar, vaguely yellow, some scarlet oak, barely hanging on, and, oddly situated further back, a limb of red maple. Ned immediately knew that the photo could not have been taken at Music Lagoon. There was no maple stand at all on "his" property, and precious little left on the island at all, due to the depredation of man, of course, but also to the dominance of scrub oak and pitch pine in the island woodlands.

Ned closed his eyes and concentrated, conjuring the mental images he had collected, over the past couple of years, of the island's natural landscape. The variety of trees seen in the photograph, with that level of foliage still intact, was not common. Ned mentally cross-referenced this information with his knowledge of the island topography, figuring in the angle of the shadows and the lapwing's preferred, sheltered habitat, mixing and matching all these factors until... *West Chop*, realized Ned; the slope that ran down to Lake Tashmoo. Ned was certain all three trees were present there, in a specific ravine facing Northwest—not unlike the ravine at Music

Lagoon—that would be sheltered enough to keep the leaves on the trees this late in the season and still find direct light at dusk. There would certainly to be other spots, Ned understood, other locations Ned didn't know about which were also possible sites for the photograph. But… this was something. A place to start.

Lake Tashmoo.

Ned looked at his clock: five after five. Nora and the Refreshment Committee had, miraculously and through the use of many elaborate lies, convinced the dozen special contributors to come by the sanctuary at staggered times, in the hope that they might not trip over each other in the "closed" section of Music Lagoon. The first and by far pushiest of them, Dr. and Mrs. Hedge, were not scheduled to come by for their personal birding session until six thirty.

Ned dressed as quickly as he could, bundling up less than usual since the weather was still unseasonably warm. He pulled a pot of yesterday's coffee from the refrigerator, microwaved it in a big insulated mug, then packed up his binoculars, camera with long lens, and portable tape player. Ned pulled on his Bean boots and headed out into the dark, early morning. In the warm, dark cab of his truck, heading up the North Road toward Tashmoo for a pre-dawn birding sortie, he reflected fondly on the circumstances of his very first attempt at bird watching.

Ned had taken the reins of the Music Lagoon Wildlife Sanctuary soon after his arrival on the island three years earlier, on the lam and anxious to find a role on the island that would give him some cover. He had lucked into an opportunity right away, seizing on the open job created when the previous Director of Music Lagoon, Walt Frost, had mysteriously left the island on Halloween Night, a few months earlier, and never returned. Ned had been hired for Music Lagoon under completely false pretenses, having faked his credentials as an educated and experienced naturalist. Ned's only real asset on the job, back then, was his extensive knowledge of the sanctuary land. As a young boy, he had spent months every summer roaming those very acres — back then known as MacDougal Farm, his grandparents' home — from dawn until dusk, nearly feral in his daily existence and defiant against all attempts by his grandmother to civilize him. Ned had suddenly and sadly lost his appetite for nature, however, on one particular August afternoon more than twenty years ago. Ned's only real experience in the wild, since then, had been a brutal thirty mile forced march over a snowy Rocky Mountain pass, led by Veronica Lodge, in order to avoid some inconvenient road checks set up by the Sheriff of Aspen, Colorado. That luckless experience had confirmed in Ned's mind that he was no longer the outdoor type.

Once Ned had become Director at Music Lagoon, though; he was determined to educate himself for the work. He applied himself to studies of biology, geography, geology, botany and any other field that would help him pass as a naturalist. Fortunately, Ned had begun the job in January of that year, and the quiet, low-traffic winter months at the sanctuary provided just the window of time that he needed to bring himself up to speed, science-wise. Ned read his way through the Nature sections of every library on the island, also covering primers on emergency first aid, animal tracking and wildlife photography. Finally, Ned pored over the works of Muir, Whitman, Emerson and Thoreau, so that if he was ever stuck on a specific scientific point, he could distract visitors by waxing philosophical on modern man's need to reorient himself within the natural world.

Ned's crash course did not turn him into a true expert in any of these fields, not nearly, but he did accumulate a working vocabulary that would prove good enough to fool all but the most educated sanctuary visitors. By the end of March that year, there remained only one field that Ned had yet to tackle. He had put off his bird-related studies until last, for personal reasons, knowing all the while that he would have to cover that ground before the first birders of spring arrived at the sanctuary. On April Fools' Day, Ned finally began his ornithological studies, poring over every text book on birds he could find. Ned learned much in a short period of time, but also recognized that there was a huge gap between the bird-related knowledge he could absorb from books and that which he would need to experience first-hand, in the field.

One reasonably clear April morning, Ned dug out a beat-up pair of field binoculars and a dog-eared guide book left behind by Walt Frost, and headed out onto the sanctuary grounds, determined to master the art of bird watching as quickly as possible.

There were problems, immediately. First, Ned was followed into the woods by a tabby cat named Rudy (it said so on its collar) from some nearby house or farm, who had taken up residence at the sanctuary in the days since Ned's arrival. Rudy had figured out that Ned was not so strict a defender of wildlife as Walt Frost had been. Distracted by his nature studies, Ned had allowed Rudy to encamp himself under the sanctuary's feeders and consume his daily fill of the local bird population. For his part, Ned liked cats well enough and appreciated the company, since by that point he had done little to establish any meaningful friendships on the island. That morning, though, Ned realized that he wasn't going to have much luck getting close to birds with a feline escort in tow, so he chased Rudy away in no uncertain terms.

Ned's next bird watching problem, once he had supposedly rid himself of the cat, was even more troublesome. It turned out that the word "watching" barely applied to the practice at all. The natural world was huge and birds were relatively tiny, plus the damn things never, ever stood still. Ned could scarcely even *find* a single bird in the woods, much less get a look close enough and long enough to tell what actual species it was. The birds were more stationary and easier to pin down when stopping at the sanctuary's feeders — as Rudy had ruthlessly demonstrated every day for three months — but that was a cheat. No, Ned had to learn how to find, follow and identify birds in their free and natural habitat, or he would soon be revealed as an imposter.

Standing alone in the woods of Music Lagoon Sanctuary, Ned opened Walt Frost's old guide book, in search of… guidance. He found help immediately in the table of contents. In the opening chapter, "Tips for Beginning Birders", the first section was entitled "Listening". *Okay*, Ned thought immediately, *of course*. Birds didn't seem to have any problems finding each other, and that must be because of their calls and songs.

Ned had sat down on a fallen log and closed his eyes. The warmth of the early spring morning brought with it many stirrings in the forest, and so it was some time before Ned heard a single bird call distinct enough to isolate from the other sounds of nature. But then it came, a clear call if not quite a loud one. It sounded like this:

"Cheek-wee. Cheek-wee cheek-wee."

Okay, Ned thought at the time, a Tarzan-movie tropical jungle call this was not, but it would have to do.

Without opening his eyes, Ned slowly rotated his head, using what turned out to be his own natural instincts, of all unlikely things, to zero in on the source of the call. When he was sure his head was pointed directly at the bird, Ned opened his eyes, rose from his seat, and walked, as slowly and quietly as he could, directly ahead through the forest of oak trees.

Ned only needed to walk thirty or forty yards, stopping now and again to close his eyes and re-listen, before he found himself standing less than twenty feet away from the actual calling bird. To Ned's surprise and pleasure, the bird was not some dull brown sparrow-like thing, but a semi-dramatic looking, bright yellow and black... *something*. That should make it easy enough, Ned had thought. He picked up his binoculars, got what he thought was a good look at the bird, and immediately began poring over the pages of the guide book.

He leafed straight through to a section of the book that featured yellow passerine birds, expecting to find a handful of possibilities, at most. Instead, Ned was surprised to find page after page of yellow birds — there looked to be a couple hundred of them — and at first glance they looked nearly identical to each other. What features did his bird have that would distinguish it from these others? Ned had no idea. He thought he had noticed what the bird looked like, but it turned out he had noticed nothing. Ned looked up just in time to see his bird flit away into the woods.

"Shit!" Ned had yelled aloud.

Ned followed the bird further into the woods, using the listening method more than a few times to relocate his target, and stopping on several occasions to re-shoo away Rudy the cat, who had doggedly followed Ned on his safari through the woods. Ned gradually realized that in most cases, he could only expect to get a clear look at his quarry for a second or two before it flitted away, so he had to concentrate on those two or three details about the specimen that would help most in identifying it, including beak length and color, leg length and color, mottling patterns on the head and wings, etc..

After trailing the bird for more than an hour, Ned finally put together a short list of specific details about this elusive yellow bird: short pale colored beak, black cap on top of head, full yellow body except for blackish wings with two horizontal white stripes. Ned found the bird in his guide almost immediately, identifying it as an American Goldfinch, year-round resident of Martha's Vineyard. It turned out not to be the most exotic of birds, but Ned was pleased and proud that he had successfully completed his task. It had to get easier, he figured, and there could only be so many kinds of birds around anyway. Before long he would have most of them memorized. Ned ambled back to his cottage, feeling a warm sense of accomplishment, and rewarded himself with a mug of cocoa.

As it happened, an ensuing event had badly tainted the positive memory of that first bird watching day. The following morning, Ned had emerged from his cottage to find *an* American Goldfinch, if not *the* American Goldfinch, presented on his doormat entirely dead, its head twisted in such a way as to indicate a broken neck. Nearby sat Rudy the cat, wearing an expression on his face which, if Ned were inclined to project human expression upon the cat's thinking, conveyed this sentiment:

"Ned, there's really no need to go through all that trouble. We're friends. If you ever want another one of these, just say the word."

Upset and feeling guilty at the slaying, Ned resolved at that moment to change his policy *vis a vis*

Rudy's hunting permit on sanctuary grounds. Over the next few weeks, Ned harassed Rudy with a nonlethal but steady barrage of peas from pea shooters, squirts from squirt guns, and even BBs from a weak, hand-pumped BB gun, until Rudy abandoned the Music Lagoon Wildlife Sanctuary for friendlier hunting grounds. Since the unfortunate demise of his first identified bird, though, Ned had referred to all American Goldfinches as American *Dead*finches. Other Music Lagoon faithfuls, such as the Refreshment Committee and the hundred or so kids from the local grammar school, had eventually started using the Deadfinch nickname without ever knowing the story behind its inception.

Ned reached Tashmoo, parking just off the main road about a quarter mile away from the ravine he was headed for, and made his way out into the woods. The forest floor was clear and easy walking. Because of the unseasonable warmth, there was some activity even though the sun had not yet risen: squirrels hustled along the forest floor, birds foraged and even managed a few calls, and a family of white-tailed deer bolted into the dark depths of the forest at the sound of Ned's approach. Once he had trod halfway to his destination, Ned stopped in his tracks, quieted himself, and listened.

Ned had come a long way as a naturalist and a birder since those first days at the sanctuary, but some things had not changed. On this warm January morning in West Chop, on a mission to locate a bird infinitely more exotic than an American Deadfinch, Ned did not plan to look at all; he planned to listen. An important part of the legacy left by Walt Frost, Ned's predecessor at Music Lagoon, had been a collection of cassette tapes with the recorded calls and songs of every bird that had ventured onto Martha's Vineyard in the last sixty years. The collection included an excellent recording of the

Caucasian Lapwing, issuing both its distinctive mating song (the same recording that Angela played during Leonard Smallwood's visit to the sanctuary) and its more informal, conversational call, used for everyday cross-forest chatter.

Ned reached into his bag and selected the tape of the mating song. He made the choice with a significant misgiving; if, by some miracle, there was a Caucasian Lapwing alive and on the island, it could well be the only survivor of its species on Earth. It had likely spent many mournful years sending out its own song in a desperate attempt to find a mate and end its sad, solitary fly-about. To lure this lonely bird with the mating song of a fellow lapwing — a fellow lapwing that had, in reality, long since expired — would make Ned Donlin a prick tease of immense proportion.

Tough luck, Ned had decided. There were too many variables in his life, just now, and it was time to start nailing down a few details. The resurrection of the Caucasian Lapwing, or lack thereof, was the most compelling question of all, and Ned wanted an answer. He inserted the tape into his small hand-size tape player and started it, holding the player high over his head and slowly circling the forest floor, sending the call in every direction:

"Too-da hooweee! Too-da hooweee!"

It was a solemn and mournful plea, resonating much differently now than it had two mornings earlier at Music Lagoon. Back then, Ned had been focused on the task of duping Leonard Smallwood. Now, as Ned stood all alone in the cool, pre-dawn silence of this wood, the call sent a chill up Ned's spine like a voice from the grave. The still morning air was a good medium, and the song carried well in every direction. Ned let the tape roll.

"Too-da hooweee! Too-da hooweee!"

After several calls, Ned stopped the tape and listened. There was no sound at all. Even the squirrels, hustling about busily just minutes ago, had fallen silent under the spell of the song. After a few moments of listening, Ned felt his chest tighten, and was surprised to discover that he had been holding his breath.

"Jeez, Ned," he whispered to himself, "get a grip."

Ned walked on, about half the distance to the ravine where the photograph might have been taken. There were some houses here, spread apart by stretches of a couple hundred feet or so. Many of the West Chop houses were year-round residences, but in these early hours there were no lights in any of the windows. Ned turned on the tape again and held the player high over his head, turning again in slow circles as the song wafted out over the forest.

"Too-da hooweee! Too-da hooweee! Hoowey hoowey hoowey!"

Ned stopped the tape and listened again. Still nothing. Ned walked on, drawing closer to the ravine. He could see Lake Tashmoo now, a hundred feet below and a few hundred yards to the West, where a low, tenebrous mist hung over the water. A pair of swans glided effortlessly over the pond, entering deep into the blanket of fog until only the graceful curve of their necks could be seen. A year earlier, the male of this pair had become caught in a loose fishing line tangle, breaking one of the delicate bones in its wing. Doc had patched the wing and, within two months, returned him to the female. He would never fly again, and so neither would his lifelong mate, but Ned figured that Tashmoo was as good a place as any on earth for a pair of swans to live out their years.

Now within view of the edge of the ravine, Ned raised the player again and projected the song. From where Ned stood now, the sound carried over the woods and far out over the surface of the lake.

"Too-da hooweee! Too-da hooweee! Hoowey hoowey hoowey!"

Again there was no answer. Of course. Ned checked his watch; it was almost six o'clock, and he would need to be back at the sanctuary, before very long, to meet up with the Hedges. Unfortunately. Things around the sanctuary were not going to be any fun, today, but Ned had to do what he had to do. As thoughts of his many responsibilities took hold of him, he suddenly felt pretty silly, standing out here in the middle of the woods, in the dim pre-dawn light, playing the tape of a mating song more than twenty years old, half expecting to hear some sort of —

"Too-da hooweee!"

When the call came, Ned was just plain confused, at first. He looked at the tape player in his hand, checking to see if the tape was running. It was not, obviously — the song had come from a place at least fifty yards away, further up the ravine, near the path that Ned had just taken. Ned was frozen, just for a moment, his mind immobilized by shock, but within seconds he was fumbling with the player, desperately trying to press the "play" button to answer the call.

"C'mon, goddam it, c'mon!" Ned chastised his fingers.

Ned accidentally hit the "fast forward" and "play" buttons at the same time and tape raced over the heads, emitting a high pitched *screech!* that shattered the tranquility of the morning.

"Shit! Shit!"

His fingers fumbled some more, finally striking the "rewind" button, but his thumb he had never let go of the play button, so now the player was screeching the call in reverse, breaking the stillness of the morning yet again.

"Oh crap! I-am-an-idiot I-am-an-idiot…" Ned growled the mantra.

Finally the tape reached its beginning. Ned, taking a deep breath, focused on the buttons and hit only the "play" button. Success! The tape rolled forward and the call sang out from the machine.

"Too-da hooweee! Too-da hooweee!"

Ned raised the player over his head, but this time directed it only toward the ravine area above him. The tape played on for five seconds or ten seconds or however long—Ned's perception of time was now completely disconnected from reality. He played at least three cycles of the call—he knew that much—and it must have been enough. The answer rang out from up the ravine:

"Too-da hooweee! Too-da hooweee! Hoowey hoowey hoowey!"

Ned began walking, using all his effort to keep his pace to a relaxed, unthreatening creep. The tape player continued sending out the mating call as Ned drew nearer and nearer to the ravine. Each cycle of Ned's tape was answered by an identical song, the opposite source drawing ever closer to Ned. The northern lip of the ravine was now thirty feet ahead. As nearly as Ned could tell, the other lapwing was approaching from beyond the edge of the ravine, converging from the opposite direction.

"Holy shit," Ned hissed excitedly, to himself.

Ned's arms were beginning to ache from holding the player so high overhead, his elbows locking and cramping. His shoulders began to tremble. The edge of the ravine was less than ten feet away now, and the other lapwing's call drew nearer, making it likely that if Ned continued on, he would meet the bird just over the nearest rise. Ned dropped to his knees, crawling forward as quietly as he could and keeping the lowest possible profile, worried that a shocking encounter with Ned, here in the Tashmoo ravine, might scare the lapwing away for another twenty years. The bird and Ned were close now, echoing each others' calls identically, loudly and clearly.

Ned reached the lip and lowered onto his belly, slithering the final few feet to the edge. Ned was so close, and the lapwing was so close, it seemed it would just be seconds before they were finally face to face.

"That's it, c'mon…" Ned coaxed in an inaudible whisper.

"*Too-da hooweee! Too-da hooweee!*"

But just as Ned was about to peek over the edge, he heard a loud thump, a metallic crunch, and then a woman's bleated cry…

"Ow!"

Ned jumped to his feet and stepped over the edge. There lay Billie Jensen, in her beige game warden's uniform, upside down and on her belly, her ankle twisted under the branch of a fallen log.

"Oh, no…" groaned Ned.

Beside Billie, on the ground, was a small tape player like Ned's, broken open and spewing tape from a smashed cassette. Ned turned off his own tape player, slumped down onto the log and buried his face in his hands.

"Hey, I'm hurtin' here, Ned," snapped Billie. "You gonna help me up or what?"

14.

"You're such an asshole, Ned," said Billie.

She was seated on the log that had tripped her, and Ned was at her feet, bandaging her mildly twisted ankle with a blue bandana.

"I take it we're talking about Thanksgiving, now?"

"Yep," she said.

"You sure we should get into this now?"

Her answer was "yes", apparently…

"After I got my family all ready and excited to have you visit, softened them up, praised you generously — to my father, especially — you suddenly come up with some mysterious 'conflict', just two days before we're supposed to go. You know, Ned, I had to reel all that groundwork back up. It was humiliating. And you know my dad…"

"Well, actually…"

"No, that's right, you don't know him. And I suppose you never will, now," said Billie. "But he was pretty positive about meeting you. I mean, there were no unrealistic expectations, as I told you an infinite number of times, which of course you didn't believe. But my father was happy that I was bringing someone home who at least had a stable job and no facial hair. That's the kind of openness I haven't experienced from him very often, and it was big. I just had this feeling, I don't know, that maybe as a group we could all get through a nice meal without strife. I was looking forward to that."

"I was in the wrong," said Ned, speaking in his calmest and most reasonable tone. "I want to communicate that to you, now, and make amends somehow. My real mistake was much earlier, though, before the planning stage. I should have expressed more clearly my misgivings—"

"Shut up, Ned."

"Okay."

Ned finished her ankle wrap, slid her heavy wool sock back on, then rose and sat next to Billie on the log.

"What's with the relationship-speak, anyway?" Billie asked. "Who have you been hanging out with?"

"I've just been trying to think of a way to unhurt your feelings. Turning words over in my head, you know? In a vacuum, which never works. I guess I didn't really expect it to take."

"Nice try, though," she said. Billie pulled out a tin of black Russian cigarettes, lighting two of them. She passed one to Ned and he inhaled the thick, sweet smoke. They sat quietly for a short while, the smoke hovering in wisps around their heads, undisturbed in the absolute stillness of the morning air. Ned had missed Billie a lot, over the past few weeks of their separation, and he felt the full force of her absence now, strangely enough, that she was sitting right there beside him.

"So what do you think?" she said.

"About the bird?"

"Yep."

"Bogus, don'tcha think?" he said, suddenly sad to hear those words coming out of his mouth.

"Bogus, definitely," she said.

"Yet here we are," said Ned.

They chuckled under their breaths, quietly, so as not to disrupt the delicate tranquility of the ravine.

"You and me, the Optimist's Club," she said.

"Irony."

"But we're both pretty sure that photograph was taken here," Ned ventured.

"*Faked* here," she said. "But yeah, from the foliage in the background and the light, I think this was probably the spot. Just some stupid prank, I guess. "

"Stupid," agreed Ned.

They smoked in silence for a moment, contemplating stupidity and folly in their various forms.

"How are things at the sanctuary, by the way?" she asked.

"Scraping by, I guess."

"Yuck. Give me government work, every time," Billie shook her head in commiseration. "Gimme that regular check. Life is hard enough without the elusive dollar factor."

"Plus you get the uniform," he ventured.

"And benefits. Yeah."

They sat for a few moments in silence, comfortable together. Ned took a long draw on the cigarette and sent out a thick stream of smoke through puckered lips.

"No bird, but it's nice here," he said.

"Yeah," she agreed, "who needs the lapwing, anyway?"

I need the lapwing, Ned thought. Then suddenly a telephone rang. Or at least that's what it sounded like to Ned.

"You changed the ring on your cell phone," Ned said.

"No, that's not mine." She dug out her cell phone and confirmed this. The ringing came again, a slightly muted, electronic sounding pulse.

"It's definitely a cell phone," she said with an accusatory glance.

"Don't look at me," said Ned, "You know I hate those things." The phone rang again, and Billie leaned toward Ned, listening to his jacket.

"What are you doing?" asked Ned.

"It's you, Ned," she said. "It's coming from you."

"It absolutely is not," he protested, but Billie was already rifling through his pockets. In the lower left hand-warmer pocket she found was she was hunting for, a tiny little folding cellular phone. It was still ringing. Billie flipped the phone open and pressed the answer button.

"Hello?" she said.

"Um… hello," came Veronica's voice on the other end of the line. "Who's this?"

"This is Billie," she said, a slight flush blossoming in her cheeks. "Who's this?"

"Billie, huh?" came the reply. "Nice. This is Veronica."

The hint of a breeze edged up the hillside from the lake, sweeping the sweet cloud of Russian cigarette smoke away from Ned and Billie.

"Well, I think there's been some sort of mix-up…" said Billie into the phone, a hurt tone slightly noticeable in the back of her voice.

"What do you mean? Isn't my Nedly there?" asked Veronica.

Billie did not reply. Without hesitation, she hurled the phone at point blank range, striking Ned with a sharp knock on the head.

"Ow," he said. "What's your problem?"

"You are such an asshole, Ned," said Billie, fighting back tears.

She rose, gathered her gear together and limped away as best she could with her wounded ankle. After only four steps, she tripped and fell again, striking the forest floor with a dull thud, but picked herself up

134

immediately and continued on, disappearing over the lip of the ravine in the same direction the smoke had gone.

"Billie?" Ned called after her, but she didn't answer him.

Ned rubbed his head, still puzzled by Billie's violent outburst, and picked up the cellular phone at his feet.

"Hello?" he said.

"Hello, darling," came Veronica's reply. "We need to talk."

"Hold on a second. How did—"

"Oh, I slipped the phone into your pocket when you were chopping all that wood. So we could stay in touch."

"There is no reason we need to—"

"By the way," she cut him off, "that's a very attractive thing for you, Ned—chopping wood, I mean. Your own very masculine, athletic scent, combined with the aroma of freshly hewn firewood. It's a terrific effect. What time is it, anyway? Six thirty in the morning? God, I am wired. I haven't slept all night, and now I've put down at least a quart of really strong coffee that Clive—"

"Shut up!" shouted Ned, his voice resonating through the once-still woods.

"Okay, hold on," she said. Ned could hear Veronica taking a series of deep breaths, releasing the air slowly through her teeth. When she came back on the line, her voice was much more controlled.

"I'm better now," she said. "You know how I get when a job is starting up. Plus all that java."

"Why are you calling me?" Ned asked angrily.

"So let's see," she said, ignoring his question. "It's six thirty in the morning, and you were with company. Nedly, you bad boy! What was her name again? Betty?"

"Stop it, Veronica," he said.

"We really do need to have a chat, Ned. An urgent one. Where should we meet?"

"Nowhere."

"Someplace centrally located. I know — how about The Cooler?"

"The Cooler? You think you can find The —"

"Let's make it lunch, okay? Say noon-ish? That'll give me time to put a few things together."

The line went dead as Veronica hung up on Ned. He flipped his phone closed, sat motionless for a moment, then hurled the offending instrument all the way to Lake Tashmoo, where it disappeared with a splash.

← ← ←

After the early morning debacle at Tashmoo Pond, Ned had spent five hours at the sanctuary with several of the contributors, one at a time or with their spouses, guiding them on hasty strolls around the sanctuary. They were, as a whole, a pushy and ill-tempered bunch, so demanding and clamorous out on the trails that they could not sneak up on road kill, much less a rare and endangered bird. The stress of near-misses, when contributors came within seconds of meeting each other during their walks, had worn Ned to the nub. By the time Ned reached The Cooler, at noon-ish, his nerves were in a sad state.

Ned scanned the bar, cheered slightly to find that Veronica Lodge was nowhere to be seen. She had been joking, certainly, about meeting here for lunch, just having a little fun with Ned. Veronica had not even been on the island a week; there was no way anyone would give her directions to The Cooler. Ned himself had been in residence for almost a year before he had even heard the name of the bar mentioned.

Deputy Lemuel Keene sat at the bar, sulking, and pretended not to notice as Ned entered. Ned stepped over and nudged his friend on the shoulder.

"I see you, you see me, Lem," said Ned. "C'mon over to the table. I could use some friendly company, but I guess you'll have to do."

"No, thank you, Ned," said the Deputy.

"C'mon, Lem. I've had a really shitty day. Just get over here and let me buy you a beer."

The moody deputy did move over to Ned's table, but made it clear that he wouldn't go out of his way to be friendly with Ned. His pain was still too fresh.

"Here's to old friends," Ned toasted hopefully once Gigi had brought over two draft beers. Lemuel drank but said nothing.

"Hey, I oughtta be ashamed," said Ned. "I'm corrupting a law officer, forcing beer on him when he's on the job."

"I'm not on the job, Ned, as you should well know. I'm strictly graveyard now. At the desk. On the phones."

Ned sighed. The problem had begun right there, at Ned's table, a few months earlier. Lem had sat down with Ned and the others for happy hour, and described his consternation over a report he had filed that day. Caroline Laguna, the librarian at the West Tisbury Free Public Library, had come into the Sheriff's office in a snit, whining about some summer visitors from France who had checked out several books and then left the island without returning them. Lemuel had tried to brush her off, of course, since there was zero chance the books could ever be recovered. But Ms. Laguna had refused to back down. She had "had it up to here with these thoughtless off-island delinquents", and would not allow Lemuel to talk her out of filing an official police report.

"This is just the kinda shit the Sheriff hates," Lem had moaned to Ned and the others, later that day at The Cooler. "That report will sit in our files for all eternity, with my signature on the bottom. It'll piss him off for years."

"Have you called Interpol?" Ned had asked, in a whimsical mood after a couple of happy hour drafts.

"What's that?" Lem had asked.

"This is just the kind of problem they take care of," Ned replied. "It's an international group dedicated to prevention of library book theft. I'm surprised Ms. Laguna didn't suggest them."

"What does 'Interpol' mean?" asked Lem innocently. He was a smart and effective law enforcement officer, but he was not overly experienced in the world beyond Martha's Vineyard, and there was a guileless, even naïve aspect to his nature that made Lem highly suggestible.

"It stands for something like, International Agency for the Prosecution of Library Offenders," suggested Doc.

Lem had thought about this for a moment.

"Prosecution of Library Offenders. That would be P-L-O, not P-O-L, Ned."

"It's those romance languages," Tommie had chimed in, "like Italian, French, like that. You know, Lem — they get all the words backwards. It's like *'Prosecution de Offendeurs Librarie'*, ya see?"

Deputy Keene had thought about it some more.

"And they would take care of this for me?"

"Why not?" Ned encouraged him. "That's what they're there for. You go back to the station, I guarantee that somewhere is a directory of law enforcement agencies worldwide. You get the address for Interpol, their offices in France, and send them a request on the

Sheriff's Office letterhead. I bet they'll track down these people and get the books back. Give it a shot."

So Dukes County Deputy Sheriff Lemuel Keene had typed a formal request and sent it via registered U.S. Mail to Interpol. The first development had occurred just days later, when Lem had arrived at The Cooler with a self-satisfied air about him.

"Well," he had told the others, "the wheels are in motion, boys."

"What wheels would those be, Lem?" Doc had asked.

"The Interpol wheels," said Lem, proudly.

"The efficient and vengeful wheels of the international library crime-fighting machine?" Tommie had mused with a twisted grin.

"Yep. They got my request and are taking care of everything."

"Uh… what exactly happened, Lem?" asked Ned, suddenly a little concerned.

"Well, I got a call from Interpol," related Lem, "a little guy sounded French or something. He said he had received my email request for help with the library books. He asked were the books evidence in a crime or whatever. And I figured, sure they are, there's a police report filed, right? So I say 'yes'. Then he asks what sort of priority should they rate the request. And I figure, hey, our library books are as important as any others. Folks are here on the island all winter, and they need their reading. So I say 'highest priority', of course. We went over a bunch of other stuff, honestly half of which I couldn't understand very well. He wanted to make sure I had proper authorization and put in all the right paperwork and so forth. Boy, those French library guys are thorough. I bet they never lose books over there, ever. Anyway, we got everything cleared up. And at the end, you know what he said?"

"What did he say?" Ned asked with a sense of dread.

"He said '*C'est bon!*'", Lem boasted with a strong smile but a weak French accent. "Just like that. *C'est bon!*"

Lem had then called out to Gigi, ordering a round of beers for Ned and Doc and Tommie, his good friends who had helped him so much with his annoying library book problem.

"Wait 'til the Sheriff gets a load of this," Lem had said. "All on my own I get this turkey out of our case files, forever. This is gonna be great."

Ned, Tommie and Doc had exchanged dubious looks at that point, together wondering if they should jump in and nip this potential disaster in the bud. But the wordless consensus had been that Lem had misunderstood his contact with the Interpol detective, that most likely nothing of consequence would end up happening on the European side or, if it was going to, then it most likely had already happened, so why alarm Lem prematurely? Such was the logic of their catastrophic cop-out.

Four days later, a bonded courier from Paris had arrived on the island, heading straight to the Dukes County Sheriff's office and to the desk of Deputy Lemuel Keene. The courier—his name lost to posterity amid the chaos that soon followed—presented the deputy with the two library books in question, plus a packet of papers that included: 1. Copies from the daily logs of the two Paris *gendarmes* assigned to observed the suspects, undercover, for a period of two days; 2. A set of unflattering, groggy-looking mug shots of the two French library book delinquents in question, Monsieur et Madame Philippe Forté, taken by the officers who had kicked down the couple's front door at two in the morning; 3. Transcripts of the intense eight hour interrogation of the offenders; 4. Blank extradition forms(should they be *'necessoire'*) and 5. A bill for expenses that totaled thirty-two thousand, seven hundred and forty two dollars, American. Payment was expected on delivery — right then and there — in the form of a money order or certified check.

Ned looked at his friend now, just a few months after the incident, and was actually impressed at how well the deputy was holding up. Here he was, back at The Cooler, sharing a drink with the very man who had set the unfortunate series of events into motion. Ned hoped that Lem would continue to improve, state-of-mind wise. The severe sentence handed down by the Sheriff — thirty years behind a desk — was sure to be commuted at some point in the future, and Ned was constantly on the lookout for an opportunity to improve on the deputy's situation.

"I've said it before and I'll say it again," Ned piped up now, reaffirming an oath to his friend, "one day I'll make it up to you, Lem, I swear."

"Uh huh," Lem replied.

The door of The Cooler swung open several times over the next thirty minutes, and Ned was relieved each time to see only regular patrons entering, including Doc and Tommie.

No way could Veronica find the place, Ned reassured himself.

"Why are your eyes stuck on the door?" Tommie asked.

"For no reason, it turns out," Ned replied.

They had just begun eating their lunch specials — the dubious tuna salad plate — when the front door of the bar swung open and Veronica entered, sashaying confidently into The Cooler as if she had been a regular all her life.

"Hi honey," she said to Ned, leaning over to kiss him wetly on the lips as she sat down at his table, propping the heels of her boots on an empty chair. "Thanks for coming by."

15.

Upon Veronica's appearance at The Cooler, all eyes had turned to Ned, with accusatory, unforgiving looks.

"No!" Ned said loudly to the room, defensively. "I did NOT tell her how to get here."

"What's the big deal?" said Veronica. "A few obscure driveways, a few nasty potholes. Gimme a break."

"It's nice to see you again, Veronica," smiled Tommie.

"Likewise, Tractor Tommie. Hi to you too, Doc. And who is this strapping young thing? I love a man in uniform," she said, looking at Lem.

"Deputy Lemuel Keene," said Lem, "and I was just leaving."

"Must you?" Veronica asked convincingly.

"Yeah, I must," insisted Lem, rising from his chair and removing his hat from the nearby rack. He had picked up on the palpable aura of larceny that surrounded Veronica, and was not in the market for more trouble.

"Nice meeting you, Deputy," Veronica said.

"Yep. See you fellas," Lem said, and left the bar.

"Well, darling," said Veronica, picking up Ned's fork and stabbing a bite from the tuna salad in front of him, "like I said on the phone, we need to talk."

"We're happy to use another table," said Doc, halfway rising from his seat, but Ned grabbed him by the shoulder and forced him back into his seat.

"Please stay, guys. I don't wanna be alone right now," he said.

"But you'd be with me, Ned," Veronica protested with a sly grin.

"Exactly."

"It's your call, Ned," she said and looked to Doc and Tommie, "because any trusted friend of Ned's is a trusted friend of mine."

"Thanks," Tommie said cheerfully.

"Then just go ahead and say your piece," Ned said, getting antsy. "And please try to keep your voice down."

"Then here it is," Veronica began. "The Friendships have been taken into custody."

"The brothers arrested?" said Ned. "Huge surprise."

"Not arrested yet, exactly," she answered, "but just in custody. With the Secret Service."

"The Secret Service?"

"Oh, yeah," said Tommie, "Didn't you hear, Ned? The island has got a certain visitor."

"At the Tarpaulin Center, isn't he?" Doc asked.

"Well yes, Doc," said Veronica, very interested. "Do you know the place?"

"I suppose," he answered. "I've been there a few times—"

"Hold on," Ned interrupted. "Don't say any more, Doc. What's this about, Ron? Spill it all."

Veronica munched another big bite of Ned's tuna salad.

"All right, Ned. The boys and I are here for a job, and now they are unavailable. If I'm going do the job, which I am, I'm going to need some help."

Ned looked at her in total disbelief for a moment, then broke out chuckling, a slightly maniacal chuckle that was so oddly out of character that it seemed a clear harbinger of dementia. His friends regarded him with concern.

"See? Too much carbon," Tommie whispered to Doc.

"The thing is, Ned, I didn't suggest you for the job," Veronica said evenly once Ned's initial wave of giggling had ebbed. "My employer did."

The maniacal grin faded from Ned's face.
"Your *what*?"

"I told you this was a commissioned job. When I informed the buyer that the Friendships were out of the plan, he handed me a rather extensive file on you, Ned, and told me to sign you up."

Ned reflected on this for a moment. Tommie and Doc exchanged confused looks.

"He knows…" Ned's voice trailed off.

"About your time working with me. With the brothers. He knows about your warrants, plus a few interesting escapades of yours here on the island. He knows your whole history, Ned."

"Hold on," said Tommie. "Even *we* don't know your history, Ned. Do we, Doc?"

"No, we don't," replied Doc.

"Who is this client of yours?" Ned demanded of Veronica.

"His name is Arnold Speck," she replied.

"The slimy developer?" asked Doc.

"Hey," said Tommie, "I did some tree trimming for that guy. Big bucks. Kinda weird."

"So sorry, Ned," said Veronica, apparently sincere. "I mean it. I had no intention of involving you. From the looks of things—I've seen his database—this Speck guy has got confidential files for half the people on the island. He's says you're to join up and help me with the job, or he's going to turn over your file to '*the relevant authorities*'."

Ned groaned dreadfully, burying his face in his hands and rubbing his eyes until they teared up.

"He mentioned, as a footnote," added Veronica, "that the property at Music Lagoon had '*an enviable ocean vista*'. Ripe for development, I think he was suggesting."

The others remained quiet, giving Ned some much needed time to digest all the new information. He was cornered, and he knew it.

"And the job?" he finally ventured.

"We're gonna take off the *visitor*," she answered.

"Whoa," said Tommie. "You're gonna take off the *visitor*…"

"Meaning…" said Ned.

"Yep," Veronica confirmed. "The Vice President."

When Roger Paulson returned to the main building of the Tarpaulin Center, he was sopping wet and shivering, but exhilarated.

"This place is marvelous," he said to Agent Hipps as she helped him dry off. "It has everything. I think I could live here, Hipps. Maybe I will."

"Yes Sir," said the agent, fluffing the Vice President's hair with a thick towel. Paulson had spent the early morning hours exploring the center, ignoring the sheets of warm rain that had drenched him as he strolled from one structure to the next. Hipps had kept track of him through the myriad security cameras placed throughout the compound, but had otherwise granted him the solitude he had asked for. A solid perimeter had been set up by the grounds detail, and the property was very secluded.

"Have you been in the Blue Building?" he asked. "There's a full theater down in the second sub-level, with stereo sound and one of those things that makes the floor shake." Paulson sneezed loudly. "And there are bowling lanes the level below that."

"Yes Sir. There are also underground walkways between all the buildings," she said with a hint of reprimand in her voice. "Should you want to stay warm and dry and avoid pneumonia."

"Why would anyone want to walk underground in such a beautiful place? I can't wait to get out on the nature trails."

"At the very least, Mr. Vice President, please take an umbrella next time. We've got enough sickness to deal with as it is."

"Oh yes — how are the boys doing?"

"Some symptoms of the bug have continued, Sir."

In fact, several of the men in Hipps' detail had had a rough night. The bug had brought about severe dehydration, which had caused some of them to hallucinate, though rather harmlessly. Special Agent Silva was found in the Center's library at three in the morning, in his underwear, using one of the computer stations to study for a Psychology 101 mid-term which he was convinced he had to take the next day. It turned out he had slept through the very test during his freshman year at UVA, and felt that his career ambitions had been side-tracked ever since.

"Is the doctor looking after them?"

"She is, Sir. She's got them popping antibiotics, plus IV drips for rehydration. They'll come around eventually. In the meantime, I'm going to call D.C. and get another team up."

"Don't be ridiculous, Hipps. I'm perfectly safe here, of all places. And as you say, the boys are getting better..."

"Sir, we only have two dozen agents on the entire detail, and between them they haven't got enough body fluids left to fill a water balloon. It's standard protocol to—"

"Please, Hipps? No more guns?"

The Vice President gave her a plaintive look, and Hipps was sympathetic. She understood that Paulson was, in most ways, a very private person, and the adjustment to public life had been difficult for him. Only five years earlier, Paulson had been an uncelebrated mid-career Economics professor at Reed College in Portland, single and something of a loner but popular enough with students. A coincidental series of "only in America" events had landed him, reluctantly, in the U.S. Senate as the junior Senator from Oregon, then, three years later, as second banana on the Democratic ticket. The sudden loss of privacy was threatening to drive him over the edge. Dealing with the public at large was tough enough for Paulson, but having his personal time and space invaded by an omnipresent cadre of bodyguards was almost unbearable for the man.

On top of that, Paulson and the President had endured some acrimonious disputes over the administration's fiscal policy, early on in their term, and since then Paulson had been completely stonewalled by the Oval Office, preventing him from having any meaningful involvement in the administration. Alone and marginalized, Paulson had drifted numbly through his second year of office before finally discovering a survival strategy that would restore his sense of self.

The Vice President had realized that he had unlimited resources at his disposal and every reason to take full advantage. After all, it was widely assumed that the Vice President was constantly engaged in missions that were obscure, inexplicable, highly symbolic and, ultimately, meaningless. That was his job. No one ever asked Paulson to explain what he was doing at any given moment, or why; it was too embarrassing for everyone concerned. Thus, the possibilities were endless. To remain sane, the Vice President aggressively turned his attention back to his life's true passion — bird watching — and had managed to attach birding adventures to almost all of his official duties, traversing the globe on minor diplomatic missions and simultaneously becoming the best traveled bird enthusiastic in the world. Paulson's situation was, if looked upon with the right attitude, a dream come true, and in Agent Rhonda Hipps' estimation Roger Paulson had just the right attitude.

"Please, Hipps, no more guns?" Paulson pled. "I have full confidence in you. And the Center has extensive security measures, no?"

"Extensive, Sir. Yes."

"We'll be fine, especially if this incredible warm spell keeps up. I want to get out and hunt down that lapwing."

"This bird is a big deal, I guess…"

"For an official sighting, you would need at least one qualified witness, but preferably a good quality photo or video of the bird. None of that has happened, yet, *vis a vis* the lapwing. Of all these birders, the one who first spots the lapwing, officially, after all these years, will go down forever in the annals of bird watching."

"Hmm."

"I know, Hipps. It can sound a little esoteric — or plain ridiculous — to someone outside the birding community. But for us enthusiasts…"

"It's the cheese. It's an accomplishment they can never take away from you. I think I get it, Sir."

"Good. Well, I might as well get on the clock, then. Do I have an office set up?"

"On the second floor library, Sir, with a lovely view of the grounds. There is hot tea waiting for you, plus some lemony pastries from a local bakery that I think you'll like."

Hipps is so good to me, thought Paulson. So good. And something about her down-home Bayou drawl always put him immediately at ease.

"Thank you so much, Angel Hipps."

"Sir?"

"*Agent. Agent* Hipps, of course. Thank you."

Paulson made his way to the library upstairs. A playful fire burned in the fieldstone fireplace, just beside the oak coffee table where his breakfast had been artistically arranged. Soft, hand-woven carpets covered the floors, and all the furniture was upholstered with smooth, buttery red leather. The built-in desk ran the full length of the window, offering a panoramic view of the spectacular Tarpaulin grounds, still being drenched by the relentless downpour.

"I would like to see this in snow," Paulson pronounced to himself, out loud.

The Vice President took off his shoes and sat on the floor beside the coffee table, warming his bare toes by the fire as he munched down two delicate, lemony cinnamon croissants and sipped the hot chamomile tea. A small table beside him held a stack of papers — his for the day. On the top of the pile were the environmental consultant' reports that dealt, coincidentally, with the disposition of a federally owned properties in the Cape Cod area, including an island less than a mile from Martha's Vineyard — called "Noman's Island" — that had been used for years as a target practice site for Navy bombers. Paulson had remained influential in several environmental committees, and his input on which property should be open to public use would almost certainly be the deciding vote. The Vice President opened the folder and was greeted with a dizzying selection of environmental impact reports, military assessments, color-coded graphs estimating potential public usage, evaluations of the Cape Cod economy and a seemingly endless amount of other materials, all apparently designed to give Paulson a headache.

He slammed the folder shut, set it aside and reached instead for a heavy black valise, carefully removing a thick, leather-bound portfolio filled with one hundred leaves of acid-free drawing paper. This was Volume VI of the Paulson Codex, as it had been affectionately named by the bird watching community. The scope of Paulson's work was impressive. The leafs contained a collection of fine drawings executed by the Vice President himself, in both watercolor and colored pencil, featuring some of the rarest birds in the world. Paulson had been making these drawings since the age of six, only sketching birds that he had personally sighted. His earlier entries, of course, were mostly of common birds, ones that would come to eat at the feeder in the backyard of his childhood home. As he grew older and more mobile, however, his collection came to include renderings of much more interesting and exotic species.

Since his political ascendancy, Paulson's sketchbooks had garnered a great deal of public attention. Flattering comparisons were made to the seminal work of John James Audubon. An exhibit has hung at the National

Gallery, featuring Volume I of the Codex, Paulson's precocious drawings from his elementary school years. The Smithsonian Institute had asked Paulson to bequeath the art works to their collection, and Volumes I through V were already in their vaults.

Volume VI, however, was the most spectacular collection of them all. These were the drawings Paulson had created since assuming office, and his ability to span the globe at will had produced sketches of the rarest birds in the world, some of which had scarcely been captured in photographs, much less watercolors.

Paulson leafed through the volume now, reviewing his greatest birding achievements of the past year. He had sighted and drawn the newly discovered Udzingwa Forest Partridge in Tanzania and the Demoiselle Cranes of Khichan. On the island of Mauritius, Paulson had stalked and finally sighted an Echo Parakeet—possibly the rarest bird in the world with only a dozen still on the wing—and on the Sulu Islands of the Philippines he had successfully tracked down the Hooded Pitta. Finally, on this last trip, the Vice President achieved perhaps his greatest coup yet, rendering in pastels the Laotian Elephant Goose, a bird so rare that it was once thought by Western ornithologists to be mythical.

Not bad for a couple weeks' work, Paulson congratulated himself.

16.

Ned and Veronica crouched low behind an old stone wall, the barrier marking the furthest edge of the Tarpaulin property. The rain had stopped at sunset but heavy clouds remained overhead, providing a cover from the moonlight. Veronica was ready for work, dressed in a snug black flight suit and carrying a shoulder pack with the equipment she would need for light recon work. Ned was dressed in gum boots and an old pair of dark grey painter's coveralls, as close as he could or would bring himself to covert fashion.

"Wow," said Veronica, upon first sighting the impressive Tarpaulin Center, every window on the compound shining brightly. "What happens here, usually?"

"It's one of those out-of-the-limelight think-tank places," said Ned. "Where the rich and powerful and smart come to secretly decide what will happen to the rest of us."

"We don't get a vote, huh?"

"Not here."

"Huh. Let's get a closer look, Nedly," said Veronica.

She hopped acrobatically over the ancient stone wall and Ned followed, clambering over the top somewhat less nimbly. They moved quietly across a broad, open pasture that had been groomed close to the ground so that it looked more like a great lawn than a farm field. The only sound was the squishing of their steps on the grassy turf, muddy and slick from the rains.

Ned and Veronica reached a stand of low brush, still two hundred yards or so from the Center's main buildings. Squatting out of sight and re-surveying the terrain ahead, they detected no human movement. There were no outward indications of a security perimeter, but they kept a close watch for the team of Secret Service agents they knew would be somewhere on the grounds.

"Yesterday I was a simple and happy sanctuary director," Ned whispered to Veronica. "Now I'm skulking around in darkness, scanning for Secret Service agents. This is not a good development for me."

"Quit your whining," Veronica hissed back. "And the way I hear it, your 'duties' as a Sanctuary Director have included some fairly dubious activities."

"Like what?" Ned protested, knowing she was right but doubting that she knew any damning details.

"Well, Ned, a couple of nights ago you were scouring the grounds of a local golf course, looking to find and bury a murder victim. Let's start there."

"A murder victim *you* brought to the island, and who, by the way, turned out to be not actually dead," Ned retorted, grudgingly impressed that Veronica had sniffed out the narrow link between the Friendships' misadventure and Ned. The girl had skills, and always had.

"The ground ahead, it's too empty," Ned whispered as they scurried across the open field.

"No," she answered quietly, "it's consistent with our information. They're undermanned, for whatever reason, which probably means that they're depending too heavily upon the Center's built-in security measures. We find a way in through those, we could be sitting very pretty."

After a few hundred yards out in the open, they reached a second stone wall, just inside the stand of trees. On the other side of the wall was a dirt road that circled this inner perimeter of the property. From here they had a relatively close view of the entire Center, about a hundred yards away. Every light in the place was burning, including flood lights around every building.

"By the way," said Ned, "I've been thinking it over and Speck's plan has a major flaw."

"Yeah?"

"Yeah. You said he wants to switch out a fake Environmental Impact Report for the real one. What if Paulson has already read the authentic report? Then this whole thing is a waste."

"First of all," Veronica answered, "I already brought that up with Speck. Seems the V.P. is a notorious procrastinator, especially if there are watchable birds within a thousand miles. He doesn't have to submit his decision until next week, so he almost certainly has not read the report yet."

"Hmm," said Ned, dubious.

"Not that I care, personally."

"Because you get paid either way," said Ned, "whether his fucked-up plan works or not."

"Correct, Ned. That's the beauty. Like Merrill Lynch, I get paid either way."

"You get paid and you leave. Whereas I, as a local resident, will find myself permanently sharing the same small island with a disgruntled, imbalanced and possibly vengeful Arnold Speck."

"I'm genuinely sorry about that, Ned."

"Right."

"Over there," Veronica said, pointing to the largest building. Two men in suits and rain coats strolled past the front entrance, sweeping their flashlight beams about them with obvious disinterest. Their patrol course carried them toward a cluster of cottages at the northern end of the compound, where they disappeared.

"They look pretty relaxed," Ned observed.

"Good of them," she agreed.

"Get down," Ned whispered suddenly, and they ducked low behind the wall, their knees digging into the muddy ground. There was a crunching of tires on gravel as a large American utility vehicle, dark blue, appeared around a bend in the road, its high beams panning the area and passing just inches over their heads. The bright lights burned through the open spaces in the stone wall, but not enough to reveal Ned and Veronica. The vehicle passed within feet of their position, the heaviness of the bulletproof Suburban audible as it compressed the road beneath it. Within twenty seconds, the vehicle was out of sight. Ned and Veronica rose slowly from behind the wall and resumed their study of the grounds.

"Pathetic," she said. "We've been here almost ten minutes, and that's only one walking patrol and one rolling. These boys are napping."

Veronica raised her binoculars and scoped the compound again, quickly registering and remembering every inch of the territory until it was no longer foreign. Ned watched her as she analyzed and schemed. It would not take long. Veronica was a purely instinctual operator, bordering on recklessly impulsive. She would determine an approach and go with it. That had always been her style, to hit the target with such brazen speed and audacity that only the most fearless and unequivocal response could hope to deny her. In most cases, the job would be over before the mark ever knew what was happening.

Ned was different. In the two years he spent heisting with Veronica and her cohorts, he would try to point out the obvious risks and flaws in her plans, and offer suggestions that he hoped would enable them all to survive the day. In Veronica's crew, however, the Voice of Reason was largely a ceremonial position. The cohorts tended to listen to Ned's arguments politely — perhaps only because he was sleeping with the boss — and then reject his ideas out of hand. Veronica had encouraged Ned to continue the futile voicing of his ideas, which he thought was strange until he figured out why: the saner and more rational his suggestions, the bolder she seemed by comparison.

Ned remembered objecting once, when the two of them were alone.

"A symbiotic relationship, that's what we have," she had insisted, back then. "It's checks and balances. Your opinions check mine, my views balance yours. It's a very beautiful thing, and so natural."

"It's not symbiotic, Veronica. You always win."

"So, it's a one-way symbiosis. It's semi-symbiotic."

"*Parasitic* — I think that's the word you're looking for," Ned had observed. "You get all the benefits."

She had answered by straddling Ned atop a squeaky motel bed, slowly unbuttoning her shirt as she leaned over and teased his face with the silky tips of her long, dark hair.

"Okay, cowboy — you wanna talk about benefits?"

Crouched in the cold night air behind a stone wall on the Tarpaulin property, Ned was suddenly enjoying the memory.

"I'll bet this place was landscaped by a local," said current-day Veronica, continuing to scan the Tarpaulin Center with her binoculars.

"Huh?"

"Where are you, Ned? Try to focus."

"I'm with it," insisted Ned.

"Good."

"I have been wondering about something, though—how long have you been here? On the island, I mean."

"Almost a week."

"Ready to take off the Vice President."

"So it would seem. Why?"

"And how did you know he would be here? He's never stopped on the island before."

"I don't know," Veronica admitted after thinking about it for a second. "Speck seems to be very well informed."

"But according to your information, the man is here because of the lapwing."

"That bird you all are so worked up about, yeah..."

"Which was not reported on the bird site until barely two days ago."

"Hmm..."

"Several days *after* you arrived on the island, ready to go to work."

"I suppose that's right," agreed Veronica.

Veronica's information confirmed a suspicion that Ned had been harboring since he first heard that the target of her heist would be the Vice President. He figured it this way: the Vice President of the United States was the most famous birdwatcher in the world, known to traverse the planet in the slightest hope of a rare sighting. As Veronica's week-long presence on the island indicated, Speck knew that Vice President Roger Paulson would be visiting the island, even before Roger Paulson himself had known.

So... there was no lapwing. Arnold Speck had faked the photo on the Rare Bird Alert site. That was why the sighting had gone unclaimed. With the Vice

President's arrival on the island, Speck had successfully lured the mountain to Mohammed, and had simultaneously arranged to have Veronica Lodge, mistress of audacious pilferage, lying in wait and ready to do her thing. Minor footnote: Speck's plan had also turned Ned Donlin's safe and serene island existence into chaos. Because of Speck, the previously reformed co-conspirator named Ned Donlin found himself crouched behind a wall on private property, stalking the Vice President of the United States and listening to a very attractive yet notorious felon say things like:

"No serious security man would have done the landscaping this way."

"Why?"

"You see the marshy side of the pond? Where the reeds lead right into those bushes, or whatever they are?"

Ned looked where Veronica was pointing, and immediately understood. The landscaping provided cover to within thirty feet of the main building. Any good security consultant would have put the kybosh on that arrangement, but the work had probably been done after the security system was set up, and probably by a local landscaper who did not have crime prevention as his first priority.

"No way would they wire motion detectors in that wet area," said Veronica.

Ned agreed. And as he watched Veronica pack away her binoculars and recheck her gear, he had a frightening realization, the latest of several he had experienced in the last several days.

"Shit," said Ned." You're going in now, aren't you?"

"Don't be silly, Ned. *We* are going in now. Audacious, huh?"

"Shit."

"It just feels right. Think about it — the place is huge, security is understaffed; they've just come off a long international flight and are probably still lagged. We jam on in and catch them off guard, and this whole supposedly monstrous gig is over in fifteen minutes."

"Or we get caught and our lives are ruined forever."

"Don't bring me down, Ned. I'm really feelin' this."

← ← ←

"Ricky? Are you awake?" asked Bobby Friendship, in darkness.

"Yeah," Ricky answered.

"I wish I had somethin' to eat."

"Yeah."

"I wish I had a mattress to sit on or a pad or somethin'."

"Uh huh."

"I wish —"

"Shut up, Bob."

"Okay."

There was ten seconds of silence.

"Ricky?"

"Yeah."

"What do you think it means we got black bags over our heads?"

"Help yourself on this one, Bobby. Go over all the reasons possible that someone would chain us to a cold cement floor and put bags over our heads."

Ricky gave Bobby a minute to think.

"Got 'em," said Bobby.

"Now how many of those reasons mean good things for us?"

A few more seconds to think.

"Zero," said Bobby.

"And how many are gut-screamin' awful?"

Ten more seconds.

"The rest."

"Right. Now shut the hell up."

Suddenly they heard approaching footsteps in the outside hall. The steps paused at the heavy metal door to their cell, keys jangled, and the door swung open, bathing the room in a light so bright they could feel it under their black felt hoods. Without warning, the hoods were whipped off, nearly blinding the Friendship brothers after almost twenty four hours of complete darkness. They squinted tightly, only able to make out the single tall, lanky silhouette standing before them.

"It's her, Rick! Hey lady, are you gonna hit us again?"

"Shut the hell up. I haven't hit you once."

"You pushed my head and it went hard against that wall!" Bobby protested.

"And your head won," said Agent Hipps. "There's a crack in the cement now."

"We want to speak to our lawyer," said Ricky with a practiced air of formality.

"A lawyer? For what?" asked Hipps.

"If you are going to charge us with-"

"No no," Hipps said, "you can put your minds at ease about that. There aren't going to be any charges. I have no interest in that."

The brothers' demeanor brightened slightly.

"Okay," said Bobby, "then can we go now?"

"Absolutely not."

"But those are the choices," Ricky said, a little weakly. "You charge us or you let us go."

Hipps laughed out loud, a cruel laugh in the shared judgment of the Friendship brothers.

"Oh, there are lots more choices than that. Let me give you an example. There's a big pond out on the property here, you must have seen it on your way in? It's surprisingly deep for such a small body of water. I could get a big, big burlap sack, stick you both in it, toss in a few heavy stones and dump you in the pond. That's just one example of something that could happen."

"There's nothin' legal about that," said Ricky.

"Legal, schmegal. No one knows you're here, except those under my command. I can do anything I want and no one will care. Seriously."

The brothers considered this for a moment.

"But you wouldn't really do that," suggested Bobby Friendship. "Not the pond."

"Sure I would," asserted Hipps. "That's how we get rid of unwanted litters in Cajun country. You know, kittens and puppies? Put 'em in a sack and toss them in the swamp."

"No! Not kittens and puppies!?" shouted Bobby.

"Shut up, Bobby," Ricky finally said. "So, it's your rules, lady. What do you want from us?"

"That's easy. I want to know why you're here."

"That's easy, too," said Ricky. "It's mostly just a misunderstanding. Some friends of ours were havin' a costume party, you know? And we were going as Secret Service agents, but we musta mixed up the—"

"Before you go on," said Hipps, "I should mention that my men found your stash of stolen goods outside the perimeter of the property. Quite a haul. And I've faxed your fingerprints to the FBI. We should be hearing from them any time now."

Again, the brothers thought for a moment.

"So what the hell do you want from us, then?" said Ricky with a sudden burst of anger. "You know everything there is to know, it seems like, and you got us chained to this goddam cold floor and we ain't eaten in a whole day, and you want something from US?"

It was a fair question, figured Hipps. In many ways, it seemed like all the issues relating to these men were simple. They were bad, and now they were caught. But from the moment they had appeared at the front door of the Center, Hipps had had an uneasy feeling. No, that wasn't quite true, she now realized; she had had the uneasy feeling since she first arrived on the island, dragging with her an entire detail of perilously ill Secret Service agents. The Tarpaulin Center, with all its spectacular security bells and whistles, should have felt airtight, but somehow it did not. It felt big and cold and remote. And then there was the appearance of these two-bit burglars who, by the sound of their accents, were from somewhere in the Southwest, not this area. Small timers like these worked their comfortable home turf, most usually, and their presence here did not fit. But was there really more they could tell her? She could wait for the FBI computers to cough up their sheets, but that process had already taken far more time than usual—there was some problem with the digital filing codes, she had been told.

"Look, Agent…" said Ricky, pausing to give her an opportunity to fill in her name. She did not.

"Anyway, you got us. We steal shit, and boy did we make a mistake when we knocked on the door of this place. But you've got way bigger fish to fry, is my guess, and we would be the most happy fellas in the world just to get the hell away from here, as far and fast as possible. You kick us loose now, that means you get us outta your hair, no hassle and no paperwork and no explanations, plus we promise to be in a different time zone before the sun rises again on this fuckin' hell hole."

Straightforward, thought Hipps, and she appreciated it in a way. The fella had a point. In the final analysis, these skels were probably nothing more than an inconvenience. Dealing with them by the books could clutter up what might otherwise be a relaxing week in the woods with minimal bullshit. She could just let them go. It might even make her feel good. The Friendship brothers watched hopefully as she mulled the situation over. They could see she was almost there.

Suddenly a message came through Agent Hipps' radio earpiece.

"Agent Hipps? This is Calmus. The dogs on the South grounds are going ape-shit."

"By the marsh?" Hipps asked into the microphone at her wrist.

"Yeah."

In her first check of the grounds, Hipps had found a mistake in the perimeter detection system, a marshy area that ran almost to the main building with no power source and thereby no electronic security measures. The oversight provided a perfect opportunity for Hipps' standard perimeter tactics; she liked to set up an apparent weakness in one area, giving intruders a predictable ingress to shoot for. She had posted a dog team nearby, completely out of sight.

"What do you see, Calmus?" she asked the agent.

"Nothing, ma'am," the agent answered in her earpiece. "It's probably just a raccoon or something. This place is crawling with varmints."

"You're probably right. Just to be sure, let them go."

"The dogs?"

"Yes. Release the hounds. I'll be up in a second."

"Roger that."

Hipps regarded her prisoners, considering. How generous was she feeling?

"Boys," she finally announced, "I could let you go now, but I would really miss these moments we spend together. Would you please remain as my guests for a little while longer?"

"Dammit," said Ricky. "So close..."

Hipps pulled the black bags back over the heads of the Friendship brothers, switched the lights off and slammed the metal door behind her as she left.

Ned's lungs were burning. He couldn't remember the last time he had run ten feet, much less a couple of hundred-yard dashes back to back, but the sound of the vicious patrol dogs, barking the alarm at the Tarp's main building, made for a persuasive motivator. At least they weren't running loose.

Veronica waited on the other side of the wall, smirking a little as Ned wheezed and panted up to her and flopped over the wall, landing on his knees in the mud.

"Nedly, you don't look so good."

"Shut up, Ron," Ned gasped for air, "you don't get to say anything. Audacious, my ass."

"Uh, Ned?" She smiled whimsically.

"What, goddamit?"

"Do you hear that?"

Ned listened — it was the dogs. Suddenly, their barking was growing louder. Ned pulled himself up on the wall and looked back toward the Center. Four dark shapes were racing along the grassy field, headed in their direction at break-neck speed.

"Oh, Christ," Ned groaned.

"There oughtta be a leash law on this island," Veronica said, and then took off across the next pasture, sprinting in long, graceful strides with no difficulty. Ned charged after her, colorful spots flashing in his eyes as oxygen deprivation began to kick in. He slipped and skidded on the slick pasture, falling twice as his gum boots struggled for footing. He could hear the dogs breathing now, all wet and slobbery with drool as they gained ground at a terrifying rate.

Ned reached the far wall just ahead of the dogs and used his last bit of energy to vault over in stride and dive into his truck, which was waiting with Veronica at the wheel. He slammed the door behind him just as one of the dogs hit the side window, leaving a slobbery smudge on the glass. Veronica peeled out the truck, kicking up dust and gravel as she sped away along the dirt service road. The dogs continued to follow, looking like they would rather die than give up their quarry.

"Take the wheel, would you Ned?" she said, and Ned reached out an exhausted arm to steer as he coughed deeply and painfully, half expecting to see one of his burning lungs flop out onto the dashboard. Veronica pulled a plastic zip-loc bag out of her vest, rolled down her window, and spilled a full half pound of chili powder in the truck's wake. The dogs immediately howled in agony, stopping in their tracks to spit and hack and rub their noses into the dirt, desperate to get the burning powder out of their sinuses. Veronica took the wheel again and hit the gas, racing off into the dark woods with no one left to give chase.

"I guess we need a new plan, Nedly," she said.

17.

Ned worked hard, packing the snow, shaping it, spraying it down with water until its hard, icy surface gleamed. For the beak, Ned used a broomstick, covering it with layer after layer of snow until the wood was no longer visible — just the long, lethally sharp pecker. After hours of work, Ned stepped back to admire his creation: a ten foot snowman — no, snowbird — a faithful rendition of a Caucasian Lapwing, standing tall in the middle of the Music Lagoon Sanctuary clearing. Satisfied with his labors, Ned set about cleaning up his sculpting tools, but was soon startled by a cracking, crunching noise behind him. Ned turned back to his creation, just in time to see a live, much-larger-than-life lapwing emerge from inside the snowbird, angrily shaking off the prison of its icy outer layer. Ned and the bird met each others' eyes, and Ned saw that the bird was enraged. Terrified, Ned turned away and ran off through the sanctuary grounds, the giant lapwing in hot pursuit, stabbing mercilessly at Ned, with its sharp beak, again and again and again...

Ned awoke, in a start, and immediately sensed that he was being watched. He turned his head toward the nearest window and discovered the assassin, gazing calmly at him through the glass. The killer blinked his eyes once, very slowly, so as to convey complete indifference.

"Go away, Rudy," said Ned in his scratchy morning rasp.

The big orange tabby watched Ned's lips move through the window pane, but would not have reacted even if he could have deciphered the words. Ned was harmless without his morning coffee. Even the cat could see that.

A sound came from out on the grounds and Rudy disappeared in a flash. Ned listened as truck tires pulled to a stop in the gravel parking area, followed by the slamming of a truck door and footsteps on the walkway to his cottage. Nora gave a peremptory knock on the door before entering, not even giving Ned enough time to croak out a reply before she was sitting at the foot of his bed and passing him a hot cup of coffee.

"Come in," said Ned.

"How are we this morning?" Nora asked.

"Dandy," said Ned, sipping the coffee with relish. "Do you have any of those—"

"Cinnamon croissants?" Nora cut him off as she pulled a small paper bag from her coat pocket and presented Ned with the exact pastry in question.

"What was yesterday like?" he asked between bites.

"A nightmare, of course. The heavy rain ruled out birding, so the towns were jammed with visitors, including some of our contributors. They were antiquing, noshing, etc., mostly in Edgartown. Rubbing elbows in all of the major taverns."

"Any problems?" Ned asked with his mouth full.

"Not until Howard got loose," Nora said casually.

"Until what!? Howard got loose? Not in costume…"

"I'm afraid so. Angela was fitting him with some new stilts—you know, tuning up the wardrobe. Howard got restless and made a break for an open window. He flew right down the middle of Main Street in Edgartown, during lunch hour."

"Shit. Who saw him?"

"A few birders. But it was just a flash and he was gone. Just a tease. It got the birders pretty excited, of course, but there was no harm done in the long run. In fact, it might help—the appearance suggests that the bird might appear somewhere else on the island, other than here at Music Lagoon. We might convince some of our birders to search elsewhere."

"And Howard is back at home now?"

"Yep."

"Tell Angela it's over," Ned said. "However all this turns out, we have run the lapwing operation for the last time. Tell Angela to burn the stilts, burn the beak, burn her airbrush."

"Are you sure?"

"I'm sure."

"Angela's going to take it hard. She's very proud of her and Howard's contribution to the sanctuary."

"I understand that. We'll find something else for her. God knows there's more than enough to do around here."

"And you'll have a word with her personally."

"I'll give her a plaque or something."

Ned sipped his coffee, trying to calm himself after this latest apoplexy, and munched down the last of his croissant.

"How's the weather now?" Ned was almost afraid to ask.

"Clear. Lovely. A perfect day for birding."

"Shit. And they're coming?"

"Oh yes, they're coming. The first wave will be here in twenty minutes or so."

"So I'm looking at least twelve exclusive birding walks in my very near future?" Ned asked.

"That's right, Ned. You can handle it. At least I think you can, but I can't really say because I'm not clear about what other obligations you have these days."

Ned studied Nora. She was loaded for bear in full field gear, including all-weather shell, camouflage Army boots, polarized sun glasses and high-powered binoculars. She was a tough gal, that was for sure, a real trooper, and she devoted a sizeable chunk of her personal time to Music Lagoon. Her loyalty to the sanctuary and to Ned, by extension, knew no bounds. And now her feelings were hurt. She could tell that something major was going on with Ned, which might or might not involve the sanctuary, and Ned had told her nothing about his involuntary conscription for the Veronica Lodge heist.

"The thing is," Ned said, "I have some things going on, Nora, which are really bad news, for me. As much as I can, I want to keep you and the Committee insulated from—"

"You told Doc and Tommie all about it," Nora blurted angrily. "They were all whispers and nudges at The Cooler last night, chatting in secret like spies. It really pissed me off."

"I discussed some things in their presence before I realized what sort of path these events would be taking. That was my mistake. But just because I screwed up with them doesn't mean I should put you in the line of fire also." He paused. "What did they say to you?"

"Nothing. I tried to pry it out of them but they were uncharacteristically mum, which leads me to believe you are in a really deep shit-hole. Ned, if this problem involves the sanctuary, I think it's only fair that I should be informed, and that goes for the rest of the Committee as well."

"Okay, Nora. I'm gonna give this some thought."

"Okay," said Nora.

170

Out on the grounds, they could hear vehicles arriving in the parking area, and chipper chattering among peppy early morning birdwatchers.

"It's starting," said Ned.

⊢   ⇐   ⊦

Ned pulled into the Sweetwater Golf Club lot and parked his truck next to the only other car in the lot, a gunmetal grey Range Rover with the vanity license plate that said "WINKLE". Parked beside the Rover was a golf cart, all powered-up and ready to go. There was a note pinned to the cart's steering wheel, written in dark purple lipstick, which read:

> You're late, Ned. Come find us!
> Love, Dan & Sharon

Ned climbed into the cart and hummed out onto the golf course. The Winkles had requested that Ned meet them at Sweetwater instead of the sanctuary, and it wasn't a bad idea. Golf courses made excellent birding sites, and they would have the vast, manicured grounds virtually to themselves. That would not have been the case at Music Lagoon today, of course; Ned had spent the better part of the morning guiding bird walks for the special contributors, in shifts. The closed area of the sanctuary actually had two separate trails, and at several times that morning there had been more than one set of contributors on the property, with Ned and the women of the Refreshment Committee deftly maneuvering them out of each others' line of sight with only a few close calls. Plenty of other birders had been drawn to the sanctuary on their own, and were crowding various parts of the grounds not cordoned off.

No lapwing sightings had been reported.

Sweetwater's first fairway was covered with a slight frost, a white powdered-sugar dusting, broken only by the recently made tracks of another golf cart. Ned obediently took up the trail, speeding his cart across the fairway and into the woods, following the tracks toward the furthest reaches of the Sweetwater grounds.

The Winkles were well known figures in the birding community of the American Northeast, famous less for their bird spotting talents than for their unorthodox antics in the field; the Winkles were practicing nudists, and though they usually kept their clothes on during treks at the most popular birding sites, the Winkles were still known to drop trousers, occasionally, if they found themselves in more remote circumstances. When they came to visit their "private" parcel at Music Lagoon, for example, they always birded *al fresco*. This sometimes made Ned feel uncomfortable — standing in the woods, fully clothed, with a completely naked middle-aged couple — but he liked the Winkles a lot, personally, and they were certainly his favorites among the special group of contributors who had access to the closed section of the sanctuary. This was partially due to the fact that the Winkles had never been fooled by the lapwing scam, at all, but had donated money to the sanctuary anyway, figuring that such an extreme contrivance revealed how desperate the financial situation had become.

Ned sped his cart across the twelfth fairway, still following the Winkles' cart tracks, but his tour was suddenly disrupted by the sound of a large, thunderous engine, and soon Ned came upon none other than Tommie Krupa, mounted on a red twenty-ton back hoe, patrolling a small area just west of the fairway. Tommie killed his engine as Ned approached.

"Ned," Tommie nodded, looking exasperated.

"You don't look pleased, Tommie," said Ned.

"I've been working on new sprinkler pipes," said Tommie. "We're trying to get the work done before the ground freezes up again, but some time during the digging I must have broken through to a spring head. Tapped right into the aquifer, is my guess. The water is breaking out everywhere, at least five spots so far. I just can't find the source to stop it up, so I'm havin' to dig up a week's worth of work. Fyodor is with the club manager now, getting his ass chewed off."

"I'll keep my eyes open for problem areas," Ned offered.

"Thanks, Ned," Tommie said, then revved up the back hoe and motored off.

Ned continued on in his golf cart, crossing over to the sixteenth hole where he reacquired the Winkles' tire tracks. Beyond the sixteenth, Ned topped a small rise which gave him a clear vista of the surrounding acreage. Ned stopped to survey the view. A quarter mile away, beside Sweetwater's eighteenth fairway, stood the grove of trees where Ricky Friendship had been buried alive by General Hoak. To the West, very near the ocean, Ned could make out the series of peaked rooftops at the Tarpaulin Center, where soon-to-be burglary victim Roger Paulson was currently in residence. A little further West stood the Music Lagoon Wildlife Sanctuary, the current epicenter of Ned's universe.

The view to the South was no less complicated. Though of course Ned couldn't actually sight all these locations, he knew they were there and that was enough; there was the Makoniky Inn, where Veronica Lodge was undoubtedly sleeping in late, wearing little if anything under the thick wool camp blankets featured on all the Inn's four poster beds. Ned sighed. Two miles east of the Inn, The Cooler was buried somewhere in the dense woods of the island's center. That was one place where Ned could generally expect to find some sort of peace, but that was not necessarily true, any more, since Veronica had figured out how to get there. Last but not least, at the furthest Southern reach of the island lay the series of ponds frequently patrolled by Massachusetts State Fish and Game Warden Billie Jensen.

Ned was just beginning to muse yet again—groan—about his life here on the island, and whether or not it was worth fighting for, when suddenly he spotted the Winkles near the edge of the twelfth green, only two hundred yards away. Ned floored his cart's accelerator and hummed over the crest of the rise, quickly closing the gap and reaching the Winkles. The couple were, as Ned predicted, naked, except for walking boots, watch caps, gloves on their hands and binoculars around their necks. They wore smiles, also, at Ned's arrival.

"You're going to catch pneumonia," said Ned as he climbed out of his cart. "I know it's a warm spell, but it's still January, after all."

Sharon Winkle held up her gloved hands. "Head, hands and feet, Ned. As long as those are warm, we'll be fine."

"How are you Ned?" asked Dan. "You look a little stressed."

"Maybe a little," said Ned.

"The lapwing?"

"Among other crises, yeah."

"Well, you won't have trouble from us, on that account," said Dan. "If the lapwing is really back, great. If we see it, great. If not, we're always happy to visit the island, Ned, and to see you."

"I appreciate the support," said Ned, meaning it.

"You suffer from a lack of outlets, Ned," said Dan. "Whatever happened to that nice shellfish constable, the blonde one? Billie something, wasn't it? Do you see her anymore?"

"We run into each other," Ned answered truthfully, "from time to time."

"Ugh, Ned," said Sharon. "That whole running-into-each-other romance scenario is a complete dead end. You realize that, right?"

"I guess," said Ned.

"Modern love is difficult," said Dan. "To make it work you sometimes have to get creative. I think the four of us should get together and hang out some time, maybe go on a nature walk—"

"Nix," said Ned.

"Fine, Ned," said Sharon. "Keep your pants on, but you have to make some sort of a change. Toss out some of that old baggage. It's compressing your spine. I'm serious—I think you're actually getting shorter. Lighten the load and get on with things. At your age, Ned, everything else is just excuses. Be bold and decisive! You can do it!"

"Okay, Sharon. Thanks."

"She's a peach, is she not?" Dan asked, regarding his wife with loving eyes.

"She is," said Ned.

"Makes my blood boil, Ned. You get it?"

"I get it," said Ned. "So what do you say? Let's head to those water hazards over yonder. There might be something worth spotting."

"Super," said Sharon.

Dan forged ahead excitedly, moving toward a cluster of small ponds nearby, while Sharon hung back and strolled with Ned. At one point, Dan opted to take a short route toward the ponds—a deep sand trap on the near side of the fairway. He took three steps across the sand, reaching the center of the trap, and then dropped suddenly and completely out of sight. In mute shock, Ned and Sharon sprinted ahead toward the spot where Dan's wool hunting cap sat atop the patch of sand. There were Dan's footprints, leading up to the cap, but no other signs of his passing. Ned had to grab Sharon to keep her away from lunging at the treacherous spot.

"Oh my god!" Sharon cried.

"Quicksand?" said Ned, equally stunned.

"DAN!!!" Sharon wailed. "NO!!!"

Several bubbles popped to the surface of the sand, in the vicinity of the hunting cap, then stopped altogether.

18.

As she approached Speck's house, Veronica noticed a small group of three or four men and women, gathered across the street from Speck's gate. She recognized them as the process servers who had been dogging Speck for weeks, each trying to serve a court order that would initiate one of the dozens of law suits being brought against Speck's corporation and him personally. These process servers were behaving differently today, though; they gathered closely together in a defensive posture, speaking in whispers, eyes darting frantically between each other and the Speck house. Their body language was twitchy and tense, like a small herd of deer at a watering hole that had suddenly caught the scent of a predator but did not know which way to run. One of the men was bleeding from a minor neck wound. Another of the servers, a thin, mousy woman, dabbed sympathetically at her friend's wound with a handkerchief.

Suddenly, as Veronica neared Speck's front gate, the door of the house flew open and a boy charged out, carrying a rifle of some kind. Short and wiry, with a buzz-cut mat of bright red hair and hard, piercing grey eyes, the boy certainly had the gift of speed — he hit the front gate in a flash, kicking it open as he flew past a startled Veronica, ignoring her, and headed straight for the group of process servers across the street. The "herd" broke ranks and scattered in all directions, but the hunter knew his trade; the boy had already chosen his mark and it was the runt of the herd, a waddling, middle-aged man who breathed with a constant smoker's wheeze.

Cocking his rifle on the run, the boy aimed at the retreating target and squeezed off a shot. It was not an explosive crack, like that of a regular rifle, but the sharp popping sound of a pellet gun. The pellet struck the retreating man in the ear and he yelped, grabbing the side of his head in pain as he ran on, rounding the corner at Cottage Street and disappearing from view. The relentless boy immediately changed directions, nimble as a cheetah on the Veldt, never slowing as he veered down the street, charging toward a public beach path where the mousy woman had sought refuge. The boy hit the path entrance in a blinding rush, motoring down the walkway that led down to the shoreline. Veronica could hear the frantic wails of the woman, growing further away toward the water, as she sensed the hunter on her trail and labored to escape.

Veronica stepped through the now wide-open front gate of the Speck house and up to the front door. There on the threshold stood young Ripley Speck, a perplexed look on his face.

"Good morning, Ripley," said Veronica.

"Good morning, Miss Lodge," responded the boy, making an effort to put on his usual brightness but unable to hide his consternation.

"Ripley, who was that kid?"

"That was Patrick O'Herlihy," the boy replied. "Remember I told you that Poppa and I were going to visit the unfortunates at the Boy's Home?"

"I remember."

"Well, we did."

"I see."

"Poppa invited Patrick to come home with us. We're just his foster family, for now, but he's going to be my new brother."

"Wow. Huge development."

"Uh huh."

The two of them stood for a moment in silence, considering Ripley's new domestic situation.

"Did you ever have any brothers, Miss Lodge?"

"I had eight," answered Veronica.

"Eight?! Wow," said Ripley, impressed. "Did you like them?"

"Some yes and some no. There are a couple that I like a lot and a couple I can live without. Brothers should be judged on a case-by-case basis, I think. Does that help you at all?"

"I don't know," Ripley answered.

The popping sound of the pellet gun echoed up from the direction of the beach, followed immediately by a woman's faint scream. Veronica looked at the soft, oddly charming boy before her, comparing him to the image, in her mind, of the red haired hellion who had flashed by her on the street, cocking his long-barreled weapon on the fly. This was a fraternal pairing of dramatically stark contrast, figured Veronica, a nature vs. nurture case study drawn in broad strokes.

"Ripley, would you welcome some advice?"

"Yes, please."

"Watch your back."

Veronica left Ripley and headed toward the den, where Arnie Speck lay quietly in his recliner, soaking up the benevolent rays of twin UV sunlamps. His bathrobe was spread wide open, revealing his naked body from head to toe, interrupted only by the black bikini briefs he wore in anticipation of receiving company. Speck took a drag off his inhaler and held the breath in as long as possible, determined to let the calming mélange flow deeply into his system.

"What's all this, now?" asked Veronica as she entered the room, taking in Arnie's sunning rig.

"UV rays," said Arnie, feeling the rush of his pain medicine. "Just an hour a day, September through April. It'll change your life. I'm going to give you one today. Try it for a week and tell me if you're not a happier person."

"What do they do?"

"Everything. It's all about your circadian rhythms. If you can keep those in order, especially this time of year, then everything else follows—sleep, digestion, mood, alertness—every biological function, plus an overall sense of well-being. Anyone who stays here during the winter should have one. This would be a much happier island."

"Good pitch. You should be selling the things."

"I do. After my first week of using the lamps, I bought the company."

"Must be nice."

Veronica observed as Arnie took another deep hit off of his inhaler. She wondered how much of his "overall sense of well being" had to do with Arnie being heavily dosed, all day long.

"So, you tried to storm the castle," Arnie said finally. "With disappointing results."

"I took a shot, and it didn't work out. It happens."

"I've brought you a long way, Veronica, and paid you a great deal of money, in the hopes that you would get the job done right the first time. Your effort was sloppy and reckless."

"It's not sloppy, Arnie. It's messy."

"This is your defense?"

"I've got nothing to defend. I like a good mess. I like to make shit happen, then toss it against the fan for full splatter effect. By the time everyone has hosed themselves off, it's all over and I'm gone. Furthermore, that's why you brought me here for this job. A conventional approach was never going to get it done. It's gonna take a little chaos to bring this off, and as you well know, chaos is what I do."

True, Arnie thought to himself. The problem was, sitting back and waiting for Veronica's methods to work was very stressful.

"You're getting the appropriate help from that Donlin fellow?" he asked.

"Your threat worked, yes. Ned is going to help us a lot. He's very familiar with the island, and very well connected. You have new intelligence from the Center?"

"They've taken no new security measures," he replied. "Your abortive effort the other night made some impression, but they still have serious personnel problems. This bug they brought back — from Thailand or Burma or wherever the hell they were last — continues its rampage through the ranks of their Secret Service detail."

"Good," said Veronica. "And the Friendships?"

"Do you care?"

"No. Fortunately, they know nothing about the job, so they can't really hurt us. They could name me, but the brothers observe a sense of honor among thieves. I'm fairly sure they won't rat me out."

"Well, the Friendships are still in residence at the Tarpaulin Center — a holding cell on one of the sub levels, as far as we know. They haven't even been identified by the FBI computers yet, which seems odd."

"Not really," replied Veronica.

She and her crew had made a speculative purchase, a few years ago, that had paid great dividends. A computer geek in Boulder, Colorado had designed bar code patches which the crew had stitched on all their shirt collars, appearing to be designer logos. Months later, when scouting a job in South Lake Tahoe, the entire crew had been spotted and picked up by the local police. There were no charges brought, but new mug shot photos had been taken to update their criminal files. From that moment on, any time AFIS—the national fingerprint database—called up their files, the bar codes launched an insidious micro-virus that caused the entire computer network to crash. Sooner or later the FBI's own computer geeks would figure out the glitch, but it hadn't happened yet. Any attempt to identify her crew through fingerprints, in the meantime, was futile.

"So, you are confident the job is on track?" Arnie asked.

"I am."

"Very well," he said. "Continue the reports, twice daily. I'll feed you new intelligence as it comes in."

"Right," said Veronica, and she was gone.

Things were going well enough, Speck mused to himself once Veronica had left. She did bring chaos, but she almost always brought results, as well. The past couple of years had been a financially disastrous period for Speck, his corporate life a landscape of disgruntled investors and litigious former partners, but it would only take one good bit of news about the Noman's Dunes development to reverse everything. The stakes were high and the downside steep, but that was the game Arnie had always played and won.

On top of everything else, he had been to the Myles Standish Boys' Home, in nearby Carver, and brought back a rough diamond in the shape of young Patrick O'Herlihy. No one else wanted a kid with a record like Patrick's, so the adoption process would be smooth and quick, and then the boy's education in Speckhood would begin. Patrick had already passed a crucial test when, during their first meeting at the Boys' Home, Speck had directed Ripley to read aloud—for Patrick—his school paper on the legend of Devil's Bridge. When asked whether he would have voted for or against a bridge to Martha's Vineyard, Patrick could barely contain his enthusiasm.

"Bridge!" Patrick had said to Arnie. "*Obviously.*"

Arnie would have preferred, in fact, to have left Ripley behind at the Boy's Home, thereby completely clearing the decks for Patrick's ascension. As it turned out, the Boys' Home did not take trade-ins; Arnie had hinted about it to the Director, and had been rebuffed. Ultimately, it would make no difference. If Arnie read Patrick right—and of course he did—Patrick soon-to-be-Speck would not tolerate competition for first position in the Speck legacy. Where would that leave little Ripley? It would be fun to watch, figured Arnie, and decided to reward his optimism with another thirty minutes under the UV lamps. He took a hit off his inhaler, and settled back for a nice roast.

19.

By ten o'clock that night, The Cooler was full of Ned's closest associates, gathered there by appointment to hear Ned speak or explain or confess or do whatever it was he planned on doing. Neither Billie Jensen nor Veronica Lodge had been invited.

"Okay, we might as well get started," said Ned, and the assembly quieted. "There are some troublesome things that are happening with me which may eventually affect some of you. I've decided the best thing is to go for complete disclosure with you all and hope for the best. First though, and very sadly, most of you have probably already heard that one of Music Lagoon's best donors — by far our favorite, really — got sucked into a pit of quicksand out on Sweetwater this morning. His name was Dan Winkle, and I was a witness to the incident. Tommie, do we have an update on that situation?"

"Sure," said Tommie, looking downcast. "Obviously, Mr. Winkle is presumed dead, given the generally poor living conditions underground. We've been drilling and digging out there all day, hoping he might pop up so that there could at least be a proper burial service, but we've had no luck so far. Mrs. Winkle has handled it about as well as one could expect, and is not hot to place blame or anything like that, which she could easily do. It was my earth mover, after all, that opened up the spring head…"

"It was an accident," Ned stated unequivocally. "Sharon Winkle understands that. She's planning a low-key memorial service — out by the sand hazard in question, as a matter of fact — for the day after tomorrow."

"Keep your chin up, Tommie," said Doc.

Tommie nodded solemnly, thankful for the support.

"Okay. As for my mess…" Ned hemmed a little.

"You're among friends, Ned," said Angela.

"Impatient friends, though," said Nora.

"Okay," said Ned. "First, as you already know, we've had a mad rush of birders on the island, with much of the activity focused at Music Lagoon, the last known residence of the Caucasian Lapwing. This would not be a problem at all, except we have previously leased 'exclusive' birding rights to twelve different people — or couples — all of whom are now, unfortunately, present on the island."

"What was your original battle plan, Donlin?" asked General Hoak. "How did you figure the whole lapwing situation would play out, in the long term?"

"In truth," answered Ned, "it all began on an impulse, one we didn't think through very clearly, and continued only because of our financial desperation. The long term plan — such as it was — relied on one key factor, which was the continued total absence of the Caucasian Lapwing from the face of the earth. This seemed like a reasonable enough strategy since the damn thing is, after all, *extinct*. It just goes to show you. Anyway, the members of the Refreshment Committee are doing a great job handling the contributors, so far. With luck, their paths will not cross, and they will eventually give up their search for the lapwing, at least for the time being, and return to their lives on the mainland."

Ned's throat ran dry, and he paused for a deep gulp of beer before continuing.

"So… as for the other front of activity… some of you have noticed that my attention has been somewhat divided lately…"

"Yes we have," said Nora.

"So, the deal is this," continued Ned. "You all know Vice President Roger Paulson is on the island. He's one of your more avid birders, drawn here by the alleged lapwing sighting, like everyone else. Anyway, I'm being blackmailed into burglarizing the Tarpaulin Center, where the VP is staying, by Arnold Speck, island resident and unrepentant developer of pristine public lands. So that's that."

There was a long moment of silence as the group digested this last update.

"You're being blackmailed to rip off the Vice President of the United States?" Nora spat in disbelief. "What could Arnold Speck possibly have on you that's bad enough for you to try something that stupid?"

"Excellent question," said Doc. "The next order of business, Ned, is for you to spill your guts about this shady past of yours."

"That is definitely *not* on the agenda," said Ned.

"I'm with Doc," said Tommie, as the rest of the group murmured their agreement. "Just the idea that these strangers on the island know all this shit about you and we don't… it's not right."

"Here here," rallied Nora. "If we're going to help you break into the Tarp, then it's only fair…"

"No no no," Ned cut her off. "You all are NOT going to help me break into the Tarp. I made my own stinking bed and I will lie in it, but there's no sense in dragging you all down with me."

"If it affects Music Lagoon, it affects the Committee," Angela piped up. "Of course we're already involved."

A voice arose that had not been heard in at least three or four months, taking everyone somewhat by surprise. It was the taciturn owner and bartender of The Cooler, Gigi Malveaux.

"If you want to know about the Tarpaulin estate," suggested Gigi, "then the guy you want to talk to is Nelson Aurelio."

"Hmm," Tommie mused, "you might just have an idea, there, Gigi."

"Nelson Aurelio?" asked Doc. "The stone mason? I was sure he'd died a long time ago. How old is he now?"

"A hundred and four," said Tommie.

←   ↙   ←

Ned drove along Shallow Bottom Road, his headlights on high beam as he swerved all over the road, avoiding the deep pits that had formed during the autumn rains but had never been graded flat.

"That's it there," Tommie said, pointing to a two story post-and-beam house just off the road. One of the cars in the driveway was a red 1963 Ford pick-up, on blocks, looking like it had not moved in more than a decade. On the door of the truck was a hand painted sign: "Aurelio Stone Masons".

"Sorry to drop in on you so late," said Ned, but Karen Aurelio, great-granddaughter-in-law to Nelson Aurelio, dismissed his apology with a wave and invited the men in. Karen was in the middle of kitchen cleaning, which in this instance meant mopping up a mass of dinner scraps hurled under the kitchen table by her twin four year old boys, Troy and Aurelio the Fifth, thankfully asleep now on the living room sofa, a Disney movie playing mute on the TV screen before them.

"Opa never sleeps, anyway, and he likes company," Karen said.

Ned and Tommie passed through to the rear of the house and entered a cozy, wood-paneled den, where Nelson Aurelio sat dwarfed in a big reclining lounge chair, his slippered feet propped up by the fire of a cast iron wood stove. Ninety-plus years of hard work had taken their toll on the old man, who had shrunken to under five feet tall. His legs, once stout and muscular, were almost skeletal beneath the hand knit blanket thrown over them. Nelson had held on to a full head of thick, black hair which he wore slicked back over his head, but constant exposure to the island weather had wrinkled and darkened his skin to a leathery oxblood tone.

"Who's that?" asked Nelson as the two visitors moved into the room.

"It's Tommie Krupa, and my friend Ned Donlin. He's the Director out at Music Lagoon. How are you, Nelson?"

"I'm still here," said Nelson, motioning toward two chairs. Tommie and Ned pulled up the chairs, close by the stove so that the flame threw light on their faces.

"An honor to meet you, Sir," said Ned.

"What can I do for you boys?"

"For starters, old man, you could return my phone calls," said Tommie. "How many foundation jobs have I tried to bring you in on? At least ten."

"It's my pins…" Nelson looked down at his legs, little more than sticks under the blanket. "They give out under me. God damn it."

"I'll carry your ass piggy-back, that's what it takes," said Tommie.

"Maybe I just don't want to work again," said Nelson. He fixed a distant gaze on the stove fire at his feet. "Now what is it I can do for you boys, really?"

Tommie gave Ned a go-ahead nod.

"I'm very interested in the Tarpaulin estate, Mr. Aurelio," said Ned. "I was hoping you could tell me about it."

"Tarpaulin. That's a long time ago." Nelson squinted, remembering. "I did the original foundation work."

"Did you know Tarpaulin himself?"

"I did," said Nelson. "Not a bad man. A bootlegger—I guess everybody knows that. He was known back then as a violent man, a hothead, but I never saw it. He always treated me right."

"What was the original house like?" asked Tommie.

"It was first class, all the way. Mr. Tarpaulin insisted on good craftsmanship, regardless of cost. All the best stone, all the best everything—and I mean *everything*…"

A sneaky, mischievous smile appeared on Nelson's face.

"What are you grinnin' about, old man?" asked Tommie.

Nelson leaned closer to Tommie and Ned, speaking in a low, hushed tone.

"I remember girls," said Nelson with a gleam in his eye. "Dancing girls. And enough champagne to fill a water tower."

"What are you talkin' about, Nelson?" said Tommie with a laugh.

"I'm not lying. The beachfront of the Tarpaulin land, it's on Talbott's Cove. You boys ever heard of Bubbly Bay?"

"No, I haven't," said Ned.

"I think I have, actually," said Tommie, remembering. "I heard some of the Menemsha lobstermen talking—I can't remember when—and they were going on about where to set traps in Bubbly Bay. I didn't know what they were talking about."

"Yeah, well, that's an old timers' nickname for Talbott's... *Bubbly Bay*," said Nelson, becoming more animated as he spilled the story. "See, in Tarpaulin's rum runnin' days, he brought most of his booze down from Canada, or had the rough stuff cooked in mash plants in upstate New York. But his favorite trade—the side he took pride in—was the champagne. His champagne customers were upper crust, you see? He really liked rubbing elbows with fancy folks, wanted really bad to become one of 'em. Which one day he did, I guess. Anyway, Tarpaulin brought ships over from France with the good stuff, and unloaded them right here on the island."

"No shit," said Tommie, surprised.

"You need to understand," Nelson explained, "back then, the Vineyard got no attention whatsoever from the revenuers. Tarpaulin moored his boats there in the bay, and his crews lugged the stuff right up to his house. See, there's where the dancing girls came in."

"The dancing girls again?" said Tommie. "I don't get it."

"Like I said," continued Nelson, "Tarpaulin wasn't real worried about the authorities. It was his neighbors. The old Christian missionaries were gone, by then, but there was still that missionary way of thinking, in some folks' heads. It was a real pain in the ass, especially during prohibition. So, you asked if Tarpaulin could haul that booze right up to his house. The answer is 'no'. His snooping neighbors would go crazy. So once construction on the main house was done, Tarpaulin calls in me and Mauricio Battaglia—you remember him, Tommie?"

"I've heard the name."

"Oh, my. I suppose… Mauricio's been dead since before you were born. He was my partner—an artist with stone. Those friggin' Italians know their rock."

Karen entered the room, delivering bottles of cold beer to Nelson and his appreciative guests.

"You happy to have visitors, Grandpa?" asked Karen.

"You're talkin' to me like a little kid again," Nelson said grouchily.

"Sorry, Opa," said Karen, giving Tommie and Ned a grateful smile on her way out of the room.

"So Tarpaulin calls us in," Nelson continued, "and tells us he's got an extra job for us on the q.t., and it'll be hard work because it can only be the two of us working, no one else, 'cause he only trusts me and Mauricio. Tarpaulin wants us to put in a tunnel, under the ground, with stone walls, that goes from the bluff at Talbott's Cove to his house, where we had built deep storage space in his basement. That's almost two hundred yards from the bluff to the house. And we do the work. It takes us two months, the whole time Tarpaulin telling his nosey neighbors that he's fixing drainage on his property, or some shit like that. When the tunnel is done, it's real good, and Tarpaulin was happy. He used that to load the champagne up to his house, in secret."

"Ahem," Tommie cleared his throat loudly.

"What?" said Nelson.

"*Dancing girls?*" Tommie said impatiently.

"Oh, yeah," said Nelson, the mischievous smile reappearing on his face. With a peek out to the kitchen to make sure Karen was not listening, he continued his story. "About three weeks after the work was done, me and

Mauricio get a message from Tarpaulin to come over that night, and don't come right from work — you know, clean up first. We get there in our church suits and ties, and a party is going on. Not a high society thing, you see, but more of a rum runner affair. I guess Tarpaulin's first boat came in from France, 'cause there was champagne everywhere, and lots of music..."

"*And...*" Tommie insisted...

"And yeah, Krupa, there were dancing girls," Nelson's eyes widened with pure, childlike wonder, "A lot of 'em! And they really could dance, you know? They weren't just for shakin', they moved with beauty. I guess Tarpaulin must have had a word with them, because the girls were nice to us — *real nice.* They had soft skin, and soft round bodies..."

Nelson stared straight into the fire at his feet, his mouth hanging open just slightly, his breathing deep.

"Oh, God," Nelson said in a quiet voice, his words a reminder to himself. "Life is good."

Ned had one more question, but he hated to break Nelson's private train of thought.

"Nelson?" Ned spoke softly. "Is the tunnel still there?"

Nelson broke out of his reverie and gave Ned an insulted look.

"Are the pyramids still in Egypt?" he asked Ned. "Is the Great Wall still in China?"

"Right," said Ned. "Stupid question."

"The bluff is probably eroded away, by now," said Nelson, "and maybe the Bubbly Bay opening has caved in. But somewhere in the clay of that bluff, my tunnel is still there."

20.

Special Agent Daniel Webster Trang turned his back to the ocean, closed his eyes, and directed his face toward the eastern horizon, where the first rays of the morning sun were just now creeping up over the tree line. The warm rays touched Trang's numbed cheeks and the benefits were immediate. The agent grunted his approval and rotated to the left just an inch or two, making sure that as much of his body as possible was facing the light directly. As the sun inched higher into the morning sky, Trang could feel the glow spreading down along his chest and legs and finally arriving at his toes, the spot where relief was needed most.

"That's better," Trang said to himself, stomping his feet to stimulate an equitable distribution of the warmth.

As one of only seven agents healthy enough to stand outdoor posts, Trang had drawn the short straw for the late night shift on the bluff overlooking Talbott's Cove. The stark, windblown cliff area had seemed very harsh at first, a little too gulag for Trang's personal taste, but in truth the watch had not been all that rough. The ocean breeze, though insistent, was many degrees warmer than he expected, and the natural beauty of the sheltered cove, bathed for half the night in the delicate blue glow of a three-quarter moon, had proved a relaxing tonic.

"Hey," said a voice, and Trang opened his eyes to find Special Agent Susan Chersky emerging from the trees, a brown paper bag in one hand and a tall thermos in the other. "How's life in exile?"

"Quiet on the Western front," replied Trang. "Whatcha got there?"

"A breakfast burrito sort of thing," she said, reaching into the bag and handing her colleague the warm, tin foil covered breakfast hybrid.

"Perfect timing," said Trang as he unwrapped the foil and bit into the tortilla, his teeth sinking into the hot, mixed filling of scrambled eggs, salsa, chopped bacon and gooey, melted Muenster cheese.

"Oh yeah," he moaned with a mouth full of burrito, "oh yeah."

"It's kinda pretty here," said Chersky, looking out onto the morning calm of Talbott's Cove.

"Yep. How's things at the compound?"

"Status quo," she replied. "The bug lingers, but seems to be weakening."

Mention of the diabolical Laotian flu bug, while he was eating, suddenly alarmed Trang. He stopped chewing and regarded the burrito with suspicion.

"Who made this?" he asked.

"The Tarpaulin cook," Chersky answered with a little laugh, "it's okay."

Special Agent Trang gratefully resumed eating, relieved that the tasty breakfast treat was probably not a serious health risk, beyond the hardening of the arteries he would suffer if he ate three or four thousand of them. Trang was so far the only agent — except for the superhuman Rhonda Hipps, of course — who had not suffered any effects at all from the Laotian rainforest virus that had decimated the ranks of Vice President Paulson's Secret Service detail. Trang suspected that his Asian blood might have afforded him some special resistance, but he hadn't suggested the possibility to the other agents for fear that he might appear to be gloating.

"There's a boat out there," observed Chersky, pointing toward the water from her position on the edge of the high bluff. Trang stepped up next to Chersky and looked down onto the cove, where a medium-sized work boat was puttering along the rocky shoal about thirty yards offshore. The boat, manned by three crewmen, eased up to one of the many buoys that dotted the surface of the water, whereupon a crew member reached out with a long hook, snagged the buoy line, and proceeded to haul a large, rectangular lobster trap out of the ocean and onto the boat's work deck.

"Lobstermen," said Trang, munching down the last of his burrito and licking a messy smear of salsa from his trigger finger. "When's the last time you had lobster, Special Agent Chersky?"

"Just a few months ago," she answered, "at that fund raising dinner in the Hamptons."

"Oh, yeah," said Trang, remembering. "That didn't suck."

"I'm gonna have some coffee," Chersky said, unscrewing the cap on the thermos. "Can I interest you?"

"Twist my arm," said Trang.

↞   ↞   ↞

Tommie could see that Veronica Lodge was going to puke again. The wave action in the cove was really not so bad, he figured, but there was no mistaking the signs: her skin was an ashen green, and her eyes were rolling back in their sockets until there was only a ghoulish slit of white showing. Veronica was about to lean her head over the transom when Tommie intervened.

"It's bad if they see that, Veronica," said Tommie from his seat at the helm. "Puking from seasick is not a problem with real lobstermen."

"Got to maintain the cover," Ned chimed cheerfully from the work deck. He pulled a glob of putrescent fish guts out of the bait barrel, fastened it inside a wire lobster trap, and tossed the contraption back in the water. "It never occurred to me before, Ron, but a life in the arid west has left you woefully under-experienced in ocean travel."

"I hope you die, Ned," slurred Veronica, fighting back her disgorge.

"My observation was of a purely professional nature," said Ned, brightly. "It's important, for the sake of the job, that we all understand our limitations. While you may be highly qualified for, say, a suburban home invasion in Tucson, you aren't going to be that much help to us on Bubbly Bay."

"*Bubbly Bay* can kiss my ass," she rasped in a mocking tone. "Get me the hell offa this stinking scow."

Tommie left the helm for just a moment and ushered Veronica to the windward gunwale, where her heaving would not be visible to the two Secret Service agents up on the bluff. Hanging her head over the side, Veronica spewed what little remained of the pastry she had eaten for breakfast, followed by two waves of dry heaves before she was done.

"That's a waste of a damn good croissant," said Ned, observing Veronica's discharge as it bobbed up and down in the waves. But suddenly a school of tiny bait fish rushed up from the depths and, within seconds, consumed everything Veronica had just evacuated.

"You spoke too soon, Ned," observed Tommie. "Look at the little fellas chowing down."

"Yeah, look at that," said Ned in a chipper tone. "You know, Tommie, nothing ever really goes to waste in nature. It's the circle of life."

"I can see that."

"Screw you both," said Veronica as she dragged herself up onto the work deck and collapsed in a shallow puddle of chum juice. Ned and Tommie shared a smile.

After their late night visit with Nelson Aurelio, Ned and Tommie had agreed that a reconnaissance mission to Talbott's Cove was called for, and soon. They picked up Veronica well before dawn, with Ned taking special pleasure in disturbing her sleep a good seven hours before her preferred wake-up time at the crack of eleven. From the Makoniky Inn, the three had driven in total darkness to Espresso Love, for the obligatory coffee and croissants, and from there to Menemsha, the old fishing port in Chilmark where Jack Lebeouf moored his lobster boat.

Menemsha had been a thriving fishing village just a few decades earlier, but all the northeaster fisheries had been substantially depleted over the past several decades. These days, Menemsha brought in most of its money by encouraging a heavy traffic of summer tourists. The visitors lumbered into town in enormous, smelly diesel tour buses and wandered through the remnants of the authentically quaint old port town, buying t-shirts and crab cakes and ice cream cones, and holding their noses at the wicked stench emanating from the barrels of rancid bait that still lined the wharf's main dock.

The tourists were nowhere to be seen on the cold, dark January morning, but the slim and wiry Jack Lebeouf, at thirty two years of age one of the younger lobstermen still in business, was already up and at work, getting his boat ready for a tour up the island's northwest shore to check his string of lobster traps. On the strength of Jack's friendship with Tommie Krupa, the three had reached an amicable agreement with the lobsterman: in exchange for the temporary use of his boat, they advanced Jack enough money for a lavish breakfast at the local eatery of his choice, and agreed to check and re-bait every trap he had in the water between Menemsha and Tashmoo Pond. Jack had supplied Ned, Tommie and Veronica with three sets of unbelievably foul-smelling work clothes, waterproofed and insulated yellow coveralls that had not been rinsed of blood or rotted fish entrails in more than a year. It was hard to say whether the fish-stink or the rolling ocean swells were more noxious to Veronica, but the combination punch was more than she could stand, and she was terribly ill from the first moment the boat motored out of Menemsha harbor. Ned was enjoying every minute of her discomfort and shame.

"Could we just do this?" Veronica moaned from her prostrate pose on the work deck.

Out of the corner of his eye, Ned snuck a peek at the Secret Service agents up on the bluff. They were chatting away amiably, only occasionally turning their heads to check on the position of the lobster boat now floating just outside their security perimeter.

"We're not a threat, it looks like," said Ned.

"Apparently right," Tommie agreed. "If we move just down the cove, I think those rocks will give the boat enough cover that we can climb ashore for a few minutes."

Which is what they did, anchoring the vessel behind two large, jutting rocks, just barely out of easy spotting range, and wading hip-deep through painfully cold ocean water to the beach. By keeping their path tight against the bottom of the bluff, they could remain out of the agents' line of vision. If the agents leaned over the edge of the bluff at any point, however, the three interlopers would be spotted for sure, and that would be a problem. Ned, Tommie and Veronica reached the sand and proceeded single file against the foot of the bluff, speaking only in whispers. The rush of the ocean breeze helping to insulate any sounds they might inadvertently make along the way.

"I think we'll be okay along here," said Tommie in a hushed tone.

"Yeah," answered Ned, "Unless they smell Veronica."

Having her feet planted on *terra firma* had, apparently, put a little fight back into Veronica; she gave Ned a swift, painful kick to his left hamstring, a target choice that suggested worse possibilities, should his taunting continue.

"Ow," said Ned, clenching his teeth to suppress a louder exclamation of pain.

As the three explorers reached a point just underneath the Secret Service watch post, Tommie patted Ned on the shoulder and pointed to a spot above them, about halfway up the cliff.

"See that line of stones? Right up there in the clay?" Tommie whispered. "That could be the opening."

Ned nodded, and he and Tommie began to take their first, tentative steps up the unstable face of loose earth. Veronica, still not one hundred percent, plunked herself down on a rock at the bottom of the cliff and gave no indication that she intended to join the climb. Ned tossed a pebble of clay at her shoulder to get her attention and encourage her on, but Veronica responded with the universal one-fingered gesture of contempt and defiance. With a shrug, Ned gave up on her and continued his ascent.

The loose stonework Tommie had spotted was about thirty feet up the slope, and it was slippery going. The terrain was very similar to the famous clay cliffs of Gay Head, just a few miles west. Those cliffs had been named hundreds of years ago, by passing mariners, for the formations of brightly colored clay that were so easily distinguishable from far out at sea. Just a little rain or dewy condensation turned the clay slick as oil, and it had been just two days since that last big downpour. Tommie and Ned dug in with the tips of their fingers and the toes of their gum boots, taking care not to start any kind of earth slides which might catch the attention of the agents just above them. When they finally reached the stones, they were no more than twenty feet below Special Agents Trang and Chersky.

"See, look at these," Tommie whispered low, pointing to a series of cut stones that were stuck near each other in the clay. They had once been part of some kind of structure, obviously, but that had been a long time ago. Decades of exposure to the natural elements and broken down whatever organized form they had once held.

"You're sure this is it?" asked Ned.

"This is just where Nelson said it would be. You look at the shape of these stones; they've been worked hard, to narrow tolerance. That's Nelson. And you can still sort of see the pattern, right? There's a pattern to the mess. These stones were once the tunnel walls, and that rotted wood up there? That's what's left of the roof."

They were surrounded by all these markers, which meant that Ned and Tommie were now perched on the very earth that had filled in the opening of the tunnel.

"How much of this dirt you suppose there is?" asked Ned.

"I'd bet about eight or ten feet. The added problem is, this stuff is at least half clay, heavy and packed tight. Shovels won't help us much."

And whatever method they chose to get through this earth, it would make noise. If the Secret Service maintained the same location for their watch post, which they probably would, the agents on watch would be within spitting distance of any excavation attempt.

"Shit," Ned whispered.

"Steamed or broiled?" asked Trang.

"Steamed of course," answered Chersky.

"Served shelled or whole?"

Chersky thought about this for a moment, taking a sip of the good dark coffee she had brought in the thermos.

"My heart says shelled, but my head says whole," she said.

"I know what you mean. That whole cracking and picking thing can be a mess, but it's like paying your dues. You really gotta earn that meat."

"Plus, if I don't have to go through all that cracking," added Chersky, "I can put down a whole lobster in like two minutes."

"Not very cost effective."

"No."

"What I've always wanted to do is a real clam bake, you know? Like the local Indians did it. You dig a pit, you build a big fire with these big smooth beach stones thrown in, and that burns down to hot embers that cook the rocks up really hot. Then you lay down layers of the shellfish and veggies all mixed it with seaweed, 'cause that holds the seawater that steams up and cooks the food. On top of everything are big canvas tarps, holding in the steam. And then you just wait."

"I think Elvis did it in a movie."

"I think Elvis paid someone to do it. But you know what? While we're here, we should give it a try. A genuine clam bake on the beach. I mean, here we are at ground zero for the whole clam bake tradition, right? We should take advantage. We travel all over the damn world and we never get a chance to really experience the places we visit."

"It's too cold…"

"C'mon, Chersky, get behind this. It'll be fun."

"Where's that boat?" Special Agent Chersky asked as she scanned the water of the cove, suddenly aware that she hadn't seen the lobster boat in a several minutes.

"It's right over…" Trang searched with his eyes but couldn't see anything. "Hey — where the hell IS that boat?

"We can see the whole bay from here. No way they went that far already, even at full throttle. The last I noticed they were checking the traps over by —"

At that very moment, as the agents' focus was on the large rocks on the northeast side of the cove, the lobster boat's engine rumbled loudly, spewing a small cloud of black diesel smoke into the air above the rocks, and within seconds the boat motored out into view again, all three crew members on board. Trang and Chersky could see one of the lobstermen tossing a trap into the water with a splash.

"We should have got their business cards or whatever," said Trang. "We're gonna need some of their lobsters."

"Keep dreaming. Your clam bake is not going to happen."

"We'll see, Chersky," said Trang, his eyes following the slow progress of the lobster boat on its way out of the cove. "You know, you hear about how hard lobstermen work and all, but one of them is taking nap on the front deck. That's the life."

As soon as the boat got moving again, the rolling swells resumed their effect on Veronica. She lay down near the prow of the boat, keeping her head near the edge in case she needed to purge again. Each new motion of the craft brought a low, agonized moan from her direction.

"How am I gonna do this, Tommie?" asked Ned. "How am I going to get through all that clay?"

"You need a digger—not a big digger, but a digger. And a way to get it onto the cove. And you need to somehow get those spotters away from the bluff, or they'll nab you for sure. It's gonna be a beach assault."

"A beach assault," Ned sighed. "Sure. No problem."

"Actually, Ned, we know someone who can do one of those."

21.

Very early that morning, Dr. Orson Titus had put on his heavy flannel robe and his shin-high Ugg boots, slipping out of the bedroom quietly so as not to wake his wife. Bad enough that his old demons had stirred Doc himself, at this early hour; Colette was sleeping the deep, sound sleep of the innocent, and Doc was determined to let her enjoy it.

Doc could see his breath fog in front of him as he made his way downstairs toward the cellar, where the big wood furnace waited for him to stoke it back to life. Doc and Colette had done a lot to improve its energy efficiency in the old house, adding better insulation, double-paned windows and foam stripping to the doorjambs, but still the old wooden structure breathed quite a lot, losing its heat over the course of a few hours if the furnace was allowed to cool.

The Tituses liked it this way. Many of the newer houses on the island were cloistered so tightly in air-tight house wrap and synthetic siding that they felt like tombs. The breezy old Titus home, however, hungrily respirated the fresh sea air that blew in off Nantucket Sound, drawing it in as if the structure's very existence depended upon it. Doc and Colette had also kept the original wood burning furnace as their primary heat source. It took some work to keep going — a lamentable chore in the frigid, early morning hours of winter — but the gritty old iron behemoth was the soul of the house, warm and comforting and traditional but also loud, cantankerous and sometimes even smelly — not entirely unlike the Tituses themselves.

Doc reached the cellar and maneuvered around a massive pile of freshly split wood — the "lust logs" that Ned Donlin had unilaterally chosen to purchase, split and deposit onto the Tituses' cellar floor. As Doc tossed the split wood into the open maw of the furnace, glowing embers remaining from last night's burn spread their heat to the new fuel and the old beast slowly stoked back to life. The iron groaned as it expanded with the heat.

Doc climbed the stairs, back up to the kitchen, and was making fresh coffee when the phone rang.

"Hey Doc," said Ned, on the other end of the line.

"How was your foray?" Doc asked. He himself had begged out of the early morning maritime adventure.

"No disasters to report," said Ned. "I was actually hoping you could help us out with something…"

"Could be."

"I called General Hoak at home, but he didn't pick up. I'm not sure if he's avoiding calls or if he's out already, but maybe you could track him down?"

"Hmm. Sounds important," said Doc.

Ned explained the situation.

ᚠ   ᚠ   ᚠ

Doc Titus crossed the border between Chilmark and Gay Head, with less than a mile's drive remaining to Nashaquitsa Bridge. He kept his old Jeep Cherokee at the speed limit, rolling over the stretch of hilly, curving road he knew well; several horses in Doc's care were kept on this land during the summer months, when the grass was thick and green and the riding trails were inviting. This time of year, the area was beautiful but stark and cold and, Doc thought, very lonely. Most of the houses were empty and dark, their windows boarded against the inevitable winter storms that would make first landfall here.

General Hoak sat alone on the guard rail at Nashaquitsa Bridge, warm in his big hooded down parka with fur fringe, pen and clipboard in hand, staring out onto Squibnocket Pond.

"Hello, Doctor," said the General when Doc strolled onto the bridge.

"Howdy, General," said the doctor. "Anything interesting out there?"

"The usual, mostly," answered Hoak. "I'm just trying to stay sharp—I haven't been out looking since the annual bird count last month."

"Ned says you're his best spotter," said Doc, and it was true. At the annual bird count, most of the assigned plots on the Vineyard required a whole group of birders to complete an accurate survey; General Hoak, however, was famous for handling an entire assignment himself, bringing in a comprehensive and detailed list that rivaled the thoroughness of ten competent birders. Doc noticed that even at that moment, as the two men sat together on the bridge, Hoak continued making his list of water fowl in the pond before him, some of the birds floating on the water hundreds of yards away. Hoak was somehow achieving this feat without the benefit of binoculars.

"You're an interesting person, General," observed Doc.

"Red Throated Loon, four count," said Sergeant Bischette, "two male, two female."

"Mallard, count eleven… no, twelve," contributed Lieutenant Harmon, "four male, eight female."

Hoak made the appropriate entry onto his list. His eight soldiers were posted at various spots along the bridge railing, the crosshairs of their powerful rifle scopes trained upon the avian population of Squibnocket Pond.

"Did you come here looking for me, Doctor?"

"I did, General. It's about the Tarpaulin Center—"

"And Donlin's heist?"

"Yes."

Doc explained the tactical situation, as Ned had related it to him early that morning. General Hoak listened, attentively, but never stopped making entries to his bird count.

"King Rail, count two," announced Corporal Stanford from the other side of the bridge, "one male, one female."

"You're not on marsh birds, idiot—I am," growled Corporal Guevara. "You're on ducks. Count Pintails, pinhead."

"Kiss my ass, Guevara," shouted Stanford. "If the official count went by what you spot, half the birds on the seaboard would be declared extinct."

"Screw you, Stanford—"

"Let it go," ordered Lt. Harmon. "Stanford, help me with the ducks. We'll give you the wading birds when we get to the next pond. Your favorite, right?"

"Yes, Sir," sulked Stanford.

"So Donlin's best ingress is at the beachhead?" Hoak said to Doc. "That's a challenge."

"Yes, Ned sounded challenged when we spoke this morning."

"It's a tactical disadvantage, from the start," Hoak explained. "The troops are highly exposed on that sort of terrain."

"See, all of these things are so clear to you, General. Obviously. As you know, Ned was reluctant to involve any of us in his problems, but since you are so uniquely qualified—"

"What sort of resistance can we count on?" asked Hoak, brushing aside Doc's concern.

"They saw two Secret Service agents posted on the bluff."

"We should be able to deal with them..." said Hoak, the wheels of his profoundly strategic mind already turning.

"The major issue, it seems, is the need for some sort of earth moving vehicle. Tommie can get one, but there's the issue of how to deliver it to the beach."

"Well, Doctor," said Hoak, "it's been done before."

"Yes it has," said Doc. "Too bad we don't have one of those Army landing craft things, like for D-Day..."

"You mean a 'Duck'... like a DUKW amphibian," said Hoak.

"Yes, exactly — a 'Duck'. Too bad we don't have one of those."

"Actually, Doctor," said Hoak, "we do."

General Hoak was just about to explain when Corporal Max, a fresh-faced young soldier from Texas, jumped onto the road on the opposite side of the bridge.

"Sergeant Bischette!" Max called out with breathless enthusiasm, "That pair of shorebirds the General spotted last winter? The turnstones? They're back! They're picking at feed in the slough between Nashaquitsa and Menemsha."

"The Ruddy Turnstones?" Bischette asked as General Hoak listened. "Are they still ruddy?"

"The colors are faded some, Sergeant," answered Corporal Max, "but still detectable. Hell, yeah!"

"That's a good sighting, Corporal," said Bischette. "Go on back there and hold the mark for the General."

"Yes Sir," answered Max. The Corporal charged across the bridge and down onto the shore of Nashaquitsa Pond, sprinting all the way.

"I have to run now, Doctor," said Hoak suddenly, looking excited.

"Uh... okay," said Doc, confused about the General's sudden excitement, "but General, you mentioned an amphibious —"

"I'll take care of it, Doctor. Have a nice day."

With that, Hoak sprung up from his spot and jogged pertly toward Nashaquitsa, leaving Doc behind and bewildered. The comings and goings of General Robert C. Hoak, Doc knew, were an unending source of mystery. Doc shrugged and climbed back into his Cherokee, negotiated a three-point turn on the narrow roadway, and headed back toward town, using his cell phone to call Ned, on the way...

"Ned? I think you're good to go."

22.

By two o'clock that afternoon, the Sweetwater parking lot was nearly full, and a hundred mourners had made their way over to the infamous sand trap/quicksand pit on the sixteenth hole. Veronica Lodge, Tommie Krupa and Ned Donlin were there, lingering a few feet back from the main crowd, with Ned doing his best to avoid eye contact with any of his contributors, all of whom were in attendance. In fact, most of those present were from the bird watching community at large; a hundred or more pairs of binoculars hung from the necks of the mourners, lenses uncapped and ready for use should any interesting avifauna stumble unwittingly upon the ritual gathering.

Seeing his contributors all here, standing shoulder to shoulder, sent chills of foreboding through Ned. Nora and the Committee had successfully — so far — kept a safe distance between the contributors as they visited Music Lagoon, preventing them from discovering that they had all been similarly duped by Ned. Their proximity to each other, at this moment, amounted to a powder keg of destructive potential.

"Ugh," Ned muttered to himself, his mind churning with dread.

Sharon Winkle stood before the mourners, beside the Reverend Cecil Rice of the East Chop Unified Baptist Church. Sharon was smiling warmly as the group of mourners drew together; she was obviously bearing up pretty well, her spirits undoubtedly girded by her unwavering belief in the afterlife, reincarnation, angels, benevolent poltergeists and psychic communication with the spirit world. She was wearing a long overcoat in dark olive, buttoned snugly at the neck and draping all the way down to her ankles. This complete coverage caused a great deal of speculation about what Sharon was wearing underneath the coat—if anything. Imaginations were stoked by the memorable experiences that many of those present had had in the field, stumbling upon Dan and Sharon in the midst of their bird watching antics *al fresco*.

"That would be Billie," Veronica whispered to Ned.

"Huh?" said Ned. He scanned the crowd and did discover Billie Jensen at the opposite side of the circle, just now arriving without escort in her full Warden uniform, freshly laundered and pressed. Her eyes had immediately fixed on Ned, first, then on Veronica, then on Ned *and* Veronica. None of the looks were friendly.

"How did you know it was her?" asked Ned, mystified. "You spoke with her on the phone for maybe two seconds."

"Her aura of anger and bitterness is familiar," Veronica replied.

"You didn't need to come here today," Ned said with a tone of resentment. "Every time you pop up on this island, you disrupt my life."

"I did need to come, Ned, because this is where *you* are. I bring tidings from Arnie Speck."

"What sort of tidings?"

"Not tidings of joy. He's pretty pissed that the job hasn't come off yet. He wants us to get to work and he wants to hear that there's a plan. He figures by Sunday it'll probably be too late."

There was no response from Ned. He understood perfectly what had Speck concerned — it had now been four full days since the alleged lapwing sighting and posting on the Rare Bird Alert site and, other than Howard's accidental fly-over of downtown Edgartown, there had been no further encouragement for the lapwing seekers. Ned could sense a hint of disappointment among the birders. Within a few days, they would begin to abandon the island for more promising hunting grounds. That would be great for Ned and the sanctuary but bad for Speck, who had gone to a great deal of trouble to bring his mark to the island.

"Look..." Ned said to Veronica, "the beachhead plan has taken shape, and we're ready to go. We just need... *something*."

"What sort of something?" she asked impatiently.

"It's all about timing, Ronnie," said Ned. "You know that."

"You need an opportunity, right Ned?" asked Tommie.

"Yeah, Tommie," said Ned. "That's right. We need the right opportunity."

Reverend Rice appeared beside them.

"Hello, Doctor Titus, Tommie..."

"Good afternoon, Reverend," said Doc.

"And Mr. Donlin," said the Reverend. "Good to see you, Ned."

"Thanks for doing this, Reverend," said Ned.

"My pleasure," said the Reverend Rice, and then directed a somewhat lascivious look toward Veronica. "I don't believe we've met...?"

"Veronica Lodge, Reverend," she replied, gently taking the Reverend's hand in her own. "Nice to meet you."

Ned was annoyed to see the good Reverend so easily and so obviously falling victim to Veronica's thrall, as had Tommie and Doc and countless rubes before them.

Including Ned.

"Veronica's just a visitor," said Ned, grouchily. "Short term. She'll be gone any day now, Reverend."

"Alas," Reverend Rice sighed, and turned his attention to Tommie Krupa. "Tommie, not to dwell on the unpleasant, but... our group is safe here today, are they not? It would be comforting to know that the unfortunate, incidental portal to the Abyss has been sealed."

"Oh... uh, yeah, Reverend, it's okay. No more quicksand here—it's all dried up. Either the underground stream has been diverted, or the opening has been stopped up by—" Tommie silenced himself, deciding it would be inappropriate to mention that Dan Winkle himself, the subject of the day's ceremony, was most likely the object plugging up the spring head at that moment. "Anyway," Tommie continued shyly, "the danger is over. Play through, Reverend."

"Thank you, Tommie," Reverend Rice said, then turned his attention to the group of mourners, stepping up to the edge of the sand trap and clearing his throat.

"Good afternoon to all of you," he spoke loudly to the group in the rich baritone that drew a full house every Sunday to hear his fervent, sweaty sermons. "I myself knew Dan Winkle only casually, but I can say with certainty that he would be proud to see the fine and loyal group of friends that have gathered here today, at the very site of his premature demise, to honor his memory and support Sharon in her time of need. Sharon has asked to start us off today with a few words. Dear?"

Sharon took a step forward, the tips of her winter boots stopping at the cusp of the sand hazard. "Thank you all so much for coming, and thank you, Reverend

Rice, for presiding this afternoon. I want to let you all know, first off, that I've been in constant contact with Dan, psychically, and he says 'Hi'."

A few "*Hi Dans*" trickled out of the assembly and Sharon acknowledged them with a nod.

"It's so fitting," Sharon continued, "that many of you attending today are members of the birding fraternity. Bird watching is Dan's second favorite thing in the world — next to me, of course — and so to pass to the next dimension while he and I were birding together would certainly be, in Dan's eyes, a blessing. Also, Dan hated golf, so in a way it's an appropriate irony that a golf course was the instrument of his evolution to a higher plane."

Sharon then encouraged the guests to offer their own memories of Dan and, after some shyness, they did. Most were stories about encountering the Winkles in the field, naked, and going through the traditional six stages of N.E.T. (Nudist Encounter Trauma): shock, blushing, stammering, wandering eyes, resignation and, eventually, acceptance. As the offerings continued, Ned snuck a glance at Billie, on the other side of the circle, to see if her anger was still in full bloom. It was — her look had never left Ned at all, except for the occasional quick, angry glance at Veronica. When Ned's eyes met Billie's she silently mouthed the now familiar phrase, '*You are such an asshole.*' Ned understood, and certainly could not offer a convincing argument to the contrary.

As the mourners' remembrances of Dan finally trickled to a halt, Sharon stood before the group again, aglow with the warmth of everyone's esteem for her husband.

"Thank you, everyone, so so much," she said. "I know that Dan is with us today, and that he feels blessed to be remembered so fondly by all of you. I sense so strongly, as many of you probably do as well, that he is right now feeling fulfilled by the sense that he led a good, complete life on this earth."

The mourners nodded and mumbled their agreement, encouraging Sharon in her comforting thoughts.

"In fact," she continued, "I'm quite sure that Dan's only regret—and no doubt you can all appreciate this—is that he never had a chance to see the Caucasian Lapwing, again…"

"Oh no…" groaned Ned, quietly and pitifully, a silent shank of pure panic slicing through his gut.

The mourners were dead silent for a long moment, until someone repeated the word that had so completely caught everyone's attention.

"Again?"

"Oh…" Sharon covered her mouth with her hand as she suddenly realized her indiscretion. She glanced apologetically in Ned's direction. "Oh my… I'm sorry, Ned. I guess I let the cat out. But it is true, I'm proud to say… we haven't got a photo or officially confirmed our sighting, yet, but last year, at Music Lagoon, Dan and I caught a fleeting glimpse of the Caucasian…"

"Like hell!" shouted Dr. Devin Hedge. "I saw—"

"WE!" corrected Mrs. Hedge. "*We* saw! Don't you dare try to muscle me out, Devin!"

"Of course not, Dear." Dr. Hedge said as if mortified by the suggestion. "*We* saw the lapwing TWO years ago!"

"That's bullshit, Hedge…" shouted Leonard Smallwood.

"Oh no," Ned said to himself, again. Nora and Doc and Tommie and the others watched him now, sharing his horror as the contributors all turned on each other, shouting accusations and epithets and repeating at higher and higher volumes that they had seen the lapwing first.

"WE saw the lapwing!"

"Liar! Bastard! I saw it!"

"Ladies and Gentlemen, please calm yourselves…" Reverend Rice pleaded, to no avail.

"But WE saw it first!"

"Screw you!"

"No, screw me," Ned groaned to himself and anyone else within close earshot.

The dispute among the birders continued, threatening to escalate to violence—Dr. Hedge and several other contributors had begun a shoving match— when all of a sudden the proceedings were silenced by a stentorian roar…

"CHILDREN OF GOD!"

The birders turned to face the good Reverend Rice, his eyes now afire with indignation.

"Is this how you honor the memory of a fallen comrade?" boomed the Reverend.

The chastised birders remained silent, out of actual shame or the vague sense that they *should* feel ashamed…

"I know not what your grievances are," continued Rice, "but this is neither the time nor place to be distracted by such worldly issues. We are here today for Dan Winkle…"

"Amen!" shouted Sharon Winkle, her own visage flushed with rare distemper as she stared down the alleged mourners. "We are here today for Dan."

If any of the birders had a response to this chastening, it was destined not to be heard; at just that moment, everyone's attention was captured by an unexpected sight: a convoy of white-gloved, motorcycle-mounted police appeared on the service road, headed straight toward the memorial service, preceding a lordly procession of six huge, dark Chevy Suburbans with blacked out windows. The impressive fleet motored right up to within fifty feet of the memorial service, stopped, and immediately disgorged the Vice President of the United States, Roger Paulson, surrounded by a modest entourage of Secret Service agents. Paulson — dressed *a la mode* in a nylon field parka, duck pants, hiking boots and with a pair of binoculars hanging from his neck — motioned for his security detail to remain with the motorcade; he approached the memorial service with just a single Secret Service agent at his flank, the fearsome Rhonda Hipps.

The once-quibbling mourners remained mute, humbled into silence by the unexpected presence of the world's most powerful, famous and prolific bird watcher. Paulson noticed their reaction and was clearly embarrassed by it.

"Oh, no," Paulson spoke gently to the mourners, "No no, this always happens. Don't let me interrupt the sanctity of these services, please. I'm just a birder, really, like all of you, here to pay respects to a valued member of our special community. Please continue."

"You're very welcome here, Mr. Vice President," said Sharon, stepping up to Paulson and giving him a hug. For a moment it looked as though Rhonda Hipps might wrap Sharon in a choke hold and throw her to the turf, but the agent managed to keep her protective instincts in check.

"Thank you," said Paulson, returning Sharon's hug. "Thank you very much, Ms. Winkle. I'm so glad I could be here for you today."

"Excuse me, Mr. Paulson," said Sharon, "but... how did you know who I was? We've never met..."

Paulson blushed slightly and let his gaze fall to the ground, toeing the dirt nervously with his hiking boots.

"Well," he said, "we didn't meet, exactly. I went with a group of friends, just a year or two ago, down to the Everglades to find some nesting Wood Storks. We, well… we saw something through our binoculars, but it was not storks. It was you and Mr. Winkle, enjoying nature to the fullest."

"Oh, that was a great trip," said Sharon wistfully, with the first real hint of sadness in her voice. "Except for the leeches."

"I apologize in retrospect, Sharon, for our unintended voyeurism," said the Vice President sincerely, "but let me say and you and Mr. Winkle added some much needed spice to the sometimes overly staid world of birding."

"That's very nice of you, Mr. Vice President…"

"*Roger*. Please."

"Okay, then… *Roger*. It's a classy move for you to come out here and honor Dan's memory like this. It means a lot."

Paulson was genuinely moved. It was hard, these days, to find places where he felt comfortable, and people to be comfortable with. Neither could be found in D.C., that was for sure. Not in the White House, definitely. He looked around at the impressive group of mourners, at the hundred pair of binoculars and hundred pair of field boots, and he knew with certainty that he was among his own kind. This, he realized, was just what he needed.

"You know," said Paulson, "this is a fine memorial, a really first class gathering, but if I may say so, I think we can do even more."

"How do you mean, Roger?" asked Sharon.

"Well, I'm staying alone in this big old place, maybe you've heard of it—the Tarpaulin Center? It's a big fancy compound with just about every luxury and convenience a person could ask for. A really capital location for a party."

Special Agent Rhonda Hipps, and the other agents in her detail, shot each other looks of dread. The last thing they needed now was a new security headache.

"A party?" squealed Sharon. "That sounds great!"

"Tomorrow night, then? Saturday night? Probably most of us will be leaving the island after the weekend, so it will make a great celebration in Mr. Winkle's memory. And we all deserve a bonus in honor of our cold weather birding efforts, whether we end up spotting the coveted Caucasian Lapwing or not."

"Fantastic!" said Sharon. "And everyone's invited?"

"Everyone!" Paulson shouted to all the birders, carried away with his own enthusiasm. "Flash your field guides at the door and you're in!"

Veronica shared a look with Ned.

"Did you hear that sound?" she asked.

"I did," said Ned.

"What sound was that?" asked Doc.

"That was opportunity," said Veronica. "Knocking."

←   ←   ←

Dominating Arnie Speck's hobby room was a large table supporting an enormous, highly detailed topographical model. The model included the entire "Cape and Islands" landscape in full relief, including Martha's Vineyard, Nantucket, the Elizabeth Islands, the shoreline of Cape Cod and, notably, Noman's Island, the former target for Navy bombing practice, poking out of the ocean just Southwest of Gay Head. Perched on a high work stool, Arnie hovered over the scale model of Noman's, where he was meticulously constructing a model of some sort of development project, using a large magnifying glass to properly place one of the thirty or so buildings included in the plan.

"A resort?" asked Veronica, examining Speck's model. "A colonial Club Med?"

"Mind your own business," said Arnie, never taking his eyes off his work. "Tell me you have good news."

"We go tomorrow night," she said.

"Excellent. That's all I needed to hear." He looked up from his work and gave Veronica a smile. "See how happy you've made me?"

"I see," said Veronica. She turned her attention to the opposite side of the model, where yet more construction was taking place. Ripley Speck sat motionless in a folding chair, looking on dejectedly as Patrick O'Herlihy, his scrappy, red haired nemesis, toiled away on the area of the model that depicted the Vineyard Sound, the stretch of water between the island and the mainland. The former 'unfortunate' had at his disposal several dozen boxes of toothpicks and a tall plastic bottle of Elmer's glue. Leaning against the model table, within easy reach, was his pellet gun.

Veronica stepped over to the boys.

"Hi, Ripley," she said.

"Hello, Miss Lodge," he replied glumly. "How are you today?"

"Great, thanks. And you?"

"Fine," answered Ripley, but share a secret look of misery and consternation.

"I'm Veronica," she said as she turned her attention to Patrick. "I don't think we've met."

"I'm busy," answered Patrick with an insolent expression.

Veronica felt the sudden urge to throttle the little urchin, but Arnie intervened before her impulse took hold.

"Patrick!" said Arnie, getting the boy's attention. "Be courteous with people."

"Why?" Patrick asked, genuinely annoyed and put-out.

"At first, anyway," said Speck." You never know — she might have something you want."

The boy seemed to understand that much.

"I'm Patrick," the boy said to Veronica, then cast a sideways glance toward Ripley as he added, "Patrick Speck."

Veronica and Ripley shared a sympathetic look.

"Right," said Veronica to Patrick, "you're the new family member. What's that you're building?"

"It's my new project," said the boy, returning to his task. "A bridge from Martha's Vineyard to the mainland. So everyone can come here whenever they want. As many people as we want."

The boy looked across the island to Arnie, his new patron, who gave him an approving nod.

"That's quite an undertaking," said Veronica. "Do you think it's really possible?"

"Oh yeah," the kid answered with a forceful determination. "You'll see. Everyone will see."

"And the little houses on either end, what are those?"

"Those are the toll booths."

"Toll booths on both ends?"

"Toll booths on both ends, you bet," Patrick answered smartly. "Coming and going, going and coming."

Veronica glanced again toward Ripley, and he returned her gaze with a look of profound despair.

23.

At one o'clock on Saturday afternoon, Ned went to his storage shed and pulled out the chaise lounge that he had stashed away back in October, sure that he would have no further use for it until the following spring. The mid-Winter warm spell had held strong over the past week — the island was now a clear blue and windless sixty four degrees — but the weather services predicted a dramatic turnaround within the next few days, with a cold front moving in by Monday afternoon to mark the true and final onset of a long winter. Ned was determined to take advantage of these last few hours of warmth and, very possibly, his last few hours as lord and master of Music Lagoon.

Ned carried the chaise to the lawn outside his cottage and settled into lounge mode, a bottle of beer in one hand and a black Russian cigarette in the other, his body basking in the solar rays. Relaxation came with surprising ease. Ned did not even raise his head when Veronica's rental car pulled into the sanctuary lot.

"Hi Nedly," whispered Veronica when she reached his spot on the lawn.

"There's another chair in the shed," he said without opening his eyes. "I can get it if you like."

"No, the grass is fine," she answered, sitting down beside his lounge chair and appraising him. "You look reasonably calm, all things considered."

"It's a beautiful day."

"Yes, it is. And a good opportunity to rest up for tonight. We're set to go at sundown."

"Right," said Ned. "A raid on the Tarpaulin. Just what the doctor ordered after yesterday's debacle at the golf course."

"Yeah, I half expected to find you fighting off a lynch mob."

"Soon, but not quite yet," answered Ned. "The indignation of Reverend Rice and the unexpected hospitality of the Vice President have shamed the contributors into silence, for the moment. They're so excited about the party tonight at the Tarpaulin..."

"That gives you some time to maneuver, I guess."

"Yes, though it would help if I actually HAD a maneuver in my pocket, which at the moment I don't. From what Nora and the others have been able to gather, the contributors haven't yet figured out the part about me leasing them all the very same exclusive parcel of land. Plus, they're all still certain that their lapwing sightings were the real deal. They haven't figured out yet that the damn bird doesn't exist, period."

"Yikes. Mass delusion?"

"Or wishful thinking. Same difference. They're all absolutely certain the bird is out there, somewhere, and they're still in the running to bag the sighting. Once they finally work out that there never was a lapwing, at all, and that they've been fleeced by me, well... then I expect you will see your lynching, and right quick."

"But then... where are they now?" Veronica wondered, taking in the empty sanctuary grounds around her, her car and Ned's truck the only ones in the lot, the Visitor's Center closed and dark.

"There was a rumor that the lapwing's song had been heard down around Tiah's Cove, on Great Pond. All the birders went there."

"You started the rumor?"

"Yes."

They sat for a long moment in silence, soaking in the perfection of the day.

"By the way, Ned, there are a bunch of birds sitting on you. Perched, I guess you'd say. In case you hadn't noticed."

"Yeah."

"Pets?"

"Not exactly. People find birds around the island, adult birds that have been hurt or chicks that have fallen out of nests, that kind of thing. They take them to Doc to get patched up, or they raise them up themselves."

"That's nice."

"They're not supposed to do it," said Ned. "All the naturalists and so forth, they say to leave them where they lay and let nature take its course. But people do what people do. When the birds are grown or mended, folks bring them here for release, but by then they're stuck on human contact. They hang here, close to the buildings, eating from the feeders. Mostly, though, they're just waiting for me to come outside. It seems like they can't really relax unless they're perched on a person."

"The red one, I know, is a Cardinal, right? Like the baseball team?"

"Uh huh."

"The red is so bright. What about the little one curled up inside your collar? With a peak on its head."

"Tufted Titmouse. Angela raised that one, and she was very doting, I guess. Very affectionate bird."

"And the big grey guy?"

"That's Harry — a Great Blue Heron."

"Quite a collection. It's a menagerie."

"Yep."

"So, Ned, are you gonna give me a tour, or what?"

Ned considered it — a tour of Music Lagoon.

Maybe his last, ever. He nodded 'yes' and rose to his feet, gently shaking off his menagerie.

They started along the main trail, a one mile loop which took them along a ridge on the Northeastern border of the sanctuary. The path cut through a wood of oak and beech and maple as it steered the walkers in the direction of the beach. Though the grounds were vacant of human visitors, the temperate weather had stirred activity among the sanctuary's bird population; they hopped and flitted all over the grounds and trees, foraging for insects that had been lured into emergence by the unseasonable warmth.

"It's really stark with all the leaves gone," Veronica observed. "Everything is so gray."

"It's my favorite time of the year, and not just because the summer people are gone."

"The crowds are a nightmare?"

"Death by minivan," Ned confirmed. "The population jumps to over a hundred thousand. I wouldn't begrudge them their time on the island, really. Everyone should have a chance to enjoy the place. But by the time Labor Day rolls around, it's enough already."

"I can imagine."

"What I like is all the leaves gone," said Ned. "In the spring and summer, when the trees are all full, it's like a wall of green, right in your face all the time. It can get kind of claustrophobic. This time of year you can see for a long ways. I like that."

The path dropped them down along the ridge, switching back and forth along the steepest slope as it made its way down toward the beach. Ned and Veronica reached a bench that was positioned with a high view over the lagoon, a popular vista for birders who were out to spot marsh birds.

"That's Music Lagoon, down there, and Glover's Beach just beyond that. All this used to be my grandparents' land—their farm house stood up in the clearing where my cabin is now. Once they passed, their will created a trust, establishing the Music Lagoon Sanctuary on their property."

"Why *Music* Lagoon?"

Ned nodded toward a point of land that jutted out at the southern end of the beach, with a perfect view back across the beach and lagoon.

"On that point, there used to be a great old house, with a great view over the Sound and Cape. It was built more than a hundred years ago, by a whaling captain who moved here when he retired. His wife was a piano teacher. She used to give lessons up in the parlor, which was facing this way. Often times, when people would be walking along the beach, or when fishermen sailed their boats along this beach, they would hear the sound of her piano drifting toward them, over the lagoon."

"So, Music Lagoon. Nice. What happened to the house?"

"It stood until forty-some years ago, when a big Nor'easter finally took it down, so I never got to see it. My grandfolks' old house was up where my cabin is now, and I'd stay with them for a couple of months each summer. My parents were out here for a few of those weeks, usually, but the rest of the time it was just me and the grandparents. I spent most of my time just wandering the property—the woods and the beach and the lagoon. It went that way until the summer when I was twelve. After that summer, I didn't want to come back, and by then my parents were in the middle of a divorce, so no one pressed the issue."

"So your last time here was... what? Around twenty years ago?"

"Just over," replied Ned, with a certain undercurrent of tension in his voice.

"Then that extinct bird must have still been here. It was last seen on this land, right?"

"Uh huh. Two of them. A mated pair."

"And you saw them?"

"Yes," said Ned, quietly, after a pause.

"Wow. Cool. It's so sad, really, that they're gone. When you think about it, the idea of 'extinct' is pretty heavy. Just gone, you know? Forever. Hopeless. Never coming back—"

"Enough already," said Ned, crossly. "I think we both understand the concept."

"But, I mean, you seem so sure that they're really gone for good? How can you know?"

"I have a pretty good idea."

"How?"

"Well…without a pair of them—a male and a female—the species is done for. And I know for sure that the male is dead."

"How do you know that?"

"Because I killed him," said Ned.

←   ←   ←

Veronica and Ned continued along the path, following it parallel to the shore of Music Lagoon then circling around until they were headed east, back up toward the sanctuary entrance. The path took them up a gentle slope, tracing along the lip of the ravine where, less than a week earlier, Ned and the Refreshment Committee had performed the lapwing scenario for the benefit of Leonard Smallwood.

"So how did it happen?" asked Veronica. They had walked in silence until then, Veronica taking that time to digest the full impact of Ned's confession.

Ned sighed deeply. He had confused himself, a few minutes earlier, by suddenly blurting out his confession — to Veronica Lodge, of all people — but after taking the time to collect his thoughts, he realized how intense his need had been, over these past years, to unburden himself by telling someone — *anyone* — about the events of that awful day.

"I found a slingshot," Ned began. "At Pilot Pond. A powerful slingshot...with the wrist support?"

"I know the kind you're talking about," she said. "A weapon can be an intoxicating thing, especially one's *first* weapon."

"It was. My first. And intoxicating."

"So... you started plinking up a storm."

"I did. I plinked my ass off that afternoon, for a couple of hours straight, shooting rocks at everything I could find. There are limited thrills, though, in shooting at inanimate objects. Sooner or later, when a live target presents itself, a boy might be tempted to take a shot."

"Uh huh. Some girls might be tempted, too."

"I thought you might be able to relate. So I'm walking through the woods — these very woods — and I hear a strange, screeching bird call. I look up into the trees, and I see these two odd looking, whitish birds with long spindly legs and long beaks, sitting there on a branch. I put a rock in my slingshot, pull back, and let the rock fly. I mean... I didn't even think, I swear. I just did it. It never crossed by mind, even for a second, that I might actually hit one of the birds, or what the fallout of that would be."

Ned paused for a moment to catch his breath, adrenaline involuntarily rushing through his system now as he relived his nightmare.

"Wow, Ned," said Veronica, watching him. "You're really worked up over this. Try not to sweat it. You were a dumb kid, like all kids are. It's water under the bridge."

"Doesn't feel like it. Feels like a whirlpool." But Ned managed to settle himself a little, and continue. "So, the rock cut through the air with theretofore unrealized speed and accuracy, and struck one of the birds square on the head. I mean, *square* on the head. The hit made a clear, popping sound, like two pieces of wood knocking against each other. Pop!"

"Jeez."

"Yeah. The bird just drops right to the ground, and the other one flies off, to destinations unknown. I run over to the tree. The bird is lying there on its back, wings still tight into its body, and it's still alive. At least for a second. It looks up at me, and its beak moves up and down, almost like it's trying to talk, and then nothing. It's dead, stone cold dead."

"That sounds truly awful," Veronica said, sincerely.

"Without question, the worst moment of my life," Ned lamented, shaking his head. "Then and still now, the absolute worst moment of my pathetic life. I was sick, completely sick to my stomach. I sat down and cried like a baby."

"Oh, god. And it was this lapwing bird?"

"I didn't know it then. That night I looked through my grandmother's bird books, and found it. *Vanellus Caucasus*, the Caucasian Lapwing. I had killed the male, that much I could tell from the pictures. '*Extremely Endangered*', it said next to the name. I had sometimes heard people talking about this bird, because it was famous on the island, but I never knew what it looked like. Grandma looks over my shoulder and sees what I'm looking at, in the guide. 'Did you see it?' she asks, and I say 'no', and she just shakes her head. 'So sad, Neddie, there were so many and now they're nearly gone,' she says. 'This land right here, our land, was their original home.' And I'm thinking, 'Oh, shit. Oh, crap.'"

"Wow, Ned."

"These days everyone knows that those were the last two Caucasian Lapwings, anywhere in the world, but back then people figured there were others, somewhere. There was talk about a colony of them in the South, near the Grand Banks, or on a peninsula up in New Brunswick. But apparently not. The moment that female flew away from me was the last sighting of a Caucasian Lapwing, anywhere. Ever. Twenty-some years and not one goddam bird."

"The female never returned?"

"Nope."

They stopped on the trail, and Ned pointed to a spot just up a small hillock, around twenty yards away.

"They were sitting right up near there," he said. "In that very tree."

"Wow. That's quite a yarn, Nedly."

He shrugged. They remained silent for a moment, as Veronica meshed all this information with what she knew already about Ned and about Martha's Vineyard.

"And now, all these years later, here you are."

"Yeah. Strange, huh?"

"Not really," she said. "You couldn't help yourself,"

"I think you're right," Ned said, excited by Veronica's perception. "I couldn't stop myself from coming back here. Why do you think that is?"

"It's the number one taboo, but we all break the rule, sooner or later."

"What rule?"

"The scene of the crime, Ned. You returned to the scene of the crime."

Together, they returned to another scene. Back at Ned's cottage, with little more than an hour of sunlight remaining, Ned and Veronica lay down on his double bed, ostensibly to grab a cat nap that would reenergize them for the night of work ahead. Instead, they hungrily stripped each other down and... had sex? Made love? Ned only knew that it was different than any sex they had shared before. More intense, somehow, which—considering their shared history of passionate, physical, outlaw sex—was saying something.

"Wow," Veronica finally said, after they had lain in silence for a good fifteen minutes after the encounter. "What was that?"

"I don't know," said Ned.

But Ned did know, actually, and so did Veronica. She peered out the window of Ned's cabin—the sky was nearly dark.

"Sun' down," she said. "We're on the clock, Nedly."

"Okay," said Ned. "Let's go."

24.

Vice President Roger Paulson gazed dreamily out the window of his second floor office, lulled into reverie by the beautiful row of trees — now adorned with strings of Christmas tree lights — that lined the entrance road of the Tarpaulin Center. Upon learning that Paulson had invited guests for the evening, the Tarpaulin staff had immediately leapt into action, expertly handling all the details for the celebration, including food, drink, music, and decoration of the Center and its grounds.

The small pine trees along the entranceway had been adorned with tasteful strings of the simple white lights, weaving a lovely half mile course from the front gate to the door of the main building, where the gala event was to take place. The effect of the lights, combined with the bath of delicate blue moon glow, gave the Tarpaulin grounds an eerie beauty that had distracted the Vice President from his work.

The sound of a throat-clearing "ahem" gently ushered Paulson out of his musing. He turned to find Major Foxbrite standing in the office doorway, with the "football" — actually a wide, square black sort of attaché case with a handle — manacled securely to his wrist, as always.

"Good evening, Major," said the Vice President, "Aren't the grounds lovely?"

"They are, Sir," agreed Foxbrite and adding, strictly to himself, if *you are limp-wristed, spotted owl-hugging civilian liberal drone.*

"I hope I can convince you to join in the festivities tonight, Major."

"You cannot, Sir."

"No. Of course."

"Sir, the guests should be arriving any minute. We should establish an operating procedure, *vis a vis* the location of the football in relation to yourself. In the unlikely event of crisis."

"I want the guests to have free access to the entire Center," said Paulson. "It's no fun sharing this place with others if they're to be herded like cattle. The Center has too much to offer for us to keep it to ourselves, in my humble opinion."

"But free access, Sir?" gritted Foxbrite, trying hard not to betray his impatience and contempt.

"All right, Major, all right. This room will be our..." he searched his memory for the correct term.

"Operational command center," offered Foxbrite.

"What you said," agreed Paulson. "This room will be yours alone. Should the world be in need of nuclear annihilation, at any point during the party, I'll know exactly where to find you."

"That's all I ask, Sir," replied Foxbrite. "As for your personal papers, Mr. Vice President, I'd like to secure those, as well."

Paulson regarded the documents that he had spread out on the desk, still unread. It really was shameful, he thought to himself, how unproductive he had been during his four days on the island. Most of the work on his plate was unimportant, but the environmental impact report on disposition of public lands on Cape Cod was critical. The hearings would start Monday, in Washington, and Paulson would be required to cast his deciding vote by Wednesday at the latest. First thing tomorrow morning, the Vice President promised himself.

"Fine," agreed Paulson. "Secure these things in whatever way to see fit, Major."

"What about the Codex, Sir?"

Paulson considered Volume VI of his sketch books, the largest and most significant tome in the series. He really should bring it downstairs to the party—after all, his guests tonight were just the sort who could actually appreciate his work—but he was tired of being the center of attention all the time, and the presence of his famous sketches would only focus the spotlight on him further. No, tonight he was determined to be just another one of The People.

"Secure the Codex as well, Major. Highest priority security whatchamacallit. Thank you."

"Consider it done, Mr. Vice President."

Something in the window caught Paulson's attention, and he looked out the picture window to see a series of car headlights, winding slowly up the driveway toward the main building.

"Our first guests!" he exclaimed. "Hooray!"

Special Agent Rhonda Hipps made her way down the steps, ready to finish the last item on her pre-party check list. She was mostly satisfied, considering the circumstances, with the security situation on the grounds. All eighteen agents were now ambulatory, more or less recovered from the Laotian bug. Once dressed and polished, all were ready to stand post and present at least the appearance of normal security.

Hipps had initially been angry with the Vice President for his hasty party idea, and had bluntly told him so, but his boyish enthusiasm for the event was reason enough to forgive him. Part of Hipps job was to recognize Paulson's particular needs and find a way to accommodate them without compromising his safety. The party idea had made him happy, the kind of anxiety-relieving happiness which would in turn would make him a better Vice President. That simple equation was all the reassurance Hipps needed. Plus, Roger Paulson was, when he got excited, kind of cute.

Hipps reached the lower level and swung open the third door on the left, immediately discovering that the cement walls of the cell had been splattered all over with hurled food; it was a Jackson Pollock-esque, multi-colored work of angry impressionism.

"Good God," she said, "what have you two been doing in here? This looks like a monkey cage at the zoo."

"Hey!" yelled Bobby Friendship, "let us go! Please oh please let us go!"

"What is all this mess?" asked Hipps. "Eggplant Parmesan? That's the chef's specialty. What were you thinking?"

"That stuff was gawdawful," said Ricky, "that's what we were thinking. There's no meat in that shit! We asked for salami sandwiches and chips — what could be easier? — but you hadda bring us this. We're goin' on a hunger strike."

"We are?" asked brother Bobby. "I don't know, Rick..."

Hipps pulled off their hoods, and they recoiled from the bright light.

"Ow," said Ricky.

"I'm going to have buckets and brushes brought in here, and you two are going to scrub these walls until they are pristine white."

235

"Geneva convention! Geneva convention!" yelled Bobby.

"What about it?" asked Hipps.

"I learned all about it from Hogan's Heroes. Don't you ever watch classic TV?"

"Shut up," said Hipps.

"And what's with the shitty music, anyway?" asked Bobby Friendship.

"You can hear it?" asked Hipps, surprised. After all, the prisoners were two levels underground, on the opposite side of the building from the ballroom.

"It's comin' in through the vents," said Ricky, "and it stinks as bad as the food."

"We're having a little party upstairs," said Hipps. "Good food, open bar, a little waltzing music. You boys are missing out."

"Not if they're eatin' this shit, we ain't."

"So," said Hipps, "I received an interesting message from the FBI. Their computers have been crashed for three days, and they traced the problem to the attempt to trace your fingerprints. You care to shed any light on that?"

There was no response from the Friendships.

"Fine," said Hipps, "be that way. You should know, however, that you will not be leaving my custody until this is all straightened out. There's plenty of room in the cargo hold of the jet, though it can get mighty cold in there and sometimes the hatches fly open, strictly by accident, at high altitudes."

Still no response.

"Have it your way," said Hipps. She put their hoods back on and moved for the door. "Your cleaning utensils will arrive soon."

"Hey lady," Bobby spoke up, and Hipps turned back.

"Yes?"

"What's today?"

Hipps considered the question for a moment, and decided there was no harm in an answer.

"Saturday."

"So tomorrow is gonna be Sunday."

"I'll double check our itinerary, but I think that's the plan."

"Could you get me the New York Times crossword? It's the biggest of the week. Have a heart."

"We'll see how clean you get those walls," she said, and with a slam of the door Hipps was gone, her steps retreating down the hallway outside their door.

"Hey, Rick?"

"Yeah, Bob."

"I can't take it anymore, Rick. Should we do it?"

"Do what?"

"I'm getting awful hungry and tired of sittin' on this floor, and who knows how bad tomorrow is gonna be. Should we give up Veronica?"

Ricky thought for a moment.

"We'd wanna make sure it would stick. If we ratted her out, and Ronnie got clear anyway…"

Just the thought of vengeance, visited upon the brothers *a la* Veronica Lodge, sent a shiver through the brothers.

"Besides," added Ricky, "we don't know anything, and whatever the job is, it ain't been done yet."

"How do we know that?"

"We know 'cause this badass Fed lady hasn't asked us any specific questions yet. Get it? Veronica only does big jobs, right? And this is a little island, right? So once the job has been done, this Fed lady'll know about it and she'll have some real specific questions for us and ideas she wants to talk about. That's when she'll need the Friendship brothers. That's when we can get a deal."

Bobby was silenced, yet again, in reverent awe of his older brother's intellect.

"You're my brother," said Bobby tearfully from behind his black hood. He reached out for his brother, but his arms stopped short with a clanging sound, wrists still firmly manacled to the bolt on the floor.

"Okay, Bobby," his brother said in a soothing voice, "okay."

←   ←   ←

"Dukes County Sheriff's Department, Deputy Keene speaking. How can I help you?"

"Lem? It's Willard? Down the Harbor Master's?" Willard Lawler, the Oak Bluffs Deputy Harbor Master, always spoke in questions.

"Evening, Willard," said Lem. "What can I do for you?"

"Isn't the deputy gig a bitch? Hard at work on Saturday night?"

"My cross to bear, Willard."

"You know the Master's office? The temporary one?"

"Yeah, what about it?"

"Can you believe it? That someone would move it? What would anyone need a dredge for on a Saturday night?"

Lemuel Keene sighed. It would take a very long time, working in question-only format, to get the information he needed from Willard. Besides, Keene could use an excuse – *any excuse* – to get out from behind the phones. With the Sheriff in Boca Raton for the next two weeks, Lem could get away with it.

"Stay there," said Lem, "and I'll be right down."

Lem forwarded all calls to the State Police switchboard and headed for his cruiser. He hadn't expected much action this evening, though it was Saturday night. There was usually a late autumn, early winter activity lull on the island, maybe the quietest time of the year, crime-wise. The tourists were long gone, and most of the local trouble makers had not yet plunged into their winter season underemployed alcoholic funk. It took Lem only about ten minutes for his drive from Edgartown to Oak Bluffs. He parked outside Mocha Mott's, on Main Street, and picked up a cup of fresh coffee there before walking down to the harbor, where he met Willard, standing alone at dockside.

Construction was in progress on a new Harbor Master's office, so a temporary office had been set up in a small trailer, which was placed on an old dredge platform tied up at the docks. The platform was actually a retired U. S. Navy LCM 6, a fifty foot beach landing craft that had been purchased by the town at a military surplus auction, and it had capably performed a myriad of water-based duties over the last twenty years.

But now it was gone. Lem and Willard stood on the dock examining the crime scene, which amounted to an empty space beside the dock, where the retired marine landing craft had been moored for the past few months. The temporary Harbor Master's office — the trailer — had been removed from the missing craft and placed up on the dock, apparently undamaged. Lem and Willard tried to put together a timeline for the theft.

"I took a dinner break at around… six thirty?" said Willard apologetically. "Up at Linda Jean's? I was only gone for maybe… what? Forty five minutes? And I have to come back to this? You think the Harbor Master's gonna have my ass?"

Examining the displaced trailer, Lem could see that it easily weighed a ton, and it was on skids instead of wheels. It must have made quite a racket, Lem figured, being hauled off the landing craft. All the cables for power and phone had been disconnected carefully and without damage. There was no evidence to indicate where the landing craft had gone. It was a functional boat, Lem knew, so in theory it could have been sailed out of the harbor and taken in any direction, at a top speed of around ten knots. According to the time line he and Willard were working on, whoever had stolen it had a few hours head start.

"Willard, you said you ate dinner at Linda Jean's..."

"Don't you love their crab and corn cakes? Aren't they the best?"

"And is that your routine, Willard? You usually eat there?"

"I usually just have a sandwich right here at the office, right?" asked Willard. "But who knew I would win a free dinner at Linda Jean's?"

"A free dinner?"

"Did you even know they were having a raffle? You'd think I would remember buying a ticket, wouldn't you? What are the odds that they just call me up and invite me for free chow?"

"Hmm," answered Lem. For no particular reason, at least no reason he could logically explain, the Deputy had a sudden desire to know the whereabouts of Ned Donlin. He stepped to a pay phone on the dock, dropped in a quarter and dialed a number.

"Yeah?" came a voice on the other end of the line, some low-volume swing music playing in the background. The phone at The Cooler was usually answered with just this sort of terseness, and always by

240

whichever random customer happened to be closest to the offending ring. Gigi Malveaux never spoke on the telephone, ever.

"Who's this," asked Lem.

"Billie Jensen. Who's this?"

"It's Lem Keene, Billie. How are ya?"

"Fine, Lem. You comin' over?"

"Can't tonight. Is Ned there with you?"

"Ned and I aren't seeing each other anymore, Lem," Billie replied angrily, "and I can come here whenever and with whomever I want—"

"Take it easy, okay? I'm looking for him, that's all."

"Well, he hasn't been here. Or maybe he was and I just didn't notice."

Right, thought Lem.

"Tommie? Doc? Nora?" he asked.

"Nope, nope, nope," confirmed Billie. "Probably all getting ready for the VP's party. I'll be heading over there soon enough myself..."

"*Who's* party?"

"Roger Paulson. A little fling for the birding community, honoring the guy who sunk into the temporary quicksand at the golf course."

"Right—the temporary quicksand. And this party's being held at the Tarp?"

"Yep."

"Thanks, Billie," he said, and hung up the phone.

Lem checked his watch, which read nine thirty. Nine thirty Saturday night, and a beach landing craft had suddenly and mysteriously gone missing from Oak Bluffs Harbor. The usual suspects in any such strange and inexplicable case—Ned Donlin and company—were allegedly engaged in legitimate, above-board pursuits, rubbing elbows with the Vice President of the United

States, no less, under the close scrutiny of the U. S. Secret Service. This knowledge did not make Lem feel any better. Deputy Keene had a gut feeling that his investigation of the missing landing craft would go nowhere until he ascertained, formally, the current location and activity of Ned, *et al.*

"Do you think I'll get fired, Lem?" bemoaned Willard, on the verge of tears as he stared out at the empty berth.

"Don't worry," said Lem. "I'll be sure the Harbor Master knows it wasn't your fault. Us deputies gotta stick together."

"Ain't it the truth?" asked Willard, but Lem was already in his cruiser and gone.

25.

When the landing craft struck the submerged rock, everyone pitched forward onto the cold, wet deck.

"Sorry about that," said General Hoak, "didn't see that one until it was too late."

Ned Donlin, Veronica Lodge and Tommie Krupa pulled themselves back onto their feet, holding tight to the side rails and nursing their bruised knees and elbows.

"Excuse me for asking, General," said Tommie, "but are you sure you're up to this? I'm pretty good at the helm, so if at any time —"

"Stow it, Krupa," ordered the General. "It's just like riding a bike. I got us this far, didn't I?"

And indeed he had; Hoak had captained the ungainly craft to a successful semi-circumnavigation of the island, motoring the crew all the way from the Oak Bluffs harbor to a point just West of Talbott's Cove. Most impressive about this achievement, perhaps, was that by his own admission, Hoak had not even been a passenger on such a boat since the Korean War, some forty years plus gone by. Of course, the real test of the General's skills still lay ahead. It was one thing to navigate relatively open water, and quite another to manage a full beach assault. The margin for error would decrease significantly with the next phase of the operation.

The sea was relatively calm, thankfully, with only medium sized swells to rock and roll the boat, and visibility under the three-quarter moon was excellent. Too excellent, as far as Ned was concerned; the lumbering craft would be clearly visible from several points along the North coast of the island, especially with the moon reflecting so brightly off the water. For this reason, they had decided to hug the coastline as closely as possible, hoping to find some cover among the rocks and points along the way. The strategy had worked, so far, except for the occasional bump against a submerged rock; a small price to pay.

"How are you holding up?" Ned asked Veronica.

"So far so good," she answered, and popped yet another Dramamine.

Ned shuffled along the side rail and out to the bow, where he stepped up to get the best possible view of the bluffs to the East. He could not see the Secret Service post, but knew that it was still there and manned by at least one agent. Ned was hoping the guy was a smoker, so that his position might be given away by the careless lighting of a match, but that didn't seem to be the case. There was no sign of any light at all, up there on the bluff; the agent was a boy scout, complying with the Secret Service's strict no-smoking-on-duty policy. The first light Ned would see on the bluff — if everything went according to plan — would be the beam of a small flashlight, blinking three times, then pausing, then blinking once more. Ned remained standing on the bow, the boat gently rolling back and forth under his feet, and waited for the signal.

A twig snapped nearby. Special Agent Trang drew his gun and spun around in one fluid motion, lowering himself into a well-rehearsed shooter's crouch as he aimed the muzzle of his Sig Sauer automatic in the direction of the sound. The woods just off the bluff provided cover from the brightness of the moonlight; as Trang scanned the tree line, his eyes could distinguish no human shapes or movement.

"United States Secret Service!" shouted Trang, using the sharp, percussive bark of authority that his trainers at the Academy had drilled into his vocal repertoire. "Stop and identify yourself!"

"Oh!" came one tremulous voice from the woods, with the inflection of a frightened old woman. "Oh my!"

"Don't shoot, for God's sake," came a second voice, also an older woman also but this one seemingly not intimidated.

"Identify yourselves," repeated Trang, his tone softening to a low growl as his state of alarm subsided.

"Nora and Angela," came the second voice again. "Point that thing somewhere else, would you?"

Special Agent Trang ignited his flashlight, a massive black aluminum thing nearly the size and heft of a Louisville Slugger, and pointed its powerful beam toward the woods. This action would have made him an easy target under hostile circumstances, but Trang did not anticipate sniper fire. The light revealed two older women, one slightly frail and one not even remotely so, standing just at the edge of the woods. The frail one held a large plastic coffee mug. Trang clicked off his light, reholstered the Sig, and waved the women over.

"C'mon out, ladies. It's all right," he said. "Sorry for the scare."

Bastards, thought Trang, thinking of his fellow agents, posted at the main Center, whose job it was to alert the perimeter men if there were walkers out on the property. Holding back the alert was their idea of a joke. All very funny, until a couple of little old ladies get blown away…

"You gals are awfully quiet on your feet," said Trang as Nora and Angela approached. "That's what got me. I never heard you coming."

"We're birders," said the slighter woman, the fear gone from her voice now. "Lots of practice sneaking up. Maybe *too much* practice."

"Not to worry," Trang reassured them, "not your fault. You ladies just out for a walk? How's the party going?"

"It's a full-on birdwatchers' blow-out," said Nora. "A total hoot."

"A hoot," Trang nodded. "I get it."

"We brought about ten gallons of our chowder, for the party crowd," continued Nora, "and we started thinking about how some of you boys and girls were out here in the cold, keeping the Tarp safe for the Vice President and us guests. We thought you might appreciate a nice hot taste of the good life."

"Homemade chowder, huh?" said Trang, his mouth already beginning to water. For the most part, he had found the local cuisine to be bland and monotonous, but the islanders could crank out some mean chowder. "Unfortunately, regulations are such that I can't… hold on a sec, ladies…"

A voice had come in on Trang's earpiece, calling for all the perimeter posts to check in and verify. Trang held the left cuff of his parka up to his mouth and spoke into the hidden microphone fastened there.

"This is seven. Trang, green," he said into his cuff, then turned slightly away from the women and added quietly, "and screw you, DeHaven. Nice heads-up on the walkers."

"Heh heh," came a sinister chuckle over Trang's earpiece, and then the line went quiet.

"Pardon that," Trang said, turning back to Nora and Angela. "Anyway, as I was saying, I really can't accept any kind of food or beverage while I'm on duty. The rule is pretty hard and fast."

"That's what they said you'd say," answered Nora.

"They?"

"The boys back at the Center. They figured you for quite a stickler."

"Did they?"

"Even tried to talk us out of your mug, once they finished theirs," said Angela, "but we decided that wasn't fair, not even giving you a chance."

"The agents at the Center got to try the chowder?"

"Sure," said Nora, "said they were glad to have something to wash down the lobster rolls, since they hadn't worked up the courage to have any champagne. Yet."

"Lobster rolls?"

"Yeah," said Nora, "we caught 'em sneaking a few dozen of them away from the buffet table. But we won't rat. They told us about how they'd had some sort of illness, and were trying to get their strength back up."

"Here," Angela offered, removing the cap from the insulated mug. "If you can't eat, you should at least get a whiff. We won the First Night Chowder Cook-Off last year, but we tried to make some improvements for this year's contest—strictly in the interest of progress. 'If you're not moving forward, you're moving back.' That's what my ex-husband used to say, and those are wise words, I think, even though the last time he moved forward was out the front door of our house and down to Sarasota with Meg Riley, that skank."

"Oh," said Agent Trang, otherwise speechless.

"Sorry for that," said Nora. "Angela's healing process is ongoing."

"Yeah, don't mind my rage," added Angela, as she waved the steaming mug of chowder under Trang's nose and he inhaled deeply, welcoming the magical aroma.

"Oh, my God," said Trang.

"Yeah, we get that sometimes," said Nora.

"Lemongrass?" Trang asked, hungrily breathing in again.

"Good nose," applauded Angela.

Trang sniffed some more.

"Lemongrass, celery seed and… what's in the roux?"

"*Masa harina*," Angela replied. "Gives the texture a sort of Mayan vibe, we think."

"Wow," said Trang, impressed.

"It's really just corn meal," said Angela, "but you have to grind it up very fine, otherwise—"

"*Secret* recipe, Angela," Nora interrupted, sneaking a look of annoyance in Angela's direction, but then turning her attention back to Trang. "Anyway, we respect your commitment to duty, Agent…"

"*Special* Agent Trang."

"*Special* Agent Trang, then. We just thought that, between friends, there wouldn't be any harm, especially since your colleagues saw fit to have a little soup themselves. We'll just leave the mug in case you change your mind. We know you won't, but it will make us feel better, knowing we completed our appointed rounds. It's a 'little old lady' thing, silly us. Would that be all right, dear?"

"If you like," answered Trang. "I mean, if it'll make you ladies feel better."

"It will," said Angela.

"Okay then," said Trang, eyeing the mug as Angela set it down on the ground near the bluff. "I've enjoyed your company, but I wouldn't want to keep you ladies from the party."

"We'll just be going, then," said Nora. "We know you have an important job to do. Good night, dear."

"Good night, Secret Service man," said Angela, "and oh, take some napkins, just in case." She reached out and stuffed a handful of paper napkins into the right front pocket of Trang's parka.

"'Night, ladies. Thanks for the visit."

Nora and Angela shuffled off into the woods, leaving Trang alone once again. He stepped to the bluff and scanned the ocean. Empty, of course. Nothing here, thought Trang, but the cool evening breeze, the moonlight dancing on the water, and the mug of hot, delicious chowder at his feet.

↦   ↤   ↤

"There it is," said Ned, seeing three quick blinks of a flashlight up on the bluff. "We wait six minutes and go."

"What if he isn't tempted by the chowder?" asked Veronica.

"I'm gonna do you a favor," said Ned, "and not mention to Nora that you asked that." Ned put away his binoculars and turned to General Hoak at the helm. "You ready, Sir?"

"Just gimme the signal, Donlin."

Six minutes later they were underway, motoring around the last point of cover and into Talbott's Cove, also known for the past seventy years as 'Bubbly Bay'. General Hoak deftly maneuvered the landing craft until it faced the beach squarely, and then gunned the engines forward, driving the craft onto the sand and dropping its

249

bow ramp onto the beach with a huge splash. A second engine roared to life with a blast of diesel smoke, and Tommie Krupa drove down the LCM's ramp in a Bobcat compact excavator, a tiny but powerful earth mover with just the right qualifications for the evening's activates.

Ned, Veronica and General Hoak followed the Bobcat down the ramp, both with knapsacks slung over their shoulders, their eyes scanning the bluff for signs of unexpected resistance.

"Doesn't seem sporting, really, without German artillery," said Hoak. "Too easy for my taste."

"Careful what you ask for, General," said Ned. "The night is young."

Tommy powered the Bobcat up the beach to the base of the bluff and kept going, steel treads struggling for purchase on the steep slope of sand and clay. General Hoak clambered up the slope behind the Bobcat, with Ned and Veronica following a few steps later. After less than a minute of work, the Bobcat reached the target location, about three-fourths of the way to the top of the slope, where large cut stones from the mouth of Nelson's original tunnel had been scattered about by the forces of erosion. Reaching this spot, Tommie locked off the Bobcat's treads and set the back hoe into motion, digging away at the soft earth of the bluff.

Ned and Veronica stood by to help guide Tommy's digging, while General Hoak continued climbing. Reaching the top of the slope, Hoak slowly peered over the crest just to make sure there were no unexpected developments in the security situation. Nope—everything had gone off as planned. A single Secret Service agent was stretched out on the ground, dozing peacefully, an empty plastic cup at his side. Hoak topped the crest and kneeled down by the fallen agent. He reached for the man's neck and checked his pulse.

"Is the agent all right, sir?" asked Lt. Harmon.

"He'll be fine, Lieutenant," answered Hoak. "Man your posts."

His men fanned out, setting a watch perimeter in every direction. General Hoak reached into Agent Trang's pocket and pulled out the handful of napkins Angela had stuffed there just a few minutes ago. One napkin was crumpled very tightly—Hoak opened it and found a message there in Angela's handwriting:

This is seven. Trang, green.

Hoak collected the empty paper cup at Agent Trang's side and stuffed it in one of his coat pockets. From another of his own pockets he retrieved an identical paper cup wrapped in a plastic bag. Hoak unwrapped the plastic and placed the new cup beside Trang—one that contained traces of clam chowder that would test "negative" for drugs of any kind, should anyone be interested. Hoak then removed the agent's radio, including the tiny earpiece and the microphone at his jacket cuff, then zipped up Trang's parka and carefully propped up the agent's head with a soft clump of dry leaves. He placed his hand gently on Trang's forehead, a comforting gesture.

"Sleep well, Special Agent Trang," said the General, softly. "You will have better days."

"Our perimeter is in place, Sir," said Harmon, appearing beside the General.

Just as Hoak inserted Trang's earpiece into his own ear, a call came in over the com. Hoak placed his finger on the earpiece to make sure he heard the incoming message. After a moment, Hoak responded into the tiny microphone with the best young man's voice he could muster.

251

"This is seven," Hoak said into the mike. "Trang, green."

Ned stood near the furiously digging little Bobcat, taking a moment to note Tommy's expression as he worked; the guy was focused, that was for sure, and Ned knew where that was coming from. Tommy had been struggling, privately, with his role in the recent mishap at the Sweetwater Country Club, where Tommie had apparently broken through to the aquifer while digging with a back hoe, turning a challenging but usually non-lethal sand trap into a Van Winkle-eating suck hole. Ned was glad to see Tommie exorcising his guilt constructively, anyway; Tommie was digging like a man possessed, and it wasn't more than two minutes before the teeth of the back hoe broke through the tunnel opening and a blast of stale air rushed out of the breach.

Here we go, Ned thought to himself, and wondered how things were going at the party.

The conga line, with the widow Sharon Winkle leading up front, snaked through the Great Room of the Tarpaulin Center, passing the immense Fieldstone fireplace and heading back toward the wet bar as the Andrews Sisters blasted away on the jukebox.

> *"Ay-Ay, Ay-Ay-Ay-Ay!*
> *Have you ever kissed in the moonlight?*
> *If you've never kissed, oh boy*
> *What you've missed, oh boy*
> *of that South American Way!!!"*

The song was playing through for the fifth time, and by now the revelers were shouting along with the inane lyrics.

"Ay-Ay, Ay-Ay-Ay-Ay!
Have you ever danced in the tropics?"
Where they thrill the bull
With the gauchos full of that
South American Way!!!"

Nora Gardner stood at entranceway to the Great Room, one eyebrow arched as the conga line passed in front of her. Ned had asked her to foster a certain amount of anarchy at the party, and with that end in mind Nora had introduced a gallon of good Mescal into the massive crystal punch bowl by the buffet table. Nora decided that a conga line was well within the level of rumpusness required for Ned and the others to do their work, but she also had her concerns. She and Angela had been gone from the party for only half an hour, making a little soup run out to the bluff, and in that time the gathering had transformed from mostly sedate cocktail festivity into a full blown south-of-the-border fiesta—a regular Rio *Carnivale*. At this pace, Nora figured, the party was just one more hour—and one more gallon of mescal—from complete saturnalic dissipation, which should be perfect. Chaos would be Ned's friend tonight, if his plan stuck, but the timing of that chaos was critical.

"We'll need a little luck," Ned had said, when he and Nora had reviewed the assault plans that afternoon.

Nora figured that to be the understatement of the winter season. Between the evening's heist and the crisis with the special contributors—all of them in attendance at the Paulson party—Ned had so many balls up in the air that some would inevitably come crashing to Earth. As for what would happen at tonight's party, there was no point in worrying; Nora and the Committee would carry out their prescribed role, and Doc was in the Great Room to lend a hand with the contributors. There was little else they could do, other than closely monitor the punch bowl.

"Bunny Hop!" shouted Sharon Winkle when the Andrews Sisters had finished their number on the jukebox, and her fellow mourners obliged.

> *"Dance this new creation*
> *It's the new sensation*
> *Do the Bunny Hop*
> *Hop, hop, hop!*
>
> *Let's all join in the fun*
> *Father, mother, son*
> *Do the Bunny Hop*
> *Hop, hop, hop!"*

Right, thought Nora. No more mescal.

26.

"We were all invited to the party, Ned," said Veronica, grouchy as she followed him through the long dark tunnel, a halogen miner's lamp on her forehead, swiping the endless nasty spider webs out of her way.

"So what's your point?" asked Ned.

"Paulson said everyone was welcome. I heard him. We could have walked right in through the front door."

"Always your first choice, Ronnie," recalled Ned, trudging along in front of her, a heavy pick-axe on his shoulder.

"Damn right."

"They'll have video of everyone who enters the Center. How long do you think it would be before they figured out who did the job?"

"Figuring isn't proving, Nedly."

"I know how comfortable you are being on a list of suspects, but you know I can't afford to let that happen. My life here on the island is already on tenterhooks as it is."

"Wait—what's a tenterhook again?"

"Let's just keep moving, Ron."

A tenter is a frame used for stretching cloth after it has been milled or dyed. The hooks along the frame hold the cloth taut as it dries, thereby in a state of "uneasiness, strain, or suspense", according to Webster's. Ned reflected on the definition and knew that it described his current situation perfectly: uneasy, strained, suspenseful.

Reflecting on the events of the past week, Ned was amused by the irony of it all; he had been jumping through seemingly endless felonious hoops to preserve a life on the island which, just a few short days ago, he had been ready to abandon all together.

The opportunity for a quiet, low-impact exit from Martha's Vineyard was long gone, of course. Even if Ned turned around and left the island forever, right now, his new life on the run would be much worse than before; the lapwing scam would be revealed in short order, and Ned's fingerprints would be run through the system. The feds would finally have a face and a name attached to an anonymous set of fingerprints they already had on file, associated with at least seven felonies throughout the Western states. Ned would be featured on his very own "Wanted" poster which — Ned forced himself to be realistic — would guarantee an unhappy ending, sooner or later.

"How long does champagne stay good?" Ned asked.

"Not long," Veronica answered authoritatively. "No more than ten or twelve years."

"What a waste."

They were halfway through the dank, dusty tunnel now, and piled up against both walls were hundreds of cases of fine, expensive French champagne that were at least seventy five years old.

"Hey, hold on a sec..." Veronica aimed her headlamp at four wooden wine cases that had a different label than the others: "Latour blanche – 1927" was branded onto their faces.

"We're in luck, boyfriend," she said. "No bubbles in this nectar."

With her gloved hands, Veronica tore open one of the cases, pulled out a bottle and cracked it open by whacking its neck against the stone wall of the tunnel.

"It might need to breathe a little," offered Ned, "after so long down here in the —"

Without waiting, Veronica tipped the bottle up and poured the wine in her mouth from a height, keeping the jagged broken glass away from her lips. She passed the bottle to Ned, who shrugged and did the same.

"Mmm," he moaned, swishing the fine wine around his mouth for a few laps before swallowing.

"Yeah, that's nice," agreed Veronica. "Come on, Nedly, we're on the clock."

ᚠ　ᚠ　ᚠ

"Little Bunny Hop Hop Hop
Don't you ever stop stop stop
All the live long day
you hop your little life away;
you hop your little itsy bitsy life away
Hop hop hop!!!"

Though tempted, at this juncture, to fully review the career choice that had landed her at this party, on this night, completely sober, Special Agent In Charge Rhonda Hipps instead decided to review the present security situation at the Tarpaulin Center. Guarding a public figure always involved a certain amount of uncontrollable elements, but the variables in this particular situation were legion, to wit: from her position on the main staircase, Agent Hipps had a full view of the Great Room, where no fewer than a hundred and fifty drunken mourners had taken full leave of their inhibitions. Due to the last minute nature of this party/wake, there had been no time to run security checks on the guests. For all

Hipps' knew, there could be Chechen terrorists or Vatican assassins mixed in the conga line. Secondly, a makeshift dungeon in the Center's basement held two as-yet-unidentified skels, whose entry into the national AFIS identification process had inexplicably crashed the entire system. Also, some sort of assault had been launched a few nights ago against the Center's security perimeter. Neither the goal of the assault nor its perpetrators had yet been discovered.

On the positive side, her Service detail was almost back up to strength now, with a full perimeter crew on patrol and the balance of agents posted here inside the Center, preventing guests from wandering too far from the buffet table or stealing any silverware. The Center's own security system had proven to be sufficient as well, with its own backup power source and decent coverage from a system of video cameras throughout the buildings and property. Special Agent Hipps listened in on her com set as her perimeter posts checked in. Five, Carson, blue… Six, Bernstein, periwinkle… Seven, Trang, green…uh oh.

"Trang?" Hipps spoke into her com.

"Uh… yes ma'am?" Trang answered in a raspy tone.

"You're smoking again. I can hear it in your voice. Put it out. And never call me 'ma'am'."

Trang coughed loudly into his com, and then replied.

"Yes, Sir."

As she listened to the rest of the posts checked in, Hipps watched the bunny-hopping conga line make another round of the first floor, with the Vice President of the United States right behind the leader, the widow Winkle. It was an education to see Roger Paulson in this context, surrounded by those of his own stripe as opposed to the school of rapacious barracudas on Capitol Hill. In the past year, he had been caused to smile only by things with feathers, but now there he was, grinning from ear to ear, his face flushed with booze and gladness at this wealth of sympathetic human company. He was in pretty good physical shape, too, for an older guy. Hell, he must've hopped a good two miles over the last hour, and he wasn't the least bit out of breath.

Plus he's kinda cute, thought Angel Hipps, for the second time that day.

"Little Bunny Hop Hop Hop
Don't you ever stop stop stop
All the live long day
you hop your little life away;
you hop your little itsy bitsy life away
Hop hop hop!!!"

← ← ←

"Make 'em stop, Ricky!"

"How do ya want me to do that, huh Bob?"

"You're my brother. You can do stuff."

Despite Ricky Friendship's alleged ability to "do stuff", the pounding from the floors above continued unabated.

"It's only dancing, Bobby. Can't you hear the music?"

"That's not dancing! Dancing doesn't sound like that at all! She's beating someone up there."

"Awww, Bobby, please shut up…"

"Thump thump thump! Thump thump thump!" Bobby yelped. "Why won't it stop?! It's like that story you used to read me when I was little. About the guy who kills someone and he's gonna get away with it but he starts to hear the guy's heart beating under his floor. Which, I hate

to tell ya, Rick, was not a good story to read to a kid only four years old."

"The Tell Tale Heart. Yeah, that's a good one."

"It's scary! Why'd you do me like that, Ricky?"

"There's a lesson in that story. I was teaching you."

"What lesson, Rick?"

"That some people have consciences and you can use that against 'em."

"*Thump thump thump! Thump thump thump*! I can't stand it!"

"Christ, Bobby. Just take a few deep breaths, alright?"

"It's hard with the hood over my head. It's dusty inside here."

"Bobby…"

"Okay okay."

Bobby Friendship took several deep, cleansing breaths.

"Chowder! Crab cakes!" Bobby yelped this time. "Can't you smell 'em, Rick? I am so hungry!"

"Oh my God, Bobby. Will you please—"

Ricky Friendship was interrupted by the sound of their cell door being unlocked and opened.

"Hey Secret Service lady, we're ready! We're ready to give it up!"

"Bobby…"

"I don't care anymore, Rick. I'm cold and I'm hungry and I can't listen to this upstairs *thumpin'* anymore. She'll ID us eventually and then we're going away. I don't want that and we don't owe nothin' to no one!"

"Yeah," said Ricky, and sighed. "Okay, Bobby."

"So here it is, lady," began Bobby Friendship, "we came here to do a major heist. Some guy, some 'Mr. Big' —

we don't know who he is — put up the expenses and we get a payoff when we deliver. But we're not even big players, here; we're just hired hands for the job. The real player is called Veronica Lodge, which is not her real name which we never found out but your guys will know about her, in your records and stuff. And she's working with a guy from here on the island name is Ned Donlin, some kinda tour guide for birds or somethin'. They worked together before, some years ago, and we can tell you about those jobs too. Secret Service lady, we know you are very tough, but this Veronica is even tougher than you. She is one nasty piece of work and if you ever plan to meet up with her you better be ready because she is mean as a snake and she will hurt you."

Veronica and Ned gave each other a look. The two men before them were a pathetic sight: they had black hoods on their heads, with ankles bolted to the cement floor with a few feet of chain attached, just barely long enough to let them use a piss bucket in the corner of the dark, empty, smelly room. Food trays lay upside down beneath the far wall, where they had been thrown. Gobs of dried food were caked on the walls.

"Well, aren't you gonna say somethin'?" asked Ricky.

"Boys boys boys…" sighed Veronica. "What am I gonna do with the two of you?"

"AHHHHH!!!!!" Ricky and Bobby screamed in unison.

Veronica gave each Friendship a quick kick to the solar plexus, which shut them up. They doubled over on the floor, their faces contorted in pain.

"No more shouting, boys," Veronica said calmly and then, sniffing the air, added "What is that smell?"

"I squirted in my pants a little," wheezed Bobby Friendship.

←   ⊢   ⇇

"Please don't shoot us, Ronnie," pled Ricky Friendship, now kneeling upright on the ground with his brother beside him. Both had tears streaming down their faces.

"Yeah," chimed Bobby, "don't shoot us."

They were out in the basement hallway now. The Friendships had been freed from bondage, but cowered meekly before their mistress as they awaited sentencing. Veronica had her Beretta out, and he pointed it at the heads of each brother in turn, as if deciding who to shoot first.

"What do you think, Ned?" Veronica asked. "They ratted us out and I've gotta think they'd do it again..."

"I think you should kill them," said Ned. "Just to be sure."

"Ned! We're friends!" the brothers squawked. "And what are you doing here anyway? This ain't your heist! What—you want our cuts? Fine! Just let us go!"

Ned and Veronica had arrived in the Friendships' cell after making two other stops in sub-level; their first errand had been in the Generator Room, which contained the source for backup power when—not if—the Chilmark area electrical transformer was blown, due to Semtex explosive being detonated by the remote control device nestled patiently in Veronica's jeans pocket. Veronica and Ned had disabled the back-up generator and then moved to a second room, which contained the surveillance recorders for the Tarpaulin's security cameras. Veronica had demonstrated for Ned, who after all had been out of circulation for a while, how easily the jolt of a stun gun could completely destroy a row of computer hard drives. The recording devices would be inoperative.

"We were crazy to rat you out, Ron, that's all we can say," pled Ricky Friendship, still on his knees.

"Yeah, we were crazy," Bobby added.

"There are circumstances here," Ricky continued, "I forget what you call 'em…"

"Mitigating?" Ned offered.

"Mitigating! I was shot in the head and buried, and we both've been chained up here for like a week —"

"Stop," said Veronica. "I'm thinking…"

"Think, Ronnie, think…" Ricky encouraged her.

As Veronica ruminated, the nose of her automatic wavered carelessly in the vicinity of the Friendship brothers' faces.

"Ned, they're part of the plan, right?" she asked. "I mean, it's *your* plan. You tell me — who else can we get to do their part?"

"No one, I guess," Ned shrugged. "Still. After hearing them betray us like that, it'd feel good to see them dead."

"Ned!"

"I just don't think the gig works without them," countered Veronica. "I vote they live."

"Yes Ron!"

"Yeah, all right," Ned agreed reluctantly. "Whatever."

"Yes Ned!"

"You boys ready to work?" asked Veronica.

"Yes yes yes!" chanted the brothers. "Whatever you say, Ron."

"That fishing boat you fellows have waiting?"

"You know about the boat?" whined Bobby.

"We're all gonna use that boat," Veronica stated. "You two need to make it to the docks and get the boat ready to go. I've got a map here to get you out of this place safely, and here's a second map that will lead you to Menemsha, where your boat is docked."

The Friendship brothers were delighted. They stood and faced their benefactress with the bowed heads of supplicants.

"Ronnie, we've been locked up before, and we never rolled on you then, right? But this tall lady, this Fed? She was scary and we had the hoods on and—"

Veronica spun around and flashed two arcing windmill kicks, first with her left foot and then her right. Her boot heels caught each Friendship brother squarely in the chin and they dropped to the ground, moaning in pain and holding their jaws as blood spewed from their mouths.

"Owww!!!" shouted the brothers.

"Have I made my point?" asked Veronica.

"We understand, Ronnie," whined Ricky Friendship, a blood bubble inflating and popping on his lower lip.

"Wait three minutes, boys," Veronica said as she pulled out a stopwatch, set it, and handed it to Ricky Friendship, along with two hand-drawn maps, "then follow the maps. Right?"

"Right!"

Veronica turned back to Ned. "Shall we?"

Ned and Veronica turned away from the wheezing Friendships and proceeded down the hallway.

"It's not too late to change your mind," she cautioned Ned as they moved on. "If they get caught, they will give us up so fast—"

"They won't get caught," said Ned, because he needed to believe it.

264

"One hundred and sixty, one hundred and sixty one, one hundred and sixty two—"

"Stop it, Bobby."

"She said count to two hundred before we go."

"Is she here now? Can you see her anywhere? Is she listening to you count?"

"Ricky, don't take this personal—you're still my smart brother—but maybe we should just do what Veronica says, this once. Doin' otherwise, at least on this rock, has not brung us good things."

Ricky opened his mouth, prepared to argue the point, but stopped himself. In truth, he agreed with Bobby. All the problems the brothers had experienced on the island had come where they had ignored Veronica's explicit orders. Now, miraculously, Veronica had granted the brothers a new lease on life, and Ricky would not even blink at this gift horse. They would follow Veronica's instructions, to the letter, and escape the island.

"Lemme see the map, Bob."

Bobby produced the hand-drawn map of the Tarpaulin Center, across which had been plotted, in a dotted red line, the escape route that Veronica had chosen for them.

"Two hundred!" said Bobby. "I was counting inside my head."

"Good work. Let's go."

The brothers followed Veronica's map through the warren of passages in the Tarpaulin Center's sub-levels. After a few minutes of walking the circuitous route, the map brought them to a narrow spiral staircase that rose up into an area of complete darkness. According to the map, the staircase would wind upward for three levels until it reached a doorway. That door would open directly into the outside of the Center, at a place where the brothers could hide behind some heavy brush and wait for an opening between the Secret Service patrols that were covering all the grounds. If they followed her instructions exactly, Veronica had promised, the brothers might still earn their cut of the heist money.

"These stairs are smelly," said Bobby as they climbed upward into complete darkness.

"'Cause it's so old and damp here," said Ricky. "Nobody musta used these stairs in years."

As they climbed higher, the musty closeness grew more stifling, and they disturbed a dense network of spider webs that now clung to their skin. Ordinarily, the brothers might have been squeamish about such a dark, creepy and buggy journey, but they were so close to earning escape that nothing would deter them.

"Almost there, brother," said Ricky. "Keep climbing."

"I can almost taste the fresh air," said Bobby. "I can't wait."

27.

Doc felt useless. He had volunteered to play an active part of the evening's plans, the way Tommie and General Hoak were contributing out on Bubbly Bay, but it was not to be. Ned's greatest fear, apparently, was that he would bring ruin upon his friends' lives if they became too involved in his problems; he had insisted that no one from the island do anything inside the Tarpaulin Center that night that might later be construed as criminal. So there was Doc, babysitting a pack of drunken birdwatchers and waiting to carry out a single part of the heist so innocuous that even if the Secret Service noticed it, Doc would never be considered suspect in the evening's wrongdoing. He stood at the Center of the Great Room and checked his watch: one minute and counting.

At least the annoying bunny hopping had stopped; a good half of the mourners were over sixty, and not even the mescal-laced punch could take the sting out of that many arthritic knees. The guests seemed satisfied with good music and inebrious mingling, now, with much of their adoring attention directed toward their host, Vice President Roger Paulson, who was regaling the revelers with yarns from his most exotic bird sighting expeditions.

"Then I moved on to Tasmania…" Paulson recounted.

As the Vice President continued to hold forth, however, Doc noticed that the birders' looks of admiration for Paulson soon evolved into something else entirely: resentment. Here was a man, after all, living their fantasy, jetting from one exotic locale to another, racking up an endless series of career sightings for himself and paying for it with the hard earned tax dollars of everyone else in the room; of course that pissed them off. Soon, their competitive spirits rose to the surface.

"Black Throated Blue Warbler," shouted out one guest in the back, "on the Cape in winter. Have you seen that, Mr. Vice President?"

"Well, no I haven't," Paulson answered politely, a little taken aback that his Tasmanian story had been interrupted. "That's a fine sighting. There was one time, though when I—"

"Black-Capped Vireo!"

"Well, yes, I've logged that sighting, but it's not in the Codex. They're quite difficult to draw because—"

"Summering Whimbrel!"

"In summer? No, I suppose I haven't—"

Suddenly bird names were being shouted out from every corner of the Great Room, accompanied by imitations of their calls.

"Red Knot! *Knut Knut Knut*!"

"Plain Chachalaca! *Cha-Cha-Lac*! *Cha-Cha-Lac*!"

"Northern Wheatear! *Chak Chak Chak*!"

Wow, thought Doc, *these people are nuts*. The birders had ceased listening to each other at all, and the room was so full of calls now that Doc could barely hear himself think. This went on for some time until one voice rang out and caught their attention.

"Snow Goose!" shouted Leonard Smallwood. "*Honk honk honk*!"

The birders around Leonard cast amused grins in his direction.

"Good grief, er… Smallwood, isn't it?" said Dr. Hedge. "Everyone's got the Snow Goose."

Leonard flushed red. The room was quiet now, and all eyes were on him.

"Yellow Rail?" Leonard offered meekly. "*Tik tik tik tik?*"

There were a few patronizing chuckles.

"Yellow Rail?" snorted Hedge. "Their migration last year brought them to every marsh on the Eastern Seaboard! You'll have to do better than that, Smallwood."

Leonard cleared his throat as he scanned his memory.

"Um... um... Semipalmated Plover? *Chee-wee chee-wee?*"

"Good Lord, Lenny," sneered Hedge, "Semipalmated Plover? They winter in Florida by the jillions. I think a family of them actually rented the condo next to mine in Boca."

There was a roar of derisive laughter at Leonard Smallwood's expense. Cornered and humiliated, Smallwood lashed out desperately with his only remaining ammunition.

"Well... I DID see the lapwing!"

The claim erased the smiles from the other contributors. Suddenly the group was thrust right back into their irate dispute from the previous day.

"My ass, you did!" countered Mrs. Hedge. "Devin... tell him!"

"Her ass you did," obeyed Dr. Hedge.

"I did!" howled Smallwood. "And that Ned Donlin, and those ladies..." his eyes searched the room for any present members of the Refreshment Committee... "Those Refreshment ladies, they were there, too. I saw the lapwing at Music Lagoon, in a ravine. And now it's MY ravine, so none of you will ever get to—"

"YOUR ravine?!?!" shouted Mrs. Hedge. "OUR ravine...!"

At that point, the other contributors chimed in with their individual claims…

"MY ravine…"

"What the hell—?!?!"

"You're all full of SHIT!!!"

"No way! We leased private rights!"

Suddenly, a wall of the Great Room swung open: it was secret doorway, concealed among the wooden wall panels, a vestigial souvenir of Horace Tarpaulin's colorful—and paranoid—lifestyle. As the confused guests looked on, in stunned silence, the Friendship brothers marched into the room, filthy and smelly and looking as though they'd been bolted to the floor of a dungeon for at least a week. The brothers gazed around the crowded room blankly, mystified to find themselves in the middle of a crowded party.

"Ricky," said Bobby Friendship, turning to his brother, "these people are not on the map."

Half a dozen Secret Service Agents—led by Special Agent In Charge Rhonda Hipps—appeared from all directions and converged on the Friendship brothers.

Then the lights went out, and the screaming started.

↞   ←   ↞

Ned and Veronica waited in the stairwell for their cue; they were close enough to the Great Room to hear all the festive sounds of the party. The sounds *had* been festive, that is, until the contributors renewed their hostilities over their lapwing sightings, now with fresh confirmation that they had all been scammed by Ned. Until that moment, Ned had harbored the secret hope that, once they figured out the specifics of his illicit but well intentioned money raising strategy, the contributors would do the best thing for Music Lagoon and overlook his transgression. As he listened in on the fracas, however, an absolute realization gripped Ned; the Music Lagoon contributors were fanatics — ruthless, vain and entitled — and they would forgive him nothing. Ever.

"Damn it," muttered Ned.

"Problem?" asked Veronica.

Before Ned could answer, he and Veronica heard the secret door burst open in the Great Room, followed by the sudden hush of Paulson's guests as they regarded the Friendship brothers, all smelly and filthy and surprised. Not surprised at this turn of events were Ned and Veronica, who had marked a route on the Friendships' "escape" map that delivered them right into the middle of the party, a necessary diversion that had occurred exactly on cue. Veronica pulled the remote control device from her jeans pocket and touched two of the buttons.

Somewhere out on North Road, a mile or so away from the Tarp, a transformer atop a power pole exploded in a hail of sparks and shrapnel. One second later, every light in the Tarpaulin Center flickered and went dark. There was screaming now — this was Nora and the rest of the Refreshment Committee, stationed throughout the ground floor, their howls contributing to the sense of chaos as other guests picked up on the sense of panic and started screaming, themselves. Two seconds later, after the backup generator failed to restore power, the battery-charged emergency lights finally came on, halfway blinding everyone in the Center with their stark light.

Doc Titus' moment had arrived. He hurried to the dining room, where an emergency exit door stood in the corner. Doc pushed the door open and that door's alarm began to shriek. Doc propped the door open and moved calmly to the three other emergency doors on the ground floor, pushing them all open. Now the screeching alarms sounded in stereo, their echoes blaring throughout the facility. Party guests spotted the open doors and hurried toward them amid the sudden chaos. On their way out of the Center, the partiers collided with and otherwise hindered the corps of Secret Service agents who had immediately split into two teams, each with a pre-determined task: first, secure the Vice President and remove him from the location as quickly as possible and, secondly: hunt down and neutralize the threatening parties, in this case the escaped Friendship brothers, who by that time had spotted the open emergency exit in the dining room.

Ned and Veronica stayed put in the basement stairwell, waiting.

"First priority," Veronica said, as if reciting from a Secret Service training manual, "get the man OUT…"

She and Ned could hear the Secret Service agents barking into their com sets; the code name "Sparrow Hawk" was repeated endless times, as in "Do we have Sparrow Hawk?" or "Sparrow Hawk on the move!" or "Transport team awaiting Sparrow Hawk!" Through a crack in the staircase door, Ned and Veronica watched as a squad of agents thundered past them, all tightly clutched together in a tight circle. At the very center of the squad, Special Agent in Charge Rhonda Hipps wrapped her ample arms around a crouching silver-haired figure: the Vice President himself. She and her team hustled Paulson through the entrance hall and out the front door of the Center, into the waiting motorcade. The Vice President was barely inside his heavily armored Suburban when the vehicle raced off in a shower of dust and gravel, one more black Surburban leading the way and two more to the rear.

The remaining Secret Service agents changed their focus immediately.

"Do we have a twenty on the intruders?" one agent barked into his com set.

"They're still on the grounds! Converge on the Eastern perimeter…"

There was a rush of movement as the remaining agents evacuated the building in pursuit of the Friendship brothers.

As chaos ruled the night on the Tarpaulin Center's ground floor, Ned and Veronica calmly but quickly made their way up the rear stairway to the second floor. They had memorized the floor plan for the Center's main building, so the bare beams of the emergency lights were all they needed to find the second floor library, where Roger Paulson's temporary office had been organized. Ned and Veronica turned on their tactical flashlights and scanned the room. The library's far wall featured a long panel of windows facing Southeast on the Center's property, with an excellent view of the grounds and entrance roads. A long built-in desk sat right up against the windows to take full advantage of the serene setting, and here Ned and Veronica found the Vice President's papers.

"It'll be one of these," said Ned, pointing to the several leather valises sitting together on the desk.

"Check them," said Veronica, and Ned searched through the valises. As he did so, he snuck a look out the picture window to the Tarpaulin grounds below, where he could see a unit of Secret Service agents moving across the front lawn. The beams of their flashlights haphazardly searched the grounds for the escaping Friendship brothers, leading them directly away from the main building—just as Ned's plan had predicted. The Vice

President's motorcade was no longer in view; it had undoubtedly cleared the grounds already, at speeds far surpassing the local limits, and relocated Paulson to Air Force Two. If his security details followed protocol, the Vice President would be off the island and in the air within ten minutes.

"Got it," said Ned, discovering the files he was looking for in the second valise he checked; it was the extensive environmental impact report on Noman's Island.

"Okay, good," said Veronica, placing a set of files from her own knapsack onto the desk with the others, "switch 'em out and let's go."

"See? It all comes down to planning, Veronica," Ned explained with self-satisfaction as he carried out the file switch. "Planning—that's something you never really appreciated about my—"

"What the hell…?" a gruff voice sounded behind them.

Ned and Veronica turned to find a uniformed Army Major standing in the doorway of the room, a valise manacled to one wrist and an MP-5 machine gun in the other, a flashlight mounted above its barrel. The Major studied the two felons, for a moment, before a cruel, gleeful sneer appeared on his face.

"Heh heh," Foxbrite chuckled, then raised his machine gun and blasted in Ned and Veronica's direction with the MP-5. They dove to the ground as the guns muzzle blasts ignited the room, a hail of bullets shattering the big picture window and tearing through the red leather sofa set.

"Come and get it, bastards…!" Foxbrite shouted, his maniacal grin illuminated like a jack o' lantern by the muzzle blasts as he strafed the room wildly with more gunfire.

Foxbrite marched around the edge of the sofa, raking the path ahead of him with a steady stream of bullets. The Major's movements were encumbered, somewhat, by the large attaché case still manacled to his wrist, but his one-armed marksmanship was still plenty lethal. The MP-5 bullets tore up the floor of the room and would certainly have riddled Ned and Veronica, except Ned chose that moment to haul back on the edge of the oriental "runner" rug that lay in the space between the leather sofa and the window. The rug pulled from under his feet — literally — Foxbrite tumbled backward, never letting go of the machinegun's trigger; a stream of bullets ripped across the room, up the far wall and across the ceiling. The surprisingly agile Foxbrite jumped back to his feet in a flash, completely consumed with rage now and swinging the "football" — the attaché case manacled to his wrist — as a make-shift weapon as he searched the room for his quarry, but Ned and Veronica had leapt over the massive sofa and were now lying prone on the other side, temporarily out of sight.

"How's your plan workin' now, Ned?" snarled Veronica, now belly down on the floor beside Ned.

Foxbrite charged the sofa with murderous intent. He swung his attaché case at Veronica, but she ducked and the case smashed and tore apart against the wall. Veronica reached into her jacket and pulled out a set of *nunchuks* — a martial arts weapon of two heavy sticks attached by a short chain — and swung the weapon in the air twice before releasing in the direction of the approaching Foxbrite. Her aim was dead-on; one of the sticks struck Foxbrite in the nose, while the second whipped around and caught him in the ear. Foxbrite dropped to the ground, shrieking in agony.

There, on the floor beside the sofa, Foxbrite looked up, blood gushing down his face, and found himself face to face with Ned Donlin. Foxbrite lunged at Ned but Ned rolled away and kicked backward, the heel of his boot catching Foxbrite on his already broken nose.

"Fucker!" yelled the enraged Major, before a fresh wave of his own blood spilled down over his eyes, blinding him. Foxbrite used his shirtsleeves, trying to wipe the blood away from his eyes, but as he did this the "football" valise kept striking his head, painfully.

"Yaaa!!" howled Foxbrite. "Fuckers!"

Ned spotted Paulson's files on the floor, scattered about during the melee, and shoved them into Veronica's knapsack.

"Let's go!" Ned shouted. Ned charged out of the room, Veronica right on his heels as he raced for the rear staircase. Major Foxbrite rose up and came after them yet again, blood still pouring down his face and out of his left ear as he charged out of the room in hot pursuit. Foxbrite fired semi-blindly with his submachine gun, the auto-blasts tearing into the historical photos in the hallway and raining shards of glass down on Ned and Veronica before they finally made it to the staircase and raced down toward the ground floor.

They emerged into the downstairs hallway, only to have their path blocked by a team of Secret Service agents who burst through the front door, drawn back to the main building by the sound of gunfire. Ned and Veronica veered off toward the Great Room, just steps ahead of the team of agents, but Major Foxbrite unwittingly came to their aid—he had just made it to the first floor hallway and was still blazing away with his MP-5. The agents hit the floor just in time, a spray from Foxbrite's gun tearing across the entranceway—just over their heads—and bringing down with a CRASH! a rustic chandelier fashioned from driftwood and sea glass.

Ned and Veronica raced through the Great Room on their way to the basement levels, but as he passed the buffet table, Ned suddenly skidded to a halt on the hardwood floor. Ned stood before the buffet table, his mouth agape, his eyes focused on the spectacular object placed in the very center of the massive crystal punch bowl: it was a large, artfully fashioned ice sculpture of Vanellus Caucasus, the Caucasian Lapwing. One of the emergency lights on the wall illuminated the sculpture from behind, lending an ethereal glow to the glistening, melting form.

"NED! What the hell are you doing!?!?" yelled Veronica.

"I have no idea," said Ned, seemingly in a daze.

Ned was abruptly ushered back to reality as the ice sculpture exploded, shattered by blasts from Foxbrite's machine gun. The Major was still on their heels, ignoring the drawn weapons of the Secret Service agents that he had passed in the entranceway.

Veronica hauled Ned by the arm and they charged onward, circling back through the myriad rooms of the Center's ground floor until they reached the basement stairs and dropped from sight; Foxbrite raced through the back rooms of the Tarp, just a few steps behind. The crazed Major reached the top of the basement staircase and aimed his gun at the retreating figures of Veronica Lodge and Ned Donlin below him, squeezing the trigger of his MP-5 once more.

An audible "click" signaled that his gun was out of ammo.

"Nooo…" the Major wailed, as a pack of angry Secret Service agents materialized from the entranceway and swarmed Foxbrite, wrestling away his gun and tackling him to the ground.

28.

Ned and Veronica set off on the hike together, headed away from the Tarpaulin Center and marching along the coast toward Menemsha, three miles away, where the Friendships' fishing trawler was waiting. The coastal route to Menemsha was the safest choice, they had figured, since the main roads on that part of the island would be crawling with Troopers and Sheriff's Deputies and Secret Service units. Common sense dictated that Tommie and General Hoak should have travelled with them, but the two men had refused to abandon the Bobcat or the landing craft on the beach of Bubbly Bay; they had motored the little earth mover back onto the boat and sailed off along the Northeast side of the island, headed toward the harbor at Oak Bluffs.

"So, Veronica," said Ned, "about your excellent inside intelligence on the Vice President's staff..."

"Yeah?"

"The guy with the blazing submachine gun..."

"I don't know for sure," said Veronica, "but he had that attaché case handcuffed to his wrist the whole time he was trying to kill us, so... maybe he was the guy who carries the 'football'...?"

"The football?"

"You know, with the nuclear launch codes and so forth."

"Arnie Speck's intelligence overlooked that, I guess..." said Ned, angrily. "The whole point of my plan,

Veronica, was to use the Friendship's escape as a diversion, so no one would even know we'd been messing around with Paulson's work papers. Now, since we encountered that maniac with the machine gun, everyone's going to know someone was up there..."

"But when they take inventory, Ned, they'll find nothing missing, 'cause we traded one set of papers for another. No harm, no foul. We're going to be fine; you're covered."

There was a hint of wistfulness in Veronica's reassurance, as if part of her had hoped for another outcome; an outcome that would result in Ned having to leave the island with her. Veronica knew she had no right to these feelings, and she did her best to hide them from Ned.

"Except for the fact that the maniac saw my face."

"Oh..."

They had chosen not to wear masks because it would limit their options if they encountered problems during the heist. A quick-talking crook could hustle his or her self out of many tricky situations, especially in a crowded, party situation like the one at the Tarp. Wearing a ski mask over one's face, however, usually eliminated that option.

"The maniac saw me up close and personal, Ronnie."

"I'm sorry, Ned." Veronica tried her best to mean it.

And Ned was sorry, too. Already he had the problem with the contributors, darkly clouding his future on the island and with no obvious solution. Now a member of the Vice President's staff would be able to identify Ned, on sight.

"Shit," he said.

"You can't stay here, Ned."

"Shit," he said.

"Maybe..." and here was Veronica trying to soften the blow, "...maybe it's just for a few days, Ned. Maybe you check back with your friends and find out there's no heat on and you'll be able to sneak back into your life. It doesn't have to be the end of the world..."

Right, thought Ned... just the end of *my* world.

The bullshit Veronica was spouting about Ned maybe returning to the island at a later time... Ned knew it was just that: bullshit. If he ran, he was on the run. His absence on the island would be noticed immediately, and uncharitable presumptions would be made about his involvement in the Tarpaulin raid, not to mention the depth of the corruption at the sanctuary.

"Shit," said Ned.

The two of them were silent and contemplative for the remainder of their journey. After an hour or so they arrived at Menemsha harbor, where they were mildly surprised to find Ricky and Bobby Friendship waiting for them.

"You boys actually made it," Veronica said when they came upon the brothers, waiting beside their fishing trawler on the main dock. "We were worried when we heard all the commotion downstairs at the Center..."

"Yeah, we musta made a wrong turn on the map you gave us," said Bobby Friendship. "Boy, did things get ugly, and fast."

"Regrettable," said Veronica.

"Can we go now, Ronnie?" whined Ricky. "I've about had with this damn place. We had Secret Service people chasing us and there was this Deputy with a gun too and—"

"We're going right now, Rick," said Veronica, and she turned to Ned, who by now was looking and feeling deeply forlorn. "Nedly, sweetheart, I'm truly sorry for the part I played fucking up your life here, but that is what has happened. Your life here is, in fact, fucked. Beyond repair. I know a part of you feels like you can't go, but Ned… you really really really cannot stay. Period. Let's get on the boat."

The certainty of Veronica's appeal had an immediate numbing effect upon Ned. At this moment, pressing himself to think of a single smart reason not to flee the island, Ned thought hard, then harder, and came up with exactly… nothing.

"Shit," he said.

Ned followed Veronica's lead and climbed, almost zombie-like, onto the trawler. As the boat's diesel rumbled into gear and motored off toward the dark waters of the Vineyard Sound. As the trawler continued its progress onto the water, Ned turned and faced Martha's Vineyard one last time. Specific details of the island were mostly lost in the darkness; all that remained in Ned's view were a small number of scattered house lights and the barest silhouette of the island against the starry sky. Even those reference points disappeared, eventually, as the boat motored into a swirl of fog that hung low over the water.

Three years, thought Ned. *Gone*. The Cooler, gone. Billie Jensen, Doc, Tommie, Nora and the Refreshment Committee, gone and gone. General Hoak, Espresso Love and its lemony croissants, Deputy Lemuel Keene, secret champagne tunnels and incidental quicksand. Rudy the cat.

Gone.

And, of course, the Music Lagoon Wildlife Sanctuary. It had once been MacDougal Farm, the home of his grandparents and a summertime paradise for Ned most every year of his youth. As a boy, he had foraged its forests and mucked through its swamps and collected periwinkles in the tiny stream that trickled down from Music Lagoon into the brisk waters of the Sound. Ned had dug clams with his grandfather and steamed them, with hot rocks and seaweed, in the sand of Glover's beach. He had learned to swim. He had learned to skip stones.

He had found a slingshot on the shores of Pilot Pond.

The land had become Ned's once again, decades later, restored to his rightful sovereignty by sheer chance or, perhaps, destiny. It truly had been his sanctuary, the long and narrow plot of four hundred and ten acres, stretching from its hilly woodland down through easy slopes of dense brush. There was a clearing, there was a cabin, and there was a small, annoying flock of wild birds that flitted about Ned's head at the most unwelcome times, begging for his attention.

Gone.

"Shit," said Ned. Suddenly feeling sick, he slumped back against the transom.

"What?" asked Veronica.

"Shit."

"Ned… *what?*"

"What if she comes back?"

"Who?"

"The lapwing. The female. She flew away. What if she comes back? And I'm not there?"

"The female lapwing? From twenty-odd years ago?"

Veronica regarded the piteous Ned. He was pale and beginning to hyperventilate.

"Easy now, Ned," she said, trying to sound patient but not feeling that way, at all. "This little panic thing, it happens, okay? Just a little dose of regret. It's natural, when we pull up stakes. Calm yourself."

And he did, taking a moment to will his breath back to normal.

"There will always be a reason," said Ned.

"A reason for what?" asked Veronica.

"There will always be a reason to leave," said Ned. "I'm tired of all the leaving."

"Just stop it, Ned," Veronica now regarded him with her characteristic impatience. "If you had stayed there, you'd have been served up to the law on a platter."

"So now I'll be on the run for good? I've been there. It sucks."

"Oh come on, Ned, stop with the drama. It's not so bad…" said Veronica.

Ned gave her a look, calling her lie.

"Well, regardless," said Veronica, unwilling to argue the point, "this here is what's called an *academic* discussion. We are motoring south. If you want to die of exposure trying to swim back, be my guest. Otherwise, you're in for the duration. Once we get off the boat, where you go is your business, but I surely hope that by that point the cold night air will have restored enough of your senses for you to realize that there is no future whatsoever left for you on that damn island."

That was the truth, and Ned knew it.

Gone. Ned really was.

"Shit," said Ned.

"Ahoy there!" shouted Tommie Krupa.

Everyone on the trawler turned their gazes across their starboard bow to discover Tommie and General Hoak, at the helm of the stolen vintage landing craft, emerging from the fog and motoring slowly toward them from a distance of fifty yards.

"Tommie?" Ned called out. "General? What are you doing out here?"

"We decided to take the Southern route," Tommie shouted back. "There were some Coast Guard boats sailing across from Wood's Hole, which might've been trouble."

Having explained their own presence there, at that moment, Tommie and the General now took a moment to consider the very same issue regarding Ned.

"But why are you here, Donlin?" Hoak asked. "What are you doing on the getaway boat?"

"Jumping ship, it turns out, General," said Ned. "Can I trouble you?"

"Our pleasure," said Tommie.

Tommie steered the landing craft up alongside the trawler, drawing near enough for Ned to make the trans-craft leap. Before his jump, Ned turned to face Veronica and they regarded each other, each of them deciding how to play out their final moment.

"I say we go with the fond farewell, Ronnie," said Ned.

Veronica considered this.

"Better than anger and resentment," she said.

"Lots."

Veronica looked in Ned's eyes and found no room for persuasion or compromise. She sighed.

"At least tell me you've got a plan."

"Nope," said Ned. "Not yet."

Veronica handed Ned her rucksack.

"Then you may as well take this," she said. "When you get a chance… Speck wanted to keep Paulson's original file. As soon as he gets it, I get the rest of my money, so…"

"Okay," said Ned.

"And that, my dear Ned, should close the book on our little enterprise."

"I guess so," said Ned.

Ned and Veronica stood face to face and regarded each other. They smiled.

"Always a good time, Ronnie," said Ned.

"Back atcha, Ned." Veronica leaned in to Ned and gave him a slightly wet but mostly chaste kiss on the lips. Turning away from her, Ned made the leap to Tommie's landing craft.

"Motor on, Ricky," said Veronica, with the slightest lump in her throat. And the trawler did motor on, continuing its course across the Vineyard Sound. Ned snuck one last look in the trawler's direction, only to find that Veronica did not, herself, glance back.

Ned turned to his new captain, Tommie Krupa.

"Motor on, Tommie," said Ned.

↤   ↤   ↤

Ned returned to his sanctuary by two in the morning, and was surprised when, just a few minutes later, Billie Jensen pulled her constable truck into the sanctuary parking lot.

"What are you doing here, Billie?"

"I don't really know. I wasn't even sure you'd be here. I only know scattered details about what's been going on, Ned, but from what I've put together... it's a mess, right?"

"Pretty big trouble, yeah," said Ned.

"Sorry."

"Yeah, thanks," answered Ned. "I was actually thinking of... I don't know... standing vigil tonight, sort of? Maybe put some wood in the fire pit. Interested?"

"Yes, please," said Billie.

Ned went to the storage shed and retrieved a chaise lounge for Billie to use—Ned's own chaise was still sitting on the lawn—and then gathered some kindling and split dry wood from the firewood shelter under the eaves of his cabin. Within a few short minutes, Ned had built up a nice tall, warm flame in the sanctuary's fire pit. Billie rooted through Ned's pantry and found a bottle of Kentucky whiskey—a Christmas gift from General Hoak. Ned and Billie reclined on their chaises, quietly sipping whiskey as they stared into the fire, its flame casting a circle of orange light around them. Beyond the circle was pure darkness, as dawn would not arrive for three more hours.

"You know," said Ned, "when I first moved in here, there was a stag, big white tail, six points at least, in residence on the grounds. He was used to roaming around freely at night, master of the sanctuary. It was as if we were working in shifts, he in the darkness and me during the day. When I first put in this fire pit, and started using it at night, it was like I was encroaching on his territory. He was absolutely incensed. He would hang out there in the woods just beyond the reach of the firelight, huffing and stomping his hooves and trying to scare me off. I couldn't see him at all, but from the loudness of his sounds he was only a few feet away. It gave me chills. Sometimes I would get up and mimic him, stomping my boots and huffing in his direction, and he would answer, and that could go on for ten minutes or so. If anyone around here had been out wandering and had witnessed this, they'd have had me committed."

They sat in silence for a while, enjoying more of the whiskey and the fire and the night.

"I wonder what became of that buck," Ned thought aloud.

Billie looked at Ned, reading the inescapable worry in his features.

"Music Lagoon is a fine place, Ned, and you have done good work here."

"I will remember it fondly."

"Don't talk that way," said Billie, and she left her own chaise, climbing onto Ned's, curling up against him. "This is where you belong."

Billie Jensen was not the only one of Ned's friends who had felt drawn to the sanctuary in the wee hours of that night. Over the next several hours, a procession of Ned's friends arrived to lend him their support. The night's chaotic events at the Tarpaulin Center had crystallized the impression, for most of Ned's close community, that Ned's days at the sanctuary were almost certainly numbered (that number possibly being just one, or even less). Coming and going from the grounds, alone or in groups, they shared Ned's whiskey and brought along even more, nuking hot toddies in Ned's microwave and soaking up the warmth of the fire as they related memories of Music Lagoon during the Donlin administration.

Nora and Angela and the rest of the Refreshment Committee arrived, naturally, with food, including two dozen warm cinnamon croissants from Espresso Love's first pre-dawn batch, and several gallons of exquisite chowder left over from the Tarpaulin party.

"You came away with leftovers?" said Ned, astonished. "From THAT party? In the middle of all the chaos, with bullets flying and angry Secret Service agents storming the grounds, hungry for retribution, you saved the soup?"

"Well," said Nora, "by that time the gunplay had stopped."

"Color me impressed," said Ned. "And by the way, the chowder is worth it."

"Unfortunately, Ned," said Nora as Ned slurped up his soup, "along with excellent chowder we also bring not-so-good tidings. From the contributors."

"Lemme have it," said Ned.

"The contributors—every one of those who thinks they saw the lapwing—have scheduled a meeting right here at the sanctuary, for five o'clock this afternoon. They'll give you a chance to defend your actions—we were able to convince them you deserved that much respect—and then they will decide amongst themselves what actions to take next. I probably don't need to tell you… they are not much in the mood to cut you any slack. That's just not who they are."

Nora was certainly right about that, thought Ned. The very characteristics that had made the contributors easy marks for the lapwing scam—greed, competitiveness, vanity—made it unlikely that they would show Ned any mercy.

The last visitors to arrive at the sanctuary were Doc Titus and Tommie Krupa. As dawn approached, Ned's other visitors drifted away, leaving him alone with Doc and Tommie. The three men sat together by the fire, drinking and munching and enjoying the unexpectedly harmonious flavors of clam chowder and Kentucky bourbon.

"Well, boys," said Ned, "this is where we formulate a brilliant strategy to keep me out of jail and preserve the blissful lifestyle to which I have become accustomed."

"I've been thinking about that very thing," said Doc.

"Yeah?" said Ned, hopefully.

"But I got nothing," said Doc.

"Sorry, Ned—me either," added Tommie. "Can't just bury this one."

29.

Special Agent in Charge Rhonda Hipps stood at the bluff overlooking Talbott's Cove, retracing with her eyes the most likely course of the crew who robbed the Tarpaulin Center during the Vice President's party. A retired U. S. Navy landing craft had been stolen the previous night from the harbor in the town of Oak Bluffs, which meant it had sailed — if that term could be used for a seventy-ton slab of steel — around the north end of the island and down to Talbott's cove.

The tracks of the digging machine were still evident in the beach's sand, leading from the water's edge to the steep slope of the bluff itself. The measurements of the digger's track width and wheelbase revealed it to be a Bobcat, a small but surprisingly powerful little earth mover.

"Special Agent Hipps?" came a voice from behind her. Hipps turned around to find a local Deputy Sheriff standing behind her, a youngish guy with a world-weary heaviness to his demeanor.

"You're Deputy Keene?"

"Yes, Ma'am."

"Thank you for coming, Deputy. I understand you had an exciting time, last night."

"Which was the last thing I was looking for, I can promise you."

"You drew a weapon on several of my agents," Hipps said, matter-of-factly. "The standoff between you and the agents allowed two burglary suspects to slip away from us."

"I was one officer facing seven heavily armed men who made no effort to identify themselves," Lem said, giving no ground. "Are you suggesting I did something wrong?"

"No. It was an understandable misunderstanding. Start working for the federal government and those situations are pretty much a daily occurrence."

Lem shrugged and followed Hipps as she climbed down to the newly dug opening in the bluff. They entered through the freshly excavated opening and into the dank, ancient tunnel, lighting their path with flashlights as they followed several sets of footprints. After a minute of walking, Hipps discovered an empty wine bottle with its neck cracked off. Hipps placed the wine bottle in a plastic bag and set it off to the side where it would not be trod upon.

"What were you doing at the edge of the Tarpaulin property last night, if I may ask?" said Hipps.

"Your boss was putting on a fairly high profile social event," said Lem. "Seemed the right thing for me to patrol the outlying the area, head off any trouble."

"Hmm. But you weren't particularly *expecting* any trouble, were you Deputy Keene?"

Duh, thought Lem. First Willard Lawler had called him about the missing landing craft, and just minutes later a State Trooper had spotted the open gate at the Motor Pool, where a Bobcat earth mover was suddenly missing, as well. Missing boat, missing Bobcat, and no Ned, Doc, Tommie or Nora at the Cooler. On a Saturday night in the middle of winter?

Trouble. After reaching this very conclusion, the night before, Lem had slipped away from the Sheriff's Office and headed to the only hub activity on the island that night — the Tarpaulin Center — in the hope that he might be able to prevent Ned and the others from whatever perpetrations they had in mind. Lem had not been able to figure out, at the time, what sort of calamity Ned was cooking up, but he'd had the feeling that it would involve the scarily sexy raven-haired woman that Lem had seen with Ned at the Cooler.

"No, I was not expecting any trouble," said Lem.

Hipps regarded the Deputy as he answered. He was not a good liar.

"So, demonstrating an abundance of caution, you abandoned the desk at the Duke's County Sheriff's Office — by the way, where *is* the actual Sheriff? Sheriff Melvin, isn't it?"

"Sheriff Melvin is bonefishing in Boca Raton," answered Lemuel. "I haven't been able to reach him, yet."

"So you abandoned the desk at the Sheriff's office, where I understand you have been on permanent assignment for the last several months, even though you did not anticipate any trouble..."

Lem's face flushed with embarrassment at being reminded — by someone from the outside world, no less — of his disgraced status within the Sheriff's Department.

"I needed some air," replied Lemuel Keene, casually.

"All right, Deputy." said Hipps as they continued through the tunnel, closing in on the main building of the Tarp. "We'd like you to be on the lookout for a Bobcat tractor—"

"A Bobcat was stolen from the Dukes County Motor Pool, near the airport, at about six thirty last night. No prints, no witnesses. No clues."

"Huh. You know what jumps out at me, Deputy? It's the remarkable efficiency of this crew. They seem to know exactly what they want, exactly where to get it, and exactly when and how to do that without attracting unwanted attention. *That* jumps out at me. It says the crew is at least partly local. You see my point?"

"Yes, I see your point," said Lem Keene.

Hipps waited for more, but none was forthcoming.

"In a community of this size," she continued, "you can't have many folks capable of taking on this type of work. You understand that if you have any ideas that might be of use to us, we would expect full cooperation?"

"I understand," said Lem.

Hipps stopped and pointed her flashlight directly into Deputy Keene's face, nearly blinding him. She took a good long look at Lem as he squinted into the bright beam. After a moment, Hipps pointed her light down the tunnel again and continued walking.

"This case has taken on something of a personal nature for us. There's going to be a strong distinction to be made, by the time this is all over, between those who were part of the problem and those who were part of the solution."

Lem contemplated Hipps words as they reached the end of the tunnel. A narrow hole had been pick-axed into a plaster wall at the tunnel's end. One step through this hole brought them into the basement hallway of the Tarpaulin Center's main building.

"I promise you, Special Agent Hipps, the Dukes County Sheriff's Department is eager to be part of the solution."

Special Agent Hipps continued along the hallway — with the Deputy close behind her — retracing the path of the crooks as it led to the make-shift dungeon just off the hall. Hipps' mind was most heavily engaged in a review of her current career prospects. She had botched her job badly, allowing the second most powerful man in the free world to be placed in jeopardy, and she would pay dearly for that mistake. No matter that Roger Paulson was completely safe now, holed up in a hotel in Edgartown that Hipps had commandeered for his use. In defiance of Secret Service protocol, which demanded that Paulson be evacuated from the island immediately, the Vice President had refused to leave the island until Codex VI had been recovered.

Hipps and the Deputy continued through the bowels of the Tarpaulin Center in silence, climbing the hidden, narrow staircase that Hipps' prisoners had taken during their escape, finally emerging—just as the skels had—through the secret door in the Great Room. As they crossed the now-empty room, the Deputy's walkie talkie squawked.

"Lem," came a voice over the talkie, "come in, boy..."

"That you, Sporto?" answered Lem into his talkie.

"Yeah. Heard you people are lookin' for a trawler? We got one."

The Deputy and Agent Hipps both perked up at this news.

"This guy Sporto is with the Coast Guard, out of Wood's Hole," said Lem to Hipps, before answering Sporto on his talkie...

"Tell me all about it, Sporto," said Lem.

"It's not pretty, Lem," Sporto answered. "Whoever was at the helm wasn't from around here, I'll reckon that. Looks like they were trying for New Bedford but didn't know there were rocks outside the point at Penikese Island. They wrecked up pretty good."

"Any survivors?" Lem asked into his talkie.

"That'd be the 'not pretty' part," answered Sporto. "Looks like the boat had full chum buckets, and they spilled into the water during the wreck. The blood must've brought in some predators. When the crew

293

abandoned ship, well... Lem, we've got some spare body parts floating around the boat."

Lem and Agent Hipps shared a look.

← ← ←

Arm in arm, they skate across the frozen surface of Pilot Pond, the very small one that has brown water and no fish and smells like tree sap. Veronica is on one side, Billie on the other, with Ned in the middle. Their skates describe a perfect figure "8" across the ice, every move graceful, the three of them working fluidly as a team. The smiles on their faces are calm and vacant. Now Veronica pulls Ned a bit more tightly, Billie answers with her own pressure. Ned, beginning to panic, struggles and pulls away from them but cannot contain his momentum. He tumbles to the ice and slides on his belly, across the ice, finally coming to a stop at the center of the pond. As the thin surface begins to crack beneath him, Ned looks down through the clear ice, into the water below. A bird, a Caucasian Lapwing, looks up through the ice, its sad eyes looking straight into Ned's. Now the ice cracks for good, splashing Ned down into the murky depths of the frigid pond...

Ned's chaise lounge jolted, suddenly, waking him. He had to squint his eyes against the bright sunlight — what time was it anyway? — to identify the wearer of the boot which had so rudely disturbed his sleep.

"Lem?" said Ned, discovering the Deputy, standing above him, his eyes hidden behind his dark aviator sunglasses. "What time is it anyway?"

"It's two o'clock in the afternoon, Ned," Lem answered with an accusatory tone. "Late night?"

With a disapproving sneer, Lem looked back and forth between the slowly waking figures of Doc Titus and Tommie Krupa.

"Late night for you boys as well?"

"Very late," said Doc.

"Morning, Lem," said Tommie.

Lem noticed a few other details of the scene: the last wisps of smoke coming from the dead fire in the portable fire pit, several empty bottles of whiskey, a large pot of what looked like clam chowder, many dirty coffee mugs and several empty pastry bags.

"I can't believe how badly you've fucked up this time, Ned," said Lem. "Even for you, this is unprecedented."

"What time did you say it was?" Ned asked.

"Two o'clock."

"In the afternoon?"

"The sun is up, Ned."

"It sure as hell is," said Tommie, covering his aching eyes.

"Two o'clock," Ned repeated, with a tone of dread. "All the contributors will be here at five. Chickens coming home to roost."

Ned sat up in his chaise, rubbed his eyes, and addressed the angry Deputy.

"You were saying something about me fucking up, Lem?"

"This is so bad, Ned," said the Deputy. "First off, do you know anyone who was sailing a trawler late last night?"

"Uhhh…"

"Well, I hope it wasn't anyone you were particularly fond of," continued Lem without encouragement. "The boat wrecked off Penikese Island. All hands lost. Well… that's not exactly accurate. They recovered one hand and one leg, with the potential of more parts to come."

"Sharks?" asked Doc.

"No, Doc. Grizzly bears," snapped Lem.

"Well, *excuse me*, Deputy…"

"Geez, Ned," said Tommie, looking at Ned with compassion, "I'm really sorry about Veronica."

But Ned betrayed no emotional reaction to the news of Veronica's alleged demise.

"Whatever," he sighed.

Tommie and Doc were visibly taken aback by Ned's nonchalance, and shot accusatory looks in his direction.

"Pretty chilly of you, Ned," said Tommie.

"Oh, please," said Ned dismissively. "Veronica versus a shark? Not even close. As for the Friendships… that's the circle of life, ya know?"

"So it *was* your friends in the boat," said Lem. "I had figured that much out. Now, there's a Secret Service team scouring the wreckage, but they are not finding what they're looking for."

Ned contemplated this.

"What?" asked Ned, sincerely at a loss. "What are they looking for?"

Lem was puzzled by Ned's response; either Ned had become a better actor/liar than Lem knew him to be, or Ned really did not know about the missing items.

"Just a small question of some nuclear missile launch codes," said Lem, "and a book with bird pictures in it. Weirdly enough, the Secret Service seems more interested in the bird pictures."

Ned froze for a moment, thinking hard.

"Wish I could help you, Lem…" said Ned with a shrug. "But I'm completely at a loss. I don't know what you're talking about."

The deputy studied Ned some more. There were some wheels spinning pretty hard in Ned's brain—Lem could tell that much—but he couldn't figure out what that meant.

"Well, Ned," Lemuel said, "I can tell you this much: these Federal guys are scouring the island, looking for this stuff, and sooner or later they're bound to sniff around here, as well. If you have any kind of custody of those missing items, then you'd better fix that, and soon."

With that, the deputy climbed back into his cruiser and roared off. Ned remained in his chaise, calmly reclined, until he was sure Lem was out of view. At that point, Ned sprang up out of the chaise and raced over to his cabin.

Tommie gave Doc a look.

"Uh oh," said Tommie.

"You got that right," said Doc.

Ned emerged from his cabin a few short moments later, a somewhat dazed look on his face, carrying Veronica's knapsack from the night before. He ambled over to his friends and sad down on the edge of Tommie's chaise.

He reached into the knapsack and pulled out three items; the first was the only item he had expected to find: the stolen environmental impact report on Noman's Island, which he was supposed to hand over to Arnie Speck, ASAP, at Veronica's request. The next item was a simple yet somehow menacing black folder labeled: "EYES ONLY" and "TOP SECRET".

"Oops," said Doc. "If I were to design a folder containing top secret, incredibly dangerous nuclear missile launch codes, I think it would look a lot like that."

"Shit," said Ned.

"No doubt those codes have already been changed," said Tommie.

"Certainly true," Doc agreed. "Recovering that folder and meting out justice to the folks who stole it, however, would still be a high priority and a question of pride for the agents involved."

"Perfect," said Ned. At that point, he removed the final item: it was a large, leather bound portfolio, about one hundred pages of thick, with acid-free, artist-quality paper inside. Tooled into the cover in gold letters was a label: "Roger Jones Paulson – Collected Drawings, Volume VI".

"Fuck me dead," said Ned.

Ned opened the portfolio and, with Tommie and Doc looking on over his shoulder, leafed through a dozen or so enchanting drawings of exotic birds, many rendered in brilliantly colored pastels, others in ink, pencil and even watercolor.

"Wow," said Ned. "I mean, I'd heard about these, even seen a few in magazines and whatnot, but…"

"Pretty striking," said Doc.

"The man is talented," agreed Tommie.

After admiring every bit of artwork in the volume, Ned closed the album and sat in silent contemplation.

"Not what I needed, at this juncture," said Ned.

"You gotta get rid of that stuff, Ned," said Tommie.

"Yeah. I was thinking about your rule, Tommie… about burying problems under six to ten feet of good soil, but—"

"Can't do that, Ned. At least not with the album," said Doc.

"That would be a real crime," agreed Ned. "And I'm not in the mood for more of that, at this time."

Ned checked Doc's watch. Two thirty, already.

"The contributors won't be here for three and a half hours," said Ned. "I'm gonna go take care of these."

30.

Ned drove at exactly the speed limit on his way to Edgartown, seeking to minimize the chance that he would have any sort of run-in with the law; in the rucksack beside him were the same three items that Veronica had carried away from the Tarpaulin raid: the original environmental impact report for Noman's Island, Major Foxbrite's lost missile launch code packet, and Volume VI of the Paulson Codex.

Ned's first intention was to deliver the environmental report to Arnold Speck, as demanded, thereby ending their business relationship for good. As for the other two hot items, Ned figured that a certain Duke's Country Sheriff's Deputy might reap career benefits by "discovering" them and returning them to the Feds. With the escape trawler wrecked, its inhabitants presumed dead, and the loot returned, Ned hoped that the search parties would call off their pursuit and depart the island.

Ned rang the doorbell of the Speck mansion. A wiry, feral-eyed redheaded boy with freckles answered the door with what a pellet gun slung over his right shoulder.

"You would be young Patrick O'Herlihy," said Ned.

"Speck," the boy corrected Ned, "Patrick Speck."

"Of course."

Without asking Ned to identify himself, Patrick O'Herlihy Speck motioned him inside and slammed the front door loudly behind him. The boy led Ned down the home's central hallway toward a bright, airy great room with massive picture windows, providing an enviable view of Edgartown, the marina and the island of Chappaquidick beyond. Just below the house, on the slope of Arnie's property leading down to the water, Ned could see a swimming pool, a pool house, twin guest houses, a private dock, and fifty-seven foot motor yacht.

Arnie Speck stood in the middle of the great room in a thick cashmere cardigan, tall and strong with slicked back silvery hair, double-checking the contents of a matched set of leather luggage. As Ned arrived to meet him, Arnie reached into the pocket of his cardigan and pulled out a portable inhaler, taking a long hit of medication before he addressed Ned.

"You're Donlin?" Speck asked. Without waiting for an answer, Speck snapped his fingers and held out his hand, commanding delivery.

Ned set down Veronica's rucksack — with Patrick O'Herlihy Speck eyeing his every move like a hawk — and pulled out Vice President Paulson's genuine environmental impact report, handing it to Speck.

"Where are you headed?" Ned asked, indicating the heaps of luggage.

"None of your business," said Speck.

Arnie leafed through the document quickly, scanning the contents. What he saw in that brief perusal gave him smug satisfaction.

"As I thought," said Speck, mostly to himself. "Eco-Nazi bullshit. My project on Noman's would have been doomed." Speck packed the report away in one of the leather suitcases. "And a smart move, Donlin, taking the launch codes and Paulson's Codex, as well. That was a

300

master stroke. Now they figure that one or both of those things was the target. They won't even look at another motive for the job."

Ned felt no need to mention that he had lifted the extra items strictly by mistake. What he wanted most was to get out of Speck's house as soon as possible. Just a few short moments in the vile man's company made Ned feel low and slimy by association.

But no—Ned knew that he was being too easy on himself. It wasn't just a question him *feeling* slimy; he actually *was* slimy, by association with Speck and by his own actions. All through the planning of the Tarpaulin heist, Ned had avoided thinking about the consequences of his involvement in the scheme; in trading out the fake environmental report for the real thing, Ned had helped this eco-villain in his campaign to corrupt Noman's Island, a beautiful stretch of land that one day, once it had recovered from its tenure as a bombing target, could be a much-deserved refuge for the Cape and Island wildlife. The fact that Ned had abetted Arnie under coercion didn't really matter, at that point; the results were all that counted.

The results made Ned feel sick. Ned dismissed his worries about his own situation, for the moment, and wondered how it would be possible to trip up Speck without screwing himself in the bargain. No obvious solution presented itself, just yet.

"As for wrecking the escape trawler," continued Speck, "that was part of the plan? To throw the Feds off Veronica's lovely scent?"

"No," said Ned, "Not as far as I know. I suppose that was improvised or accidental."

"And Veronica?"

"I like her chances," Ned shrugged, "Sharks or no sharks. Speaking of which, you and I are done."

"For now," said Speck as he took another hit off his inhaler.

"What do you mean, *for now*?" objected Ned.

"It's a small island, Mr. Donlin," said Speck with a vague, unctuous smirk. "You and I are bound to do business, again..."

Ned seethed inside, but disguised his feelings as best as he could; whatever actions he took against Arnie, they would be more effective as a surprise attack. What to do?

"I'll show myself out," said Ned, grabbing the rucksack and heading back out through the main hallway.

"Nice of you to drop by," Arnie called after him.

Ned had almost made it to the front door when a voice sounded from a side hallway.

"Are you Veronica's friend?"

Ned turned to discover young Ripley Speck standing outside the door of his bedroom, beckoning him. Ned ambled down to hallway to meet the kid.

"I *am* Veronica's friend, in fact. You must be Ripley. Veronica told me about you."

"What's your name?"

"I'm Ned."

"Do you think Veronica is okay, Ned?"

"I guess someone told you about Veronica's boat..." said Ned.

"No one tells me anything," said Ripley, "but I'm a good listener."

"A listener is a good thing to be," said Ned. "And I'm sure Veronica is just fine. You shouldn't worry about her."

"Okay."

"Ripley, I saw your father was packed for a trip. Where are you all headed?"

"Off-island somewhere, but I'm not going," Ripley answered with a look of consternation. "I have school. It's just Poppa and my new brother Patrick taking the plane. Poppa says Patrick is going to learn all about the family business."

"Doesn't Patrick have to go to school?"

"Poppa says Patrick already went to school, on the streets of South Boston. I guess he doesn't have to go anymore."

Ned wasn't sure how to respond to this. He peered into Ripley's room and noticed distinct spaces where various items seemed to have been removed: sets of books had volumes missing, discolored spots remained on the wall where posters or pictures had been taken down, and stripped wires hung loose from the computing and entertainment center, where components had been roughly extracted.

"Ripley, have you been robbed?"

A dark little cloud descended upon Ripley, a stark contrast from his naturally cheery disposition.

"I know all about sharing," said Ripley, "but you're supposed to ask first if you want to share something."

"That's right," Ned agreed, "you're supposed to ask."

"My new brother, Patrick O'Herlihy, was an unfortunate, so he didn't have many things of his own. I have too many toys and books anyway, and I want to share them, but he still should ask. Each day more things are gone. They're all in his room, now."

"That sucks, Ripley," said Ned. "You should mention this to your father."

"I did tell him," said Ripley with the perplexed look again. "But Poppa said if I want my things I need to take them back for myself. And he gave me a long talk

303

about a bunch of stuff I didn't really understand. Ned, what does 'natural selection' mean?"

"Uh…"

"I'd look it up on the Wiki but I don't have a computer anymore."

"Natural selection means 'survival of the fittest', more or less," said Ned.

"Dog eat dog?" asked Ripley.

"Exactly."

"Oh," said Ripley, remaining silent for a moment as he considered the primal law of nature and its potential impact upon his home life.

At this point, Ned became aware of a presence, lurking somewhere nearby. Reflected in the stand-up mirror in Ripley's room, Ned caught the shadowy image of Patrick O'Herlihy, out in the hallway, mostly concealed by a corner wall.

Patrick was listening. And Ned was thinking.

"Ripley, I almost forgot…"

"What?"

"Veronica asked me to give you something. It's a special present, from her to you. It's something really really cool and it's just for you and not for sharing with anyone, especially Patrick."

The boy's face lit up like sunrise.

"Yay!" whooped Ripley.

Deputy Lemuel Keene parked his cruiser at the furthest edge of the Martha's Vineyard Airport tarmac, surveying the terrain as he arrived. The first thing he noticed was the high-pitched whine of a jet engine. He figured the sound might be coming from Air Force Two, which was constantly undergoing maintenance by its full time crew, but a quick glance toward the Vice President's plane, parked three hundred yards away beyond the West end of the terminal, revealed it to be sitting quietly, engines shut down, a detail of two Secret Service agents patrolling nearby. Lem's eyes followed the jet engine sounds to a private jet now taxiing to the far end of the runway, just moments away from departure.

Lem switched his radio over to the airport tower's frequency and listened to the chatter. It was Lydia Stokes' voice that sounded over the channel, directing the afternoon's leisurely air traffic. A Cape Air flight was approaching from Logan Airport, in Boston, just three or four minutes from touching down, and the pilot of the private jet was calling in for clearance to take off. The tower instructed the private jet to wait for the Cape Air flight to touch down.

There was a break in Lydia's chatter, and Lem chimed in.

"Hey, Lydia…"

"Is that your cruiser, Lem, out on the tarmac?" Lydia answered over the radio.

"Yep. Anything unusual going on?"

"No, except for you being here. What's up?"

"I don't know yet," said Lem. "I'll keep you posted."

"Uh… okay," answered Lydia, puzzled. "Roger that."

Lem set out his radio just as Ned Donlin arrived in his pick-up truck, on the service road outside the airport grounds, separated from Lem by a cyclone fence but still just a few feet away.

Both men rolled down their windows.

"Hey Lem," said Ned.

"Uh huh," answered Lem, suspicious — as ever — of Ned, but interested to know why Ned had called and asked him to meet up at this particular spot.

Ned took a moment to survey the activities of the airport.

"Whose jet is that, about to take off?" Ned asked, innocently.

Lem gave Ned a look, but picked up his radio.

"Tower," Lem said into the radio, "Who's private jet is that, taxiing to take off?"

"That's Arnie Speck," Lydia answered.

"Has his jet been searched?" Ned asked Lem.

Lem gave Ned another look.

"Has Speck's jet been searched?" Ned asked again, ignoring Lem's admonishing glare. Lem sighed, and relented.

"Lydia, has Speck's plane been searched?" Lem asked into his radio.

"There's a team of Feds," answered Lydia, "though what particular brand of Fed I cannot say, down by check-in, going over everything and everyone leaving the island. I think they gave Speck's jet the once-over."

"A 'once-over'?" Ned reacted. "Hmm. I don't know much about airport security, Lem, but a 'once-over' doesn't sound very thorough, to me…"

"Ned…"

"Lem," said Ned, "I know I'm a few weeks late, but… Merry Christmas."

←   ←   ←

Inside Arnold Speck's jet, Patrick O'Herlihy Speck looked out the porthole window beside his seat and saw the flashing lights of the Sheriff's cruiser, charging at high speed across the runway median, headed straight for the jet. Patrick silently considered the implications of this development. Patrick was not given to panic or even fear, but...

"Dad?" Patrick said to Arnie, who was reclining across the aisle in a plush leather flight chair, chuckling to himself as he gloated over the text of the authentic Noman's Island environmental impact report.

"Nesting plovers, my ass," snickered Arnie as he read.

"Dad," Patrick said again, more loudly this time.

Arnie looked up from his work, a warm smile on his face as he regarded his new son. Arnie had not yet noticed Deputy Keene's flashing cherry top outside the jet, growing closer to the plane every moment.

"It's so nice to hear you call me that, Patrick," said Arnie. "*Dad*. It makes me very happy. You're like the son I never had."

"That's great, Dad, but..."

Patrick pointed out the window of the jet, and Arnie noticed the approaching cruiser for the first time, growing nearer by the second. Arnie quickly and calmly calculated what the problem might be.

"We're covered," Arnie said to Patrick. He had decided to immediately start including Patrick in his business workings. How better for the kid to learn? "All angles of the heist have been tied up, from our end. The Feds haven't caught any of our associates, and their investigations so far have gone nowhere. I'm very confident about all this; our sources inside the Federal agencies are first-rate."

"What about that?" Patrick asked, pointing to the stolen environmental impact report sitting before Arnie.

"Excellent thinking, son," said Arnie, beaming, "but there are two very hot contraband items on the island, right now, and this is not one of them. Plus... we commissioned our own report, so we're covered. We can always say this is the one we paid for—the cops won't know the difference. You see?"

But Arnie couldn't help noticing that his reassurances had not really landed home with Patrick.

"Is there a problem, son?" Arnie asked.

"Uh… no."

"I'm your father," Arnie assured the boy, sensing that Patrick was holding something back. "You can tell me anything."

"Well… Dad, the two missing things… you were talking about them with that Donlin guy?"

"Yes…" Arnie experienced a phantom tic of his eyebrow, a warning that his medication was starting to wear off. He took a quick hit off his inhaler and confronted Patrick again.

"What is it you want to say, Patrick?"

Without another word, Patrick reached into his small computer bag and pulled out the Paulson Codex, Volume VI.

Arnie's eyes grew huge with fear and rage.

"The HELL you did!" shouted Arnie.

The door to the pilot's cabin opened.

"Sir?" the pilot said to Speck, "the tower has asked us to stand down, and there's a Sheriff's cruiser off our starboard wing…"

"Arnold Speck!" came Deputy Lemuel Keene's voice, blasted over the PA speakers on his cruiser. "Shut down your engines and open your aircraft for inspection!"

"Shit! SHIT!" yowled Arnie. He jumped to his feet and scurried around the plane, desperate for some miraculous solution to present itself. None was forthcoming.

"Mr. Speck?" said the pilot. "What do you want us to do?"

Speck fumbled through his pockets until he found his inhaler. He took a deep haul of the drug, but halfway through his breath the inhaler went empty. Arnie howled in frustration.

"That worthless bastard Fyodor!" He hurled the inhaler away and then, in that despairing moment of pique, an idea struck Arnie which, in retrospect, he would question, over and over again, for the rest of his life.

"Open the door! Right now!" Arnie yelled to the Pilot.

"But Sir, the engines are still..."

"OPEN THE FUCKING DOOR!!!"

The Pilot turned to his control panel and complied with the order. With a gentle humming sound, the pressure door of the jet's main cabin slowly opened outward, and the automatic staircase folded out and down. The flashing red and blue lights of the Deputy's cruiser now poured into the cabin through the opening.

Arnie grabbed the Codex from Patrick.

"Anything *else*...?" he growled at the boy.

With a defiant, unrepentant look, Patrick reached back into his bag and pulled out the missile launch code packet.

"SON OF A..." Arnie, enraged at the sight of the newest contraband, snatched the codes from Patrick and stepped to the open door of his jet. With one heave, Arnie launched the codes and the Codex out the door. As soon as they hit the air, the force of wind created by the still-running jet engines ripped the two items apart, scattering their pages into the air.

"Now GO!!!" Arnie yelled at his pilot.

31.

From his parking spot on the perimeter of the airport property, Ned watched events unfold on the runway with deep satisfaction. By flinging Volume VI of the Peterson Codex out the window of their private jet—a well-conceived diversionary tactic—Arnie Speck and his would-be scion, Patrick O'Herlihy, bought themselves an opportunity for escape, and had made good. The Gulfstream maneuvered around Lem's cruiser and sped down the airport runway, successfully taking off while barely avoiding a collision with the descending Cape Air prop plane.

The circumstances of their flight to freedom, however, were such that they—well, Arnie himself, at least—would never be able to return to the United States without going to jail for a very, very long time. Noman's Island was safe, now, from Speck's aspirations, and the Feds would not need to look further for any Tarpaulin heist suspects. With the Codex and the launch codes back in the hands of their rightful guardians, the search teams would be leaving the island soon. Ned was concerned for the well-being of the Codex—the individual leaves of the album had scattered about the runway in every direction—but a pack of Federal agents had soon emerged from the small airport terminal and mobbed the runway, corralling the drawings before they would be too damaged.

The rescue of Noman's Island from Arnie's scheme was particularly satisfying for Ned; soon, his own sanctuary enterprise would sadly come to an end, but the bright future of Noman's would help balance that loss. Ned could live with that—from behind bars, unfortunately—but fair enough. He checked his watch: three o'clock. Two hours to kill before Ned returned to Music Lagoon to face... well, the music.

Ned sighed deeply. He was exhausted, his tank completely drained by the events of the past week. He slumped down in the seat of his truck and closed his eyes, not necessarily wanting to sleep at that moment but willing for sleep to take him if it was so inclined. He immediately felt himself plunging into the abyss of REM and there, in the first flashed frame of a dream, saw something that immediately jolted him back awake...

It was the ice sculpture from the previous night's party at the Tarp: a beautifully crafted representation, in crystal-clear ice, of a Caucasian Lapwing. Ned had caught sight of it during his chaotic escape from the Center. It had transfixed him at the time, inconveniently and much to the annoyance of Veronica Lodge.

"NED! What the hell are you doing!?!?" Veronica had yelled, as Ned had screeched to a halt in the Tarpaulin great room, his eyes focused on the giant lapwing.

"I have no idea," Ned had replied, and he had immediately relented to her appeal, following her as they continued their escape from the Tarp. The image of the ice sculpture had never really stopped haunting Ned, however, since that odd encounter.

Why? Ned wondered. What was it about the lapwing on ice that made the image so compelling? Ned thought hard, now, sensing a distant memory tickling against his conscious mind but then shyly retreating back into the darkness.

"Huh," said Ned to himself. "Weird."

Ned started up his truck and drove for a whole fifty feet before it finally hit him. He slammed on the brakes, skidding his truck to a dead stop.

"Holy shit," Ned said aloud, jolted by the stunning realization.

Ned checked his watch again; it was three ten. An hour and fifty minutes until his show-down at the sanctuary…

✦ ✦ ✦

Ned left his truck on the shoulder of Lambert's Cove Road and walked the hundred yards through the woods to Pilot Pond, a spot he had not visited in twenty years. The quiet morning air was still unseasonably warm, though the radio news had claimed that real winter was on its way back to the Cape and Islands. As he approached the shore of the pond, he could see that the water was as brackish and lifeless as it ever was. The pond itself seemed smaller, as childhood landmarks often do to adult eyes, but Ned suspected that it actually *was* shrinking, like many of the still water ponds on the island, slowly turning from pond to marsh and ultimately to dry land as layer upon layer of fallen autumn leaves brought the bottom of the pond closer and closer to the surface.

Ned was relieved to see the old ice house still standing and intact on the opposite shore of the pond; he knew Miss Daly was still churning out ice sculptures, but he wasn't sure she was still using the ice house as her studio. Ned noticed that the building had been well maintained over the decades and, as he drew nearer, saw a thin slice of orange light peering out from under the doorway. The hum of an electric chainsaw could be heard from behind the door. Ned tried the doorknob but it was locked, and then knocked hard several times, but no one answered and the sound of the chainsaw continued uninterrupted. Finally Ned picked up a rock and pounded on the door until the chainsaw went silent.

"Go away," came a voice as Ned knocked once on the door.

"Miss Daly? It's — "

"I don't entertain visitors at my studio," came the voice, again, from inside the ice house. "Everybody knows that."

"I forgot," answered Ned.

The door squeaked open, and a thin, peevish-looking woman of fifty-five appeared in the doorway with an electric chainsaw in her hands, her safety goggles propped up on her forehead.

"Do I know you?" Miss Daly asked Ned. "Were you one of my students?"

"No, ma'am," Ned answered, "I'm Ned Donlin."

"I've heard your name around the island. You run Music Lagoon, is that right?"

"Yes, ma'am. But also..."

"Yes, when I heard your name for the first time, a few years back, I wondered if you were the same little Ned — the summer boy — who used to play the little scamp around here. From the embarrassed look on your face, right now, I can see that you are."

"It was mostly just little pranks... wasn't it?"

"You'd better come in, Ned," said Miss Daly opening the ice house door all the way and ushering Ned in.

She shut the door behind him. There was only one room, not very wide but reaching back a good twenty or twenty five feet to where the rear of the building was set inside the hill. In that dark, rear area, a stock of ice blocks filled the space, with a heavy coating of frost on the walls and ceiling, like in a kitchen freezer that hasn't been cleaned in a long time. The area in front of the ice house was Miss Daly's work area. A big block of ice sat on a platform three feet off the ground. The artist's work had just begun; it was too early to see what its final representation would be.

"May I ask what this sculpture will be?" Ned asked.

"It's going to be a bouquet of camellias. Polly Hill's birthday is coming up in a few weeks, and they're doing a little memorial gathering at the arboretum. She loved camellias, so I'm work-shopping a few ideas before the day arrives."

Polly Hill was the famous horticulturist who had worked for decades in near obscurity, doing ground-breaking work at her West Tisbury arboretum.

"Cool," said Ned.

"You once stole one of my ice blocks," said Miss Daly. "You used it to sled down that little slope on Black Brook Road, in the middle of August. Do you remember that?"

"You bet," Ned smiled. "It was great. So fast and smooth and… I remember it was so nice, in the middle of the hot, humid summer, to come in here and sit in the cool air. I am sorry about the stealing, though."

"No, you're not," Miss Daly rather sternly, but then she shrugged. "It's all right. You were only a kid, after all, and it was only ice, after all."

"But the things you make, they're not just ice. They're works of art."

Miss Daly paused, thinking back.

"Do you remember any of my work from back then? I'm afraid I wasn't very good. I was just starting out. Bulky things, mostly. Santa Claus. A map of the island. A striped bass, perhaps, leaping out of the ocean. I believe I've improved quite a bit."

"You have. I saw your lapwing at the Tarpaulin party. It was…*magnetic*. I couldn't take my eyes off it."

"Thank you," said Miss Daly, obviously pleased. "I worked hard on that one."

"It paid off."

"Tell me, Ned—did you see it melt?"

"Your lapwing?" Ned wondered whether or not to share the sculpture's violent end with her—it had been blown apart by the errant autoblasts from Major Foxbrite's machine gun. "No," said Ned, choosing discretion. "I didn't see it melt."

"Too bad. That's my favorite part, the melting. Things are more precious, aren't they, when their time is measured?"

"And how," agreed Ned.

Miss Daly seemed caught in a reverie for a brief moment, but rose out of it and watched Ned closely for a moment.

"Why are you here, Ned? I'm assuming you don't have an ice sculpture emergency? A naked punch bowl sitting somewhere at a brunch buffet? Or did you just feel like going sledding?"

"Well," Ned ventured hesitantly, "I guess I'm wondering about the ice in this place."

"In what context?" Miss Daly asked, confused by the strange inquiry.

"I mean, I know this ice house is old," said Ned, "but it's refrigerated, isn't it?"

"Oh, yes. In the old days, these walls were insulated—with seaweed and hay, of all things. That was long before refrigerators changed *everything*. Back then, great slabs of ice were harvested in the winter, from the ponds nearby. The blocks could stay frozen for a year or even more. For my purposes, though, the heat from my machinery would melt the blocks too quickly. I need to keep my ice heavy and hard, all year round. I run power down from my house for a refrigeration unit in the back of the cave. It's done the trick for over twenty years now."

Ned felt a sudden tightening in his chest, an intense feeling of anticipation.

"Miss Daly?"

"Yes, Ned?"

"I need a private moment."

"I don't know what you mean, dear."

"Here, in the ice house. I need a private moment in here."

↜   ↜   ↜

The parking lot was completely full when Ned finally pulled into the Music Lagoon Wildlife Sanctuary. He was forced to park on the shoulder of the central clearing, a hundred feet away from where the Sanctuary buildings stood and a crowd of at least thirty visitors waited for him. Before exiting his truck, Ned checked out the crowd from the relative safety of his driver's seat; these afternoon visitors were the special contributors to Music Lagoon, whom Ned had scammed for many thousands of dollars. By the looks on their faces, their collective mood seemed akin to that of a lynch mob.

The two passengers in Ned's truck scrutinized the crowd also.

"Those are friends of yours, Mr. Donlin?" Melvin Tullidge asked dubiously from the passenger seat.

"They don't look very friendly, as birdwatchers go," added David Sanger, who sat between them, a hefty, professional-looking camera bag on his lap.

316

"It's a difficult time for them," said Ned.

"Yes, well," Tullidge sounded impatient, "we wouldn't know anything about that, since you haven't yet explained—"

"Please bear with me, gentlemen," said Ned.

He climbed out of his truck and the two men got out as well, following him as he approached the crowd at the center of the clearing. As he walked, Ned's personal flock of birds descended upon him, perching on his head and shoulders as usual.

"It's looking bad," the cardinal whispered into Ned's ear.

"You've really done it this time, Ned," said a robin. "You're going down hard."

"Run away, Ned," said the tufted titmouse. "Run away now."

But the birds dispersed, shyly, as Ned neared the restless assembly of contributors. The group also included the ranks of the Music Lagoon Refreshment Committee and General Robert C. Hoak, U.S. Army, Retired, plus Doc and Tommie, reclined in chaise lounges off to the side of the clearing, where they could spectate at an objective arm's length. Deputy Lemuel Keene was no longer present.

"Good afternoon, folks," Ned nodded to the crowd.

"Good afternoon, Ned," said all of the Refreshment Committee in their peppiest voices, hoping to influence the angry contributors with their cheerfulness. This tactic did not appear to work—most of the group continued to glower angrily at Ned.

"You have some explaining to do, Donlin..." Leonard Smallwood spoke out first.

Ned calmly raised a "give me just a moment" index finger to Smallwood and the others, then motioned

317

for Nora to join him in a brief side-conference. She stepped forward so the two of them could speak privately and noticed, for the first time, that Ned was carrying with him a small cardboard box.

"Don't open it here," Ned in a whisper as he passed Nora the box. "I need you to go into my kitchen and nuke it in my microwave. I don't know for how long. Use your best judgment."

Nora was clueless but nodded her head in agreement and scurried off toward the cabin. Ned turned his attention back to the angry and anxious assembly.

"I want to introduce you all to these gentlemen," he said, gesturing toward the two men who had arrived with him. "This here to my left is Melvin Tullidge..."

Among the assembled group, more than one eyebrow was raised.

"The same Melvin Tullidge," asked Mrs. Dr. Devin Hedge, "who writes for the Smithsonian Magazine?"

"Indeed," said Mr. Tullidge with a regal bow.

A hum of excitement and curiosity rose up from the group. Ned received more than a few nervous glances from the Refreshment Committee, wondering what dangerous game he was playing now.

"This could get interesting," Tommie whispered to Doc.

"Ned has a talent for theater," agreed Doc. "Any idea what's he's about to say next?"

"No," said Tommie.

"Exactly," said Doc. "Me either. But you can't wait to hear, can you?"

"I really can't," said Tommie.

"Also here with us," Ned continued, "is Mr. Tullidge's frequent collaborator, the renowned nature photographer, Mr. David Sanger. Mr. Tullidge and Mr. Sanger are on-island to cover the lapwing story, and I thought it was important for them, at this sad juncture, to meet you all."

The introduction of the two men had a profound effect upon the contributors, and for good reason; Tullidge and Sanger were the most renowned journalist/photographer team in the birding sphere, a veritable Lewis and Clark of ornithological trail blazing. Their expeditions—sponsored by the Smithsonian Institute, among many other deep pockets—came close to challenging the tax-funded travels of Vice President Roger Paulson.

"Mr. Sanger," Audrey Winkle spoke up, "didn't you shoot those photographs of the Sandhill Cranes migrating in the blizzard? Those were beautiful!"

"Thank you very much," the burly Sanger answered softly, blushing.

"Gentlemen," said Ned, addressing Tullidge and Sanger, "these folks before you now are the most generous and loyal contributors that the Music Lagoon Wildlife Sanctuary has ever known. They are unsung heroes of the birding movement. For the past several years, they've helped us keep a secret from the outside world—a very significant secret—and they've done so at tremendous personal expense."

"A secret?" said Tullidge.

"A big secret. I'm referring to the return of the Caucasian Lapwing," Ned said.

There was absolute quiet in the clearing as everyone present weighed Ned's pronouncement. The contributors cast wary glances amongst themselves, unsure what Ned was up to, now, or what their reactions should be. For the moment, they chose to remain silent.

"Donlin," cautioned Mr. Tullidge, "the alleged lapwing sighting on Martha's Vineyard has been, by now, debunked. A prank of some kind, perhaps... who's to know? But for several days now, hundreds of experienced birders have been scouring every inch of this island and have not made a single verifiable sighting of the bird. That is because — in case you hadn't heard — the Caucasian Lapwing is extinct."

"As for the alleged sighting that was posted as a Rare Bird Alert," responded Ned, confidently, "I have to agree with you, Mr. Tullidge — it was probably some sort of hoax. Certainly, no one associated with our sanctuary posted that photo."

"Then what are we talking about here?" asked Sanger.

"As you may know," Ned continued, "Music Lagoon is the ancestral home of Vanellus Caucasus, but the last pair of the species disappeared suddenly — and so sadly — over two decades ago. Then, just shy of two years ago, these folks were all here for a spring migration bird walk, scoping out the South Ravine, when what did they discover but a single, lonely, but very much alive male Caucasian Lapwing, miraculously resurrected."

"Wow," Tommie whispered to Doc.

"Yeah, but hold on. Is it just me," observed Doc, "or is Ned right now digging himself an even deeper hole?"

At this juncture, the mystified looks on the faces of the dozen contributors took on a new urgency — even panic — as they wondered what sort of game Ned was playing and to what degree they were all complicit. Leonard Smallwood, who had struggled to contain his rage thus far, was becoming very agitated.

"What the hell is this…" he hissed to his fellow contributors.

"Shut up, Smallwood," snarled Mrs. Hedge. "At least until we know what he's up to."

"These folks," continued Ned, indicating the contributors again with a broad sweep of his hand. "These folks — all together, as a group — were the first to spot and correctly identify the new lapwing. For the record, we have that sighting thoroughly documented. Now, these good people could have rushed off and let the world know about the sighting. Who would have blamed them? The discovery was a momentous achievement. Instead — and this will tell you what kind of people these are — they came to me, as a group, and announced that they had other ideas. You see, Mr. Tullidge, given the number of fanatic birders around these days, a rare bird is a very vulnerable target. Once news of the lapwing's return spread, Music Lagoon would have been inundated by birders and scientists from all over the world, which would have placed incredible stress on the bird."

"Theoretically true..." agreed Tullidge, certainly not yet convinced by Ned's story, but eager to hear more.

"Definitely true," asserted Ned. "For that very reason, these good people — these *heroes* — were determined to keep the sighting a secret. Their greatest hope was that the new bird was the first of a secret lapwing colony, thriving in a remote location, somewhere, which was feeling the itch to return to their ancestral grounds. These folks wanted to make sure the birds had a quiet and welcoming place waiting for them here at Music Lagoon. Everyone here made generous contributions of time and money that allowed the sanctuary to close off part of its land — the South Ravine — in order to keep it a calm and pristine home base for the lone lapwing. For the past two years, that's been the situation here."

Ned paused and gave Tullidge a chance to digest the story. The stunned contributors watched him, and Ned, closely, still looking confused and suspicious, but also at least partially seduced by Ned's narrative.

321

"You said today was a sad day…" Sanger the photographer finally said.

"A very sad day, yes," said Ned. "Two years we have all waited, hoping and praying for other lapwings to arrive. Alas, they have not. We were graced with just the one bird, a magical, profound vestige of a lost tribe. And now… just this morning, he breathed his last…"

Ned motioned to Nora, who had re-emerged from his cabin a few moments earlier. She herself wore a look of stunned reverence as she stepped forward and handed Ned a folded towel.

In full view of Tullidge, Sanger, Doc, Tommie, the Refreshment Committee and all the special Music Lagoon contributors, Ned gently unfolded the towel to reveal the lifeless carcass of one actual, legitimate, verifiable Caucasian Lapwing.

"I found him just this morning, lying quiet and motionless at the base of a holly tree," Ned said in a reverential tone.

Silence now ruled the Music Lagoon sanctuary as the dumbfounded crowd all leaned in for a closer look at the deceased bird. Even Doc and Tommie, theretofore content to play the role of heckling peanut gallery in Ned's drama, rose from their chaise lounges and stepped in close.

"*Quietus est*," murmured Tullidge, as he gazed upon the lapwing's abandoned mortal coil.

Poof! Sanger's camera flash went off, preserving for posterity an image of the world's last Caucasian Lapwing, with all of Music Lagoon's special contributors—looks of wonderment plastered on their faces—visible in the frame. It was an historic photo which, within weeks, would be featured on the cover of the Smithsonian magazine, guaranteeing each of them the everlasting admiration of birdwatchers all over the world.

Tullidge reached out and ever-so-gently stroked the bird's silky plumage with the back of his hand.

"My God," Tullidge gasped, "he's still warm."

32.

Special Agent Rhonda Hipps rapped gently on the Vice President's door, and entered. Paulson sat at the desk in the suite's sitting room, staring with a bereft look at the blank first page of a thick leather album. In his hand was a freshly sharpened pastel pencil, in the color of ochre.

"It's no use, Hipps," said Paulson. "I guess it's just too early to start drawing again. I'm still grieving."

"Lost your muse, Sir?"

Paulson looked at Hipps and gave her a shy smile.

"I wouldn't say that, necessarily…" he said.

"Well, Sir, I think I can brighten your day."

"You mean…?" Paulson perked up.

Hipps stepped forward to Paulson's bed and held out Volume VI of the storied Paulson Codex, tattered but intact. Paulson was speechless with joy. His hands caressed the leather of the album, and he began leafing through its pages, excitedly checking to make sure that every drawing and journal notation was in its rightful place.

"It's battered, Sir," said Hipps, "but unbowed."

"Thank you, Hipps, thank you so so much…"

"Actually, Sir, a local lawman, Deputy Lemuel Keene, recovered the album, single-handedly. I'll spare you the details for now."

"A Sheriff's Deputy? How can we show him our appreciation?"

"A word to his boss, Sir, has sufficed. Plus a signed and framed Vice Presidential commendation."

"Very good. And the perpetrators — they've been brought to justice?"

"Justice of a sort," said Hipps. "They've been lost at sea, presumably, though we may never know for sure. The only person to actually set eyes on them was Major Foxbrite, but his head was pretty well cracked when my team tackled him. I don't think his recollections will be of much use."

"Whatever," sighed Paulson. "As long as it's all over."

"It's over, Sir," Hipps reassured him.

Paulson cradled the volume to his chest and closed his eyes, a look of bliss upon his face as he relished the embrace.

"It's just a book, Hipps — I know that. But…"

"I understand, Sir."

"We can leave now, yes? I feel like I've been away from home for a year…"

"I'm very sorry, Mr. Vice President…" said Special Agent Rhonda Hipps. Paulson's heart sank just a little.

"Not home?"

"The Comoros, Sir. The President of the archipelago is dedicating a suspension bridge or some such. The President has suggested that you might attend the ceremony."

"Suggested."

"Indeed, Sir. As a visible way of bringing positive attention to the fruits of the Comoros' burgeoning democratic movement."

Paulson sighed. He had so been looking forward to sleeping in his own bed, for a change. Instead, he was off again to some god forsaken foreign destination, serving at the whim of an idiot Commander in Chief who had absolutely no regard for —

"Who knows, Sir?" Hipps interrupted Paulson's train of thought. "You might bump into a Baganga-Anjouan Scops Owl."

"What's that, Hipps?"

"The Batanga-Anjouan Scops Owl. *Otus capnodes*. Tiny little thing. Critically endangered. Lives right there in the Comoros. Hardly anyone has seen it. You don't have that one on your Life List, do you, Sir?"

Paulson regarded Hipps with a beaming smile of gratitude.

"You light up my life, Angel Hipps," he said.

"Sir?"

But the Vice President did not shy away, this time. Paulson looked directly into Hipps' eyes, and Hipps looked back.

"You heard me, Rhonda," he said.

It was dark when Ned pulled into the parking lot. As he stepped out of his truck, he felt a welcome chill in the air; real winter had returned to the island. Ned scanned the lot, and was cheered to see so many of his friends' cars parked there. It would be warm inside The Cooler.

"So," said Tommie, once Ned had taken his seat and had a cold beer delivered by Gigi Malveaux, "Arnie is gone."

"As gone as gone gets," said Ned. "With the diabolical Patrick O'Herlihy Speck in tow."

"And the contributors?"

Ned looked to Nora for confirmation.

"Also gone, *en masse*," said Nora. "Thank god."

"And yet," said Tommie, "I cannot help but notice that you, Ned Donlin, against all goddam odds, are still here."

Ned could only shrug, barely able to believe it himself.

"A miracle resurrection," he said.

"And all because you pulled a *bone fide* Caucasian Lapwing out of your ass," observed Angie Ventura.

Ned shrugged, again, as if the feat had been no big deal.

But it was a big deal, after all. Twenty three years earlier, after his slaughter of the male lapwing, a panicked young Ned had decided to put the dead bird's carcass on ice, literally. In some dark reach of his theretofore immature mind, perhaps, there was hope that the terrible deed could somehow be reversed through a miracle of comic book science. In any case, he had known of only two freezers that he could access: his grandparents' basement freezer (unthinkable) and Miss Daly's ice house/ sculpting studio on Pilot Pond (usually locked but easy to break into). Because of the horror and shame that had plagued him since that fateful day, Ned had subconsciously shoved that macabre element of the lapwing story back into the furthest reaches of his memory. For him to recall that detail at the last desperate moment, and found the bird's carcass still there—in the depths of the ice house, those many years later—had been a stroke of good fortune almost beyond imagining.

"Seems like mostly good tidings, all around," said Nora, "though I'm wondering what will become of the surprisingly sweet and delightful little Speck boy…"

"Ripley," said Ned. "I checked with Lem on my way over. The kid's maternal grandparents are headed here to pick him up."

"He seems like a resilient little fella," said Tommie. "In any case, he's better off without Arnie."

Doc Titus arrived and took his seat with the others.

"Where've you been, Doc?" asked Nora.

"I drove the General home. We picked up fifty pounds of bird seed on the way and I helped fill all his feeders. Then, of course, I had to leave pretty quick."

"You got the creeps over at his house, right?" asked Angie.

"Not the creeps so much as the heebie-jeebies," said Doc.

"Like you were being watched…"

"Yes," said Doc.

"I was worried the General might be wiped out after last night," said Ned.

"On the contrary," said Doc. "He seems ten years younger, thanks to the beach landing."

"That's nice," said Nora.

"See, a guy like that needs challenge or he shrivels up," Tommie said. "That's how he burns off his extra carbon."

"Oy, Tommie," said Ned, "please don't start with the carbon again."

"I'm just saying, Ned," answered Tommie. "You're as cooped up tonight as you were a week ago. We still need to do a road trip."

Sometime later, after the group had harmoniously quaffed their way through three rounds of cold tap beer, Pres Gibbons entered the bar; he was a rare visitor to The Cooler but a familiar face nonetheless. Tall, lanky and a bit shy, Pres was a painter who specialized in watercolor landscapes of the island.

Pres bashfully approached Ned's table, looking quite sallow and drawn, as if he had not slept in some time.

"Hi, guys," said Pres softly.

"Pres," Ned answered.

"I wondered if I might get your advice on a certain matter," said Pres, looming over the table.

Ned and the others exchanged wary looks.

"Normally," said Ned, "we'd be happy to help in any way, but the last few days have been kind of harrowing..."

"I've got new neighbors," began Pres, ignoring Ned's hint.

"You still up on Quansoo Road?" asked Tommie.

"Yeah," said Pres. "I've got new neighbors to the southwest, a large house with two outbuildings. I have never seen them, not once, even just coming or going from the property. Not once in two months."

"Then how do you know they're there?" asked Doc.

"The dog," answered Pres with a sudden heaviness.

"The dog?" asked Tommie.

"I think it's a dog, anyway. Something big, whatever it is. It growls, or roars or whatever, absolutely all night long. It sounds vicious, and I haven't slept in a week. I've left notes at their gate, asking politely for them to control their animal, but the growling continues."

"Are the notes still at the gate?" asked Nora.

"No, the notes disappear."

"And still with the yowling?" Doc asked.

"Still with the yowling," answered Pres, forlorn. "The sounds move around a lot, now, like maybe it's stalking the grounds. It's really freaking me out. I don't think I can take much more..."

"The Sheriff's office takes care of animal control issues all the time," Ned said. "I'm sure Deputy Keene would be happy to—"

"Calling the cops is a problem for me, fellas," said Pres, cutting Ned off. "It's a little complicated…"

"Of course it is," Tommie said.

"Have a seat, Pres," sighed Ned, "and tell us."

Epilogue

Spring, four months later...

How many days had they been flying? Three? Five? They had lost count. It had begun as a simple, unambitious sortie; she and the young male — her selected mate — had left the colony before sunrise, eager to avoid the disapproving scrutiny of the elders. The two young birds were headed for the archipelago that was rumored to exist, according to colony lore, just beyond the southeast horizon. According to the pair's plan, the hop should have taken two hours — three, at the most — and landed them in a remote territory rich in nesting grounds and abundant with the food sources that had become, over the past few years, more and more scarce at the home colony.

Their flight calculations, however, had proved to be in error. They discovered no archipelago, no pristine nesting grounds, no life-sustaining groves of oak or maple. They were, instead, lost at sea. Finally realizing their mistake, too late, they had turned back toward home, calling forth the dormant powers of navigation that their kind had not put to use in countless generations. Their return voyage, however, had proved equally fruitless. Instead of piloting their way back to the safety of their home, they instead found themselves circling

331

uneasily above an open, empty sea that was darker, colder and more turbulent than any they had ever known. Home was nowhere to be found. With this loss, the pair's desolation was so great that when an ominous looking storm front arrived and swept them into its grasp, carrying them at high speed toward foreign skies, they did not resist; they yielded willingly to its force and soared together into the unknown.

How long had they flown in the storm's embrace? Darkness had come and gone, more than once. How much distance had they traveled? Unable to measure the tumultuous sea below them, they could not know. Just as they began to feel despair, however, a gap in the weather front appeared beneath them. Without hesitation, they tucked their wings and dropped down and down and down further until they were liberated from the storm and gliding easily in clear air. A patch of land suddenly appeared ahead — an island. Soaring above the land mass, they scouted for a safe place to touch down, finally spotting a heavily wooded patch of forest a short distance from the island shore. To one side of the wood, a deep, dark ravine presented itself with a surprising, magnetic allure.

"There," she said.

"Why?" he asked.

"Just because."

They folded their wings and dropped into the ravine, where they immediately found a suitable tree and lit down. The young female looked around, appraising the forested area around their perch and finding it very much to her liking.

"We'll be safe here," she said.

Below them, lurking in the dense brush at the base of the tree, sat Rudy, an orange tabby cat, watching and listening as the two young birds lay claim to their new domain.

"*Too-da hooweee,*" said the male.

"*Hooweee hooweee hooweee,*" she replied.

The End

5684547R0

Made in the USA
Charleston, SC
20 July 2010